ATOM INC

Book Three of The Race Is On Series

OC Heaton

Rookwood Publishing

Join The Race is On Readers' Club

In return, you'll receive a free novella plus loads more gifts, occasional e-mails from me about my life in rainy Leeds and first notice of when a new book will be out.

If you want to unsubscribe at any time, it's simple to do and I promise never to share your details with anyone. To join the club just scan the QR code below or enter this link into your browser: https://ocheaton.com/atominc-mad-offer/

Contents

"Technology is neither good nor bad; nor is it neutral."
Dr Melvin Kranzberg First Law of Technology

Kabul, Parwan Province, Afghanistan

8th April 2010, 20:21 hours AFT

Hamid Shirzad stepped off the Bagram Air Base bus onto the service road which ran parallel to Kabul Airport. Overhead, a 747 thundered into the night sky, its huge Pratt & Whitney JT9D turbofan engines roaring with relief as they lifted the enormous aircraft above the city. He always felt nervous, stepping from the relative comfort of the air-conditioned interior into the chaotic familiarity of Kabul. Even though the bus was unmarked, someone could easily follow the fifteen-seater from the American Air Base, forty odd miles north of the city, and pick off the men as they disappeared home to their families. The job at Bagram offered riches they couldn't have imagined just five years ago, and that was the problem. Each one was a target, of envious friends and family who hadn't benefited from the Americans' largesse, but also of the Taliban. Attacks were common in Kabul. People vanished all the time. He was right to feel nervous.

Hamid popped an M&M into his mouth and hurried down the airport road towards Aria City, a huge development of mid-rises that had recently sprung up, fuelled by American cash and Afghani corruption. He didn't care though. His family had been fortunate enough to secure one of the apartments, courtesy of his job at the air base. They were tiny but felt like palaces compared to the poverty of Khost, his hometown on the Afghan-Pakistan border. He couldn't wait to tell Asal of his promotion. He was now head of service at the main mess hall. In charge of five servers no less. An extra fifty dollars a month. He felt rich. Like a king. At this rate, he would have enough to bring his mother to Kabul. Maybe even get her an apartment next to theirs.

To access the complex, he needed to take the underpass, a pedestrian tunnel which avoided the chaos of the airport road. It was normally well lit, but tonight, the steps disappeared into a gloomy blackness. He reached for the packet of American candy, debating whether to risk the road, but at this time of night it would be impossible to navigate the traffic on foot. He crunched down on the coloured candy, took a deep breath, and hurried down the steps. It was cooler down here, but not enough to explain his involuntary shudder. Up ahead the warm glow of the exit propelled him forward, but fifty feet in, a low rumble from behind dissolved his sugar-fuelled courage and he broke into a run. Was this the night? The night when he failed to come home, leaving Asal with four children under five at the mercy of the Taliban, his family and friends. By the time his boot hit the first step of the exit, Hamid was panting heavily and, as he emerged into the warm night, he stopped to catch his breath. He risked a glance back, down into the dark underpass, but there was nothing. For the love of Allah, he chided himself. His neurosis was getting the better of him and he popped another sweet into his mouth as he hurried through the security barriers into Aria City.

As he crossed the road, a van pulled out of a side street up ahead, turning towards him. It was American. A battered Ford transit van, every window blacked out, its red paint scoured pink by the harsh Afghani terrain. Hamid barely gave it a glance. These vans were everywhere, driven mainly by the private security contractors that swarmed

Kabul. It rumbled past him, heading back towards the concrete blast blocks of the checkpoint. Hamid half heard its worn tyres protesting as it U-turned. He waited for it to pass, but the engine idled noisily behind him at a walking pace and his heart quickened. He popped one, two, three sweets into his dry mouth and eventually risked a glance back. As he did, the van roared forward, its side door screeching open. Two men appeared, one holding a heavy sack, whilst the other pinned his arms back, causing the brightly coloured packet to spill from his right hand. He felt a tiny pinprick on his arm. Hamid looked down in confusion, his head already woozing over, but all he could see were the brightly coloured sweets scattered on the weed-scrubbed concrete on the street.

When he came to, Hamid was bound and gagged. Face down on a carpet. It smelled of smoke. And something else. A rancid festering odour that burned his nostrils and paralysed his mind with images of death and torture. He groaned in despair at his first thought—that he would never see Asal again. Or any of his children: dear sweet innocent Paak, her soft brown eyes, always so thoughtful; Aalem, tall for his age and fearless like a black bear; little Fateh, forever reading books, waiting patiently for him to return home so she could curl up in his lap with her favourite story; and, finally, young Mukhtar, already speaking English, head bursting with big thoughts that Hamid could only dream of. He suppressed a sob, trying to control his breathing. Why had he accepted the job? He should have remained in Khost. They would be dirt poor, but at least they would be alive and together. Actually, that wasn't true. Under the Taliban, they all faced daily dangers: he could be forced to fight; his wife married off to another fighter, effectively sold into a lifetime of sexual slavery; his girls would suffer the same fate. He realised with a start that he shouldn't be alive, and the thought made him feel better. His abduction didn't make sense: kidnappings were rare. Whilst he had a good job by Afghani standards, he wasn't wealthy. Certainly not worth all this trouble. Most people at his level were simply executed, their bodies left in the street as a warning to others that they should not work with the Americans. So why was he still breathing?

He had barely asked himself the question when he heard low voices talking in Dari. It was too low for him to catch anything, but he thought he heard an accent. What was an American doing here? With the Taliban? He assumed that's what they were. Who else would kidnap him? The voices approached. He shifted, trying to sit up. Strong arms hauled him to his feet. The hood came off, a bright light burning his eyes as Hamid stood, swaying and blinking. Slowly, shadows solidified, and he found himself standing in an apartment. It felt familiar. With a start, he realised it was exactly the same layout as his. He glanced towards the windows which weren't covered, the bright lights of Kabul twinkling below. They were high up, probably top floor. It must be within the Aria City complex. The thought gave him strength. To think that his family was close by. One of his captors gave him a shove, and he stumbled forward, only now taking in the men. Two were clearly Taliban: heavy beards, rifles strung across their backs, their unassuming white-leather Cheetah high-top sneakers, the clincher. Beloved by Taliban fighters, they were seen as a status symbol. Everyone avoided wearing them. How had they even got here without attracting attention? The third man was the most mysterious: clearly American; tiny, like a small mouse, his bald head gleaming in the single light of the apartment. He was sitting at a table, tapping away at a keyboard.

'I'm ready,' he muttered to no one in particular. 'Please, prepare the prisoner.'

They led Hamad to the doorway around which a metal frame had been constructed. His captor stopped, but continued to hold him tightly.

'OK, now. Put him through the gate.'

The guard roughly pushed Hamad forward and, without a sound, he disappeared.

'OK, you next.' The American nodded at one of Hamid's captors, who also stepped through and disappeared.

The man turned back to the keyboard. Seconds later, two men came back through the gate.

Hamad stumbled forward into the room, dimly aware of the American still sitting at the table, still tapping away. He sensed another figure behind him, but didn't get the chance to turn, instead, sinking to his knees as candy-coloured bile soaked the cheap carpet. His mind was whirling with unanswered questions. What had just happened? Why did he feel so sick? He groaned, trying to calm his stomach. Had he eaten too many of those sweets? He'd found them at the base. They were free in the kitchens and he now consumed three packs per day. With a groan, he eased himself into a standing position, and as he did, the man behind him stepped forward. Into Hamid's line of sight. He'd assumed it was one of the fighters, but something about him looked familiar. The realisation nearly made him sink to his knees again. It was him—Hamid—standing there, staring back. For a ridiculous moment, he thought he was staring into a mirror, but as his hand reached forward and touched the man's face, no hand came to meet his. How was this possible? Had he died? Had he entered Barzakh, a state of waiting, until the Day of Judgement? And was this an angel sent to question him? If so, why did it look like him? Was he an angel?

'Come on, we haven't got all day,' the American grumbled.

Hamid's double gently removed his hand and went over to the table, where a gun lay. It had an overlong barrel and looked menacing. How had Hamid not noticed it before? Had he been gone a long time? The man picked it up, flicked a switch on the side and returned to Hamid, who stood there, staring dumbly at his double. As the nozzle pressed gently to his skull, Hamid stared questioningly at himself. The barrel puffed quietly and the back of Hamid's head exploded. As he crumpled to the floor, Hamid's double stood there, staring at the corpse, his face expressionless.

'Clear up this mess,' the American said, standing up and gathering his laptop. 'You know where to leave the body, and once I've gone, dismantle the gate.'

Without waiting for an answer, he stepped through the doorway and disappeared.

Townhouse, Camden Town, London

8th April 2010, 17:11 hours GMT

Ed Fox studied the pickets gathered in small groups around him, shifting from side to side as they struggled to keep warm against the biting wind, the cold air having long since silenced their protest. A woman in a ragged sheepskin coat slalomed through the crowd with a large tray, on which cups of hot soup steamed. Ed rested his placard against a lamppost and accepted a serving as she passed by – he wasn't cold, but he was hungry. As he sipped the scalding liquid, he asked himself the same question that he'd posed on his first night, ten days ago: what was he doing here? The answer was simple, but also complex. He shouldn't be here. He should be in California with Jo's parents, getting his head straight, preparing for a return to work. His command had given him an extended leave of absence. It finished in three days. Ample time for him to complete his new mission, but then what? He had no desire to return. There was nothing there for him anymore.

A man approached. He was wearing a heavy parka, the hood pulled low, face in deep shadow. He nodded at Ed, a friendly nod, one borne of camaraderie on the picket line. Ed recognised him from his first night.

'It's Ed, right?' the man held out a hand.

'I'm sorry, I don't remember your name.' Ed did. He just didn't want to talk.

'James Forsyth,' the man said. 'With PCA. Or at least I was until yesterday.'

Ed frowned.

'It's a private plane charter company. Based out of Stansted. They laid off half the workforce yesterday. Because of—' The man glanced up at the building. Ed followed his gaze. '—Uma Jakobsdóttir and Ethan Rae.' He spat on the pavement. 'And you?'

'Ostend Ferries. Out of Dover. Same problem.' Part of his story was true, at least. The bit about boats. He always found it easier to lie if there was an element of truth.

James scowled.

'Why bother with a ninety-minute journey, eh,' he said sarcastically, 'when you can be transported from your home instantaneously.'

Up ahead, some of the group stirred. One of the organisers blew into his megaphone and started to chant. Others around him put their cups down and grabbed their own placards. James and Ed did the same, electrified by the collective energy that rippled around the crowd. The chant started slowly. It always did. Just one voice, then others joined and suddenly hundreds were chanting as one.

'Keep your LEAP,' they screamed.

The room was growing dark, its tall ceilings swallowed up by the advancing gloom, as the wintry sun surrendered meekly beneath the London rooftops. Uma pulled the sheet tightly around her shoulders as she watched the pickets below. She couldn't hear what they were chanting. She didn't need to. They'd been there all day and would be there all night. It was the same in DC, outside her apartment, and in every other major city: a ragtag bunch of religious nutters and others opposed to the LEAP rollout. They'd appeared the day after the Copenhagen Treaty, where she'd stood with President Jamal Williams to announce that LEAP would be available globally. For free. At first it had been a few lonely protesters, but over the weeks, as the ramifications of the rollout had become clearer, they had grown in number. So much so, that Ethan had persuaded the Met Police to station two squad cars outside the house to prevent anyone breaking through the wooden cordon the council had thrown up.

Uma shrugged in frustration and stepped away from the window. What was she doing, wasting time, watching people who weren't prepared to change? The realisation returned her to the huge bed that dominated the room. She stared down at the sleeping figure. Ethan stirred slightly, but didn't wake, his lips curled into a half smile, as if amused by Uma's annoyance. His forearm covered the rest of his face, the ragged scar from his ordeal, an angry red. It was Uma's turn to smile. Had it only been three months since she was first in this room? Waking up in this very bed, Ethan sitting beside her, cradling his shattered arm, nervously contemplating what he had to tell her: that she had died, in an earthquake at Reynolds Castle; that Ethan had restored her using LEAP. But he didn't need to explain himself. She had done the same thing years earlier, restoring his comatose body because she couldn't bear the thought of losing him. But the best thing about that night had been their reconciliation. Before then they had been at war, Ethan unable to forgive her, not for entangling him with Anderson, but for keeping it from him and deciding to cut him from the LEAP launch. After she had restored him from his coma, it had been the first thing he remembered and the perceived betrayal had infected his soul like a cancer, reducing him to a malevolent recluse, holed up in Reynolds' bleak castle at the end of the world. He had refused to help in her hour of greatest need, and it had taken Uma's death in the Hall of Steel to drag him out of his malaise. They had made love that night for the first time and the memory made her feel warm inside, for the first time in a long time. And here they now were: LEAP finally launched as Uma had intended when she had first approached Ethan all those long years ago. He was now based in London. All the better for coordinating the rollout of the LEAP technology, given the multiple time zones he was dealing with. She was in DC, busy dealing with the Americans, but it didn't matter. With LEAP, they saw each other every day, usually late afternoon in London, lunchtime on the east coast. Today was a short visit. She was heading out to Iceland. It would have been her father's birthday today. It didn't seem like a good reason to go, but she felt drawn to the island, like a moth to the flame of a flickering candle.

Ethan stirred, stretching luxuriously, sleepy eyes flickering open, his mouth breaking into a boyish grin as Uma let the sheet slip to the floor. She knelt on the bed and kissed him deeply. *God, his lips were so soft*. Ethan responded, butterflying her tongue with his own. Pangs of pleasure bolted down her spine and she groaned. Encouraged, he slipped a hand between her thighs.

'I've got to go,' she giggled, pulling away.

'Please stay,' he said, pushing his lower lip out. 'We never see each other.'

'I'd love to,' she said, trying to find her clothes under the mess of sheets, 'but I've got to go to Iceland and be back in DC for—' she glanced at her watch, trying to work out the time in Washington, five hours from now, '—one o'clock.'

'Please,' he repeated.

'I can't. The rollout is going way too slowly. The Americans are so damn cautious, mired up to their eyeballs in vested interests: airlines, car companies, trains, shipping—'

'It'll change,' he cut in, watching her bend over and then disappear beneath the bed. 'It always does.'

'You keep saying that.' Uma's head appeared above the mattress. 'But it's not just the politicians. I'm meeting a delegation of lawyers this evening from some of the biggest law firms in DC. They're worried about the privacy consequences for their billionaire clients handing over their atomic code to us. They're suggesting it be held on an escrow server into which we're granted limited access. Otherwise, their clients will stop LEAPing.' Uma stood up, holding her jeans and shirt. 'Meanwhile, the earth continues to pump CO2 into the atmosphere at an unprecedented rate because the vast majority of people are still not benefiting from LEAP.' A faint pink tinge had appeared on her neck.

'Well, it will. Remember, I've done this a few times.'

Ethan stroked Uma's thigh, pulling her towards the bed, but she wriggled away and turned on him, the blush now a deep red that blossomed out across her chest.

'Well, it's not fast enough,' she exploded. 'Every hour we delay, millions more tonnes of CO2 spews into the atmosphere where they'll sit for generations. We need to move faster.'

Ethan nodded solemnly, even as his eyes hungrily drank in Uma's nakedness.

She turned away in frustration, suddenly desperate to leave.

'Looking for these?'

Ethan was sitting up, twirling her panties suggestively in one hand. She lunged for them, but he pulled his hand under the sheets, curling up into a foetal position.

'This is important,' she yelled at him, struggling into her jeans and shirt. She spied her boots and grabbed them before flinging the door open. It smashed into a tray containing their half-eaten lunch from earlier, spilling plates, cutlery and half-eaten pot pie across the floorboards. She screamed in frustration and stormed off down the landing towards the LEAP gate.

Ethan's head appeared above the bed sheets as he listened to her stomping up the steps to the attic. Curses drifted through the open door and then suddenly it went quiet. He got out of bed and recovered the tray, carefully picking up its contents. Mrs Carr, his housekeeper, could clean this up later. He wondered whether to call Uma, but abandoned the idea. She would be mad for hours now. He'd seen it happen three times in the last week. She seemed to be carrying the weight of the world on her shoulders regarding the rollout, and despite his protestations to the contrary, he was also worried about the pace. Every government seemed gripped by paralysis and indecision, but it was too late to turn back now. Not after the Saudis had acquired a copy of the LEAP technology and declared a new alliance of other Arab nations that would have exclusive access to the stolen code. They'd been forced to counter the move quickly – it had been Uma's idea. To accelerate the rollout by announcing that they could in fact teleport humans and that it would be available free to every country on the planet: 182 countries out of a possible 192 had taken up the offer. Which was all well and good, but President Williams' plan for a controlled rollout had been obliterated in an instant. As the President had feared, it was now chaos, as countries, corporations and individuals fought for a foothold in the new world order, or tried to slow it down. Ethan was caught in the middle, battling to accelerate Uma's timeline, whilst managing a thousand vested interests. Getting dressed quickly, Ethan made his way downstairs. It was strange living in the Camden townhouse after spending so many years in Reynolds' Castle, the latter being a cold, dark and soulless – what had Uma called it? – mausoleum. It was a fitting description, whereas his London home was bright and airy and he was surrounded by people all intent on helping them with the biggest rollout in human history. He was now in the basement, his former deal room, where he had bought and sold companies at a rapid rate. At one point it had made him the richest man in the UK and was now the nerve centre for the global rollout. On the main screen, their mission boldly claimed a LEAP gate in every household on Earth by the end of 2012. That was 2.3 billion houses. Across 6.9 billion people. They weren't even close, and the team knew it. Many were slumped at their desks, staring at their screens, eyes dull with fatigue, faces creased with frustration.

Ethan entered his office and sat down, his thoughts returning to Uma. He regretted laughing now, knowing the levels of stress she was under, and grabbed his mobile, wondering what to do. In front of him his parents' photo smiled back. It was his favourite, taken when he was four. The young couple were standing outside, in their garden in Aberdeen, Ethan squeezed between their legs, looking up at his mother. There was a time when the sight would have triggered a tsunami of pain: first from his leg and then across his back. The metal pins that were inserted into his thigh after the car accident that killed them would begin to ache at the memory. Ethan had been driving that day in Saudi, where his father had worked as an engineer. He had blamed himself for their deaths. As had the Saudi court that summarily sentenced him to fifty lashes and ten years in prison. His back, now a ragtag of scar tissue, would have blossomed like a fireball whenever he thought of them. He'd spent, what felt like a lifetime, trying to atone for that one mistake. That is, until he'd met Uma, who had filled the void left by his parents and ultimately enabled him to move on. He owed her everything, and the reminder guided his fingers across the mobile screen. Ethan waited expectantly, but after four rings, the tone cut to Uma's voicemail. He ended the connection, suddenly at a loss what to do, which was laughable given everything he had to do.

His phone rang. For a joyful moment, he thought Uma had called him back, but it was his PA: The Swedish Prime Minister wanted to speak to him. Apparently, Volvo was demanding a share of the Swedish licence agreement. Ethan sighed. It was going to be a long evening.

þingvellir National Park, Iceland

8th April 2010, 21:10 hours GMT

The night was unusually clear, courtesy of a cold westerly wind rifling in off the Atlantic. Uma breathed deeply, inhaling the freezing air. It tasted good and calmed her anger with memories of a simpler time: long walks on the beach, smoking vents, and bubbling geysers. Below, Reykjavík glowed dully to the west, before the black coastline took over, but she didn't need the light of day to guide her eyes across the canvas of her childhood: Strandakirkja where they used to go camping every year, Selfoss with its annual summer festival which they never missed, its gardens decorated with brightly coloured ribbons. And further east still, the faint glimmer of Eyjafjallajökull. Completely covered by an ice cap, the volcano had flexed its muscles at the beginning of March, blasting spectacular lava bursts six hundred feet into the air. She missed Iceland, still had her father's old house, kept offices in the Technical College, but couldn't remember the last time she had made the trip over, so consuming was the push to roll-out LEAP. It filled her days and haunted her nights with suffocating nightmares that woke her in the early hours, gasping for breath, her chest tight with fear. It shouldn't still be like this. The rollout was underway. A chance for real change.

Her phone buzzed. It was Ethan, his tenth call since she had stormed out, but she ignored him, even though a part of her wanted to take the call and apologise for her outburst. Another surge of anger nixed the thought, coursing through her veins like hot lava. Couldn't he see the urgency of their situation? Instead, he was behaving like a sex-crazed teenager, content to offer condescending platitudes about how it would happen, sooner rather than later. They could be doing so much more with LEAP, but were now stuck in a morass of self-interests, all trying to protect their patch of commerce, as Ethan called it. Which they had anticipated. Or at least he had. What they hadn't expected was that the American government, their partner in LEAP, along with every other government on the planet, would kowtow so readily to industry demands to slow the rollout to a snail's pace. All the while, ignoring the obvious demand: most people seemed desperate for the technology. Who wouldn't? Turning any trip, three thousand miles or thirty, into a millisecond moment was a compelling proposition, but for that to happen, they needed to democratise the gates. Install one in every house, in every office, in every venue, but that was where the resistance came.

Everyone wanted to control the gates, especially the transport companies, but there was no point in installing a load of gates at an airport, train station, or port. Those days were long gone, but they were fighting like fury to protect their franchises and deadlock reigned like an impassable mountain range. She picked up a lump of lava and hurled it into the crevice she was standing above. It cracked unseen against the lava walls like a gunshot and the sound unlocked a memory; a memory of a winter's day spent with her father in Þingvellir National Park. They'd gone hiking for a week, at the beginning of her school holidays. They'd set off early, backs straining with the weight of their packs. On the third night, they'd stuck camp above a ravine, maybe forty, perhaps fifty feet deep. Directly beneath them, a pond had formed in a deep crevice. They'd already eaten, the stars twinkling above them, much like tonight, and were huddled around the campfire trying to keep warm. It had been her father's idea. Ten lava lumps each. See how many they could get in the pool of water. Every time they'd missed, the petrified missiles cracked against the ravine floor. She'd won that night – three splashes to his solitary one. The thought rose unbeckoned and unwanted: What would her father have said about all of this?

Why it appeared, she had no idea. She already knew the answer. He would have hated it, but she didn't owe her father anything. He was a hypocrite. A man who had spouted restraint about LEAP. Who had repeatedly said, right until the day he died, that LEAP should never be released to the world. That humans weren't able to deal with the responsibility of such a powerful technology. Yet, at the very first opportunity, he had made Uma into a perfect copy of Eva, her twin sister. *Oh poor Eva*. Now dead. Uma's heart lurched at the memory of their fight. Over eight years ago now, but still as fresh in her mind as if it had happened that morning: the fight; the boom of the gun going off and then nothing; Eva's still figure, proof that Uma had killed her own sister in cold blood. It had been the final tragedy, heaped on a succession of tragedies, and had led her to abandon LEAP and pursue more traditional ways of reducing global warming. Until the CIA had discovered Reynolds, the airline boss who had stolen the LEAP tech from her, frozen solid on a frigid plain in Iceland. Overnight, they had sucked her back into the nightmare of LEAP. Except this time, the US government was her bedfellow, along with two powerful men: Joseph Ingram and John Forsyth. The first, a ruthless spy boss who seemed to anticipate her every move and manipulate Uma to his bidding, like a helpless marionette. She was convinced he was behind the attempted assassination of the President, a masterful power grab that had left him as de facto head of the entire US Intelligence Service. The second, a magnetic presence who had started out as her mentor, but whose shiny exterior hid an evil predator that preyed on women for his own sexual gratification.

She shuddered at the memory of that night and unconsciously cradled her belly. She hadn't even realised she was pregnant until LEAP had sounded an alert, two weeks after Forsyth's brutal attack. It identified all changes in her atomic makeup. Hers was minuscule, but profound: a one-celled entity inside her fallopian tube. A zygote. She didn't even know whose it was and had no interest in finding out. Ethan's or Forsyth's. It didn't matter. She was never having babies. It was the worst thing she could do to the environment. One human being, especially a first-world human being, could produce 4,000 tonnes of carbon over the course of their lives, more if you lived in America. Converted into a solid mass of carbon, it would be 300,000 tons and need 10,000 trucks to carry it. She could feel the weight of all that carbon crushing down on her. All from a single zygote, the size of a poppy seed. Nope, she was never having babies and had aborted that same day. A simple act. The press of a button and the cell was gone, but she couldn't turn off her body straight away. Nor, it seemed, her emotions. She found herself weeping helplessly at any moment, her abdomen aching with grief, before uncontrollable rage swept both away.

She dare not tell Ethan about Forsyth or the baby. For starters, she had got her revenge on Forsyth and besides which, it was her body. She could do what she wanted with it. Even if she could have summoned up the courage to share her dirty secret with Ethan, 4,000 tonnes was an impassable barrier, even though she loved Ethan with all her heart. So, she had buried it deep, instead throwing all her energy into achieving her life-long dream of reversing global warming now that LEAP was out in the world.

Except they hadn't released LEAP voluntarily. They'd been forced to after the Saudis stole their design. It was a move borne out of desperation and, given a choice, she would have left that buried as well and pursued traditional means to reverse global warming. Suddenly, the real reason for her anger and frustration was upon her. It had nothing to do with her terminated baby. That was simply the chemistry of pregnancy. Whereas this was borne out of fear over what they had now done. Over what they had been forced to release into the world. A technology so powerful that people could conceivably live for hundreds of years, and worse. With just four laws designed to keep people in check. Four laws to keep her father's voice at bay: Thou shall not clone people, revive the dead, or merge minds or species. She either forced through the change at such a pace that she controlled the narrative and, therefore, the laws. Or, if she relented, her greatest fears would come true. Others would control LEAP, do what they wanted with it. Just like Ethan and she had done – she'd revived him from his coma; he'd resurrected her from the dead. It was human nature. Deep down she knew what would happen if others took control of LEAP: it would surely accelerate global warming as billions more people cloned, revived and merged themselves ad infinitum. That was worse than creating life itself, as lives would suddenly be measured in centuries not decades, consuming precious resources. And worse, much worse.

That was the real problem. It hovered over her like a malevolent spirit. That's what drove her to push forward the rollout. The alternative was too calamitous to bear. And as she had discovered last year with the Americans and the Saudis, there was nothing either Ethan or she could do about that.

Far off in the distance, the horizon suddenly glowed brightly. Seconds later, the reverberations of Eyjafjallajökull's bellow swept over her. Uma sank to her knees, uncertain whether she was crying for a baby she didn't want or losing a planet she was desperate to save.

Bagram Air Base, Parwan Province, Afghanistan

9th April 2010, 06:04 hours, AFT

Abdul Turabi approached the checkpoint. It was a beautiful sunny day, the sun already cresting the Hindu Kush mountain range that ringed the base. He tightened his collar against the bitterly cold wind slicing across the outer perimeter. Ahead of him, the old Russian Control Tower sat forlornly, an abandoned relic of the '76 Soviet occupation. There was already a long queue to enter the base, both men and women, waiting to first pass through a scanner after depositing what few possessions they had on a plastic tray. Behind two-inch plexiglass, American marines regarded them suspiciously through eyes that had witnessed several lifetimes of violence. Abdul glanced at his watch. It was 06:05. He had plenty of time to get to his position: serving hungry American soldiers their morning breakfast. Nearly two hundred marines from the 3rd Battalion gathered in a tight tent. Security would be high, and rightly so.

Finally, it was Abdul's turn. He placed his keys in the tray along with some notes – a few afghani mixed with dollar bills – his watch, and those damn sweets. He ran his tongue around his mouth, feeling for the right molar. It felt like a crater and hurt like hell. The man's teeth were literally rotting. Finally, he removed his jacket and slowly rotated in the holding area to show he had no hidden vest or IEDs strapped to his chest. Not that it mattered. His payload wasn't designed to explode, but it would kill. Hopefully hundreds. And finally, through the last checkpoint. Abdul stumbled slightly, his head swirling crazily, a booming brickbat hammering away at the base of his skull, but he felt calm, as calm as he'd ever felt. This was his destiny. How could he feel anxious about this moment? They'd warned him about the dizziness and headaches, the result of his supercharged blood pressure being driven to 180/110 mmHg by the stimulant he'd taken just before he got off the bus. He showed his ID to the officer on duty: Hamid Shirzad, 34, newly appointed kitchen manager at Bagram Airfield, the largest military base in Afghanistan. However, inside, in his head, he was Abdul Turabi, loyal soldier of the Taliban Islamic Movement. His mind was now sitting inside this peasant's body. It was an abomination, but his death would be glorious. He watched anxiously as the contents of his pockets went through the scanner. Nothing sounded. He walked through the gate and collected everything on the other side.

Finally, he was through the checks and Abdul paused, trying to picture the layout of the base in his head. He'd studied it for weeks, preparing for this day. Satisfied, he withdrew the bag of sweets and emptied some into his hand before discarding them on the dusty sidewalk. He repeated the exercise, and this time he saw it. A white one with a black dot in its centre. He quickly popped it into his mouth, biting down on the pill. The taste was acrid, but what it promised was sweet and the realisation he was near the end propelled him towards his final destination.

The base was already alive with activity. Several troops passed him, but barely gave him a second glance. Why should they? He was Hamid Shirzad. Fully authorised to be there. To feed the troops so they could murder his brothers, but today was his turn to strike back. He entered the dining facility and headed for the kitchens. According to his debrief, he was due to report to Ali Halimi, who was now his boss. He spotted him, standing by the large grills, talking to someone he didn't recognise. Ali looked up and nodded as he approached.

'You're late,' Ali said, glancing at his watch. 'Service started fifteen minutes ago.'

'Sorry, boss,' Abdul said. 'The queues were long this morning. It took ten minutes to get through.' The sound of Hamid's voice felt strange. He still couldn't get used to it. Would no longer have to, shortly.

'So what are you waiting for?' Ali shouted at him.

Abdul hurried over to the kitchen galley, where he grabbed a large tray of plates and followed the other servers out into the mess hall. A young man ahead of him turned and smiled. Abdul stared at him. He didn't recognise him either, but nodded back. He surveyed the room. There must have been 200 soldiers in the mess hall, perhaps more. Better than he had hoped. Than all of them had hoped. As he made his way to the centre of the large room, Abdul started serving plates to the seated men and women, being careful to keep his breathing even. Aerosol transmission was important, but droplets would be more effective. As he served his last plate, he walked to the end of the table and put the tray down. The two service men sitting in front of him looked up. He winked at one of them, a serene smile on his face.

Abdul felt two pinpricks of pain over each of his radial arteries, just enough to break the skin on the underside of his wrists. Thumb side. Nobody noticed, but he may as well have primed a five-thousand-pound bomb. This was it. He had two minutes before he bled out. Two minutes to circulate the room before his heart gave out. What had the American said? He had ten pints of blood. Exsanguination would occur after he had lost four, maybe five. He would fall into hypovolemic shock. The words felt alien in his mind, but so did these soldiers, sitting here, occupying his land, killing men, women, children. His children. The memory energised him. He lifted both wrists to waist height as his deadly payload sprayed into the hall. The aerosol effect would carry them several feet across the room. Invisible to everyone except Abdul, who was already beginning to feel the effects of both the blood loss and the virus. His footsteps felt heavy, his skin felt cold, his muscles ached and his bones were heavy. Keep walking had been the instruction, and he complied, stumbling to the end of his row and down the next. His breath was coming in shorter bursts, his heartbeat pinging at an impossible rate. He stumbled into the back of a soldier, who glanced up. Abdul mumbled an apology and kept going. He needed to move. Needed to spread his gift to every invader in the room.

'I'm OK,' he murmured to one. 'I've cut myself, that's all.'

He held up both arms, the fine spray nearly invisible in the harsh glare of the mess hall lights.

The soldier stared at him, his face reddening slightly.

A drop of blood oozed from Abdul's nose.

'I don't feel so good,' he said to another, a young woman, who stood to help him. He reached out towards her. She steadied him and he smiled back, his eyes leaking blood. She gasped in surprise and grabbed a napkin. He tried to walk away, but his legs felt like concrete posts, so he stood between the two tables, swaying like a barroom drunk.

'He's bleeding,' he heard the woman say and tried to turn towards the voice.

'I'm fine,' he gasped, his pale-lips now ruby red as bloody spittle leaked down onto his smock.

Without warning, Abdul vomited, a bright red spume that turned the woman's fatigues scarlet. She screamed and fell back onto the table, surprise turning to fear.

A soldier opposite stood and drew his gun, unsure what to do.

Two others did the same, their faces anxious with confusion.

Abdul turned away and vomited again, hosing a plume of hot crimson liquid onto the other table. Pandemonium erupted in the mess hall as men and women scrambled to escape, knocking chairs and tables aside.

'He's got a bomb,' someone screamed.

A gun boomed and Abdul snapped backwards onto the table, where he lay spreadeagled, his chest spurting blood like a crazed fountain. He tried to sit up but a cacophony of bullets patchworked across his upper torso and he collapsed back on the table, a ghoulish smile now etched across his face as his dying body continued to pump out its deadly cargo into the rapidly emptying mess hall.

Oval Office, Washington DC

10th April 2010, 09:20 hours EDT

U ma looked around the room. A new set of faces stared back at her, but the room hadn't changed. Still calm, hugely intimidating, but never judging, its cream decor and soft pastels reminiscent of a family sitting room. She remembered the first time she had sat here on this very couch: 6th November last year. That day, she had been entrapped by the people sitting around her. They knew what she had done to Reynolds and had given her a stark choice: work with them to release LEAP or face the consequences. She had nearly walked, but the President had convinced her to stay, promising a controlled rollout. Of course, thanks to the Saudis and Forsyth, that had been impossible. Now, less than four months later, the world had shifted on its axis: LEAP was out in the world. Both versions. Uma glanced over at Ethan, who smiled back at her reassuringly, their argument ancient history. She wondered what they were doing there. Hopefully to discuss the slow pace of the LEAP rollout, but deep down she knew it wasn't that. The attendees foghorned danger—Chuck Harrison, Secretary of Defense; Michael Thompson, Chairman of the Joint Chiefs of

Staff. She didn't recognise the others. Didn't need to. Their olive-green uniforms laden with colourful service ribbons told her everything she needed to know. No one spoke. They were waiting for the only person who mattered and he was running late.

One of the doors opened, and she stood, along with the others, as President Jamal Williams, forty-fourth President of the United States of America, entered. He was closely followed by Joseph Ingram, acting head of the US Intelligence Services. Uma stiffened as his lanky frame lowered itself onto the couch opposite. He smiled humourlessly at Uma, who scowled back. She detested the man, had done so, right from the first moment she had laid eyes on him. Or rather, he had first laid eyes on her, in her hotel bedroom in LA. She could still feel his cold gaze slithering across her half-naked body, and shuddered. Since then, he had manipulated her into releasing LEAP at a pace that she had been powerless to resist. Uma was still convinced that he was behind the terrorist attacks from last year, engineered in a bid for a power grab. Which had worked as far as she could see. Since the failed attempt on the President's life, new legislation had been rushed through that made him de facto head of the entire US security apparatus, with power to integrate foreign, military and domestic intelligence in defence of the United States and its interests abroad. After the President, he was probably the most powerful man in the room. Scratch that. He was the most powerful man.

The President glanced round the gathering, nodding at each person before taking his seat next to Uma. He stared long and hard at the Resolute Desk now opposite him, framed by the US flag and President's flag. Eventually, he spoke.

'What have you got for me, Chuck?'

The Secretary of Defense straightened, glancing down at a small manilla folder on his lap.

'Yesterday morning, just after 6 a.m., one of our Afghani collaborators, a kitchen team leader by the name of Hamid Shirzad, reported for work as usual at the Bagram Air Base just north of Kabul. Less than thirty minutes into his shift, he committed suicide in the main mess hall.'

'Was anyone injured?' the President said.

'Yes and no,' Chuck Scott replied. The President frowned. Uma glanced at Ethan. Where was this going? Defence wasn't their area. They had LEAP to roll-out.

'At the time of the ... incident, no one was hurt, but since then, forty-three of the service people who were in the mess hall have come down with an assortment of symptoms: fever, nausea, vomiting, asthenia, myalgia, nose bleeds and chest pains. We've cleared out one of the med centres and are using it as a makeshift incubation centre on the presumption that this was some sort of chemical attack. We've quarantined everybody that this Shirzad character came into contact with – some two hundred personnel.'

'Do we know anything about this man?' the President said.

'Given Shirzad's role in the kitchen, he was subject to a basic security check.' Chuck Scott sounded defensive. 'Nothing stood out. Grew up in Khost. Settled there with his wife and four kids before moving to Kabul. No extremist connections. No criminal record. No financial issues. He has worked for us since 2008. Never given us a problem. In fact, he had just received a promotion, that brought extra responsibility and money.'

Uma couldn't contain herself.

'Why are we here?' She nodded at Chuck Scott. 'This doesn't feel LEAP related, or environmental.'

The Secretary of Defense ignored her and continued.

'We've run an initial postmortem on the dead body and there were some, shall we say, very unusual modifications to his skeletal structure.'

'Go on,' the President said.

'Well, his internal biology had been tweaked somewhat. In his wrists—,' Chuck Scott held up his forearm as if waving at the President and tapped, thumb side, just below his palm, on the wrist bone '—here, right above the radial artery, a small valve appears to have been fused into both arteries. When engaged – our pathologists aren't sure how yet – they think that the natural blood pressure in his artery produced a fine mist of blood through the valve, rather like an aerosol effect. Normally, if you cut the artery, it will spurt in tandem with the heartbeat, but if it is just nicked, or in this case, driven through a small aperture, it will produce a fine spray with a range of up to six feet. The really strange thing is that there are no scars or puncture wounds to indicate these valves were inserted externally. In fact, they were made of bone.'

'What do you mean?' the President said.

'Well, it looks like they were created internally somehow. Or at least fitted without breaking the skin.'

'How is that possible?'

'I don't think it is currently.'

Uma felt a shiver of unease ripple through the room. Or was it just her?

'Which brings us to why we asked you to come in, Doctor.' Joseph Ingram turned slowly, his long neck swivelling in her direction. She felt the trap close. 'Could LEAP somehow be used to do this?'

Uma felt herself flushing, somehow feeling guilty with no idea why. Was it happening already, she thought? She glanced at Ethan, who smiled encouragingly, but it didn't help. He hadn't been around during Ingram's repeated efforts to undermine her.

'Of course it's possible,' Uma retorted. 'We're dealing with the building blocks of life, so atoms can be manipulated and reordered in any way we see fit, but this hasn't come from us. We monitor the system constantly for irregularities. If something like this had happened, we would know about it.'

'Except when Professor Crouch stole a copy last year,' Ingram said. Uma could have sworn his lips curled ever so slightly. *Was he behind this?* 'And Forsyth sold it to the highest bidder. Not to mention that a terrorist infiltrated your system and nearly blew up the President,' Ingram added.

The mention of Forsyth's name froze Uma to the couch. She could feel the weight of the room pressing down on her, sucking the air out of her lungs. Suddenly, she was back in the Transamerica Pyramid, the carpet sandpaper-rough on her cheek, right shoulder pulsing with pain, an unnatural burn in her groin as his cruel laugh boomed in her ears. Dear God, she had buried that memory deep, to the darkest recesses of her mind, yet the simple mention of his name had unleashed the fury of his attack on her. An attack that had left her too sore to move after he had drugged and defiled her. And filmed the act, with a threat to release the video to the public if she reported him. So Uma had kept it quiet. She had told no one and was never going to, especially Ethan. He didn't deserve to know that. She stared at him opposite. He frowned back, a concerned look on his face, his kind eyes asking her what was wrong. All she could do was sit there, willing the hurt away.

'Could they have done this?' the President asked.

'I don't know,' Ingram replied. 'As you know, Forsyth has disappeared. So has the professor.'

Uma knew what had happened to Forsyth. It was her revenge on him. She had removed every single piece of plastic surgery in his wicked body: his collagen, all his implants. His face had been stuffed with it, as was his chest, along with his fake hips and new knees. She doubted if he was alive, but the possibility that he might be made her belly ache at the thought of his cruel seed inside her.

'Even if they could,' Ingram continued, 'why would they? What are they trying to prove?'

There was a knock on the wall. An aide entered through one of the hidden doors. He looked breathless. Even before he spoke, his eyes gave the message away.

'Mr President. I'm sorry for interrupting, but we're getting reports of multiple attacks on American bases right across Afghanistan.'

Situation Room, White House

10th April 2010, 11:48 hours EDT

The room was hot, an oppressive heat that was not solely down to the number of people crammed around the table running the length of the narrow space. Uma and Ethan had been sitting there for over two hours and each update got worse.

'So, for our friends in the military, could you give a quick overview of what we're looking at, Mike?' the President said.

The Chairman of the Joint Chiefs of Staff stood up and moved to the head of the low room, until he was standing in front of a new screen that, along with most everything else in the Situation Room, had been replaced following the double terrorist attacks on the White House four months previously. He cleared his throat, and the room fell silent.

'So far, we have reports of attacks at fifteen of our bases, including Bagram and Shindand in the south, but also smaller ones such as Camp Delaram and Camp Rhino in the Registan Desert. Same method of operandi for each one. A long-standing employee enters the base and explodes his wrists in a crowded area. Ten were in the mess hall, three were in a briefing room and the other two were in the sickbay. To date, over four hundred personnel have been directly infected, but this could grow, since a further sixteen hundred were in the immediate vicinity of each incident.'

There was a knock at the door and two men entered. They both looked harried. One handed Mike Thompson a thin folder. He quickly scanned the single sheet, before speaking.

'We've just received this communication from Bagram Air Base.' He sighed heavily. 'Six of the personnel from the attack have died in the last hour. We've also received the toxicology report back from the labs. They appeared to have died from Ebola. Or at least a variant. It seems to have been modified. I'm told—' he paused, locating his place on the page, '—the virus used at Bagram is characterised by a single amino acid change in a region of the virus' surface protein. This allows it to bind to human cells more easily and therefore accelerates the infection by a factor of ten.'

A woman to the President's left spoke.

'Isn't Ebola one of the deadliest viruses known to man?'

'It is,' Mike Thompson said, 'but this appears to be on a different scale. Because of the mutation, we're looking at a 100 percent kill rate.'

'How many people were exposed to this?' the President said.

'Well, so far, we've counted two thousand, seven hundred twenty-three across the fifteen bases,' Michael Thompson said.

There was a silence in the room as everybody absorbed the number.

'Good God, that's more than were killed in the 9/11 attacks,' the President whispered.

Just then, a phone rang beside Chuck Scott, startling everyone. The Secretary of Defense answered it and listened carefully, before replacing the receiver. He turned in his seat. A screen above his head lit up, before coalescing into a video feed. It was an air shot, offering a night view of a grey highway. Cars were at a standstill across all four lanes, their headlights casting a patchwork of light on the screen. Ragged trees and shrubs running along the central reservation threw ghostly shadows over the traffic jam. The road faded from view as the drone drifted across dirty grey roofs dotted with pinpricks of light, which shortly gave way to a patch of dark scrubland.

'They've found a mass grave in Kabul,' Chuck Scott said, 'near Aria City. It contains, what appears to be, the bodies of the attackers. Each one has been shot, execution style, in the forehead.'

The room dissolved into shocked chatter as Uma turned to Ethan. She already knew what was coming, as did he, judging by the look on his face. She found her gaze drawn to Ingram. He was sitting next to the President, his long limbs hunched in the chair, perfectly still, like an oversized predator, waiting patiently for its prey. Ingram's eyes flicked to hers and in that instant she knew. She was certain. He was behind the attacks. The question was, why?

'I thought you said that each attacker had died at the base they targeted?' the President said. He sounded tired, and a little confused.

'They did. Each one is lying in a morgue at the base they attacked,' Chuck Scott continued. His tone sounded perplexed, but Uma knew what was coming and she was powerless to resist. 'Yet these men on the feed also seem to be them. They match their identification and we are just in the process of having their fingerprints analysed.' He glanced up at the screen. As everyone looked on, a rectangular ditch appeared in the centre of the screen, surrounded by army vehicles and huge spotlights which rendered the image daylight white. The feed zoomed in. Fifteen bodies came into view. All were lying face up, arms across their chests, as if asleep.

'How is this possible?' the President said.

All eyes turned to Uma and Ethan, but it was Ingram who answered.

'They must have been copied, using LEAP,' he said.

'Wouldn't that contravene the LEAP Laws?' Uma countered, her voice weak with emotion. 'Besides which, there is another system out there. That could have—'

'Let me get this right,' the President cut in, a note of incredulity in his voice. 'We're looking at a potential loss of nearly three thousand US personnel lives from a series of terrorist attacks, using men who were copied using LEAP and infected with a mutated biological weapon that they delivered through an aerosol system made from bone.'

'It would appear so, sir,' Jack Scott conceded.

'What are we going to do?' the President said.

Joseph Ingram stirred, swivelling his long neck towards the President.

'We have Operation Twin, sir. Every individual on that list is part of it.'

'What's Operation Twin?' Even as she asked, Uma already knew the answer and her heart dropped. Had Ingram set this whole thing up to point the blame at Green Ray?

Ingram looked at the President.

'Can we have the room, ladies and gentlemen?' It wasn't really a question, but as Ethan and Uma got up to leave, along with everyone else, the President motioned for them to stay.

Once the room had emptied, Uma turned on Ingram, her voice dripping with venom.

'Are you saying what I think you're saying?'

'We've been running a covert operation to copy members of the armed forces operating in Afghanistan.' His voice was condescending. It reminded Uma of how he had behaved at the White House LEAP gate the morning she and Ethan had been apprehended by Ingram's men. On that occasion, she had taken a swing at his smug face. Today was no different. Ethan seemed to anticipate what she was thinking and placed a restraining hand on her thigh. She brushed it away.

'Did you know about this?' Uma turned to face the President, but Ingram cut in.

'The President didn't know the precise details. The programme extended the one we started for the President's security detail after the bombings. It's a simple beta to understand the impact on soldiers.'

'That's OK, Samuel,' the President turned to Uma. 'I knew we were running a discreet beta programme that extended into Afghanistan involving some of my security detail who were rotated back into frontline action.'

'This is completely against the LEAP Laws,' Uma cut in, unsure if she was more upset at the copying programme or the President's duplicity. The former, she decided, turning towards him. 'You said you wouldn't.' She looked imploringly at the President who held her gaze. 'You have to stop this.'

'We're saving American lives,' Ingram continued, as if she hadn't spoken. 'Forty-two to date who were killed in action, prosecuting the war in Afghanistan. That's forty-two families. One hundred and twenty-two people plus countless others who would be mourning the loss of their loved ones had we not acted. Not to mention the unrelenting bad press. It's a win for everyone: the families, the army and, of course, the country. Besides which, it's currently a secret. No one knows about it and had this biological attack not taken place, it would have remained so.'

'But we agreed,' Uma protested, jumping to her feet, fists clenched, ready to round the table and pummel Ingram's smug face, 'that you wouldn't breach the laws.'

'Why should we?' Ingram retorted, 'when you can't even comply with them.'

'Is this true?' the President turned towards Uma, a look of disappointment etched across his face. It cut through Uma like a sharp knife. She felt herself reddening. Ingram pressed home his advantage.

'You revived your boyfriend,' Ingram said, nodding at Ethan, who shifted uneasily in his seat. 'And he revived you. Once again, it's one set of rules for you and one set of rules for the rest of us.'

'To be fair, sir, Uma didn't have any say in her own resuscitation. I did it,' Ethan said.

'And that somehow makes a difference?' Ingram countered. A laconic smile spread across his face as Ethan and Uma floundered in his trap.

'We can't allow this to happen?' Uma said. 'If everyone starts resuscitating their loved ones, we'll have a population explosion of unimaginable consequences.'

'Let me get this straight,' Ingram said. 'You want to be responsible for the deaths of two thousand seven hundred and twenty-three servicemen and women?' He paused before continuing and the lost lives hung over Uma like the sword of Damocles. 'All because of some rule you made up. One that is not even enshrined in the laws of our constitution. One that you've repeatedly breached yourself.'

There was silence in the room as Uma and Ingram faced each other. Ingram spoke first.

'If we do nothing, this could be the greatest loss of American life since the D-Day landings.'

The President broke the deadlock.

'Uma's right, Samuel. We need to draw a line under this.'

Ingram glanced at his Commander-in-Chief in surprise.

'But, sir—'

'I propose the following. Revive these personnel if they die, to avoid the fallout. Then pause the programme until we can decide how to manage this. There will be no more copies. No more resuscitations.'

'Mr President, Operation Twin could save hundreds of lives in the future. I've already kept five agents alive who would otherwise be forgotten stars on the Memorial Wall. Five agents who get to continue giving their lives in the service of their country.'

'I understand Joseph,' the President said wearily, 'but where does this stop? In no time at all, there will be pressure to resuscitate everyone killed by something: crime, road traffic accidents, cancer. Hell, what about old age? No one will ever die. Uma warned us of this last year. It's already coming true.' He nodded at Uma and stood up, the meeting seemingly at an end.

Ingram contemplated his boss' words, face expressionless, but Uma knew what he was thinking. There was no way the programme would be paused for long. The President's words were hollow platitudes to keep her quiet, whilst Ingram prepared his next trap.

'In the meantime, find out who did this and stop them.'

Saudi Arabia

11th April 2010, 21:15 hours AST

His nose looked good – not too long or too short. Angular, like a Grecian emperor, with a perfectly straight bridge. All traces of the previous kink were now gone. His nostrils were narrow, and the tip pointed. It gave him a regal bearing. He smiled, luxuriating in the symmetry of his lips, but with a slight crookedness that he had requested. It made him look ever so rakish, a hint of mischief, of hidden fun just waiting to break free. His eyes wandered to his hair. It was long, purposefully so, almost down to his shoulders, nearly white with a hint of grey. He brushed his hand through it. He'd gone to 1 mm thick with a diameter of 120 microns, the maximum allowed, but the effect was perfect. He shook his head, and the hair responded before springing back into place like a movie star. Perfect. He smiled again, this time staring into his own eyes. He'd stuck with aquamarine blue but gone heavier with the cyan, which he felt deepened the effect of a bottomless pool. Familiar, but unknown. Friendly, with a hint of danger. It was delightful, and this time he laughed, a deep baritone, two full octaves lower than previously.

He was perfect.

'What do you think, Crouch?' Forsyth said, staring past his reflection at the dumpy man sitting behind him. It wasn't really a question and Forsyth knew it, but he still expected an answer.

'It looks good,' Crouch grunted, a look on his face that suggested that he didn't care and that Forsyth should just leave him alone so he could get back to work.

Forsyth frowned, his eyes nearly disappearing as his pupils narrowed. Then he smiled, more at himself than the professor – a real sun beamer that would have lit up any heart. Satisfied, he turned away from the mirror and stared down at his CTO. He looked a mess: overweight, bald, perspiring heavily despite the air-con, his thick glasses perched precariously on the edge of his pockmarked nose. This was despite the fact that Forsyth had ordered him to stop drinking. It was a condition of his new employment. Crouch was tested weekly, but it didn't seem to make a difference to his appearance. It wasn't a good look for his new company and Forsyth had ordered Crouch to enhance himself through the machine, but the professor had refused.

'The physical self doesn't concern me,' he would say. 'It's up here that matters.' And he would tap his bulbous forehead, but Forsyth knew other people didn't think that way. The look was everything. That was how people judged you. It was all about the look. So he kept Crouch in the background, out of sight when making his pitches, but today was different. Crouch was going to have to come with him, and Forsyth was nervous about that. Except that he had no choice. Whilst he now had the means to control his looks and so much more besides, it was all thanks to this ugly little man. Today there might be questions which nobody could answer, except Crouch. And Forsyth couldn't afford to mess up. Not today. This was his big chance. One that could propel him to the top table, instead of feeding off the scraps that he had been forced to forage on since returning to Saudi Arabia.

After that bitch had deformed him, Forsyth had been stuck in Saudi Arabia for months, barely able to move, his world shrunken to a daily ritual of simple survival that he had thought he had escaped. He thought of returning to his flat in San Francisco, but that was impossible after the fallout from the LEAP theft. Money was not a problem, despite losing the clinics. However, cash meant nothing here. The real currency was power, and he had lost it all after Al Rahman's death. Poor Abdullah. Summarily executed by the Saudi warring factions for his perceived failure to secure LEAP for a one-hundred-and-twenty-billion-dollar investment, which had all been rendered worthless by that damn woman. In one televised moment in Copenhagen, she had pulled the rug out from under both Forsyth and the Saudis by announcing that LEAP would be available for free. To the entire world. In an instant, what had been a licence to print money by replacing oil production with chargeable travel had been rendered worthless. Forsyth couldn't shake that cold feeling as he had watched the live transmission. A feeling that had overridden the pain he was in, a sense of dread sliding down his weeping face and through his arthritic bones that everything he had planned for had disappeared in an instant. He had found out about Al Rahman's death shortly afterwards. For a time thought he was next, but no one came. All they took were his clinics, calling in the loans advanced to him by Al Rahman. Why should they bother with him? He was a deformed, beaten geriatric who offered no threat. His grotesque body was punishment enough. He shuddered at the memory. Never again. One moment of life on the bottom rung was a tragedy. A second would be unforgivable.

'Are you ready?'

Forsyth jumped, turning towards the man by the door. He hadn't seen him enter. Didn't know how long he had been standing there. It was Mohammed Hussain, Al Rahman's former right-hand man. Now Forsyth's. One morning, several days after the Copenhagen announcement, Forsyth had visited Al Rahman at the oil centre to pay his respects. It had been deeply moving standing there, staring at his former partner. And friend. Or as close to one that Forsyth had ever had. For all intents and purposes, he was still alive, but dead inside, eaten away by the carbon-eating bacterium. Sentinel-like, as if he was contemplating something, his face was now sallow, pinched features already beginning to decay due to lack of water and sustenance. Shortly, he would collapse to the sand like the thousands of seagulls in the centre and fade away. As Forsyth had stood there, he had felt a presence behind him. It was Mohammed. He had lost everything, too, and had a proposal for Forsyth. One that offered a way back for them both: Crouch. Forsyth had never really cared for him. Saw him as a drunken liability, even though he had never doubted his talent as a scientist. For that reason alone, he saw merit in Mohammed's idea: have Crouch rebuild his broken body and approach the Saudis with an alternative way to neutralise Green Ray and the Americans. For good. Theirs had been a bold move, but Forsyth's was bolder. As everyone was just about to discover.

Forsyth turned back to the mirror, studying his reflection one last time. He smiled, his perfectly aligned teeth flashing white against his smooth skin that made him look thirty years younger. Crouch had got the colour just right; not too brown, so it would look fake, like so many of the bronzers on the market, but also not too pasty. He didn't want to look ill. He needed to look healthy. He wanted perfection. He was selling perfection. And so much more.

'I'm ready,' Forsyth said.

The three men made their way down the short corridor towards the elevator, where they rode in silence to the foyer, Forsyth transfixed by the reflection in the full-length mirror that faced them. He had a good feeling about today. Mohammed had set the meeting up. It had taken him two months. God, the Saudis moved so slowly. Two long months during which they had effectively been stuck. Unable to roll-out their ideas meaningfully, except piecemeal, which had been deeply frustrating. But that was the point of today. If successful, it would give them speed and respectability. A chance to relaunch.

They arrived in the foyer and, with Forsyth leading the way, moved purposefully through the vast reception area of the Kingdom Centre towards the front entrance. A man behind a desk inlaid with marble nodded deferentially at Forsyth, who ignored him. As they exited the building into a covered collection point, the heat hit them. A dry, suffocating wall of hot air that seemed to suck the moisture from his skin. He began to sweat, and the realisation quickened his pace, but it made no difference. By the time he collapsed into the cool interior of the limo, Forsyth was sweating profusely. Crouch looked like he was going to have a heart attack, whilst Mohammed seemed completely unaffected. It was only April, the really heavy heat of June months away. No wonder the Saudis moved so slowly. He breathed deeply, trying to cool down as the limo whisked them south west through the crowded streets of Riyadh towards the Al Yamamah Palace, the official residence and office of the King of Saudi Arabia.

Ten minutes later, the limo slowed and stopped beside a guard house. Forsyth couldn't hear the exchange through the darkened glass that separated the passengers from their driver, but it seemed to take way too long and, for a moment, he wondered if the King had cancelled the audience. He was old and his moods were infamous. Mohammed had warned them that this might happen. The thought that they might have to wait another two months brought Forsyth out in another sweat, this one cold and clammy, but after what seemed an age, the car gathered pace. Forsyth breathed a sigh of relief, his tingle of excitement returning. *Not long now.* He felt the limo lurch slightly as it dipped down a steep incline before straightening out into a subterranean garage and pulling up beside nondescript doors. As they alighted, the first thing that Forsyth noticed was the temperature. It was cool, not too cold, and the oppressive humidity was non-existent. They could have been back in the US on a spring evening outside of San Fran. The second thing he noticed was the cars surrounding them. Forsyth understood them. Had to in his previous life as head of the clinics. All his clients drove exclusive cars, but this was on another level. He spotted a Koenigsegg Trevita beside a Bugatti Veyron Grand Sport. Opposite a Pagani Zonda Cinque Roadster nestled between two Lamborghini Reventóns. As far as he knew, just five production cars had been built, and two of them were sitting in this garage along with other limited editions: a Koenigsegg CCXR, two Leblanc Mirabeaus and an SSC Ultimate Aero. More recognisable brands stretched back towards the entrance of the underground complex like abandoned baubles. Forsyth grinned like a small boy. He felt at home around this wealth. Shortly he would be part of it.

The double doors retracted, and an Arab stepped out of a small room to meet them. Without a word, he motioned for the three men to enter what was, in fact, a large office. The man sat down at an ornate desk and began reading some paperwork as the doors silently closed. Forsyth made to say something, but Mohammed quietened him with a finger to his lips. Forsyth scowled back, but stayed silent as they all stood there staring at the man. Seconds later, the doors opened and all three of them turned. Forsyth half expected to see the garage, but they were greeted by two more men and behind them a long corridor stretching away towards two colossal double gold-leaf doors. One of the men bowed slightly and beckoned them to follow. They fell into step behind him, three abreast, with Forsyth in the middle, the other man trailing a respectful distance behind. Either side of the small party, gilded mirrors, twenty feet high, were separated by huge paintings that were just as wide. One depicted a desert scene, the dunes stretching away for miles in repeating waves of sand and framed by an impossibly large blood-orange sun that seemed to radiate heat onto the corridor itself; the other, an oasis, its cool waters reflecting three date palms that towered over the pool and which partially obscured a gibbous moon, its glowing white surface lighting up the five men with a cool breeze. Eventually, the desert scenes gave way to some civilisation: first, a small mud-brick village, the flat dirt red roofs ringed with white triangles; next, a fountain of black oil shooting impossibly high into a cobalt-blue sky; and then a swarm of oil derricks stretching into the desert, their black sucker-rod pumps reminiscent of mosquitoes hovering above the hot sand, waiting to settle on unsuspecting prey and extract their blood; a sprawling city appeared, minarets and mosques jostling for space with western high rises; and, finally, a Saudi cityscape dominated by impossible constructions – the squat elegance of the Islamic Development Bank Building; the futuristic Kingdom Centre, its two silver towers connected by a thin sky bridge; the brilliant white of the Haj terminal capable of supporting nearly one million pilgrims, sheltering them from the baking sun by high-tech canvas shades that could open and close on demand; and, finally, the tiered cylindrical structure of the Al Faisaliah Centre topped with a golden globe that radiated power like a supernova in the midday sun. And still they were only halfway down the long corridor, which had given way to mirrors, and which Forsyth realised had a slight incline. Combined with the thick pile of the carpet which sucked at his feet, he was soon out of breath and focused on their guide, who seemed to glide up the slope. As they neared the colossal golden doors, Mohammed leaned into Forsyth and whispered.

'This is a good sign. The audience with the King will be in his private quarters.'

Forsyth felt himself smiling and tossed his hair back at the thought of all this power soon to be at his disposal. He stopped and looked up at the doors, which were inlaid with intricate circular designs that interlinked and spiralled inwards like a giant whirlpool. The effect was mesmerising as was the optical illusion cast by the final set of mirrors. Forsyth couldn't resist a final glance to his left and marvelled at his new look, stretching away into infinity, courtesy of its facing cousin. The repeating pattern felt appropriate given the purpose of the meeting. He stood there admiring his reflection until the doors suddenly swung open.

Their guide stood to one side and beckoned them forward into a room bathed in darkness. As they stood there, adjusting their eyes, uncertain of which direction they should go, a glow appeared ahead of them which grew steadily brighter. Forsyth found it strangely re-assuring and, without realising, discovered he was moving towards it. As the gloom continued to melt away, two figures materialised out of the growing light. Both appeared to be hovering above the ground, but as he neared, Forsyth realised they were in fact sitting on two chairs raised six feet above the floor on a gold dais. The glow finally stabilised, now bright enough to light the two men and a five-foot circle around them, within which Forsyth, Crouch, and Mohammed now stood. But nothing beyond, just the blackness of night. The effect was both unnerving and strangely comforting; an oasis of light in a darkness that pressed in on them from all sides. An infinite blackness to match the infinite mirrors. It was another neat trick, but Forsyth reminded himself that was all it was. In his day he had been a master of misdirection and the realisation gave him strength. Shortly, he would show them what real power was.

Forsyth studied the two men sitting in front of him. Both were dressed in traditional Arab garb; a long flowing black Bisht over a snow-white thawb, their heads covered with a red-and-white che-quered Ghutra held in place with a black Agal. The older man was well into his nineties, but you would not have known. Sitting erect, his beard neatly trimmed, nothing escaped his eyes. The eyes of a hawk. His son couldn't have been more different, his round face heavy with flesh that almost concealed his eyes, dull with ... Forsyth wasn't sure what to call it. And then it came to him: excess. The man was drowning in it and his body showed it. The older man smiled slightly at them, whilst his son merely scowled. More seconds passed. Then the King nodded, almost imperceptibly. Suddenly, all three of them were sitting in chairs that had abruptly appeared behind. They were slightly too deep in the seat, which forced Forsyth to make a choice: either recline, or perch uncomfortably on the rim. Either way, they were looking up at the two Arabs. More parlour games, Forsyth thought.

Mohammed spoke first. In Arabic. Forsyth tuned out. He had never bothered to learn the language, and eventually Mohammed turned to him. Forsyth tried sitting forward in the heavily cushioned chair, but it didn't feel right so he sat back, power smiled at the two men and began.

'Thank you for your time today, your Royal Highnesses. And for the opportunity to present an alternative course for the teleportation system that Al Rahman acquired for the Kingdom.'

At the mention of his erstwhile security chief, the King scowled, causing the younger man to smile in anticipation of what was to come. Forsyth shuffled forward awkwardly in his seat. This was going to be more difficult than he had expected, but it was too late. His future was on the line.

'As you know, Green Ray, supported by the Americans, has stolen the *raison d'être* for LEAP right from under us. From you,' he cor-rected, nodding at the King, 'and the Kingdom.' Forsyth swept his arm round the room. 'Today I wanted to offer an alternative vision of what we could do with our version of LEAP. Forget teleportation,' he thundered, but his voice sounded flat in the chamber. Forsyth swallowed hard. It had sounded way grander in the privacy of his room. He sat back and pressed on. 'It is simply the crumbs of what this system is capable of in the hands of someone with the right foresight.' Forsyth nodded at the King, who stared back at him, his sharp face expressionless.

'I have three words for you.' Forsyth paused and counted slowly to three. 'Looks. Health. And BackUp.' Neither man reacted, so he ploughed on. 'These three areas are where the real potential of the system lies, not transportation.' He spat the last word out as if expelling sour milk. 'Imagine a system,' he began again, lowering his tone so his voice sounded trustworthy, yet in control, 'that monitors your health 24/7, tirelessly searching your body for any illness known to man. At the molecular level. The moment a cancerous cell appears, we can destroy it.' He clapped his hands theatrically together, but couldn't generate the power he needed while he was crunched in his seat. It sounded like polite applause, not the thunder clap he intended. 'Heart disease will be an illness of the past, as we constantly repair your arteries every time you teleport. If you get hurt in an accident, we can restore you: replace whole limbs or bring you out of a coma if needs be. Have heart or kidney disease? No problem. We can replace your old organ with a new one that won't be rejected by your immune system. Suffer a stroke – we can repair any brain injury. And also offer any cosmetic surgery to keep all our clients in a state of perfection. Look at me.' Forsyth abandoned the chair. It was cramping his style. He needed to express himself.

Mohammed shot him a warning glance, but it was too late. Liberated from his seat, Forsyth felt his spirits soar. *This was more like it.* 'Three months ago, I was a crippled old man.' Forsyth mimicked how he had barely been able to walk, stooping, curling his hands into arthritic claws and shuffling across the carpet towards the King. Mohammed looked on in horror. The King remained expressionless, but his son, now sitting straight, studied Forsyth with amusement, a grin widening across his pudgy cheeks. 'Look at me today,' Forsyth said, straightening up to his full height and spreading his arms wide. He turned in a slow circle before removing his jacket and flexing his upper body. He had practised this a hundred times in the mirror and knew it looked good, his precisely engineered physique nicely accentuated beneath a tight-fitting cashmere sweater.

'Feeling overweight? We can maintain your BMI at a constant level throughout the year, regardless of what you eat, drink or snort.' Forsyth couldn't help himself and sniffed loudly, stealing a glance at the fat prince who clapped enthusiastically, his fat jowls jiggling like a manic blancmange. 'Hangovers are a thing of the past. Follicle failure, a distant nightmare,' he swept his fingers through his own thick locks, 'as would be sagging waist lines, wrinkles, crow's feet, unwanted hair and frozen foreheads from too many face lifts. But it doesn't just stop there. Tired of your body? Hell, try a new look if you want. We can make you taller, shorter, leaner, fitter, faster or more muscular. All without ever seeing the inside of a gym.'

Forsyth laughed deeply; a sonorous chuckle that promised fun. He felt good and smiled at the two men. His most brilliant smile. A million-watt Hollywood blockbuster that would gladden the heart of even the most cynical onlooker. The King remained poker faced, but Forsyth didn't notice. He was on a roll, lost in the brilliance of his own vision. 'And finally, BackUp should the worst happen, and heaven forbid, you die: a backup. Run daily, so you are only ever twenty-four hours from a full restoration.'

Forsyth paused and studied his audience. The King remained expressionless, but his son, now leaning forward, had an even wider smile on his fat face. Crouch, as usual, wasn't even looking at him. Mohammed motioned desperately with his eyes towards the chair, but Forsyth ignored him. He would not be restrained by that thing. He had a vision to sell.

His vision of a superclass of citizens.

Not the top one percent.

Not even the top 0.1%.

But the lucky 0.001%.

The fortunate few.

His few.

'As of today, there are 1,000 billionaires globally. One level down, there are over ten thousand families with net wealth exceeding 100 million dollars. This presents a ready-made market that would generate revenues far in excess of your current oil sales. What were they last year? Two hundred billion dollars? Our conservative projections show that, if only one person from each of those second-tier families paid for the health monitoring, at an annual cost of £250,000 dollars per month, or three million per person, that alone would generate annual fees of thirty-three billion. But that's nothing compared to BackUp. Our premium service will cost fifty million per year, per person. For top-tier billionaires, that's fifty billion in annual revenue from just 1,000 people. And why would they limit that gift to just themselves? They would probably want to include their spouse, children, perhaps even the extended family. Or a girlfriend or two.' Forsyth smiled wickedly as Mohammed put his head in hands. 'As you can see, that is more than enough to replace your lost oil revenue ten times over, just from BackUp alone.

'Let the Americans keep their free teleportation. It's chump change compared to the riches available from our three services: Looks. Health. And BackUp.'

Forsyth sat down, smiling. He had nailed it.

There was silence in the room. No one spoke. Eventually, the old man muttered something to his son and then turned to Mohammed, ignoring Forsyth. He spoke for two minutes while Mohammed sat nodding. And then finally he stopped. The King stood, nodded curtly at the three men there, and walked offstage into the darkness.

The audience was at an end.

Four Seasons Hotel, Riyadh, Saudi Arabia

11th April 2010, 22:09 hours AST

Forsyth was standing in the enormous living room of his hotel suite, arms spreadeagled above his head, palms pressed against the window of his suite in the Kingdom Tower. The glass felt cool against his hands, but it made no impact on the rage burning inside him. Three hundred metres below, the city of Riyadh glittered underneath a dull night sky. Well, some of it did, he thought. The Al Faisaliah Tower gleamed majestically, its triangular shape reminiscent of the Transamerica Tower in San Francisco where he still had his apartment. And then what? The Hamad Tower was the only other building of any note as far as he could see, and then it was just flat roofs stretching away into the distance, and beyond. Nothing. Just desert. What had Mohammed called it? Rub' al Khali – the Empty Quarter. Sand stretching south for hundreds of miles until it disappeared into the Gulf of Aden. The view summed up its ruler's vision as far as he was concerned: flat, featureless and—. He whirled away in annoyance, unable to think of another adjective beginning with 'f'.

To his right, Mohammed reclined on a deep sofa watching the American, his eyes betraying nothing, much like the King's. Crouch had disappeared. To where, Forsyth didn't know. Or care. The man was a mess and was further evidence of the imbeciles he was having to deal with, all of them, incapable of seeing the boldness of his imagination. Forsyth snorted in disgust and turned to look at Mohammed.

'Tell me again,' he said. 'What exactly did the King say?'

'That he didn't need the extra revenue. That they felt certain their efforts to slow down the rollout of LEAP could be run in the courts whilst they explored more traditional means of replacing lost oil revenue. That they had five years to do it before the oil revenues would be severely affected by the new technology.'

Forsyth stared in disbelief. He had already heard it four times, but each time felt like the first.

'How can he not see the benefits of my proposal? Where's his vision? We could establish a new world order with Saudi Arabia leading the charge. How could he not see that?' he exclaimed again.

There was a soft knock at the door.

A Four Seasons bellhop appeared.

Forsyth turned on him.

'I told you, I'm busy,' he shouted at the Arab. 'That we're not to be disturbed.'

'Sir, you have a visitor.'

'I don't care,' Forsyth barked back. 'Send him away.'

'Sir,' the man continued, eyeing Forsyth nervously. 'It's the Crown Prince.'

For the first time since entering the corridor of mirrors, Forsyth smiled. He winked at Mohammed, hurried round to a large armchair that dominated the room, and sat down. After a moment, he stood up, making his way over to the cavernous windows that stretched thirty feet to the ceiling.

Two can play at his game, Forsyth thought.

'Why didn't you say so?' he said. 'Send him in.'

There was a knock at the door, and several men entered. All over six feet. All thick set. All wearing matching black suits, their tight jackets failing to hide the bulge of metal above their waists. The Crown Prince entered. Forsyth suppressed a gasp.

He was tiny – maybe five two – but what he lacked in height was more than made up for by his girth. Forsyth guessed he must have weighed two hundred pounds, most of it concentrated around his ample belly, which bulged precariously over his feet and forced his arms out wide, so it looked like he was constantly trying to regain his balance as he walked.

'Please, take a seat, your Majesty,' Forsyth suggested, staying by the window.

The Crown Prince waddled forward and sat down, seeming to roll back into the deep cushions. As he did so, his Bisht and thawb rode up.

He's wearing platforms, thought Forsyth.

'To what do we owe this pleasure?' Forsyth said, still not moving.

'That was quite a show you put on this evening,' the Crown Prince said. He had a shrill, wispy voice, as if the air was constricted in his windpipe. It was, Forsyth thought, staring at the man's impossibly large jowls that swallowed up both his neck and chin. They hung heavy, almost at his chest, which seemed to have been consumed by his belly. Forsyth thought he looked like a cherub. Yes, that was it. A small fat cherub. Already he was trying to imagine what he would look like with all that weight removed, another six inches, and his voice deepened.

'Your father didn't seem to like it.'

'He's from a different era. Trades in different currencies than you. Or me.' He glanced at Mohammed.

'I don't understand,' Forsyth said.

'Humility and deference, to start with.'

Forsyth scowled, folding his arms defensively.

'Don't get me wrong,' the Crown Prince continued. 'They frustrate me as much as you, but if you want to make any headway with my father, that's a good place to start. I thought you would have known that.' He glanced at Mohammed, who stared back at the pudgy man, his gaze implacable, before nodding his head deferentially.

'You haven't come here to tell me this,' Forsyth said.

'That is true. Your proposal has merits. I would like to explore them further. Both professionally and—' he glanced down at his stomach, '—personally.'

The Crown Prince laughed, a high-pitched cackle that shook the rolls of fat around his face and wobbled his belly. The laughter continued for several more seconds until he stopped suddenly and clicked his fingers. A man appeared, holding a plate of small cakes. The Crown Prince studied the delicacies, his fingers hovering, until he chose one and popped it into his mouth.

'As you can see,' he continued, taking another cake, 'I could do with losing some weight.' He winked at Forsyth, nodding at the plate. 'Please.'

Forsyth was just about to decline when he caught Mohammed's frown. Instead, he stepped forward and took the smallest, before taking a small bite. It was sickeningly sweet, but he swallowed the mouthful and retreated to the window, the uneaten remains cupped in his hand.

'They're called luqaimat. My favourites. My mother used to make them in the mornings. I would help her fry the dough and, once they were cool, douse them in date syrup. He smacked his lips and popped another one into his mouth. 'I can't resist them.'

Forsyth stood there wondering what to do. His instinct was to throw the fat cherub out of his suite. He was worse than his father, simply focused on reducing his waistline so he could gobble down more of these disgusting dough balls.

'Seriously, you must think me so shallow.' The Crown Prince took another of the delicacies and gulped it down. 'My father is wrong. Our oil revenue will collapse faster than he thinks. Especially if Green Ray is allowed to roll-out their tech unopposed. And we don't intend to let that happen. Do we, John?'

The Crown Prince's eyes had become black pin pricks that bored into Forsyth's forehead like laser beams.

Forsyth smiled. Maybe there was more to the cherub than he had realised.

'But without your father's say so, how can we stop them?'

'Leave my father to me,' the Crown Prince replied, popping another luqaimat into his mouth.

Transamerica Pyramid, San Francisco

12th April 2010, 12:30 hours PDT

T he sun was sparkling off the whitecaps, clearly visible on the azure waters of San Francisco Bay as life carried on below him: a cruise ship, toy-like, sitting beneath the twin towers of the Golden Gate Bridge; just ahead of it, a procession of massive container ships, their cargo stacked dangerously high as they idled towards the huge port of Oakland behind Treasure Island; two catamarans racing each other between Angel Island State Park and the smaller Alcatraz. Professor Crouch sighed. He would be happy to exchange his current prison for that. Even the icy waters of the Pacific, inside a small cell, with changing seasons, seemed preferable to the hot and dusty one he currently inhabited. A lifeless landscape, baked by an unrelenting sun that had burned away all colour and boiled off every drop of water. Where no one spoke his language, least of all his vain glorious boss that cared for no one but himself. Just like Reynolds. At least

Crouch had been able to escape the Nevada compound. Now he was stuck in Saudi, a pariah, able only to LEAP here in secret, but stuck behind plate-glass windows, nearly nine hundred feet in the air. All thanks to his US masters, ones who hid in the shadows and offered nothing except threats dressed in sheep's clothing. At least Forsyth had pulled him back from the brink. A way out of his predicament after the aborted attempt on the President's life. Even in his drunken state, he had realised it was only a matter of time before they came calling again, but the call, when it came, was from Forsyth. With an offer, even his alcohol-sozzled brain had been happy to accept. It was 113 days today since he had stopped drinking. One hundred and thirteen days clean. He liked having a clear mind. Most of the time. Until forty-six days ago, when that other call had finally come. In his heart he always knew it would: the same voice, summoning him back to San Francisco. To this very conference room, with an offer at redemption. Crouch turned as his redemption walked in through the door, his bald head hidden beneath a forty-niners baseball cap pulled low against the glare of the midday sun. The fact that the man no longer bothered to hide his face was deeply worrying. Crouch took a deep breath, suddenly nervous, unsure of how to begin.

'Admiring the view, I see.'

The man, whose name Crouch still did not know, joined him by the plate-glass windows and stared out onto the glittering bay below.

'Beautiful isn't it?'

'How did the operation go?' Crouch said, already knowing the answer. He had been monitoring the comms of the US Defense Department's command force that covered the Middle East, hoping to gain news of the attacks. Their security was childish, with so many back doors into the network. It had been a simple task to breach and then watch, waiting for the news he was desperate to receive and that would herald his return to the States. As a hero this time, but things hadn't gone quite as planned, hence the meeting.

'Well, thank you.'

'It wasn't our deal,' Crouch whined, failing miserably to maintain his cool.

'If you already knew the outcome, why ask?'

'You said that if I helped you infiltrate the Taliban strongholds on the Pakistan–Afghanistan border, I would receive full immunity from prosecution for the attempt on President Harris.'

'And you helped us. Thank you for your service,' the man answered, his tone questioning what the problem was, leaving Crouch with no choice but to plough on.

'You said the weapon would be detonated inside the Taliban's cave systems and wipe out their strongholds. You said it would kill thousands of terrorists. Shorten the war by five years.'

'You killed thousands, Crouch.'

'Yes, Americans,' Crouch said, stammering slightly, as he realised where this was going.

'Yes, and you're on the line for that. If it ever got out, you'd be finished. More so than you are now,' the man continued. 'Luckily for you, Green Ray agreed to reverse their anti-copying law, and we were able to restore every single man and woman who was killed by your virus. No harm done.'

There was plenty of harm done, thought Crouch. The prospect of returning home to America suddenly seemed as far as away as the cruise ship stuck at the entrance to the bay.

'When will I receive my immunity and get to come home?' Crouch said, staring into the bay wistfully. He could feel the cool breeze against his face.

'Soon,' the man said.

'What do you mean, soon?' Crouch said, breaking out into a cold sweat.

'Whilst Green Ray exists, there is no immunity. That's the goal. Destroy Green Ray and you get your paperwork. No one expected them to reverse that no-copying rule. We need to disgrace them so completely, that the LEAP technology passes into the full control of the US government. That's the play here. Have you missed something?'

Crouch stood there, the cold sweat now joined by a hammering heart that threatened to burst from his jacket. He had been set up.

Again. The man had just said it. They hadn't expected Green Ray to cave in so easily. Had they stood their ground as expected, Crouch would have been fingered as the architect of the virus. Along with the attempted assassination of the President, he now had the blood of thousands of Americans on his hands. It made no difference that they had lived. He was directly responsible for poisoning them.

'So, she needs to go?'

'That's always been the plan here. They both do. I thought you wanted that?'

'I do,' Crouch said. Actually, what he wanted was a drink. A long hard one to blank out the nightmare that he had never really escaped from.

Camden Town, London

13th April 2010, 02:36 hours GMT

They were late. He wasn't sure what for, but he could feel his pulse racing. No, it was worse than that: a hard block of fear wedged in his gut, his palms slick with sweat. He looked down at the cereal bowl full of Fruity Pebbles, the multi-coloured rice bits, floating forlornly in the off-white milk. Angel loved the Flintstones and would watch the cartoon on hard repeat for hours, begging Ed for a dog like Dino. He put the spoon down and stood up, moving into the hallway where Jo and Angel were running through the little girl's checklist. Ed had suggested it. He used it all the time at work. Five key things for school: homework, check; lunch box, check; ID card, check; two dollars for snacks, check; and, most importantly, her lucky pencil case, Flintstones of course. Angel screamed with frustration and stomped off upstairs to recover the project she'd been working on for two weeks – a history of Suriname, where her grandparents were from. Ed had helped her. A rare ten-day break. Jo was smiling at her departing daughter and turned it on Ed, who felt himself respond. God, she was beautiful. He reached out, drawing her in real close. She smelled good, her hair tickling his nose as it always did. She normally tied it back, but she knew Ed liked it free. Gently, she pushed him away, grabbing the car keys before exiting the house. He felt Angel run past and called out. She stopped, returning for her hug: a big squeeze that swept her off her feet, as Ed twirled round. Once, twice, and finally three times. She giggled, squirming in his arms, telling him to put her down. That they were late for school and she didn't want a tardy ticket. He set her down, and she scampered off. That feeling again – a sense of impending dread squirrelling round his stomach, up into his chest, making it difficult to breathe, as if something was constricting his lungs. He shut it down, watching Angel climb into the Camaro. Top down today. Top down every day in LA, where the sun always shone. Jo waved from the car as she turned the key.

The boom of the blast knocked him into the house, but he could still see the car engulfed in a fireball.

He got up and walked calmly over to the car.

Jo was nowhere to be seen.

Angel was still sitting in the passenger seat, hair flaming like a torch, panic and fear dancing across her skin as the flames hungrily devoured his little girl.

Ed sat bolt upright, arms outstretched, gasping for breath, heart thumping like a jackhammer. It was several moments before he realised where he was. The bedsit was as he had left it. Peeling paint and green mould peppered the ceiling, a grimy basin in the corner, above which sat a cracked mirror so pitted with chips, it barely reflected the red neon sign flashing intermittently through the window opposite. Ed lit a cigarette, hoisted himself off the creaking bed and went to stand by the glass, forcing the lower half up. It screeched alarmingly, but a six-inch gap appeared and he crouched down, blowing smoke into the busy street. Opposite, the Red Lemon was emptying, drunken students rolling onto the pavement, screaming obscenities at each other as they debated where to go next. Eventually they agreed, walking across the road, dodging the slow-moving traffic, before disappearing into the kebab restaurant underneath Ed's bedroom. He could hear them arguing through the thin floorboards, the smell of cheap mince making his stomach grumble. But he was in no mood to eat. Extinguishing the cigarette on the blackened sill, he reached the basin in two strides, opening the cold tap. As he waited for the water to cool, he urinated into the basin, using the tepid water to sluice the stained marble, before taking a long drink and splashing his face. He straightened, peering into the mirror, but all he saw were glimpses of Angel in the ruined glass, her eyes boring into his skull like twin spotlights. He grabbed another cigarette, trying to process the nightmare. Angel and Jo hadn't died in the drive of their home in Palmdale. It had been on SR-14. Late afternoon, not early morning. On the way back from a school concert, not on the way in. Ed should have been with them, but wasn't, instead laid low by a bug. God, he'd wanted to go so badly, but could barely move that day. Jo had promised to record it for him. They were meant to watch it all together that evening. Curled up on the sofa, eating Angel's favourite pizza – margherita, extra cheese, on a thin crust. There had been no explanation for the crash: no witnesses, no other cars involved, no mechanical failure. Nothing was the same in his dream, except the fire. That had been real enough. The petrol tank had breached. It was full. The police report confirmed that Jo had stopped at a gas station just off W Rancho Vista Boulevard, on the way to the school. Nineteen gallons of fuel igniting to create a fireball, burning at 1,500 degrees Fahrenheit. Ed swallowed hard, as Angel's eyes sought his out. He took a deep drag and exhaled, dropping the cigarette into the grimy washbasin.

He donned a T-shirt from the Formica closet, before turning to examine the only other item of furniture in the room. Twelve tall glass jars were sitting on the table. Six of them were filled with water, each labelled with a spontaneous combustion warning sticker. Inside, a long tube of what looked like brown chalk, maybe six inches in length, rested diagonally against the glass. It was phosphorous, an element so reactive with oxygen, it had to be kept in water. He put on a surgical mask, unscrewed the lid of one of the jars, and extracted the chalk tube with some forceps. Within seconds it started to smoke, emitting an odour, like burning matches. It wasn't unpleasant, but in large enough quantities was extremely hazardous. That was the idea, but the problem was that it took too long to react, which is where the carbon disulphide came in. He opened one of the six remaining jars and dropped the phosphorous stick into the clear liquid, before quickly sealing it. Within a minute, it had completely dissolved into a dirty yellow solution. He moved onto the next one, working methodically until he had finished all six. He recovered a cheap rucksack from underneath the table and inserted a rigid plastic divider, before carefully placing each bottle into one of the six compartments. Finally, he sealed the bag with the strapping and sat back to admire his handiwork. It was crude, and, given more time, he would have preferred something more sophisticated, but he'd made do with what he could procure locally. Besides which, it would do the job. When he broke the glass, the carbon disulphide would evaporate and, once exposed to oxygen, the phosphorous pentoxide would turn from a liquid into a gas to create white phosphorous that burned at 1,000 degrees Fahrenheit. Not quite what Jo and Angel had suffered, but it would still burn the skin off someone's body.

Ed glanced at his wrist: 03:10. The remaining night lay before him like a raging bonfire, within which his two girls twisted and turned as the flames consumed them. There would be no more sleep for him tonight, not that he slept much these days. He struggled into a nondescript hoodie and, after wedging his baseball cap low, pulled the hood tightly around his head, before making his way down the creaking stairs onto Parkway. The entrance to the guest house was marooned between two takeouts, on one side Bamboo Blossom, the other, Doner Cave, outside which the drunken students were finishing their greasy meals. They stared at Ed as he passed them. Without warning, one of the students suddenly grabbed the peak of his cap and flicked it upwards, knocking it to the pavement, whilst the other three threw the remains of their kebabs at him. Before he could react, all four of them were twenty yards away, sprinting along the pavement, howling with laughter. Ed didn't even try to follow. He stooped to retrieve his cap, quickly donning it, before slipping the hood back over his head. Satisfied, he entered the deserted restaurant. The spitting cone of meat looked disgusting, but he didn't care. It was simply fuel to feed his

body, a last supper of sorts, to get him through the days until he could
avenge Jo and Angel.

Markarfljót River, Iceland

13th April 2010, 14:34 hours GMT

The grey clouds were so low that Dagur Einarson couldn't tell where they stopped and the earth started, thanks to the grey squalls that were currently peppering the landscape. He was cold, but most of all, he was pissed off and stopped to catch his breath, wondering if he should have stayed in Hafnarfirðiat. He'd reluctantly left his warm office at midday after receiving reports of dead fish in the Markarfljót river, driving east along Route 1, before detouring at Hvolsvöllur, onto F261 and finally 250. Eventually, he'd abandoned the Shogun, hiking the remaining half mile to the head of a small escarpment which overlooked the floodplain. It was a dizzying maze of muddy brown water courses, worming their way down towards the Atlantic Ocean. Fed by the Mýrdalsjökull and Eyjafjallajökull glaciers, the outwash plain was constantly replenished by glaciofluvial deposits carried there by meltwater from the nearby glaciers. Dead fish could mean many things, but the concerning one, the one he was here to check out, was local volcanic activity increasing the meltwater volumes. He needed a sample for the Directorate of Fisheries to analyse.

If they were right, then the department would evacuate every village in the floodplain right down to the coast. He swore loudly as he checked his watch: the concert started in four hours. At this rate, he would struggle to make it on time. Which wasn't an option. Bjork was performing Voltaic tonight, in Reykjavik. At The Nordic House, no less. It only seated seventy, and Dagur was one of them. There was no way he was missing it. He adjusted his headphones, causing the industrial beat of Army of Me to grind deep into his ears. The synth bass sounded menacing in the fading light of the afternoon, but the thought that he might not see her perform this song catapulted Dagur down the steep slope towards the plain.

Dagur made good time and seventy minutes later was standing, staring at the water twenty feet beneath him. The flowing current had carved a deep swathe out of the bank he was standing on, and, in doing so, had created a pool in which he could see dead fish floating. He tracked downstream along the bank, looking for a point where the river was more accessible. After five minutes, he found his point of entry, where the steep bank had levelled out into the point bar further along the meander of the river. Here, he could access the water easily, where it was neither particularly fast flowing nor too deep. He unhitched his rucksack and removed its contents, before wriggling into the heavy fisherman's bib and oilskin trousers. Next came the bright orange oilskin smock. After assembling the fishing net, he ventured into the water. Even through the skins he could feel the temperature, which only confirmed what he suspected. Dagur walked upstream, smiling as the pounding synth of Army of Me began its fourth play of the day. The water was already up to his waist, making him struggle against the current. As the aggressive thump of the drums cut in, he pressed forward, wading deeper into the river, which was noticeably hotter. He scanned the water for fish as he rounded the bend of the river. Up ahead, several were caught in a pool of whirling eddies. Dagur beelined for it, not noticing the distant roar through the heavy drumbeat. He cast the net ahead of him, dragging trapped fish under the water, before deftly twisting the pole and scooping it up high into the air to keep them pressed into the mesh. He snagged three before turning his back to the current, leaning into it as he examined his catch. All three were cooked through. At some point, the water must have been boiling.

Behind him, a metre-high wave of glacial runoff appeared, roaring and snarling around the bend in the river, a haze of steam hovering above it like a malignant shadow. In one second, the river was around his waist, the very next, past his neck as the boiling juggernaut upended him, quickly filling the jacket and pants with super-heated water. He gasped in surprise, inhaling sulphurous meltwater deep into his lungs. Dagur vomited as he blindly tried to claw his way to the surface, but his flooded skins kept him anchored to the riverbed. His movements became sporadic, his arms jerking helplessly towards the surface. With a final shudder, he fell still. Above him, the cooked fish resumed their gentle bobbing in the eddies of the now bubbling pool, whilst beneath them, the surging techno opera faded away, to be replaced with, I Miss You.

Eyjafjallajökull Ice Cap, Iceland

14th April 2010, 07:14 hours GMT

The dirty grey sleet covered everything like a malevolent blanket, deadening the landscape with its grim touch. Hilda Borgsdottir adjusted her face mask, brushing the light ash away, but it was a losing battle. A light haze clouded her vision almost immediately, forcing her to wipe again. Around her, ghostly shapes moved slowly, like astronauts on a barren planet. A planet where the sun had been snuffed out by an otherworldly storm that emanated, not from the atmosphere, but from inside the bowels of the earth itself. She stretched cramped limbs, brushing dirty soot from her watch. No wonder she felt hungry. Her day had started the night before. Whilst others were sleeping, her team had stayed awake, glued to their seismometers as the earthquake had swarmed for over two hours, gradually building in intensity until it hit four on the volcanic explosivity index. The results had scared, excited and puzzled the team in equal measure: four was catastrophic. History making, in fact. Just one below the cataclysmic eruption that blew a hole in Mount St Helens back in 1980, but last night there was nothing to see. The fissures from ten days earlier had been more exciting, visually at least. Then they had witnessed lava pyrotechnics blasting 1,000-degree molten rock five hundred feet into the clear night sky, but twelve hours ago, they'd seen nothing. Just a swarm of volcanic activity which suggested that magma was still moving in the same conduits that had brought lava to the surface at Fimmvörduháls. That was dangerous. Very dangerous, and the team had informed the local authorities before maintaining a watching brief throughout the long, chilly night, but the ice cap had remained silent.

At 5 a.m., an officer of the Icelandic Civil Protection Department had arrived to inform them they had ordered evacuations of the towns and farms near Eyjafjallajökull. One of their observers had drowned yesterday after a sudden increase in the amount of water in the area's streams and rivers. Boiled to death, apparently. Poor man. No one deserved that death. It meant only one thing: the onset of a jökulhlaup, a flood caused by an eruption under a glacier. Hence, the fine shower of ash. Somewhere deep down, the hot magma had mixed with the ice, blowing steam out into the atmosphere. The team were safe, occupying high ground to the west of the icecap which provided them with a bird's eye view of any volcanic activity, but, after hearing from the CPD they'd given up hope of any pyrotechnics. Instead, they were all standing in a morning twilight of swirling ash, which meant visibility was nearly zero, their chance of observing the eruption equally bleak.

Her radio crackled into life.

'How long should we stay here?' It was Jökull Magnússon, her team leader. He was only standing ten feet away, but all she could make out was his ghostly silhouette.

'Maybe till eight?' she replied. 'Unless the wind picks up, we may as well head back into Reykjavík. Clean up, get some food, a shower, some sleep and head back this afternoon.'

'Agreed,' he said.

A wave of exhaustion swept over Hilda. Was there even any point in waiting forty more minutes? This was not going to clear. As the thought formed, a sudden gust of wind cleared the surrounding area. Suddenly, she could see the entire team, all five of them, gathered around her like stone-grey sentinels. She instinctively looked back towards Eyjafjallajökull and gasped in astonishment.

The mist had parted like a theatre curtain, revealing the icecap, framed against a clear blue sky which was steadily being consumed by a growing mushroom of grey billowing madness. It was as if the pits of hell were spawning a malevolent evil into the atmosphere, one that broiled and seethed like an angry spirit. One that looked solid to the touch, but moved like a multi-limbed serpent, twisting in the morning air. She craned her neck as she looked up at the towering plume. It must be five miles high, she thought, following its trajectory South-East over the iron-grey Atlantic Ocean.

Without warning, the curtain closed, blotting out the magisterial view so quickly, Hilda wondered if her mind's eye had made it up.

Orlando Airport, Florida

15th April 2010, 12:30 hours EDT

The baby's face was blue and, for a second, Alan Taylor wondered if she had stopped breathing. He winced as a strangled cry suddenly filled the restaurant, growing in strength, like an approaching police siren, until everyone had turned his way. They stared, eyes filled with a mixture of fatigue and resentment. The same fatigue and resentment that he felt. Mandy, his wife, clucked softly, rocking the small bundle back and forth, but it was to no avail. The tiny lungs fell silent for another prolonged pause, before wailing out another piercing cry. Alan stood up.

'Where are you going?' his wife asked, her tone full of accusation.

'To check the boards again. See if anything has changed.'

'Fat chance,' she muttered.

'Maybe. But if it has, you will be the first to know.' He attempted a smile, but it came out as a grimace, which Mandy met with one of her own. He didn't wait for a response, instead limping away through the passengers strewn around the restaurant. Most moved as soon as they saw him, but others were asleep, some lying across three chairs, others under tables, forcing him to carefully navigate his way around them.

Alan sighed. They'd had such a good holiday: fourteen days of uninterrupted sunshine in Orlando. A blessing after the winter grey of England. The baby loved it. Gurgling and happy, meant Mandy was happy. Which meant he was happy. They'd intended to go to the parks, but had lingered beside the pool, basking in the hot spring sun, taking long naps in the afternoon with the baby, followed by short walks along the boardwalk that ringed the lake. Some evenings, they had taken advantage of the hotel sitting service, enjoying a quiet meal at one of the many restaurants dotted around the Spring Palms Hotel complex. Then they would wind their way back to the villa, where they relaxed on the veranda, listening to the cicadas chirping as they watched the last firework display over the Magic Kingdom. For a moment, their lives had felt normal again, suspended in a bubble of calm and tranquillity, until last night, that is, when the bubble had burst.

They'd arrived at Orlando airport to find all flights to Europe had been cancelled. Something about an ash cloud over the Atlantic, but otherwise nothing: no news, no updates. Just eighteen hours of silence as passengers worked out for themselves what had happened. A volcano in Iceland had erupted. The ash was bad for the engines, so no flights. He'd looked at flights via Paris, Amsterdam, in fact anywhere, but everything seemed to be grounded. He was due back at work tomorrow. Needed to be at work for a pitch next Tuesday. If he won it, they were safe for the next two years. Without it ... He dared not think about that, and instead concentrated on the boards, which were still displaying a sea of red cancellations.

Overhead, a Tannoy suddenly sprang into life.

'Ladies and gentlemen. We regret to inform you that all flights to Europe have been grounded for the foreseeable future. We suggest you contact your holiday company or airline for further details. In the meantime, please make your way to baggage control and collect your luggage.'

A hubbub of chatter flickered out across the cavernous departure hall, morphing into an angry roar which swept over Alan as he watched the departure display flick every red entry from 'DELAYED' to 'CANCELLED'.

Townhouse, Camden Town, London

15th April 2010, 07:32 hours GMT

U ma hurried down the steep stairs of the old house, trying not to rush. It was the first time she'd returned since her argument with Ethan, which seemed months ago, but was only last week. They'd barely spoken since their meeting with the President, their world upside down following the attacks on American bases in Afghanistan. And now this. As she passed their bedroom, the chants from outside were clearly audible in the corridor. Uma felt drawn to the window. Below her, there must have been two thousand people stretching away down the street, on either side. Many carried banners. All were facing the house, chanting their stupid chant. As she looked, someone spotted her and the entire crowd moved as one, surging forward. For a moment she thought the thin blue line would break, but it held.

'Idiots,' she muttered under her breath, before turning and continuing down the grand staircase into the basement. As she skirted between the desks, someone caught sight of her. He stood and applauded. Others joined in. Within seconds, fifty people were standing and clapping. She smiled tiredly, acknowledging the team with a namaskar.

Through the crowd, she spotted Ethan in his office, phone glued to his ear. He saw her and returned it to its cradle, mouthing for her to join him. As she entered the room, he scooped Uma up in a big hug, kissing her deeply on the lips.

'God, I've missed you,' he said. 'Sorry about the other day. I was selfish. Not thinking.'

He looked tired, a grey shadow framing his jaw, eyes bloodshot with lack of sleep. They hadn't been alone since the attacks in Afghanistan. Ethan returning to London; Uma staying in Washington to firefight the internal fallout from the President's decision. Days stretching into nights. She couldn't remember the last time she had slept, suddenly realising it was 3:40 in the morning in DC. She suppressed a yawn.

'Don't worry about it.' Uma said, nodding at the open-plan office. 'Why are they applauding? What's happened?'

'We've been speaking with the prof here,' he nodded at a balding man sitting in the corner of the room. 'He said the last time, Eyja—' Ethan stumbled over the unfamiliar word.

'Are you destroying my language again?' she smiled. 'It's pronounced, 'Ay—ya, that is "ay" as in day.'

'Easy for you to say,' he smiled, and tried again, 'Ay—ya.'

'Good. Feeah—atlah. Try the "feeah" as in few.'

'Feeah—atlah,' Ethan repeated.

'And finally, yo—kootl.'

He laughed, shrugging his shoulders.

'It's the hardest bit,' Uma said. She could feel herself getting angry but wasn't even sure why. Icelandic was an impenetrable language for English speakers, containing sounds that didn't even exist in their native tongue. Why should Ethan suddenly grasp the pronunciation of some obscure volcano in southern Iceland, that, until yesterday, no one had even heard of? 'Try it again, yo—kootl,' she said, more patiently. 'Yo—kootl.'

Ethan mumbled something. It was nowhere near, and they both knew it.

'That's right, ay—ya—Feeah—atlah—yo—kootl,' she said phonetically, and then, more quickly, 'Eyjafjallajökull.'

Ethan shrugged his shoulders.

'The volcano,' he said. 'They think it's a sign. Erupting like this in our hour of need. You have to admit, it feels like one. An Act of God almost.'

'Nonsense,' she snorted. 'Volcanoes are always erupting in Iceland.'

'Not this one. It's been dormant for nearly two hundred years. It really feels like someone is smiling down on us.'

Uma thought of her few hours in Iceland, just days ago, thinking about her father. She'd seen the lava eruptions, thinking nothing of them. A shiver ran down her spine, which she brushed away. She wasn't a superstitious person. She was a woman of science. Besides which, she had barely registered the eruption. Too busy reincarnating thousands of dead soldiers, but she understood the science.

'It's just weather and geology,' she countered. 'Eyjafjallajökull is directly under the jet stream which, fortunately for us, was unusually stable at the time of the eruption's second phase, blowing continuously southeast right over European airspace. Plus, the main eruption occurred under 700 feet of glacial ice. The resulting meltwater flowed back into the volcano, where it vaporised, significantly increasing the explosive power. Add in the fact that the lava cooled very quickly, which created a cloud of highly abrasive, glass-rich ash. Which just so happens to be deadly to aeroplane engines.'

'The doctor's right,' the small man sitting in the corner interjected. 'In 1989, KLM flight 867 was on its approach into Anchorage, Alaska, when it flew through volcanic ash from Mount Redoubt, causing all four engines to shut down. The crew were able to restart two of them on the left wing and landed safely in Ted Stevens International Airport.'

Uma seemed to notice him for the first time. 'Excuse me, and you are?'

'This is Professor John Dawson at the UCL Hazard Research Centre,' Ethan interjected. 'I've retained his service to consult for us so I could better understand exactly what was happening. And for how long – timing is critical here.'

Uma stared at the man. Why hadn't Ethan asked her? She was Professor of Geothermal Studies for Chrissakes. In Iceland. Working for most of her life, less than forty miles from Eyjafjallajökull.

'And?'

'And what?'

'How long?' Uma said. 'How long could it go on for?'

The Professor stood up. 'The ice cap last erupted in 1821. It spewed ash for over a year.'

The penny finally penetrated her sleep-deprived brain. Uma smiled for the first time since entering the house.

A year!

Ethan stood up excitedly.

'It's better than we had dared hope. Governments are approaching us to work out a way of getting their citizens home. We've already received lists of all the passengers stuck at their various destinations. It's over ten million people. This is what we've been waiting for.'

Uma's legs felt weak as another wave of exhaustion hit her. And something else. Relief. The feeling washed over her as her eyes watered up. She sat down as Ethan continued.

'That number could get higher. The airlines cancelled over seventeen thousand flights yesterday. Same today. That alone is over 7.5 million passengers. Now we know where everyone lives, we're going to set up LEAP gates within two hundred yards of every single house. We're budgeting for over two thousand gates, but it could be more. One of the techies has rigged up some software that will allow us to plot in all the addresses and work out the optimum number we need. I've already got teams from the US bringing the gates through. From there they transport them out to each district right across Europe. We're doing the same at all the airports. They're saying this is the largest repatriation of passengers since the Second World War.' The words poured out of him. She hadn't seen Ethan this animated in years. The mood was infectious.

'We're doing the same with freight companies who are also grounded. There's a huge quantity of time-sensitive materials that need to be transported. Medicine mainly, but also fresh flowers and fruit. We've already contacted every single company affected and are setting up LEAP gates in their distribution centres.'

'Why not into each house?'

'We don't have time. It would take six months to do that.'

'What if it lasts a year?'

'Yes, we considered that, but it also could stop tomorrow. Then we've lost our advantage. Plus, we can't get into the houses. Everyone's away. We wouldn't even know where to put them, even if we could get in. However, I've got a team working on a post-repatriation strategy. As passengers come home, we're going to collect the contact details of their employers. We'll approach each one to install a priority LEAP gate at their premises. Free of charge, of course, and also one in the house of the repatriated passenger with priority installation given to each employee of that business. It'll create a network effect.'

Uma frowned.

'It's a virtuous cycle. Like Facebook: the more people that are using LEAP gates, the more value everyone who is already using the network will gain. It'll ripple out from the ten million data points. Before we know it, LEAP will be ubiquitous.'

'My, you have been busy.' Uma smiled. She felt like crying again. Ethan had truly delivered. But why did she feel so angry with him? She thought of him sitting there in the Situation Room as the President dismantled her LEAP Laws, doing nothing. Yet, here he was pushing forward the LEAP rollout as if his life depended on it, driving his team to take advantage of the opportunity offered by the eruption. Working days and nights, just like she was doing. Her anger suddenly dissipated, melting away like the meltwater from Eyjafjallajökull. Why was she blaming this man for everything? When all he had done since last October was love her unconditionally. Helping her navigate the viper pit in DC. And now, in what seemed like an age, they had a chance to break through with LEAP. Show the world what it was capable of. Ethan was leading the charge, full throttle. A wave of guilt enveloped her as the tears flowed unchecked now. Ethan came round the side of his desk, taking her hands in his.

'Are you OK?' he said, his eyes creased with concern.

'Thank you,' she said. 'For everything.'

Riyadh, Saudi Arabia

19th April 2010, 14:01 hours AST

'In what has been described as the largest repatriation of people since the Second World War, Green Ray continues to overcome the travel disruption caused by the Eyjafjallajökull volcano eruption. By some estimates, they are on target to repatriate over one million passengers by next week alone, through a series of LEAP gates that have sprung up overnight. We're going over to our reporter in Leeds, England, to hear about one family's experience.'

The screen cut to a couple standing outside a small terrace house. The woman was holding a sleeping baby.

'Good morning, Jane. I'm here with Alan Taylor, a war hero from Afghanistan, his wife Mandy and their two-month-old baby, Emma. They were on holiday in Florida and were caught by the ash cloud.' The reporter shoved his microphone into the man's face. 'Alan, can you tell our viewers what happened to you and your family?'

'Yes, Graham. Good morning,' Alan glanced at the camera nervously, before continuing. 'We missed our flight back to the UK, along with thousands of others. We were lucky as we managed to secure a room at a Days Inn on the outskirts of Orlando. We've been living there for the past three nights. Given some stories I've heard, we were very lucky. Having Emma helped,' he nodded at the sleeping baby. 'Families with very young children were given preference. I hear others are still at the airport sleeping on floors, tables, wherever they can. Even so, it was getting difficult. We were low on money. The worst thing was not knowing when we would be allowed to fly. I was spending four hours every day on the phone with the airline staff trying to work out a route home. But there was nothing, which was incredibly stressful. I work for myself. I had to get back to work for a meeting. A sales meeting. One of the most important in the life of our business. Without it, I ...' His voice trailed off, eyes misting slightly. His wife placed a hand on his arm, whilst the reporter remained silent. 'Until Green Ray stepped in. We received a call yesterday, about midday, from one of their service representatives. Said that they had located a gate in Leeds city centre and that we were eligible to be sent home because of the baby.' He smiled down at Emma as the camera panned in to show the sleeping child, completely oblivious to the group crowded around her.

'Were you worried about the LEAP?'

'Yes, initially, but some of the LEAP team went through the gate first to reassure us. We could see it happening real time on a video feed. Mandy was allowed to take the baby with her. I went first. They warned us we might feel some sickness, which was true, but otherwise ...' he paused, lost for words, '... you don't feel anything. It's incredible. One moment I was standing in Orlando airport; the next second, I was in The Light – a retail centre in the middle of Leeds. It was instant.' He snapped his fingers. 'No jet lag. Our bags came with us. Which is more than happens with the airlines. No waiting. No queues. No getting up early. No sitting on a plane for nine hours trying to keep Emma quiet. We could choose a time that suited the baby. Just after she had been fed. She was asleep. It cost nothing. It means I can get back to work tomorrow.' Alan paused and put an arm round his wife. 'To be honest, it's a miracle. I work for myself. If I'm not there, I don't get paid. We have a mortgage to pay. I have a pitch tomorrow, in Germany. I was facing ruin if I didn't make it. Thanks to LEAP, I can make it. They've set up a gate in Munich, Germany, so I can go. It's incredible. It would have been a three-day trip normally. Obviously, with the ash cloud, I couldn't get over.' The camera panned to the woman. She smiled. 'But now it's instant. I'll travel the day of the pitch, just one hour before. Actually, it's even better. If they want, I can bring my customers back and take them round the factory here in Leeds. If I win the business, with LEAP I can deliver their orders within a week. We've been told we're allowed to send it through the gate. If I win it, of course.'

The camera returned to the reporter.

'Well, there you have it, Jane. Just one family's experience in using the new LEAP transporter.'

The tumbler hit the television, exploding in a red burst of liquid and glass, causing the screen to flicker, but it didn't fade. Tomato juice dripped down the cracked glass. It looked like it was bleeding. Forsyth felt like he was bleeding, the memory painfully recent. The memory filled with pus and mucus bubbling from a hole that had once been his nose. The creak of his arthritic joints, so bad he couldn't walk without the aid of a Zimmer frame, unable to look in a mirror at the horror that had been inflicted on his body. Damn that woman. She had reduced him to that, and now it was getting worse. Through a quirk of fate, she was now grabbing the hearts and minds of the world's population. He couldn't turn on a channel without being reminded of it. Green Ray was everywhere, and so were their damn gates. Right on cue, an image of Uma Jakobsdóttir appeared on the TV, clear, despite the spiderweb of cracks that covered her features. The sight of her coalesced into a cry of rage, bubbling up through his stomach like a demented demon. He grabbed a lampstand and attacked the screen, smashing it repeatedly until, finally, it flickered dark.

'I thought you were happy to let them have transportation.'

Forsyth glared at Crouch, who was sitting at his desk, tapping away.

'I am,' he spat back. 'It's basic. It's boring. We want the stuff they don't dare touch.'

'This could be good for us,' Crouch ventured.

Forsyth shrugged. Crouch didn't have a clue. He had no idea what that woman had put him through, but he couldn't resist.

'How the hell is this good for us?' he spat back.

'It might force the Saudis back to the table once they realise their delaying tactics have been nullified by the eruption. This ...' Crouch nodded at the destroyed television, 'will impact oil consumption, especially if Green Ray successfully kick-starts a network effect. They could have hundreds of millions of users by the end of the year.'

Forsyth paused. Crouch had a point. This might be good for them.

'Maybe I should give the Crown Prince a call. Better yet, I'll go and see him.'

He stood up and checked himself in the mirror. He looked good. Back in control. He ambled towards the door, but before leaving, he turned to Crouch.

'You're still ready, aren't you?'

Crouch nodded.

Forsyth stared at him suspiciously. He had been so sure about the professor, but recently he had sensed a reluctance about everything he asked him to do. He was clearly drinking again. Maybe he was going soft. Forsyth shrugged. He would deal with him later. He had a backer to grab.

Crouch didn't look up as Forsyth marched out, instead adjusting his laptop as the screen metamorphosed into a TV studio. He adjusted the volume.

'What do you think, John?'

'It's quite a turnaround for Green Ray. This time last week, they were mired worldwide in legal action, Union action and self-interests. It had effectively stymied their plans to roll-out LEAP, yet seven days later they are sitting pretty.'

'So true, John. It is quite incredible how quickly the sentiment has swung. As you say, this time last week they were the big bad wolf, destroyer of industries and jobs. And now they're the saviour. Expected to repatriate up to eight million people and possibly—'

Crouch closed the screen and stood up. He felt claustrophobic in the apartment, but there was nowhere to go, particularly at this time of day. In Riyadh, it was always hot and this was supposed to be the best time of year. He couldn't risk making a LEAP to the Transamerica Pyramid now. He thought about going back to his apartment, but the thought terrified him. He didn't trust himself. His hand reached for the bottle by his side, slurping down the tepid water, which made him gag. He hadn't meant to start drinking again, but the CIA agent had spooked him. What if he was blamed as the architect of the massacres? He would be finished. Not only a tattered reputation, but a lifetime in prison.

For Crouch, it was the challenge of what was possible with the new tech. Always had been; always would be. There were no boundaries with Forsyth. For that, he was grateful, but – and there was a big but – as he slowly sobered up, his mind had cleared as if a fog had been burned away by the morning sunshine, leaving him clear-headed. He didn't want this life. He wanted his reputation back, but this type of work would not get him there. His thoughts turned back to the LEAP interview. That was respectable work. Uma and Ethan, burnishing their credentials. And reputation. However much he hated her for what she had done, she was now where he wanted to be. The irony was not lost on Crouch. He'd joined Reynolds for a chance at immortality, but instead received ridicule, a national joke bumbling about the floor of the LEAP chamber trying to find his glasses. A metaphor for everything that was wrong with Reynolds' plan. Now Forsyth and the CIA were sending him down a road from which there was no way back. It felt like the assassination attempt all over again. He was simply a pawn in someone else's plan. The realisation catapulted him out of his seat back towards his apartment, drawn to the one thing that would make him forget.

Riyadh, Saudi Arabia

19th April 2010, 15:33 hours AST

The central atrium rose above the ancient tree, two, maybe three hundred feet into the air towards a parabolic glass ceiling that was cool blue, the colour of the sky. The Crown Prince was perched on a park bench underneath the gnarled branches, sipping what Forsyth presumed to be teas from a delicate bone china cup.

'Is that real?' Forsyth asked, looking up at the towering branches.

'Of course it is, Mr Forsyth.' The Crown Prince laughed his high-pitched laugh, pleased at his visitor's reaction.

'Why an oak?'

'It was in the main courtyard of my school in England. I loved that tree. Used to hide in it when—' The Crown Prince stopped and his pudgy eyes narrowed. 'Well, that's a story for another time. The point is, I bought it from the school on my last day.'

'You brought this from the UK.' Forsyth laughed in wonder.

'Anything is possible if we turn our mind to it. That is what I want the Kingdom to become in time. Achieving impossible dreams regardless of the challenges.'

Forsyth stared up at the tree again. It must have been one hundred feet in height, its ancient branches spreading out across the courtyard like a benevolent colossus. This is why he needed the Saudis. With their money and his vision, they could achieve anything.

'Tell me, has your father's resistance thawed over the last few days?' The Crown Prince smiled, his eyes betraying nothing.

'My father is not a hasty man, Mr Forsyth. He measures his decisions carefully. Even if the LEAP tech seems to have stolen a march.'

'He does realise that if they establish this baseline, it will accelerate their rollout by years. Not just across travel, but also transport, manufacturing. Once they have those, Green Ray becomes the incumbent. They can do anything.'

'But will they, Mr Forsyth? Your proposal is not dependent on LEAP's success. In fact, it depends completely on your willingness to do things they are not prepared to do. We've all read the LEAP Laws.'

'I wasn't talking about LEAP.' Forsyth could barely keep the irritation out of his voice. 'I was referring to the impact this will have on oil production. Trust me, I know what that woman' he spat the word out, 'has planned. It will decimate the oil price, because she can start replacing food production, material production. Everything that oil currently caters for. It'll be death by a thousand cuts.'

The Crown Prince shrugged in acknowledgement, one born of many years of waiting for his moment.

'But we could slow them down.' Forsyth's eyes flashed an iridescent blue.

'Why are you so interested in stopping this woman? Surely leaving them be would build our case with my father.'

'LEAP's success is not dependent on that woman. It'll succeed with or without her. I have unfinished business.'

'Ah, the disfigurement. I heard about that.'

'It was more than that.' Forsyth's voice trembled with anger. 'She ruined me. And now I want to ruin her.'

'And how far are you willing to go, Mr Forsyth?'

'All the way,' he whispered. 'All the way.'

Forsyth stood up. Time to test the small man's ambition. 'And you?'

The Crown Prince didn't reply straight away. He sat there, seemingly deep in thought.

'Anything is possible, Mr Forsyth.' He put his cup down on its saucer and stood, reaching out a chubby hand. 'In the meantime, I've been working on something since our first meeting that will push my father over the edge and have him consider your proposal more seriously.'

Forsyth nodded. He didn't care what the Crown Prince did. He just wanted the King back at the table.

'OK. Whilst you take care of him, I need some help with stopping Green Ray for good.'

'All my resources are at your disposal,' the fat prince smiled, his eyes gleaming hungrily as he shook Forsyth's hand.

Townhouse, Camden Town, London

20th April 2010, 07:32 hours GMT

U ma woke suddenly and lay there, staring up at the high ceiling, completely disoriented. Her apartment in DC was tiny, with low lighting, not the ornate candelabra hanging above her head. And then she realised. Of course, Ethan's – their, he kept reminding her – bedroom in Camden Town. She'd been living here continuously since news of the eruption had broken, helping Ethan and his team to accelerate the rollout of the LEAP gates. It was the most time they had spent together. The realisation brought a smile to her face along with an unfamiliar feeling: happiness. The eruption seemed to have blown away all her concerns, exorcising all the poison from her body in one blast: Forsyth, Ingram, her father, the dead baby and the rollout. Especially the LEAP rollout. For the first time in years, she felt like she could breathe, sleeping a dreamless sleep each night. No night terrors. No lying awake until the early hours of the morning, wondering how she could drive her environmental agenda forward. There was no need, as Ethan's plan to leverage the effects of the ash cloud forged ahead. They barely saw each other during the day, but at night they'd tumble into bed and share stories of their day, talking for hours until one of them fell asleep or …

As if on cue, Ethan stirred, his hand closing gently on her breast, before tracing the outside of her nipple with his finger. She felt it harden, bolts of pleasure tickling out across her chest. She turned to face him, kissing each eye softly before nibbling his ear. It was his turn to groan, as she darted her tongue gently against his lobe. He responded by nuzzling her neck, gently biting the skin. She giggled at the sudden tickle. He was fully awake now and carefully straddled her, using his arms to support himself, body rigid like a plank. Slowly he lowered himself down, pressing gently along her entire torso so she felt his soft skin against her thighs, buttocks and back, his lips now nuzzling the nape of her neck. God, they were feather light. Everything was. He moved lightly up and down, cupping his abdomen into her buttocks. Soft buttery chills spidered down her legs and up her back. She felt herself moisten and wriggled round, wrapping her arms around his neck, pulling him towards her. She gasped as he entered her.

A sharp crack from the direction of the window collapsed Ethan onto Uma.

'What the hell was that?' he said, rolling off her and stumbling out of bed. He padded over to the curtain, pulling it aside. There was a jagged crack where something had hit the window. Beneath him, the crowd swelled.

'Someone's thrown a rock.'

'Let the police deal with it. Come back to bed,' she called, her voice husky with what had been interrupted, but also hopeful with the promise of what still could be.

'The crowd's grown,' he said, 'since that volcano erupted.'

'Leave them. Come back to bed. We've got to get up soon.'

He let the curtain fall back and ran towards the bed. At the last second, he dived onto Uma, who shrieked with surprise, before dissolving into giggles, then, finally groans of pleasure.

The huge crowd roared with derision as two police officers manhandled the young man who had thrown the stone into the back of a Black Mariah. It had been an excellent shot, cracking the upstairs window with a noise like a starting pistol. It was also a welcome distraction from the long night that had left the crowd in an ugly mood, steaming like a dying bonfire after a thunderstorm that had saturated them for twelve long hours. Ed Fox, baseball cap pulled low and framed by a black hoodie, barely noticed the loud jeers as he adjusted his backpack. He was too focused on getting towards the front of the crowd, but it was hard going. The numbers had swelled in the few days following the eruption. They were mainly airline staff with no prospect of a return to work. It was rumoured the volcano would spew ash for months, possibly longer. Further rumour had it that the Icelandic woman had triggered the eruption. It was nonsensical, of course, but so was LEAP. If this continued, half a million workers stood to lose their jobs from airline-related jobs alone.

Not that Ed cared. He had one job to do here. The rucksack felt reassuringly heavy, but all would be for naught if he didn't get closer to the house. At the moment, the crush was simply too great. Had been all night, which made him nervous. He had planned to do this in the early hours, when everyone was tired and police presence was at its lowest, but the throng of people had kiboshed that idea. There was no way he could complete his plans today. There were simply too many innocents. Enough had died already. He would have to abort, even though his heart, turbocharged by the grief pumping through his veins, screamed payback. No, he would return tomorrow and complete his mission, although he realised that, so long as the ash cloud hovered overhead, the crowds would never die down.

So be it. Ed had all the time in the world to avenge the deaths of Jo and Angel.

A chant started up around him.

'Down with LEAP.'

The damp crowd didn't react straight away. The long night had put paid to that. The cry fizzled out as quickly as it had started. Up ahead, a man dressed in black climbed onto a makeshift gantry in front of the townhouse. He was holding a megaphone. Two policemen on the stoop watched him warily. They could sense the mood change as well.

'We've just heard the airports will be closed for another day,' he began. The crowd stared back sullenly, the excitement of the thrown rock a damp memory. 'That's another day when you don't get to put food on the table for your families. Don't get to pay your mortgages. And what's the government doing? Nothing,' he bellowed. The crowd grumbled like a waking serpent. 'Whilst Green Ray installs more LEAP gates to replace our planes. Do you want that?'

'No,' came a lone cry from someone in front of Ed.

'I didn't hear you,' the man roared.

'No,' several more voices shouted.

'Is that all you've got?' the man screamed into the megaphone. 'Your livelihoods are disappearing before your eyes. Because of them.' He turned, pointing up at the house.

The serpent rumbled its approval.

'If this is allowed to continue, there will soon be nothing left of the airlines, but it won't stop there. Trains will be next. Then ships. In time, cars. This is the tip of the iceberg. Green Ray will destroy your lives.' Ed felt himself nodding at that last one: they'd destroyed his. 'They will rip it up, and discard entire industries like rubbish. Do you want that?'

The crowd, including Ed, roared back as one.

'No, we don't.'

'So, what are you going to do about it?'

The crowd surged forward, and Ed felt himself lifted off his feet, his face pressed into the back of a giant wearing a green gabardine. It smelled of damp dog. He felt himself gag, tried to push back with his arms, but they were pinned to his side. The crowd paused. The release of tension allowed him to worm his way round the tall man who barely glanced at him. He was bellowing something indistinguishable. So was

everyone, brandishing their placards like swords. The mood was ugly.
Ed felt the familiar surge of adrenaline he got on a patrol. A woman
stumbled in front of him, but he didn't have a chance to grab her arm.
The crowd was on the move again. Up ahead, one of the police officers
manning the barricades shouted a warning, imploring the crowd to
stop, but this time there was no stopping them. The barriers gave way
and the mob surged up the front steps of the townhouse. To his right
an electronic voice boomed out.

'Down with LEAP.'

It felt unhinged, and the crowd responded in kind.

'Down with LEAP!' they screamed as one.

For a second, the crowd parted, and Ed pushed forward. It was the
only direction he could travel in. Perhaps, if he could get to the front,
he could work his way along the street. Escape down one of the side
roads before this got uglier. The thought of being arrested with this
much explosive brought him focus.

He would go down for that.

His plans in tatters.

Jo's and Angel's deaths unrepaid.

He was almost at the steps.

Ahead of him, two protesters attacked a policewoman with batons.
Where had they come from?

They were dark in complexion, matched by their attire which was
black: black anoraks, jeans and combat boots, like his. And what
looked like body cams strapped to their chests.

A sixth sense, honed by ten years of war, klaxoned danger.

The bigger of the two men brought the heavy wood down on the
copper's helmet, and, as she put her arm up to defend herself, the other
jabbed her ribs with his baton. She screamed and fell to her knees.
Without pausing, the first man punched her full in the face, as the
other ripped her helmet off, hurling it into the baying mob. A great
cheer went up. As the woman slumped to the hard stone, the first
man brought his staff down hard on the back of her skull. And then
they were gone, pushing others aside as they forced their way up the
steps. Ed tried to kneel beside the woman, but the crush was too great.

He was swept up the narrow stoop. It was a natural choke point. A protester beside him screamed as a man toppled over the wrought-iron fence into the basement level below. Ed pushed her into the vacated space, swivelling her body sideways so he was now pressed against the fence. Suddenly, he was fighting to keep his balance as the mob surged again, forcing him to grab the woman to prevent the same fate the man had suffered. Someone had lit a red flare, and the smoke drifted up the stoop, covering the steps in a crimson cloud.

As Ed lost his grip on the woman, a man shouted in front of him.

'He's got a bomb.'

The pressure disappeared as people further up the steps pushed back against him.

There was a crack like a firework, and someone screamed.

That sounded like a standard breaching charge, he thought.

His unit used them all the time in Afghanistan.

What was going on?

Two men appeared on the outside of the fence beside Ed. They were young, dark complexioned, like the other two, unshaven, unsmiling, faces expressionless. Without pausing, they continued up the outside of the stoop, disappearing into a maelstrom of red mist, just as a louder explosion rumbled the steps.

Smoke poured from the door. It smelled acrid. Ed dissolved into a fit of coughing, stumbling over something. He glanced down. A young man was spreadeagled across the steps, face bloodied, a deep gash to his forehead.

Something was burning.

Two booms.

This time from inside the house.

Ed felt the soundwave hit him.

Ringing in his ears.

Flash-bangs.

Who were these people?

Ed shook his head, trying to shake free the high-pitched whine in his ears.

The crowd was on the move again, carrying him into the hallway.

Smoke everywhere

Past the door curtains that were flaming, shooting orange licks of fire towards the ceiling.

The crowd swarmed forward, some disappearing through a side door, others towards the back of the house. Many headed for the main stairs at the far end of the wide entrance hallway. Ed was carried with them up several steps. To his right, framed photos of a grinning Ethan Rae stared back at Ed. He felt his blood boil at the sight, struggling to break free of the crush. Someone picked up a transparent rectangular block and hurled it over the banister. It smashed against the opposite wall, showering people in the corridor with glass. Two men tried to push past him. Ed realised they were the ones who had attacked the policewoman. They were moving quickly, trying to barge past people, but the press was too great. One of the men lifted his arm above his head.

He was holding something, the black metal gleaming malevolently in the fire's glow.

Ed would have recognised it anywhere: a Beretta M9.

Standard US Army issue sidearm. Semi-automatic. Fifteen-round magazine.

It exploded into life, and on the staircase, the sound was deafening.

Once, twice, three times, it boomed.

People ahead of him started screaming, pushing Ed aside in their haste to get down the stairs. A woman, barely in her twenties, smashed into him. She was crying, her eyes slick with fear. The gun boomed again, and she disappeared over the banister.

Ed's first thought was his backpack. If a bullet hit that, he was dead. So was everyone else around him. The realisation propelled him back down the stairs, but the crush was too great as people continued to pour into the house.

Behind him, the Beretta cracked twice and the mob in the corridor paused, finally registering that something was wrong. Ed shrugged the pack off his shoulders, holding it close to his chest as he fought against the river of humanity crowding into the house, but he could barely move. Some fought their way back towards the front door, others crushed forward towards the rear, and yet more flooded off the staircase.

He felt the heavy pack twist from his grasp as the crowd surged again, driving him deeper into the house. He looked back. An arm shot up, holding his pack. He screamed for it, but within seconds it had been carried ten feet away, almost to the entrance.

Flames licked hungrily in its direction.

Ed was carried into the kitchen.

More shots, this time a low burst of fire.

Ed saw the bag puff as bullets sprayed above the mob in the hallway.

A fresh horror exploded in his mind's eye as he calculated the time it would take for the leaking carbon disulfide to evaporate in the air. Perhaps ten seconds, maybe less, and then the liquid phosphorous would react with the oxygen and ... boom. Its ignition point was eighty-six degrees Fahrenheit, but in the heat of the hallway, that was easily possible.

A phosphorous fire that would burn hot.

Upwards of fifteen hundred degrees Fahrenheit. That's why he had chosen it. To mimic a car fire.

There were six bottles and once they exploded in this packed hallway
...

What had he done? Ed thought.

It wasn't intended for these people.

Just Uma Jakobsdóttir and Ethan Rae.

The people responsible for killing his family.

They were meant to burn in the same inferno that had killed his girls.

He shouted for people to move towards the kitchen, but no one was listening.

Behind him, a new sound filled the hallway – a sound not of this world.

A sound as though a wraith from the pits of hell had materialised in the house and was announcing its arrival.

With an inhuman shriek.

A siren call that demanded he turn and look.

An inferno of flames exploded in the doorway, dousing the walls in burning rivulets of fire that rained down on the carpet.

The unmistakable odour of burning phosphorous.

In the centre of the conflagration, a figure was somehow still standing, arms aloft like the Angel Uriel.

As he watched, it sank to the ground.

The crush, now frenzied, pushed him into the kitchen, trying to escape the fire.

Ed somehow turned and began pulling more people into the room.

'Open the back door,' he screamed at an elderly lady who was standing towards the back of the kitchen. She nodded and unlocked the latch. The double-doors burst outward with the weight of people and the older lady disappeared in a scream of flailing limbs as people flooded down the back steps and into the garden.

The bag exploded.

Ethan felt the room shake beneath his feet. He instinctively sought Uma's hand as she crouched behind him beside the locked bedroom door. After the smaller explosions, they'd hurriedly dressed and tried to leave, but had retreated as gunshots peppered the stairwell below. That was two minutes ago. Already the door jambs and sill were leaking wispy fingers of smoke into the room. The tendrils felt like icy fingers around Ethan's heart as he remembered the last time he'd been trapped in the anteroom off the great hall in the castle after the earthquake. The smell of smoke had prefaced a scene of absolute devastation: the main hall destroyed, the steel tower collapsed and Uma ...

The memory of her falling slowly forward, the spear buried deep in her back, skin alabaster white, was seared across his synapses like a call to arms: that never again would he expose her to such a danger. Yet, here they were under attack. In their own home. Gun shots fired, explosions rocking the foundations. How had he allowed that to happen? Ethan checked himself. He could perform a postmortem later. First, he had to get Uma to safety. He felt his heart rate slow, a calmness dowsing his panic as he checked off their options. There really was only one: the LEAP gate.

Wrenching open the door, he stepped out into the hallway just as a bullet splintered the doorframe above his head. He fell back into the bedroom as Uma slammed the door shut and locked it.

Ethan rolled to one side of the door and motioned for Uma to get behind the bed as two more explosions shredded the panelling.

Heavy boots thundered on the thick oak as Ethan flicked the lights off and bee-lined for the curtains. Outside, flames licked up the windows, already charring the frame. He pulled the heavy material closed, plunging the room into semi-darkness. As he hurtled back towards the door, he grabbed a pair of scissors from the dresser and stabbed his left radial artery, once, twice, as he threw himself to the floorboards, wrist across his throat, warm blood pulsing down his neck and onto his chest.

He had thirty seconds before he lost consciousness.

The lock disintegrated in a cacophony of splintering wood and metal.

The door burst open. Two men entered, one moving left, the other right, almost tripping over Ethan. A flashlight lit up the gloom, playing over Ethan's body, pausing on the pooling crimson around his neck and shoulder. As Ethan felt the man's fingers on his carotid artery, his eyes flicked open and he drove the scissors deep into the man's pterion, just behind his temple.

The man grunted in surprise, collapsing on top of Ethan, the torch now illuminating his partner's lower torso. The remaining intruder turned, firing blindly at the indistinct shape on the floor.

The bullets thumped into the body, high across the back, heart side.

Ethan's good hand spidered around the floorboards, searching for the dropped weapon.

He felt lightheaded.

Two more shots boomed. This time, lower, into the dead man's waist.

Ethan's fingers closed around the cold metal.

He felt for the safety catch.

Ethan fired blindly towards the torch, pressing the trigger repeatedly until all he could hear were clicks.

And then silence in the room.

Just the smell of cordite.

Ethan could feel a heaviness clouding his skull.

He humped the corpse off his body, struggled to his feet, then inspected the other motionless figure, now illuminated by the light of two torches. The bullets had torn into the man's face, neck, and chest.

Stumbling over to the bed, Ethan tore some strips off a sheet and wrapped them round the spurting fountain from his wrist, sitting down heavily on the mattress. Uma appeared like a ghost from behind the bed, crying out as she took in the ghastly scene, throwing herself at Ethan and hugging him tightly. Eventually he gently prised himself away, showing her his wrist, which had already soaked the sheet.

'Here, let me do that.' She grabbed the material and took his arm. Ethan sat there, trying to control his ragged breathing, his heart hammering against his chest. A memory surfaced from another life: of Uma binding his wrist in the lecture theatre. It was the first time he had met her. Back then, she had been business-like, just like now, but on both occasions he had been aware of her presence: thick black hair cascading down her shoulders, delicate features, soft hands cool against his hot, flustered skin.

'Who sent them?' she said.

Ethan had no idea.

He glanced towards the curtains.

'You think they're protesters?'

He shrugged, his mind heavy, wandering. Another memory: of Uma slumping forward onto a carpet of weaponry in the Hall of Steel, a spear buried deep in her neck. The thought of her getting hurt again resurfaced the earlier terror. As she finished the binding, he took her face in his hands and kissed her gently. She pulled away, her lips now blood red, staring dumbly back at him, eyes slick with fear and shock. He had seen it a hundred times in combat. Or at least Anderson had, and he suddenly felt grateful for the scumbag. Grateful that he was two men, the other a murderous thug that had saved his and Uma's life on numerous occasions. Today was no different.

'We need to go,' he whispered.

'Where?'

'Through the gate, back to Washington. We can regroup there.'

'What about everyone else?'

'There's no one here. I sent them home last night. Half of them hadn't slept in a—' He stopped. That wasn't true.

'Mrs Carr,' he said.

Uma looked at him.

'Where is she?'

'On the ground floor. Probably in the kitchen, making our breakfast.'

The realisation propelled Ethan off the bed towards the bathroom, a blanket in each hand which he dowsed with water from the bath. When he returned carrying the sopping blankets, Uma was still standing there, gazing vacantly at the dead bodies. He gently wrapped one of the blankets around her head and shoulders like a shroud before steering her towards the door.

'Come on,' he said, silently berating himself for not taking her into the bathroom.

They inched out into the corridor where the smoke was thicker, acrid clouds pluming up from the hallway below. It smelled like decaying fish. The odour shook loose an Anderson memory.

Phosphine gas – from the phosphorous bombs used in Afghanistan.

That was heavy munitions. Had these men exploded one downstairs? If so, Uma was in more danger than he had realised. The fire alone would melt their skin. The gas would flood their lungs.

An inhuman scream wailed up the stairwell, quickening their pace down the corridor.

As they neared the doorway leading up to the LEAP gate, Ethan stopped.

'I'm going to get Mrs Carr,' he said to Uma. 'You LEAP now. I'll follow with her.'

She shook her head.

'You're not going down there?' she cried.

'I can't leave her.'

They stood for a moment, absorbing the reality of what might happen.

'Please don't wait,' he said, hugging her fiercely. Uma held onto him as he pulled away, rewrapping the blanket tightly around his head, and then he was gone, lost in the billowing smoke.

Uma stood there feeling numb.

What had just happened?

Less than five minutes ago, they had been making love. And now here she was, standing in a burning building, two men dead in their bedroom, and Ethan had just disappeared down into the pits of hell. She considered following him, but what was she going to do? She couldn't match Anderson's strength or Ethan's cunning. What if there were more assassins out there? She wouldn't stand a chance. Ethan was right. She needed to head for the LEAP gate at the top of the house and escape before this got any worse, but as she turned, the fear that fizzled in her stomach burst out as a strangled cry.

They had both agreed to no more copying. How could they do otherwise? It was one of the four laws. They couldn't be seen to breach it again. Not after what had just happened in the White House. Ingram would have a field day, and now the reality of that decision was burning around her.

A billow of smoke engulfed the landing, as a roar of flames snaked hungrily up between the banisters.

How would she survive without Ethan?

She pulled the wet blanket tightly around her head and breathed deeply through the damp material, trying to control her coughing.

'Get a grip, Uma,' she mumbled. 'Get a grip.'

She dropped low, crawling along the corridor. The smoke was still thick, but, using the wall as a guide, Uma was able to locate the door to the top floor. She took a deep breath and stood, feeling for the handle. One turn and it was open. She stumbled through, pulling the door closed behind her. In the stairwell, the smoke was manageable, and she was able to climb the steep stairs to the attic without having to breathe through the blanket. As she waited for the LEAP door to retract, she risked a glance through the dormer window into the street below: Red and white flares mixed with the thick black smoke billowed up the side of the townhouse. In the distance, she heard sirens. Uma debated again whether to wait, but there was no point. The realisation of her own inability to save Ethan felt overwhelming. What was she going to do? There was only one thing she could do. Without a second glance, she stepped through the LEAP gate and disappeared.

Gulf of Mexico

21st April 2010, 12:56 hours AST

From five miles out, the column of black smoke cleaved the blue canvas in two like a divine act of vandalism, its fiery base glowing orange like a factory furnace. As the helicopter drew closer, the horizon clarified: above, a pale early morning cerulean; below, the darker aquamarine of a millpond ocean, upon which the pits of hell burned with the ferocity of a vengeful sun. Closer still, the angry flames broiled out over the water, upon which platform supply vessels gathered like mini oil tankers, shooting ineffective plumes of water onto the conflagration. A fiery explosion bloomed out from the stricken rig, causing the pilot to bank left. For a second the catastrophe disappeared, but he circled round and it returned. This time, so close, the conflagration blotted out the sky. The rig was listing at a seventy-degree angle, one of its huge pontoons clearly visible like the pale underbelly of a beached whale. A series of small eruptions rocked the platform, sling-shotting fireballs into the ocean like a floating trebuchet. Most landed harmlessly in an eruption of seawater and steam, shooting hundreds of feet into the air, but one fell close to the rig. Within seconds a seething carpet of fire rolled out across the ocean towards the helicopter, which quickly retreated from the raging inferno. Moments later, the screen flicked to a newsroom.

'You're just seeing the latest pictures from the Gulf of Mexico, where the Deepwater Horizon, an offshore drilling rig owned by the oil giant, British Petroleum, exploded in the early hours of yesterday evening. As you can see, the rig is badly damaged and, despite over eight maintenance vessels, appears to be burning out of control. Combined with the continuing dust cloud in Europe and the repatriation scheme spearheaded by Green Ray, oil futures have slipped into negative territory in early trading this morning. Yes, that's right folks, you heard it here first. Oil is currently trading at a negative $37.63, the lowest level recorded since the New York Mercantile Exchange began trading oil futures in 1983. The low price comes amid a slump in demand for the black stuff as the market anticipates the end of oil. This has led to an unprecedented surplus of unneeded oil and fuel. I have oil trader, Max Sandwell, here in the studio with me to explain what is happening.'

The reporter turned towards a smartly dressed man, who smiled broadly into the camera. Behind them, a screen continued to show the burning platform.

'Good morning, Max. Can you explain to our viewers why events in the Gulf have affected oil futures so badly and how it's possible to have a negative price?'

'Good morning, John. Yes, sure thing. It's very simple, really. There is currently a massive glut of oil in the market following the slump in demand after Eyjafjallajökull erupted, which has caught oil producers like Saudi Arabia cold. They haven't slowed production, perhaps betting that the dust cloud will settle soon. Consequently, they have no place to store the oil and that's what's driving the price dive. They're literally paying futures traders to deal with the excess oil. The Deepwater Horizon disaster has just exacerbated that problem by showing the world how damaging oil really is: difficult to extract, a danger to the atmosphere and one blow out from plunging an entire ecosystem into environmental Armageddon. One that could make the Exxon Valdez oil spill look like a small drum leak.'

Forsyth flicked off the television and turned to Mohammad, smiling.

'How did the Crown Prince do it?' he asked. 'How did he blow up an oil rig in the Gulf of Mexico?'

Mohammad shrugged his shoulders and smiled back, raising his glass.

'You're assuming it's the Crown Prince. Maybe he just got lucky. Either way, it's going to bring the King crawling back to our table.'

'I don't see how it can't,' Forsyth agreed, then sighed. Despite his joy at seeing the burning platform, he felt flat. This would also be a leg up for Green Ray. If anything, the explosion would accelerate the take up of LEAP. What did Al Rahman used to say? That oil spills were bad for business. He was now witnessing one of the worst in living memory, with very little likelihood that it would be repaired anytime soon. Already, they were hearing reports that the wellhead had blown five thousand feet beneath the surface of the Gulf. If the Deepwater Horizon sank, there was no telling what volume of oil would escape and how long it would take to cap. An image of the black seagull arose unbidden. Quickly followed by the Sheikh. Forsyth was not given to moments of reflection, but the memory of his gutted friend left him even more melancholic.

'Shall we give the Crown Prince a call?' he snapped at Mohammed.

'I wouldn't recommend it. Let him deal with his father first. He'll contact us when he's good and ready.'

Forsyth grimaced. Mohammed was right, of course. It was just that the waiting was killing him. The longer the Saudis took to decide, the further ahead Green Ray would get. The phone rang, and he nearly knocked over the table in his haste to get to it. Ripping the receiver from its holder, he stood motionless, listening, a broad smile growing across his handsome face. Finally, he put the receiver down.

Mohammed looked questioningly at him.

'Reports are coming out of London that Ethan Rae is dead.'

Washington DC

U ma clenched the down pillow tightly to her chest and stared up at the ceiling, reliving the moment, barely thirty hours earlier, when she had been lying in their bed in Camden Town, staring up at another ceiling, cocooned in a rare moment of bliss. The memory triggered a fresh tsunami of sobs that swept over her aching body, leaving her head throbbing with a maelstrom of emotions that threatened to overwhelm her at the realisation that she might never see—. She stopped the thought, unwilling to even think his name, and sat up in bed. No, she couldn't afford to disappear down that rabbit hole just yet. Not until she had proof. So far, none had been provided. She'd been on the phone for much of the previous day and into the night, calling to see if he had escaped. The reports were not good. The inferno had destroyed the townhouse. The fire brigade was still bringing bodies out. To date, over thirty, so badly burned that they would have to rely on dental records to identify the charred corpses. She'd considered going back to London, but the thought of standing in front of that building after what had just happened filled her with dread. Not dread at never seeing him again, but at the realisation that she had the power to bring him back. That all she needed to do was flick a switch and he would be standing there. He would have no recollection of what had just happened, but for all intents and purpose he would be the same man she had been making love to yesterday. Except she couldn't. After their meeting with the President and Ingram, they had both made a promise to each other. They would honour the LEAP Laws moving forward as the President had requested. If one died, that was it. Death was death. They had no choice. As LEAP gathered pace, they had to be beyond reproach. Otherwise, there would be chaos if people felt they could copy their loved ones, and governments resuscitated their dead soldiers. It would never end.

Another thought rose unbidden, searing into her heart like an Exocet missile: her baby. If she couldn't resuscitate Ethan, she could have had the baby as a memory to him, but almost immediately, the idea exploded with the ramifications of such a decision. She wasn't even sure it had been his. Forsyth's grinning face appeared, laughing cruelly at her weakness. What if it had been Forsyth's? The shame of that night curled her back up into a tight ball. She groaned at the memory of Forsyth's stubble against her breasts, thighs. She could never have a baby. She didn't want a baby. It was her single greatest sacrifice to protecting the environment, but what if it was Ethan's? Her whole body sobbed as his name snapped into her mind, which morphed into a cry at the realisation that she might never see him again.

A million miles away, she heard a ringing phone.

The sound gave her hope. That the police had found Ethan. Alive and well. She reached for the receiver.

'Yes,' she announced breathlessly, sitting up in bed, wiping the tears from her face.

'You seem to have been impaled by your own law.'

A different emotion gripped Uma. One she was familiar with and which, on this day, she was happy to embrace.

'How dare you call to gloat,' she seethed into the phone.

'Far from it, in fact,' Director Joseph Ingram said. His voice sounded sad. 'Since you persuaded the President to ban copying, I've lost two men myself. Two men who have families. Who I now have to call and break the news that their son, in one case, and husband and father in the other, won't be coming home. I take no pleasure in any of this.'

'Why are you calling me?'

There was silence on the line that went on for so long that Uma thought he had hung up. Eventually, he spoke.

'Let's assume Mr Rae perished in that fire.' The mere sound of those words caused Uma's heart to fracture with such a great tearing sound that she was convinced the spy boss could hear. 'It's such a waste. If you were to approach the President and persuade him to reverse your ban on copying, I would be fully supportive.'

Uma was too startled to say anything. Then it came to her: had Ingram sent the two men to kill Ethan in their bedroom? To force her to breach the LEAP Laws by resuscitating him? After last year, she would not put it past him.

'Ethan brings a unique skillset to your rollout,' he continued. 'He is not easily replaced. And his loss will slow your warming reversal programme down massively.'

Her anger morphed into rage. The same old Ingram. Forever scheming like a modern-day Machiavelli.

'You'd love that, wouldn't you?' she snarled. 'To witness my volte-face in front of the President.'

'Doctor, no one wins from your intransigence on this issue. If you were to reconsider, I'd get my two men back, plus the ten marines who were killed in Afghanistan just yesterday. And you'd get your boyfriend back. Again.'

In that moment, Uma knew she wouldn't resuscitate Ethan. There were a million Ingrams out there, all looking to advance their personal agendas.

'Putting aside the moral and ethical consequences of such a de-cision, the impact on the environment would be catastrophic if no one ever died. That's precisely why Ethan and I made that pact: that we would never restore ourselves in the event of our deaths. I won't be changing my mind, Mr Ingram. So, if you'll excuse me, I'll like to mourn in peace.'

She slammed the phone down and slammed her body back into the mattress, wishing it would open up and swallow her whole.

Almost immediately, the phone rang again. She ignored it, but the shrill tone was persistent and eventually, on the third try, she answered. It was Maisie Collins, head of the environment for Green Ray.

'Have you seen the news? An oil rig has exploded in the Gulf last night. It's a disaster. You need to get down here right away.'

Uma remained silent, her mind barely registering the words, let alone their implications.

'Uma, are you there?'

'Yes. What are you talking about? What oil rig?'

'It's all over the news.'

'What oil rig?' she repeated.

'In the Gulf,' Maisie sounded frustrated. 'Uma, are you OK?'

Everything seemed to happen in slow motion. Uma recovered her remote from the bedside table and flicked on the TV to be greeted with images of a burning rig surrounded by burning water.

'You know this is another gift,' Maisie continued. 'With the volcano and the oil leak, we can speed up the transitioning of consumers to LEAP.'

Uma lay there, too tired to speak, staring at the burning rig as Maisie droned on in the background. The screen suddenly cut to a reporter in London outside the smouldering townhouse. A picture appeared of Ethan. He was grinning, his kind eyes sparkling with merriment.

Uma dropped the receiver as she tried to find the remote.

The image had cut to a video of them both sitting in a studio from last year. Ethan was talking earnestly to the camera, cradling his shattered arm. Uma remembered the day before the interview when he had finally expressed his love for her and they had made love. She could feel his soft lips on hers.

Letting out a gargled cry, she leapt from the bed, attacking the small screen with both hands and dragging it off the wall. Still, the video played.

Ethan was laughing this time.

She smashed the TV into a chest of drawers. Once, twice. Finally, it flickered out, but she couldn't escape his smiling face. Uma collapsed to the floor in tears, mourning her dead partner she couldn't resuscitate and the dead baby she didn't want.

Chelsea & Westminster Hospital, London

21st April, 2010, 14:21 hours GMT

He was blind, intentionally so, his eyes screwed shut against the smoke. He was barely able to breathe through the wet blanket pressed to his nose and mouth, but it was better than the alternative: choking black smoke that smelled like rotting fish. It was the phosphine gas. He took small sips of air to protect his lungs, but the hydrogen phosphide breached his damp defence with hot fiery fists that scalded his throat and inflamed his chest. He wheezed into the blanket, trying not to cough. Big mistake. The exhalation set off a chain reaction and within seconds, he was hacking lungfuls into the damp material. For a moment, he lost his footing on the staircase, but it was enough to pitch him forward. He braced himself for the hard marble of the hallway.

But there was no sharp pain to his elbows, just a cushioned landing. Had he made a wrong turn?

Impossible. The stairs led nowhere except to the hallway.

He reached out with both hands, grabbing the soft material. He continued his blind exploration, eventually pausing as the unmistakable outline of a face radared up through his fingers.

They must be bodies, he thought, caught in the explosion. He felt further. More faces. No one was breathing.

The realisation sent him into a fresh paroxysm of coughing. He lay there, trying to calm his chest and growing panic.

First, he needed to orientate himself. The explosion had been directly beneath their bedroom. He felt behind him until his hands traced the outline of the bottom step. Left would take him towards the entrance. Which made sense. Even through the blanket he could feel the heat of a fire along his flank. He stayed flat to the floor and started crawling over bodies, feeling for the solid wall to his right, moving towards the kitchen. If he could just reach the door. Maybe close it. Cut out the worst of the smoke. But first he had to navigate the carpet of corpses. He lost count of the bodies.

Then something grabbed his foot.

He instinctively pulled free.

He felt a hand on his face, grasping.

Another on his chest, clawing at the blanket.

Panicked, he pulled the material away from his face, opening his eyes. Beneath him was an ashen face, thick hair fanned out like a shroud.

Uma!

Her eyes suddenly opened, opaque in death.

'You left me,' she said.

Ethan screamed and spidered forward.

Ahead, a torso sat up and turned in his direction. Pointing.

Mrs Carr?

He screamed again and pressed forward as more hands reached out, clawing at his face, legs, arms, and feet.

Too many bodies.

He looked down. A woman. Long blond hair. Bloodied and burned.

Her eyes opened.

'Mummy,' he screamed.

Ethan awoke. He was coughing. Something was across his face. He tried to claw the covering away, but his hands seemed to be trapped in thick padding. Where were his fingers? The retching got worse and he thought he was going to vomit. Was he still in the dream? He couldn't escape his mum's accusatory face. His back prickled for the first time in months. Hot flicks of pain shot across his shoulders and down his spine. His head boomed in rhythm to his chest contractions. Through the coughs, he heard a door open, then the clacking of heels on linoleum. Hands on his face; something being applied to his mouth. For a moment, he thought they were trying to suffocate him. And then the cool blast of air in his throat. Almost immediately, the tickling dissipated. He inhaled deeply, feeling his lungs settle almost immediately.

A woman's voice, kind and soothing.

'You've been badly burned. To your face, hands and arms. You were lucky. That blanket saved you. Without it, you would have probably died.'

Ethan froze. What if Uma had?

'Can you hear me? Raise your hand if you can.'

Ethan obeyed.

'We need to identify you. I'm going to read some names. Please raise your hand if you recognise one.'

'James Forshaw. Graham Petty. Phil Ratcliffe. Dr Edward Forster.'

That last name sounded familiar: recollections of an elderly gentleman in his Camden townhouse kitchen, stitching his forearm after the earthquake in California. A doctor – Mrs Carr's companion. He was called Edward. Ethan was sure of it.

The possibility that it might be triggered another thought: Mrs Carr. He hadn't saved her. She may have died as well. He had failed her. The realisation reopened old wounds he thought had been long conquered. He felt an explosion of scalding pin pricks on his back, the whip head slicing through soft flesh. Warm blood running freely. Ethan inhaled the oxygen deeply, using the cold gas to focus his mind and banish the memory, but it was no good. He relaxed into the pain, counting to fifty. When it finally stopped, his body was bathed in sweat, his mind overwhelmed by what had he allowed to happen. How many people had been caught up in the fire? He should have prepared for that. Could have prevented it.

'—Rae.'

Wait, he recognised that name.

He raised both hands and waved.

There was silence, then the sound of clacking heels, and a door opening. Then nothing, just the hissing of oxygen. Ethan lowered his arms, exhausted. He felt his eyes close, his body settling into the blissful release of the cool air as it inflated his damaged lungs and cooled his damaged back.

But nothing could take away the rotting odour of his failure.

Riyadh, Saudi Arabia

22nd April, 2010, 10:39 hours AST

The images were surprisingly clear, despite being in black and white. It had been Forsyth's idea. He wanted to watch the moment when that woman died. He at least wanted that pleasure after all the pain she had put him through. However, before she did, Ethan Rae had to die first, preferably in front of her. He wanted to see the pain on her face as she lost her lover. So, the Crown Prince's hand-picked team, members of the SSF – the Special Security Forces, Saudi's supposedly elite fighting soldiers – had worn body-cams on their chests, transmitting through an encrypted local WAN network, to a van parked behind the townhouse. Crouch had organised it. The man was a hopeless drunk, but he knew his tech. The highlights had been playing on a hard loop in Forsyth's office for the past hour as they tried to work out what had gone wrong. The operation had started so well, Captain Hassan and his team quickly gaining entry to the house as instructed, using the crowd as cover. Once inside, the group had split into two pairs, Hassan taking the stairs with one of his men. Forsyth didn't know his name, just that he was called VID2 – the identifier, nestling in the top corner of each feed, along with the time and date, that showed whose body-cam they were watching. Forsyth flinched as the feed suddenly depicted a door splintering under a fuselage of bullets.

It abruptly opened, presumably kicked in by VID2. The feed cut to VID1 – Captain Hassan. The image was blurry grey, apparently down to the lack of light in the room. It scanned the interior left to right, eventually settling on a shadowy figure crumpled on the floor. Even though he knew what was going to happen, Forsyth's heart leapt as Hassan approached the body, the light from his torch illuminating the unmistakable features of Rae. He looked dead, black liquid – presumably blood – leaking from his neck and pooling on the floorboards. Suddenly, the image blurred and faded to black.

Another feed, this time from VID2, the other soldier in the room, who turned towards where Rae had been lying. Rae's body appeared, Hassan lying on top of him, the torch light briefly reflecting off the scissors sticking out of Hassan's temple. Useless, Forsyth thought. What had the Crown Prince said? "Captain Hassan and his men were the best of the best." Clearly no match for Rae. VID2 didn't react fast enough as the feed picked up Rae's hand, finding the gun and firing at the surviving soldier. Repeated flashes lit up the screen. No man could survive that. The scene changed again, back to Captain Hassan's camera, which suddenly sprang back to life. One moment it was black – presumably because Hassan's body was pressed into Rae's – the next, it showed Rae, walking away towards a bed, his wrist spurting blood. Wow, Forsyth thought. Had he cut his own artery to mimic a bullet wound to his neck? Now that was clever. As Rae shredded the bed sheets, a woman appeared. Forsyth felt the rage ignite across his body. They had been so close, but it was not enough around Rae. He fought like a gladiator, not an accountant. Forsyth watched in fascination, as she hurled herself at Rae, her face clearly visible on the dead man's feed. Her eyes were screwed shut, her features contorted in horror at what she had seen, and perhaps fearing what could have passed. Despite the fourth viewing, the scene was still electric for Forsyth: they were a couple! It was one of only two useful outcomes from the disaster – knowing that they were romantically involved changed everything.

The camera view shifted again to VID3, one of the soldiers downstairs. The feed was much harder to watch now, as smoke – presumably from the fire – obscured most of the screen with white pixels. Forsyth watched carefully. They were now in a different room, presumably the kitchen, which was crushed with bodies, fear slick on fleeting faces which appeared and disappeared like apparitions. Rae suddenly materialised, his back to VID3's camera. Forsyth hadn't known this on his first viewing, but this was a movie he had already seen. Once again, the initial viewing was promising: VID3's hands encircling Rae's neck, who somehow turned to face his attacker, slowly sinking to his knees as the life was strangled out of him. He was looking up right into the camera, staring into Forsyth's soul, his eyes bulging, but showing no fear, just defiance and rage. A rage that Forsyth knew only too well. A kindred spirit, he thought, his fingers subconsciously travelling to his own throat as he watched the life force slowly fade from Rae's face. It was glorious, life affirming. Forsyth's only regret was that the woman hadn't witnessed the scene. Maybe he should send her the feed, along with the video of them together in San Francisco. As a reminder of who was really in charge.

And then it was over. Suddenly, VID3's hands appeared to go limp and the life seemed to flood back into Rae's face, as if a switch had been flicked. The image greyed. When it settled, the body camera was facing upwards, towards the ceiling. A man appeared in frame, ghostlike, as smoke swirled around him, before he bent forward then disappeared from view. Then he was back, this time gripping Rae's still body in his hands. The man stood for a moment, as if adjusting his stance and then hinged his hips backwards, before jerking Rae's body above his head in one fluid movement, like a deadlift. For a long moment, he was motionless, as if steadying himself. Eventually, he turned, hurling Rae towards what must have been the fire. Forsyth let out a long expulsion of air, staring at the last frame on the screen. It was a headshot of the man who had both rescued Rae and then tried to kill him. Just as he bent towards the camera, before lifting Rae, Forsyth could see the man's face. It was caught in a frozen scowl, skull shaved buzzcut short, army style. His features were hewn from a slab of granite – square jaw, strong nose, hunched eyebrows. But it was his eyes that caught Forsyth's breath: they were devoid of emotion and empty of life. The eyes of a dead man.

Forsyth stared at the image for a good minute, thinking. Rae had done most of the damage, displaying skills he wouldn't have attributed to a businessman, but downstairs, the stranger had killed VID4, maybe VID3 as well, two of the best that Saudi had to offer, even though Forsyth questioned if that meant anything. However, of more interest was his connection to Rae. Forsyth rewound the video to where the mystery man had lifted Rae up like a rag doll and hurled him away, hopefully to his death. Why, was the question? What had Rae done to produce that reaction? Forsyth needed to find out. Furthermore, he needed that man on his side.

Forsyth stood up, smiling, his mind made up.

'Crouch,' he bellowed, 'Find this man.'

TV interview, Heathrow Airport, London

22nd April, 12:32 hours GMT

Katrina Hoskins watched the security guard take her bag and empty the contents of it onto the desk between them. He inspected each item, opening lipstick tubes, her compact mirror, wallet, even her phone. Nothing avoided his forensic search, but after what she had just experienced, it all seemed unnecessary. Why didn't they just put her back through the machine, she thought? It would show everything he could see and more besides. Then again, if this was the price for the interview, she would submit to every search they could throw at her. She'd received the request only yesterday – to be in London with her film crew at a secret location. It all sounded very James Bond, but understandable given what had just happened. God, Brett had been pissed. It was their first holiday in months: at the Four Seasons Resort in Hualalai, Hawaii. They'd only been there one day. They'd argued. Again. He'd left in a blaze of expletives, leaving Katrina to pack, wondering if he would be there when she got back. The thought had left a gnawing ache in her stomach, but she comforted herself that at least she had her scoop.

After leaving her suite, she'd been taken to a newly installed LEAP gate. In the actual hotel. She'd been astounded. A distance of seven thousand miles covered in a micro-second. It would normally have taken her seventeen hours minimum flight time. Plus the rest. The only thing they hadn't sorted was her jet lag. What had the doctor called it as she received a quick medical after the jump? LEAP lag. There was no getting round an eleven-hour time difference. She glanced at her watch, trying not to think about it, but failed miserably: just past one in the morning HST. She stifled a yawn, waiting for the guard to finish his pointless search.

Finally, it ended, and all five of them were corralled through to the next cabin. The irony that the interview was to take place on a plane was not lost on Katrina. She wondered who was behind that decision. Where, she wasn't certain. The windows were shuttered, and when she had tried to open one, another security guard had firmly blocked her attempt. Instead, she checked her notes whilst her team set up the equipment. Finally, a sound and image check with her co-anchor in Manhattan at Radio City where the network had its studios for the Daily Event – the highest rated morning show in America, with viewers averaging five million a day. Today they were expecting double that number. Katrina felt a surge of adrenalin at the thought. It would catapult her to new levels, just like the last one had. Unless, of course, they didn't turn up. She checked her watch, suddenly feeling nervous. What if they didn't show? The segment was timed for 08:00, hoping to deliver maximum viewing figures.

'Focus on what you can control,' she muttered, closing her eyes and slowing her breathing down. If they weren't planning to show, they had gone to an awful lot of trouble to set this up. She tried to picture walking on stage at the 2010 Emmy's to collect her award, but all she could see was Brett storming out of their suite. She opened one eye to check the large stopwatch pinned to the camera opposite: 12:58 here, 07:58 on the East Coast. Where were they, she thought?

A door behind her opened and two people entered. She stood and approached them. Immediately, one of the guards stepped forward.

'That's alright, Jim,' Ethan said, extending his hand out to Katrina and shaking it warmly. The woman with him just scowled at Katrina.

'Good to see you, Katrina,' Ethan said. 'How are you? Did you enjoy the LEAP?'

'I did, thank you. Quite incredible.'

'Do you want to buy a plane?' He swept his arm around the plush interior. 'I couldn't give this away at the moment.'

'No, I don't suppose,' Katrina said. 'I—'

'Shall we do this?' Uma interrupted, her jaw set forward, green eyes flashing dangerously, arms folded.

'Yes, yes, of course,' Katrina said, taken aback by the woman's aggression. 'Let's do this.'

Ethan smiled reassuringly at Uma. He wasn't surprised at her reaction. It had been his idea to run the interview with Katrina. It had worked well on the last occasion, just after he had resurrected Uma following the West Coast earthquake. Back then, he needed to generate some good PR to neutralise the efforts to discredit Green Ray with stories of them supporting terrorism. Today, they needed to tell the world what had just happened: that someone was out there, working to prevent them from repatriating families affected by the ash cloud. Katrina was the leading daytime anchor in America on the most watched morning show. This would get global airplay. It was a quick win after what had happened. Uma just wanted them to hide away. Which he understood, to a degree.

They all sat down, Katrina facing Uma and Ethan, two cameras positioned either side of Katrina's shoulders. Another sat between the interviewees, pointing back at her.

'Is all this security necessary?' Katrina asked.

'Someone just tried to kill us. And nearly succeeded,' Uma shot back.

'I'm sorry,' Katrina said, momentarily thrown, 'someone tried to kill you?' She had expected an interview about a fire and how it might affect the rollout of LEAP. This was going to be better than last time.

The realisation calmed the ache in her stomach. She hoped Brett was watching. Maybe he would understand now. 'I'm sorry to hear that,' Katrina repeated. The Jakobsdóttir woman looked like she wanted to launch herself across the cabin at her. What had she done to upset her? Katrina looked across at her producer, Nick Lovell, who was theatrically counting down with his hands. Katrina nodded, turning back to Ethan and Uma.

'We can explore it in the interview, if that's OK. Do you mind?' She shook her mane of blond hair and suddenly beamed at the camera, everything forgotten. It was showtime.

'Now, I've got some very important guests here with me this afternoon. Well, afternoon here. Morning for all you folks in America. If you remember, last November we invited two of the most high-profile people in the world to tell their story on the Daily Event. It was an exclusive back then. Today is no different. Except this time, we are in a secret location, for reasons that will become clear. Everyone, I would like to welcome Ethan Rae and Uma Jakobsdóttir back to my couch.'

The camera panned to Ethan and Uma, who scowled back.

'As everyone knows, they were caught up in a fire at Ethan's London-based HQ. A fire that destroyed the building and, so far, has accounted for over twenty dead people, mainly protesters, but also included was Ethan Rae's housekeeper.'

'Someone tried to kill us,' Uma said, eyes misting over. Her hand reached out for Ethan, who took it, suddenly wondering if this was such a good idea. Back in November, Uma had seemed more composed. Today, her mood was febrile. He had put it down to the attack, but there was something else which he couldn't lay his finger on. Anyway, it was too late now.

'What do you mean?' Katrina said.

'The fire was started by men who broke into the house, two of whom came to our bedroom and tried to kill us. Had it not been for Ethan, we would have died.'

'Who were these men?'

'We don't know. We're working with the CIA and British Intelligence to find out who did it. But so far, no leads.'

'Please,' Katrina appealed to the camera, 'take a moment. Start at the beginning for our viewers. Take me through exactly what happened.'

Ethan made to answer, but Uma cut across him.

'Two days ago, we were at home, in bed, when there was a large explosion downstairs. A—'

Ethan thought of that moment. He had thought about it a thousand times as he lay in the hospital bed at the Chelsea & Westminster Hospital burns unit. That he could have lost Uma. Had lost Mrs Carr. He couldn't forgive himself for what had happened. How could he have been so stupid not to have the requisite level of security in place? Was he losing his touch? If she had died ... He shuddered at the thought, skin crawling as his mother's eyes suddenly blinked open beneath him, her blond hair, normally so vibrant and shiny, a dull dirty blood red. *Dear God, not here on national TV.* He forced the image from his mind and tried to focus on what Uma was saying.

'—there were men at our door. With guns. They tried to kill us. Ethan,' Uma squeezed his hand and looked over, 'fought them off. Afterwards, I only just got out. Ethan wasn't so lucky. He got caught in the blaze.'

'How?' Katrina said.

'Whilst trying to rescue his housekeeper. She was downstairs, and he went to save her.'

Katrina turned to Ethan, who was suddenly aware of the red light on the camera opposite him, blinking like a lighthouse beacon, blaring danger, but it was too late. He was already on the rocks.

'I've known her for many years,' he mumbled, trying to focus on Katrina, but her long hair reminded him of his mother's: bloodied and burned. 'Since I bought the house, in fact.'

He felt his back prickle.

'Please, take us through it,' he heard Katrina say.

'I don't know,' Ethan said. 'I remember going down the stairs with a blanket over my head to protect me from the smoke. Uma went up to the third floor. We have a LEAP gate there. She was able to escape. I must have blacked out. Too much smoke. It was everywhere.

I remember an explosion. Then nothing. And the next thing I woke up in a hospital bed, covered in bandages.'

Except he remembered. He remembered getting to the kitchen and someone attacking him. Another of the men. This time smaller, but it didn't matter. Ethan was spent. He could feel powerful hands around his neck, slowly strangling the life out of him as he looked into the man's eyes. Then suddenly, someone else was above his attacker, his hands on the man's cheeks. A quick flick to the right and his attacker slumped to the floor. Then Ethan felt himself being lifted by his saviour except, instead of moving towards the garden, he was flying across the kitchen into the fire.

'With third-degree burns to your face and hands.'

'Pardon,' Ethan said, staring blankly at Katrina.

'You said you awoke in hospital. With burns, to your face and hands.'

'That's right,' Ethan said. 'That's why they couldn't ID me straight away.'

'How have you recovered so quickly?'

'LEAP,' he said simply. 'We can repair cells. As long as we have a previous copy to work from, we can regenerate anyone's body to a replica of what they were.'

'But you famously didn't repair your arm when you injured it in the earthquake last year. The one that destroyed Reynolds' castle. What's the difference this time?'

Ethan paused. Now there was a good question. To be honest, he had wanted to recover naturally. The burns would be a reminder of his negligence, just like his back and leg. Just like his arm. All represented his abject failure to protect those around him, but Uma had insisted. They needed him now. To push the programme forward. To make Mrs Carr's death count for something. It wouldn't, if he was years in rehab waiting for multiple operations to heal his singed skin.

'I've always struggled with certain elements of LEAP. For me, personally, life is experienced. Even injury. It forms you. Moulds you. Makes you who you are. Just like my arm.' He held it up to the camera. The scarring was clear, an ugly mark running down the outside of his forearm. 'It happened at a low point in my life. Whenever it aches, I'm reminded of that moment. That, if I'm not careful, I could repeat the mistakes that lead me to that point.'

His leg and back prickled appreciatively. He was waffling. He needed to get a grip. It was the fire. He couldn't shake the feeling he should have done more, and the consequences were now being laid bare on national TV. Maybe this hadn't been such a good idea. This time, Uma came to his rescue.

'The programme needs him,' she cut in again. 'We have an opportunity to make a significant difference to millions of people's lives through the volcano repatriations. Ethan is leading that entire effort. We need him today, fully fit, not stuck in a burns unit for months on end.'

For once, Ethan was glad to let Uma take the lead. He sat there thinking of Mrs Carr and her kind face. He had failed her. Just like his parents. And nearly Uma, but by the grace of God, she had survived, as had he. His back prickled again, causing him to push his palms into his legs.

'OK, I understand how important Ethan is to the programme. Before we move on, can you explain to our viewers how LEAP was used to repair his body. It doesn't seem possible. Or natural, for that matter.'

Ethan relaxed. Uma could talk all day about this stuff.

'Of course,' Uma replied. 'LEAP doesn't transport your body. It just scans your atomic structure at the outbound gate, using quantum computing. Then it reassembles you at the other end, atom by atom, using the scan as the blueprint – not only for what atoms make you up, but where they go. To avoid there being two of you, the system actually disassembles your original atoms at the outbound gate for later use by whatever was being transported to that gate. Meanwhile, at the arrivals gate, you are literally being created using different atoms, using the scan as a guide to rebuild you. Subsequent scans only record what has changed since the previous scan.'

'It sounds horrifying,' Katrina said. 'Like something from a sci-fi movie.'

'All science is, at some stage, fiction,' Uma shot back, 'but the immutable fact remains that we're very simple creatures really. We are composed of just three elements: oxygen, carbon and nitrogen. Oxygen is the most abundant and is found mostly as a component of water, which makes up over seventy percent of our entire body mass, including our brains. What many of your viewers might find surprising is that at an atomic level, there is very little individuality or sense of "self". None of us is ever the same person for more than a millisecond. At any one moment, billions and billions of our atoms are reforming into different compounds, molecules and cells. It's a continuous process that occurs right through our life until the day we die. In fact, there isn't a single part of us here today, atomically speaking, that was part of us twelve months ago. Your stomach lining changes every five days. Your skin will have completely recycled itself after thirty days. Every day, it sheds billions and billions of tiny flakes and underneath, it is constantly renewed and recycled. The same goes for every other part of your body. Take your skeleton. It renews every three months. Even your brain gets a full makeover. The cells you actually think with weren't there nine months ago. Think of LEAP as a super accelerator of that process.'

'Fascinating,' Katrina said. She needed to get this woman away from the science – not great TV, first thing in the morning.

'So, getting back to Ethan, what you're telling me is that without the intervention, he could have died?'

'Unlikely,' Uma said. 'His lungs were damaged from smoke inhalation and the skin across his upper torso was badly burned. We rescanned his body in the hospital then compared it to the most recent copy we took when he last LEAPed. All we did was reline his lungs and restore his skin. Everything else remained the same, including his memories right up to where he lost consciousness in the townhouse.'

'But had he died, would you have restored him?'

'No, of course not,' Uma retorted. 'The LEAP Laws forbid it.'

'What gives you the right to decide?' Katrina countered.

'We have no choice. Can you imagine the implications for everyone?'

'Well, in a way, you have. Without the intervention, Ethan could have died.'

'I didn't say that and he didn't,' Uma replied.

'But had he died, you're telling me you wouldn't have intervened, even though you have the technology that allows you to restore him?'

'We're not crossing that Rubicon.' Uma said. 'It's non-negotiable. Just like the other LEAP Laws. If we do, there will be no return. It would be chaos.'

'How so?'

'Well, this planet of ours is struggling to sustain the nearly seven billion people we already have. Can you imagine if we started restoring people? They would be eternal. We don't have the resources to sustain that. Without sounding too dramatic, it could herald the end of civilisation. If no one ever died, the population would balloon and become out of control. That's why the law exists.'

Except it doesn't work that way, Ethan thought. Look at him. He restored Uma; she restored him. And now, given the chance, he would restore Mrs Carr. She didn't deserve to die.

As if she had read his mind, Katrina turned to Ethan and smiled sweetly.

'And what about Mrs Carr, your housekeeper? Wouldn't you want to restore her? She was murdered the other morning, in her own home. An innocent victim of a brutal attack. She didn't deserve to die.'

Ethan didn't reply straight away. He was caught off guard.

'I don't know,' he said, thinking that he did. He would restore her in a heartbeat.

'Don't you think your law is too rigid? Surely there should be exceptions.'

'No, it's an absolute law for the reasons I have given,' Uma cut in. Ethan could tell she was getting irritated. They needed to wrap this up.

'What about Mrs Carr?' Katrina repeated. 'God rest her soul. A victim. Of murder. Shouldn't we restore her?' Without waiting for an answer, Katrina turned to the screen. 'And that's our poll for this morning. Let's see what our viewers think. The question is simple. "Should Mrs Carr live?" Poor Mrs Carr. Killed in a vicious fire set by assassins sent to murder her boss. Should she get to live? Calls are free. Let's see what you have to say.'

Katrina turned back to Ethan and Uma.

'Where do you draw the line?' Uma interrupted before Katrina could speak. 'If you make an exception for one death, then you could have an avalanche of claims.'

'There are a hundred good reasons why someone should live – road traffic accident victims, murder victims, victims of wars – the list is endless. And I'm not sure it should be you deciding these questions. It's too much for one person. Governments should set laws and then they should be policed by the courts.'

'Except that you'll get 147 different interpretations. It would get so messy.'

'Life is messy, Uma.'

'But—'

'We're getting our first results from the votes,' Katrina cut in. 'It's 98 % in favour of Mrs Carr living. Our viewers have spoken.'

Uma made to speak again, but Katrina cut her off with a raised hand. She appeared to be listening to someone.

'I'm so sorry, we need to take a weather break,' she said, turning back to Uma and Ethan. 'Thank you so much for your time today.'

She stood, reaching out a hand.

Uma stared at it as if she was being handed a poisonous snake.

'Why did you twist everything like that?'

'I didn't. I did my job. To examine both sides of an issue. Your law is an over simplification of what's at stake here. As Ethan,' she turned to him, 'and Mrs Carr, have shown.'

'You can make your own way home,' Uma snarled, pushing past the startled anchor and disappearing through the doorway towards the exit.

Transamerica Pyramid, San Francisco

23rd April, 2010, 13:21 hours PDT

Crouch slumped in the chair as his hand absentmindedly reached for the tumbler, pudgy fingers grasping the cool glass. He put it to his mouth, smacking his lips with appreciation as the liquid fire warmed his throat. He stared at the near-empty bottle, realising that he would need another one before long, and wondered if Forsyth had any liquor left in his cabinet. No matter, he could always nip back to Riyadh, where he had an enviable stash of Rittenhouse Straight Rye. At least that was one good thing about the Saudi elite – if you had the money, plus the right connections, you could pretty much acquire any luxury, and Mohammed had done just that for him. Crouch undid his top button, loosened his grubby tie and cracked his fingers, staring at the screen.

The mystery man should be easy to find and, like all problems that Crouch faced, he approached it as a puzzle, quickly listing what he knew: white Caucasian, could fight, was strong, probably military. It wasn't much, but now he had a photo. It should be enough. He would start with the UK and US Armed Forces personnel databases. The obvious ones first: Army, Navy and then Air-force, before moving onto Special Forces and more specialist units: the Army Rangers and Green Berets in the US; SAS and SBS in the UK. He assumed the Metropolitan Police were investigating, so he would need to understand their progress, and, given the media reports that witnesses had heard explosions, he debated whether to see if MI5 were involved. If all that failed, he would search Interpol's Face Recognition System, a global database of facial images received from over 170 countries. First things first, though.

Access was not a problem. It was how he had started out at college: hacking home PCs for suspicious wives, spying on their spouses and stealing customer addresses for rival pizza takeouts. As the jobs had got bigger, the security had improved, and he had turned to quantum computing in order to brute force the passwords quicker, not because it was difficult. Given time, any password could be hacked, but some could run into hundreds of decimal places, which required vast amounts of computational power. Quantum was the obvious choice, turning a three-month job into minutes, as the power at his disposal allowed him to run millions of calculations simultaneously. No system was safe, including the ones he was targeting today. It was no contest really, as if he had landed in the nineteenth century with a Ferrari and was racing the locals on their horses. Better still, on foot.

First, the HR departments. He had already created a simple routine that had analysed the man's face, including the distance between his eyes, the width of his nose, the shape of his cheek and the contour of his lips, ears and chin. In all, forty-five characteristics, which were as unique as the ridges on a fingerprint. All he needed to do was scrape each database for any images and compare them against his mystery man. He worked methodically, accessing each database, scraping the images and setting the routine running. There were over thirty in total and whilst he waited for the results to come in, he broke into the Met Police. It was child's play – they were running over thirty-five thousand desktop machines alone, all on Microsoft XP, which had a hundred vulnerabilities that Crouch was aware of. He didn't have time to send a virus or phishing email, so he ran a routine that scanned Met IP addresses, searching for poor passwords. Within a minute, one popped up, and seconds later, he had invaded the network, using the digital address of an XP machine in Holborn Police Station, the Borough HQ for Camden. He quickly scanned the case file for the townhouse attack. There was nothing. The police were baffled by the fire, including its causes. They were currently awaiting a preliminary report from the Kentish Town Fire Station that had attended the initial blaze. He ran the same routine and accessed the server at the West Hampstead Fire Station. Nothing again. One of his search routines pinged, and he glanced over. All the UK Armed Forces were returning a negative search across all their databases. Crouch pondered his next move. He could either search the Met, TFL and council databases of CCTV images or target the US. CCTV was a good bet – London was one of the most spied upon cities in the world, with Transport for London having over 10,000 surveillance cameras alone at its stations and bus routes, closely followed by the Met, including local boroughs. Beyond that, there were another half million CCTV cameras watching Londoners' every move, most of which were private. If his mystery man had walked, or caught a bus or tube, he might be on camera. In the end, he ran both. He was already accessing the Met and Camden Council, so it was easy to hack into the TFL database. He did the same with the US Armed Forces, targeting the HR department like he had done for the UK. It would take twenty minutes. Crouch wandered into the other room containing the LEAP gate Forsyth had used before his untimely escape to Saudi Arabia.

It was one of many that Crouch used to hack the LEAP network. Hack wasn't the correct term, since he already had access to the system, courtesy of his continuing work for the CIA. He recalled his recent conversation and shuddered. What Forsyth was currently asking him to do was a worrying development for him. More deaths would follow. This time he didn't have the CIA to hide behind with promises of immunity, however hollow they were. Fingers would inevitably point at him, placing him directly in the firing line for whatever blame would follow after they executed the programme. He could always refuse, but what then? Forsyth could hardly go out and replace him. He couldn't think of one person out there who could do what he had done. Or would want to, which brought him back to why he had agreed to help Forsyth in the first place. That woman. She was responsible for his current predicament. Helping Forsyth with his plan would finish Green Ray, a goal that the CIA also had. Maybe he should share what Forsyth had planned with them and get them to add another immunity clause to his contract. In that way, he would be covered. Crouch took a long drink from the bottle and immediately felt better. He brought up her details on the screen, staring at the data and flicking through her LEAP history. He could finish it now. Delete the woman and all her backups, then move onto Rae. He had access to their entire atomic structure, every last atom of it, but Forsyth hadn't wanted to do it this way. It was too easy. He was obsessed with making the woman pay. That was the goal. Make her hurt like she had made Forsyth hurt, and Crouch. She had humiliated him publicly, effectively ending his career. No, Forsyth was right, death through deletion was too easy.

He was just about to log out of her profile when he noticed an abnormality in her jump history. Something was not quite right. She had made a recent deletion. Crouch studied the screen carefully, his pudgy face breaking out into a smile. She had been pregnant, but had aborted it. Why? Crouch immediately assumed it was Rae's baby. They were clearly together, judging from the videos of the townhouse raid. He looked at the date of deletion. That was shortly after Rae had emerged from his mausoleum. Crouch shrugged. Maybe Forsyth would know what to do with the information.

He made his way back into the other room. The routines had finished. More importantly, they had returned two positive results: bingo! He studied the screen, staring at a short video of the man. He was outside what looked like a kebab shop in Camden on Parkway, retrieving his baseball cap from the sidewalk, before cramming it back on his shaven head and disappearing into the restaurant. Five minutes later, he appeared, his face now covered. He was holding a white plastic bag, but instead of walking off down the street, he immediately disappeared through a door next to the takeout. The other search was from the Special Forces segment, specifically the US Navy SEALs. He clicked on the file, a second smile breaking across his ruddy face.

'Hello, Commander Fox,' Crouch said, taking a long drink which emptied the bottle.

Camden Town, London

24th April 2010, 18:04 hours, GMT

Ed couldn't get used to the British weather. It was like nothing he had ever experienced, even in Afghanistan. He wasn't cold, but the dampness tugged at his spirits, pulling them down like a lead weight. His thoughts turned to LA. At this time of year, the temperature would be low seventies, zero humidity, with a cool westerly wind blowing in off the Pacific. He pictured the Camaro with the roof down. He seemed drawn to it, and regardless of what he thought about, every memory boomeranged back to that car. One moment, hurtling along; the next, consumed by a fireball. Ed stopped dead in the street, causing the following pedestrian to hurriedly apologise as she collided with him. Slowly the image faded. Ed continued aimlessly along Camden High Street towards Parkway. Around him, early evening commuters thronged the damp pavements, parting like a river around a rock as their dinners called them home. As Ed passed a store, two familiar figures stopped him dead. Arrayed before him on twenty TV monitors was the reason for his indecision – a re-run of the TV interview that Rae and Jakobsdóttir had given yesterday evening. It had been picked up by the networks as their main news story. He entered the store, watching the interview again, feeling the familiar ache as the number of recovered bodies flashed up on the monitors: twenty-six confirmed dead. He stared at the screen, trying to process the number. He hadn't meant it to be this way. Just two should have died, but they were clearly very much alive, sitting opposite the American reporter, recounting their story to her. This wasn't him. His job was to protect the weak and the innocent, fighting evil. It was what had led him to join the army against his parents' wishes. He was not evil, yet the number of dead suggested otherwise. It didn't matter that they had died in his desire to avenge the deaths of Jo and Angel. They called it collateral damage in the army. He had always hated the term, but was now hoisted by the same petard. As he stared at the number, a new resolve burned away his guilt. If anything, it made Rae and Jakobsdóttir even more culpable. If they had restored Jo and Angel, he wouldn't be standing here now. He would be home with them, probably driving the Camaro with the top down, taking a trip along Bouquet Canyon Road up to the reservoir, where they would sit watching the sun go down as Angel played in the shallows.

No, this was all their fault. The question was, how did he get to them? Had he wasted his one opportunity? He didn't even know where they were. Probably back in the States for all he knew, and he was stuck here, his leave now over. He should have reported for duty back at the Coronado Naval Base in San Diego already. At best, he was facing a full court martial; at worst, prison time. But he didn't care about his career any more. That had finished the day Jo and Angel had died, but he did care that he was stuck in London, unable to travel for fear of his passport being flagged. They would now know that he had flown into Heathrow on March 17th and, most likely, would have alerted the British authorities, who were probably trying to find him.

Ed exited the store and continued his aimless walk down Camden High Street. To his left, a man appeared on the crossing. He looked familiar. Ed could have sworn he had seen him yesterday whilst exiting the bedsit, but the man barely glanced at him as he scooted across the road and hailed a cab which pulled up ahead. Ed frowned. It was highly unlikely they were looking for him. All the reports in the Press had mentioned no one, but even so, there remained a sneaking suspicion that time was running out for Ed. He needed to make his move, before his luck ran out and the authorities apprehended him, either for the townhouse bombing or for deserting the US Naval SEALs.

Either way, it made no odds to him – he would die here in London, trying to kill the two people who might as well have lit the petrol fire that had burned Jo and Angel to death.

Riyadh, Saudi Arabia

24th April 2010, 22:04 hours, AST

The music boomed up through the courtyard, thumping so loudly that Forsyth could feel his bones vibrate. A group of women approached, pausing beneath the immense oak tree. One was barely dressed, a silk robe clinging tightly to her body. Forsyth stared, licking his lips in appreciation. God, she was beautiful. Her friends started to dance, swaying to the deep bass which thundered through hidden speakers. Strobe lights pulsed behind dropped balustrades that ringed the square, shifting through the colours of the rainbow as the song built to a crescendo. The woman swayed to the beat, laughing at something her companion said. She grabbed a magnum of champagne from a passing waiter, and drank directly from the bottle. As the song reached its climax, she shook it vigorously, spraying champagne high into the night sky. It rained down on them, soaking them. The woman's silk chiffon gown was now transparent, revealing voluminous breasts.

'You like?' a voice squeaked in his ear.

Forsyth turned. The Crown Prince was standing there, his pudgy eyes glinting flint-black in the light show. He nodded at the group less than twenty feet away. One of the girls nudged her partner, and all five looked over, suddenly aware that the second richest man in the Kingdom was watching them. He raised a glass in response.

'Who is she?'

'Who do you think?' the Crown Prince replied, licking his lips. 'I can introduce you?'

'Maybe later,' Forsyth murmured, slightly disappointed. He preferred to work for his conquests. Where was the fun if they were laid out on a platter, however beautiful they were?

'When do we make our announcement?'

'You Americans. Always in a rush. You need to enjoy yourself.'

'We need to move now. Every day we delay, LEAP gets further ahead. The more oil escapes into the Gulf and the worse the optics become.'

'That was the idea, if you remember,' the Crown Prince replied. 'I said I would take care of my father, and Allah spoke—' He smiled mischievously. '—by creating the biggest environmental disaster the world has ever known and tanking the oil price. You, on the other hand, said you would deal with Jakobsdóttir and Rae. I agreed to help, but here they are still, running around, making life difficult for all of us.'

'It was your men,' Forsyth cut in, suddenly angry. That quickly faded as the Crown Prince's eyes narrowed until they were tight slits, and in that moment, Forsyth realised that beneath the faux bonhomie lay a ruthlessness, just as perilous as Al Rahman's. His dear friend, who was now dead for failing to deliver what he'd promised the Kingdom. He wondered if the same fate awaited him. Of course, it did. This place didn't countenance failure. Anyone's. That's how it should be. 'Leave them to me,' Forsyth said in a more contrite tone. Crouch had said he could find the man that had derailed his team's attempt. That the system could hack any security in the world. Well, he needed to find him and find out who he was fast. Plus, he had something else in mind for Green Ray, something that would be significantly more effective than killing off the founders.

The Crown Prince nodded, his fat lips cracking into a wide smile that continued into a high-pitched cackle. Curious faces turned in their direction, despite the music.

'Good. We'll cement our new partnership tomorrow morning with the King,' the Crown Prince replied. 'But tonight, we celebrate a glorious victory. I suggest you enjoy it.'

Forsyth's heart leapt. Tomorrow. That was perfect. He could feel the victory. 'What time are we meeting?'

There was no reply. Forsyth glanced over, but the Crown Prince was walking away towards the main foyer. As he reached the doors, he paused and looked back at Forsyth.

'Enjoy yourself,' he mouthed.

Forsyth nodded, and as he turned back, he nearly bumped into the woman who had caught his eye earlier.

'Hello, Mr Forsyth.' She reached out a hand, which he took, his eyes drawn to her gown which clung tightly to her slender frame. Up close, it was almost translucent, and Forsyth licked his lips. 'You like?'

'You read my mind,' he said.

She leaned in close, so close that her breast was touching his right hand, and whispered huskily into his ear.

'Maybe we can find somewhere quieter?' she murmured. 'My quarters are on the second floor. Are you coming?'

She pulled away.

Forsyth smiled. He could see her buttocks through the soaked material. Champagne dripped down her olive skin.

'Do you have champagne up there?' he said.

'As much as you want,' she laughed.

Forsyth shrugged.

'When in Rome,' he muttered and followed the woman, a small vial gripped tightly in his right hand.

Camden Town, London

25th April 2010, 19:17 hours, GMT

Forsyth stood on the threshold of the room, debating whether to enter. A stale odour clawed at the back of his throat – sweat mingled with congealed lamb fat and sour yogurt. He hurriedly placed a handkerchief over his mouth and entered, stepping over half-eaten kebabs mixed with barely smoked cigarettes that littered the floor. He swivelled on his heel, wondering if he had the right place, but Crouch had been insistent. This was where Commander Fox was living. An operative had confirmed it, after following the man home the previous evening, but still, this was not the digs of a decorated war hero. Forsyth took a deep breath. Using his handkerchief, he opened the wardrobe. A pair of slacks hung forlornly from a deformed wire hanger, beneath which was a pile of dirty hoodies and T-shirts. He wandered over to the window, staring down into the street – beneath him, outside the Red Lemon, two drunks were arguing over a half-finished kebab, before, somewhat surprisingly, agreeing to split it. Forsyth grimaced. He turned away, scanning the room, looking for something, anything, to suggest that he had found his man. In one corner, underneath the stained sink, were six bottles. He wandered over, crouched down, and studied the two labels on each bottle: one showed a fire, the other a skull and crossbones. That was more like it.

There was a click in his right ear.

Forsyth quickly glanced round.

'Easy does it,' a voice growled in his ear.

He turned slowly, heart beating wildly, staring at the large gun now pointing at his chest, before flicking his gaze up to the man's face. It was unmistakably Fox, but not the clean-cut, smiling version from his service record. The man's jaw was now set in a permanent grimace that flatlined his mouth and was shadowed by a three-day stubble speckled with grey. His skin was wan, black rings hollowing out eyes that looked exhausted from lack of sleep. And something else: the light was missing from them. They were the eyes of someone with nothing to lose. Forsyth looked beyond him, through the open doorway. His two bodyguards were sitting, back to back, their heads lolling forward against their chests.

'They'll be OK, just unconscious,' the man whispered again. It sounded like gravel.

'You're a hard man to find, Commander Fox,' Forsyth said, trying to keep the annoyance out of his voice at the sight of the Crown Prince's bodyguards. They were worse than the ones from the aborted raid on the townhouse.

If he was surprised, Fox didn't show it. He just stared at Forsyth with his dead eyes.

'Who are you, and what are you doing in my room?'

Forsyth couldn't help himself.

'This isn't a room. It's a pigsty.'

'You haven't answered my questions,' Fox growled, 'and I won't ask them again.'

He holstered his gun, taking one step towards Forsyth, who hurriedly backed away until he was pressed against the sink.

'OK, OK, easy there,' he said, raising his palms outward. 'My name is John Forsyth and I'm here because I know we have something in common.'

Fox's eyes drilled into him, as if to suggest that they had absolutely nothing in common.

'You know nothing about me.'

'I know that you're a commander in the NAVY SEALS. That you have performed four tours of Afghanistan. That you are currently absent without leave. I know that you have been here since the 17th March and that you're wanted by the US Army. I know you will be apprehended shortly. I know that your family were killed in a motor accident on 10th March this year.'

That got a reaction. A flicker of pain sliced across Fox's face, his fists clenching into tight balls. Forsyth swallowed hard, imagining them bludgeoning his face.

'You're on very thin ice,' Fox rumbled dangerously, as if two tectonic plates were grinding together.

Forsyth didn't disagree.

'I know you were in Ethan Rae's townhouse four days ago.'

That got Fox's attention.

'How do you know that?'

Forsyth pressed home his advantage.

'Because I have you on video killing at least one of my men. And then hurling Ethan Rae into a fire that I think you started.' Forsyth nodded down at the bottles by his feet. 'My high school chemistry isn't great, but even I know a bomb-making factory when I see one. Creates a fire that burns hot, as hot as the petrol fire that killed your family.'

'What do you want?'

Forsyth relaxed. He had him. He stepped past Fox into the centre of the room and turned.

'OK, cards on the table. I run a rival system to LEAP called Eternity. I have three services: Looks, Health and BackUp. Rae and that woman are my competition.' Forsyth was watching Fox carefully as he spoke, realising he was losing him. Fox didn't care about Eternity, and less still what Forsyth did. He needed to help Fox understand why he wanted them dead. 'They – she – destroyed my life, much like it would seem they destroyed yours. I want revenge.'

Fox's eyes glimmered at the word "revenge".

Forsyth pressed on.

'So, that's my story. What's yours? Why do you want revenge so badly?'

Again, that reaction.

Fox stood for a long moment, staring at the floor. As if battling something. Forsyth thought he wasn't going to talk, that he had lost him.

'I was part of the government's CBL programme. Operation Twin. All active soldiers in Afghanistan were in it. If you were KIA, you were restored. It happened to me twice. I was kept alive, but when Jo and Angel were killed,' Fox seemed to choke on the names, 'there was no second chance for them, because of Green Ray's damn Laws.'

In a flash, it all became clear to Forsyth.

'It looks like we have a lot more in common than either of us realised.'

Fox frowned, forcing Forsyth to continue.

'She took everything from me. My looks, my livelihood, my life as I knew it. I want her to suffer as I suffered.'

'Why should I help you?'

'I failed this week. To kill them. So did you, but upon reflection, death was too easy for them. I have a better idea. We can make them suffer. Like we have suffered – are suffering – but in ways they can't even imagine.'

Fox nodded, listening intently.

'Your wife and daughter. They suffered for a minute. Me, a month. You,' he nodded at Fox, 'your suffering will last a lifetime. What I've got in mind will make Ethan Rae and his whore suffer for a hundred lifetimes.'

Leipzig, Germany

26th April 2010, 11:55 hours CEST

Alan Taylor stared at the crumpled note in his hand, silently repeating the words under his breath. Even after repeated attempts, they still felt unnatural in his mouth, like he was chewing an unfamiliar food. He wondered if he should abandon the idea, but Phil Davids had been insistent. He looked over at the producer who was standing by the buffet bar chatting animatedly in German to Fritz Schlossen, the owner of the distribution company which Alan had successfully pitched to yesterday. It had gone like clockwork, all thanks to Green Ray. He had made the LEAP first, followed by the camera crew, and the gate had delivered them into the boardroom of Liquid Bier, a craft beer distributor importing English ales into the German market. Phil Davids had offered to translate, but it wasn't needed – the Germans spoke perfect English, much to Alan's relief. After some pleasantries in front of the camera, they had made the LEAP back to his factory in Holbeck. It wasn't much to look at, but that didn't matter. What mattered was that they could brew 10,000 litres per month for Liquid Bier. And now, with the LEAP gate, they could deliver the output daily. The visit had been a formality, really. For the cameras. The deal had been done the previous evening, in his hotel room with Fritz. A two-year deal guaranteed to generate £15,000 a month. It was a turning point in his life. They could upgrade the factory, move the family. After the Germans had left, he'd called Mandy, breathless with excitement. They had chatted for over an hour, discussing what they would do with the money, ideas tumbling down the line. To think, less than ten days ago, he had been facing financial ruin, stuck in Orlando, watching a volcano spewing ash five miles into the atmosphere. And now look at him – a paper millionaire. Green Ray had even offered to restore his leg. Said they could rebuild it if he wanted.

Phil Davids laughed, too quickly for Alan's liking. Everything about him was too quick. Too glossy. Too southern. Phil shook Fritz's hand, sauntering over to where Alan was standing.

'Ready when you are, buddy. Remember, you go first, followed by the German. I'll come through last. Amanda will meet you on the other side with little Emma. We'll sign the paperwork there, and then I thought we could take them out for a celebratory lunch. Some fish and chips maybe? There must be a hundred chippies around your neighbourhood. What do you think?'

'Sounds good to me.' Alan smiled, but inside he was frowning: another northern stereotype. Fish and bloody chips. What a wanker. Alan's hand tightened around the paper. He couldn't resist a look down, and Phil caught his eye.

'What have you got there?' he asked.

'Nothing, just some words I wanted to say to Fritz. For the camera. To thank him. I thought it would look good.'

The producer snatched the paper from his hand and read it out loud.

'Vielen dank LEAP. Danke fritz für dein geschäft. Wir freuen uns auf die zusammenarbeit mit ihnen und ihren kollegen.'

It sounded a lot better coming from him.

'Are you sure?'

Alan nodded. 'OK, hit me with it,' Phil said, his eyes twinkling with anticipation.

'Pardon.'

'Say the words now.'

Alan looked down.

'No, without looking.' Phil screwed up the paper and tossed it behind his back. 'Go on.'

Bastard was mocking him.

'Vielen dank ...' Alan mumbled before trailing off, his face reddening.

'Thought so. First rule of TV. Be yourself.'

Phil didn't need to finish the sentence. His face said everything. A thick northerner, that's what he was thinking.

'Are we clear?'

Alan nodded dumbly, staring miserably at the ground, shifting on his stump. It itched something rotten. He wanted to rip off the prosthetic leg and batter Phil over the head with it.

'OK, in English, please.'

Alan stared at him. Surely not, he thought, but Phil folded his arms like an angry parent. They faced each other and then suddenly Alan smiled. He'd dealt with a hundred Phil's in the army. Just grin and tell them what they want to hear.

'Thank you, LEAP. Thank you, Fritz for your business. We look forward to working with you and your colleagues.'

It sounded wooden and Phil's face confirmed it.

'Be yourself,' he said, jabbing his finger into Alan's chest. Then he was gone, turning away, clapping his hands together, like a school teacher corralling kids.

'Right, people. Take your positions. We're live in sixty seconds. It's a big audience today. Let's give them a show.'

Mandy Taylor adjusted her hair for the hundredth time since they had arrived at the gate. Around her, the camera crew waited patiently. She still hadn't got used to their constant presence and wished they would go away, but Alan had reassured her the documentary would be great for the business. And them. She wasn't so sure. Things were moving way too quickly for her liking. It was as if they were on a giant conveyor belt, hurtling along at warp speed. She couldn't understand the rush. Ten days ago, they were finishing a near-perfect trip to Florida and the baby had slept well. True, Alan had been distracted, but so had she. They were acclimatising, she kept telling herself. To little Emma. She looked down at the baby in the pram who was fast asleep, a tiny fist crammed into her mouth. And then suddenly, from the moment they had arrived at the airport, their world had changed. All thanks to LEAP: their jump home; the offer to teleport Alan to Germany; the approach from Green Ray to film a documentary about them; the new contract. Alan was thinking of moving to North Leeds but the thought scared her. She liked their terraced house in Holbeck. True, it was small and the nights were noisy, but her mum was five minutes away, and her two sisters even closer.

The producer caught her eye. "One minute," he mouthed and Mandy smiled at him, adjusting her hair again, as the reporter stepped forward.

'We're here in Holbeck outside the White Rose Microbrewery. In less than a minute, Alan Taylor will step through with his new German partners and a two-year contract to supply thousands of litres of their flagship ale, Yorkshire Pride, to Germany. It will bring jobs and tax revenue to Leeds. All thanks to LEAP.' He put his hand to his ear. 'Folks, I hear they're coming.'

On the monitor, Mandy could see her husband alongside the bald German. Between them, the producer. Alan was smiling. Sort of. She knew that look and wondered what had upset him.

'Three, two, one.'

Mandy stepped forward with the pram.

The conveyor belt slammed to a stop.

Her legs buckled from underneath her.

She felt herself falling.

Someone was screaming.

Hot bile was in her throat.

A faraway rushing in her ears

Another person shouting.

The baby was awake, her mouth silently screaming at Mandy.

In front of her was a mass of ... flesh, weeping blood like a festering sore.

She knew it was Alan. His prosthetic leg stood defiantly like a lone sentinel even as the rest of him toppled forward, hitting the pavement with a sickening thwap, like a melon hitting concrete.

A hand, flayed of skin, reached out towards Mandy.

She screamed as a gargled cry bubbled from its stripped lips.

'Danke, LEAP ...'

Manhattan, New York City

28th April 2010, 07:55 hours EDT

Uma couldn't remember the last time they had been here. Was it sometime last year? She wasn't sure. She wasn't sure of anything. On that occasion, Ethan had secured the interview with Katrina Hoskins. Had pulled in a favour, which had started their comeback of sorts. It paved the way for her glorious announcement in Copenhagen alongside the most powerful man in the world at the United Nations Climate Change Conference. Now look at them, she thought grimly. Here they were again, just six days after being interviewed by this poisonous woman, this time begging to be given a forum with that same slimy reporter who cared for no one but herself. How quickly things had changed. Two days ago, outlets had begged to be given an audience with Green Ray, but now sentiment had swung. They were pariahs. The woman adjusted Uma's head, tipping it towards her as she pasted more makeup on top of makeup. Uma stared at herself in the mirror and grimaced. Just like last time, she felt as if she was wearing a mask, that if she smiled or moved her face, the mask would crack and shatter, revealing the monster beneath. The monster that was currently responsible for over four thousand deaths. The woman tried to tie her hair back, but Uma brushed her hand away.

'Leave it.'

Beside her, Ethan was slumped in his chair, similarly grim faced, also staring into his mirror as if he was trying to shatter it.

A production assistant popped her head around the door and smiled at the two of them. Neither responded.

'You're both on in two minutes. Can I get either of you anything?' She waited and then shrugged, pulling a face at the makeup woman, before disappearing.

Ethan stood up and smiled down at Uma, but it died half formed, contorting into a grimace that she didn't feel comforted by. How could she? She had the blood of thousands on her hands and knew what was coming, but they had no choice according to Ethan. It was their chance to present a different version of the story that had dominated the news for the past two days.

They walked through into the main studio, passing a metal structure. It looked remarkably similar to a LEAP gate, but she knew there were none in this building. She had seen to that as a condition of the interview. Immediately, Uma felt the glare of the lights beating down on her forehead and suddenly felt faint, reaching out for Ethan's arm. He sensed her discomfort and grasped her hand with a gentle but firm grip. This time the smile made it, one full of love, and it did the trick: her lightheadedness faded. She squeezed his arm tightly before letting go as they waited beside the raised dais where Katrina was already sitting. In her kingdom. Her rules. She didn't even acknowledge them. She was finishing up the previous segment. Something about the recent oil spill. How it was now leaking 62,000 barrels per day into the Gulf. Could this day get any worse, Uma thought? Another production assistant guided them onto the couch, Ethan closest to the anchor, Uma furthest away. She felt strangely comforted by the arrangement, as if the distance would somehow protect her from what was to come.

'And now, ladies and gentlemen.' Katrina beamed at the camera before turning it onto her two guests, who stared grimly back. 'What you've been waiting for. My specials guests have flown in from a secret location, following the destruction of their global HQ in London last week. Please join me in welcoming Ethan Rae and Uma.' Uma felt herself flush at the slight. She had started the company. It was her tech.

'Well, what a difference a week makes,' Katrina continued. 'It's fair to say you were riding high that morning, but not so much now. Can you give us an update on where we are?'

'Good morning, Katrina,' Ethan began. 'Thank you for having us at such short notice. We're here to say that we have discovered the cause of the accidents that occurred on Monday. It would appear to be a virus that was inserted into the system, that literally stripped the skin from everyone who was making a LEAP across a ten-minute period. As we speak, it has now been cleared. We are once again open for business. As a mark of our confidence in the system, we made the LEAP ourselves this morning.'

'Well, I am pleased to hear that you've corrected this virus. What do you have to say to the families of the 4,240 people who won't be coming home? For them, your words are cold comfort.'

'I understand that, but I wanted to reassure everyone that this wasn't a fault in the system. Someone sabotaged LEAP. As with the Camden Town fire, we're working with local police authorities to try and understand who did this.'

'I repeat the question, what have you got to say to the families of those 4,240 people who died on Monday?'

Uma felt nauseous again, each number driving into her heart like a hot poker. Four thousand two hundred and forty of them, all burning and sizzling with the ferocity of a blast furnace.

'We're sorry,' Uma blurted out. 'We're so, so sorry about what has happened to them.'

She dare not look over at Ethan. They had spent hours with the lawyers discussing their strategy, and everyone had been clear and in full agreement. Don't apologise. It would open the floodgates of litigation that had the potential to run into billions. Not, at least, until they had established the facts, but hearing the amount of people that had died was just too much for Uma.

'Are you going to restore them? That would clear everything up, wouldn't it?'

Uma faltered. This was the question they had feared. The question that was on everyone's lips.

'We ... we can't,' she faltered. 'It would breach the LEAP—'

'Yes, I'm familiar with the laws,' Katrina cut in. 'We discussed them last week in some detail: that you can't resurrect a person who has died. But come on, let's face it, when you conceived that law, you couldn't have anticipated this. It wasn't designed to prevent this, surely. It was designed to prevent untrammelled population growth, as you were at pains to explain to our audience. This is another Mrs Carr, multiplied by a factor of 4,240.'

Uma felt Ethan bristle with anger at the mention of his housekeeper's name, but she ploughed on with what they had agreed to say.

'We can't make an exception, even for those killed in Monday's accident.' There, it was out. They had argued long and hard about this. Back and forth. It was the thin end of the wedge. Once you allowed this, there would be a thousand exceptions. And slowly but surely, the law would be whittled back and millions would get round it. They had to stand firm, even if it set the programme back years. Already, usage had flatlined since Monday.

'I'm sure it would be very easy to sit in your ivory tower, like an omnipotent God, dispensing justice from on high. After all, it's just a number to you, but each number has a family – a wife, a husband; sister, brother; children, grandchildren; friends and colleagues – who will never see that person again, because of a mistake you've made.'

Uma took a deep breath, trying to control her rage at this woman. How could she say that? She had lost loved ones – her sister, Fredrick and so many others – but even as she thought of them, she realised she had also saved Ethan using LEAP. He had saved her. They were hypocrites, but it was precisely because of that experience that they were taking such a hard line. There was no other way.

'It wasn't a mistake. It was a virus inserted into the system. It's not our fault.'

'That's what you say, and I understand why you would, but would you like to tell Mandy Taylor that, face to face?'

As Katrina turned, Uma noticed a woman standing just below the raised dais by one of the cameras. She was holding a baby. Uma gasped with shock as she realised that Katrina Hoskins had ambushed them. Mandy Taylor made her way onto the stage, baby clasped to her chest. Katrina stood and hugged her tightly, being careful to keep the baby in shot. She looked happy, playing with a small elephant.

'As you know, viewers, Mandy's husband, Alan, was one of the first victims of the LEAP massacre.' Katrina led Mandy to the sofa and beckoned for Uma to move along, so the younger woman was sitting between her and Ethan, little Emma now facing Uma and gurgling happily.

Dear God, she was calling it a massacre, as if Uma and Ethan had gunned them down in cold blood. They hadn't. Had they?

'Uma,' Katrina said, 'what have you got to say to Mandy?'

'I'm so sorry for what happened,' Uma said, unwanted tears wetting her eyes.

The younger woman turned towards Uma, staring at her, along with the baby and her toy. Uma felt an ache in her abdomen, which rapidly radiated out across her entire body. She wanted to reach out and grab the baby, to cradle it to her chest. What was happening? Uma thought, trying to refocus. She shifted her gaze to Mandy.

'Will you restore him?' Mandy asked. 'We miss him so much.' A tear slid down her cheek.

'I'm so sorry, we can't. We—'

'Yes, we know your position on restoring victims of the LEAP massacre, but don't worry, ladies and gentlemen, we may have some help for Mandy and Emma. I would like to welcome on stage a special guest who has an unusual offer to make, not only to Mandy and little Emma, but to all the other victims of the LEAP massacre.'

Everything seemed to happen in slow motion. Through the frame she'd noticed earlier, three men suddenly appeared. Out of nowhere. It was a gate! The leading pair were tall, well over six feet, and wide with it. The one to her right, his hair buzz-cut short, glared at Uma, black eyes oozing hatred, but Uma's gaze was drawn to the third man who had entered the studio. He looked younger, and his hair was longer, but it was unmistakably him.

John Forsyth.

Uma sat there frozen, eyes telescoping in on his handsome face as he sauntered across the stage. His laugh boomed in her head until all that filled her vision were his cobalt blue eyes. She was back in the Transamerica Pyramid in San Francisco, curled up on the floor, hearing that laugh again, her sore body and foggy brain trying to process what had happened. She felt herself flush red – part shame, but mainly anger. The surge of blood cleared her head as she stood up. He was saying something, reaching out his arms. She responded, holding a hand forth, but suddenly found herself enveloped in his arms.

'I missed you,' he whispered into her hair and gave a lecherous laugh as he let go.

She turned. He was shaking Mandy's hand and then Ethan's, who looked at her, frowning. Then suddenly, he was beside her again. Uma realised with a sinking feeling that he was going to sit next to her. She looked pleadingly at Ethan, whose frown deepened, but as she sank back onto the couch, another chair appeared to the left of the anchor. Forsyth sauntered over to it.

'Hello, Katrina. It's a pleasure to meet you at long last,' he said, sitting down. 'I've been a fan for many years. A big fan.'

As Katrina adjusted her papers, Forsyth's gaze slipped to Uma and, for a millisecond, the mask slipped. Uma suppressed a gasp as his eyes burned with a rage only she believed she was capable of. Then his merriment returned, blue eyes sliding back to the anchor.

'It's nice to meet you too, Mr Forsyth.'

'Please call me John. All my friends call me John.'

'I take it you've met everyone on the couch?'

'Mandy, just yesterday. I've never met the great Ethan Rae. And of course I know Uma. We worked closely together last year. Very closely indeed.' He smirked and licked his lips. Uma's eyes welled with tears. She swallowed hard, trying to compose herself. She dropped her eyes to the baby so she didn't have to look at him, but this made her belly ache as his cruel voice boomed in her head.

Katrina looked over at Uma and smiled knowingly.

Does she know what he did? Uma thought, suddenly even more desperate to leave. How had he escaped her trap? How had he recovered his body? Where had he been? How come no one knew about him? Was he behind the attack on the townhouse? The questions rained down on her like molten lava blown from an erupting volcano, each one unanswerable, each one sizzling through her cranium.

'Viewers, I would like to introduce you to John Forsyth, entrepreneur millionaire businessman who, amongst his former positions, was, until late last year, former head of In-Q-Tel, the CIA's VC fund. Perhaps you could explain to the audience what you've been doing for the last few months.'

'Yes, of course, Katrina. I've been quite ill, if truth be known,' Forsyth said, glaring at Uma. 'I picked up a mysterious illness last October and have been convalescing at one of my clinics in Riyadh.'

'For those of our viewers who don't know John, you also run a chain of clinics across the globe catering to the elite, don't you. It's called One.'

'Actually, they went bust during my illness, but when I recovered, I was invited by my Saudi hosts to run their teleportation business. It's now called Eternity.'

'I wondered what happened to that technology. It's been very quiet since the Saudis announced their acquisition.'

'It wasn't acquired. It was stolen,' Uma blurted out.

'We paid one hundred and twenty billion dollars for it,' Forsyth said, his handsome face contorting into an ugly scowl.

'That was an investment in Green Ray,' Uma spat back. The rage had grounded her. Given her focus. She was damned if she would let him derail her. 'Why on earth would the Saudi government invest that much money in a fund dedicated to the decarbonisation of the planet?'

'Anyway,' Forsyth continued, 'our version will have nothing to do with teleportation. We will be focused on much more important matters.'

'Like what?'

'Looks, health and backup.'

Uma felt as if she was being immersed in a barrel of ice-cold water. Backup!

Dear God, she thought, the nightmare was happening.

'Before you expand,' Katrina said, 'we need to go to a ten-minute news break and when we return, we'll hear from John Forsyth on how he's going to use Eternity to transform the world in ways you cannot even imagine.'

Katrina put her papers down as two assistants raced onto the dais with brushes and makeup. One approached Uma, who knocked her hand away as she stood up and launched herself at Katrina.

'How dare you hijack us like this, inviting, that ... that monster onto your show.' She turned on Forsyth who looked up at her, a glorious smile stretched across his handsome features.

She made a move towards him, but Ethan appeared at her side and gently steered her off the stage as Katrina called out behind them.

'Remember, you've got ten minutes.'

Changing room, Manhattan

28th April 2010, 08:15 hours EDT

'What just happened in there?'

Ethan and Uma were in a small room, just off the main studio. Uma was slumped in one of the makeup chairs, head bowed, face in her hands, weeping softly. Ethan was pacing up and down the room, hands clenched into tight fists, his face a dark mask of concern and anger. Uma sat up. Mascara spidered down her white cheeks, giving her face a ghoulish glower in the soft lighting.

'What do you mean?' she said, catching sight of herself in the mirror. She grabbed a wipe, scrubbing her face viciously, but the makeup was too thick and she only succeeded in smearing the mascara into her cheeks. 'We're responsible for the deaths of over four thousand people, and you want to know what's wrong.'

Her tears started again, and she flung the soiled wipe onto the counter.

'I'm not talking about that,' Ethan said. 'Your reaction when he walked onto the stage. Do you two have history?'

Uma felt herself redden, the burn rising up her neck and consuming her face even through the makeup. All she could hear was Forsyth's cruel laugh booming around her cranium.

'Grow up, Ethan. You're behaving like a lovesick schoolboy.'

'What's that's supposed to mean?' he retorted. It was his turn to flush. 'I don't mean to,' he said helplessly, his tone softening, shoulders slumping. 'I can't help it.'

'What if we did? What difference would it make to us?'

Ethan shrugged.

'I don't know. It would have been nice to know, that's all.' He had stopped pacing and was staring at Uma's reflection in the mirror.

'I had a fling, OK.'

Ethan looked like he had been slapped.

'When?'

'When you were entombed in that damn mausoleum, refusing to speak to me and blaming the world for everything. That's when. It was a mistake.'

'I'm sorry,' Ethan said, placing a hand on her shoulder.

Uma pulled away.

'Don't touch me, OK. Please don't touch me,' Uma cried out.

Ethan dropped his arm and just stood there, clearly unsure what to do.

'What's going on, Uma?'

She stared at him in the mirror, standing there miserably, eyes fixed on hers. Kind eyes that only offered her unconditional love and protection. Eyes that didn't deserve to see this cruel man, who had suddenly resurfaced in her life with no warning. Suddenly everything fell into place: the attacks in Afghanistan, the fire, the massacre. Forsyth was responsible for all of it and would never stop until he was stopped. She knew someone who could stop him.

'He raped me,' Uma whispered. A great weight lifted as her dirty, dark secret entered the world. She was standing now, anxious to purge herself of the poison. 'He drugged me, fucked me and filmed me.'

She slumped to the floor, sobbing, her whole body shaking.

Ethan knelt down and tried again, placing a hand gently on her arm. She didn't pull away this time.

'It was the night I went to San Francisco. When the deal was announced.'

Ethan froze. He sat down heavily, head in his hands. He had sent Uma to that meeting.

'I'm so sorry, Uma,' he whispered.

'It's not your fault.'

'I insisted you go, but you didn't want to. Why didn't you say something?'

Uma shrugged.

'Forsyth's a creep. I think I knew he'd drugged me previously in—'

'He's done this before?' Ethan cut in. He sounded like he was chewing on broken glass. Uma nodded.

'I thought I was being stupid. Al Rahman wasn't even there. It was just Forsyth. I walked straight into it. He drugged me again.'

Uma blinked. She was back in the conference room, trapped on the couch, unable to move.

Sensing his desire.

Feeling him unbuttoning her blouse.

Pulling her bra up.

His stubble sandpaper course on her breasts.

Hands urgently caressing her thighs.

All Uma could do was lie there, silent tears falling from unblinking eyes.

She blinked again and was back in the changing room, Ethan beside her, his face a rigid mask.

'Why didn't you say anything?' he repeated.

Uma shrugged, arms wrapped tightly around her aching abdomen. The baby? She had forgotten about the baby. What if it had been Forsyth's? She'd carried that evil inside her, growing like a cancer in her womb. A spawning devil, conceived in an act of violence. Now violence would be visited on Forsyth.

She turned to Ethan

'I thought he was dead.'

'What do you mean?'

And then it all spewed out: meeting Forsyth in the boardroom, the rape, her waking up and hearing him with Al Rahman. The fight. Uma's discovery of the secondary teleportation system. Forsyth's fake body: his hip, knees, teeth, eyes and hair. She had removed it all.

'He must have restored himself. Got into the Saudis' favour. I had no idea he was behind all this.'

Ethan was silent, his face a thin mask of rage. Uma swallowed hard, but her eyes glittered with a nervous anticipation of what she had set in motion.

'This isn't your fault,' she said.

Ethan didn't answer. He stood up, fists clenched, staring at the mirror. And then, suddenly, he lifted the entire unit, hurling it against the far wall. The glass shattered, showering Uma with shards of mirror.

Without a word, Ethan wrenched the door open and marched off down the corridor.

Manhattan, New York City

28th April 2010, 08:20 hours EDT

'Welcome back, viewers. Just to recap, before the break, we heard from John Forsyth. He is now the CEO of Eternity, a new organisation, backed by the Saudi government, that will offer the public an alternative version of the LEAP technology, one with exciting possibilities. John, would you like to expand on what you said? That Eternity will offer looks, health and backup.'

Katrina looked away from the camera to her left where John Forsyth was smiling like a Cheshire cat. Next to him, Mandy Taylor was cuddling Emma and further along the couch, Uma and Ethan were sitting, their stares frozen on Forsyth.

'Of course, Katrina. We intend to use the technology to offer instantaneous, non-invasive plastic surgery such as breast augmentation, body sculpting, weight reduction, facial youthing and hair transplants. Anything you desire, in fact. We can also monitor someone's health 24/7, so they need never be ill again – no cancer, no heart disease, no strokes. You'll be able to drink, eat, smoke and inject whatever you want, but still look and feel perfect every day of the week. No hangovers. No danger of diabetes. No weight gain. And if, on the off chance, you, or your family, suffer a fatal accident, we can restore you from a backup.'

Uma felt like she was falling in a high-speed elevator that was moving faster, until it was approaching the speed of light. Black dots spotted her vision as snapshots of the last seven years rushed by: a bloody obelisk; Fredrik floating in the Blue Lagoon; Eva crumpled on the floor of her apartment; Ethan unconscious in Bellevue Hospital; Ingram staring at her half naked; a roaring fireplace; the earth rending in two as medieval weapons rained down on her; Forsyth's lips on her breasts, his cruel laughter mocking her as she sat there.

'You can't do that,' she heard herself say.

'And who's going to stop us?'

Uma looked over at her rapist, willing back a flood of tears that threatened to wash away her newly applied makeup. Not on live TV, she thought.

'It's in breach of the—'

'Yes, I know, your precious LEAP Laws.' Forsyth cut through her protest. 'But they don't apply to us. This is our offering.'

Uma felt Ethan shift beside her like a coiled serpent. She could feel his anger engulf her, and it felt good, snuffing out her fear like a fire blanket. It promised violence, swift and explosive, that would rip Forsyth in two, breaking every bone in his evil body and smash his handsome, perfect face to a bloody pulp.

'You can't,' Uma repeated, feeling more confident. That was more like it.

'Oh, but we can,' Forsyth cut in. 'Also, we would like to offer Mandy the opportunity to restore her dear husband. For little Emma, there, to get her father back.' He smiled at the baby. 'There is no reason for them to suffer like this. In fact, we would like to extend this offer to every family who has suffered from the massacre at the hands of them.' He nodded at Uma and Ethan.

Katrina clapped her hands with excitement.

'You can't do that,' Uma repeated for the third time, her voice now a dangerous whisper.

'Yes, we can,' he retorted again. 'You don't own their code. It belongs to each individual. It's their atomic structure. Read your licence agreement. It specifically states in Para 34 b that the code belongs to the LEAPer. Not you.'

Forsyth pointed at Uma triumphantly.

How did he know that level of detail, Uma thought?

'We won't give it to you,' Uma spluttered, her renewed confidence draining away.

Katrina turned to Uma.

'Can you do that?'

'Yes, we can withhold the code if it prevents someone from breaching the LEAP Laws.'

'Here we go again,' Katrina said, a hint of exasperation in her voice. 'It doesn't seem right that you get to be judge, jury and executioner.'

'Exactly right,' Forsyth said. 'What is it with you two and your double standards? One rule for all of us and one rule for you and your boyfriend.'

Uma froze.

'What do you mean?' Katrina said.

'Well,' Forsyth said, turning his best 100-watt smile on Uma, 'here's the thing. Ethan Rae suffered a cataclysmic accident in 2003. He was effectively catatonic. A vegetable. We've published his medical records on our website. Anyone can view them. How do you think he's now sitting there in perfectly good—'

Uma launched herself at Forsyth.

'You bastard!' she screamed, raking her nails down his face.

Forsyth didn't even try to stop her. He just stared into her eyes, a contented smirk on his face which enraged Uma even more. She headbutted him with all her strength, driving her forehead into his nose.

Forsyth howled in pain.

And then someone was grabbing her from behind, pulling her backwards. She fought like a caged tiger, limbs flailing as she struggled to free herself. Forsyth remained slumped in his seat, hands covering his nose, blood seeping through his fingers. The sight spurred her into a greater frenzy, but she couldn't break free.

'Uma,' she heard from a great distance away. 'Uma, not like this.'

She recognised the voice. It was authoritative, but kind. She felt herself being swung away from Forsyth, and stumbling to her knees. She looked up. It was Ethan who was now confronting the two men who had accompanied Forsyth into the studio. They were on the dais, standing between Forsyth and Ethan.

She saw Forsyth get up, his flattened nose oozing blood onto his white cashmere sweater. He was smiling, his perfect teeth garish red. He stepped forward, past his bodyguards, and embraced Ethan. His bloodied mouth was by Ethan's ear, whispering something, looking down at Uma, cobalt eyes ablaze with pure joy.

Forsyth winked at her, and in that moment, Uma realised what was about to happen.

Ethan tensed, pushing Forsyth away.

His fist caught Forsyth in the jaw.

She saw Forsyth collapse to the floor like a ragdoll.

Katrina screamed as the two bodyguards grabbed Ethan, one on each arm, pulling him back, away from Forsyth.

Somehow, Forsyth was on his feet, swaying drunkenly. He stepped forward towards Ethan, saying something, but he was staring at Uma, his eyes a mixture of triumph and glee. Then he stepped back, collapsing into his chair.

A guttural roar filled the studio.

Not of this world.

Ethan wrenched one arm free, driving his fist into the other bodyguard's trachea. The man howled in pain, dropping to his knees, holding his throat as he slowly collapsed like a felled tree.

Forsyth stood, stumbling down the steps of the dais.

The other bodyguard swung a huge fist towards Ethan's face, but he stepped lightly back. The giant stumbled as his haymaker missed its target, allowing Ethan to deliver a flurry of punches to the man's head, finishing with an uppercut that snapped the man's mouth shut like a bear trap. As he fell forward to join his partner, Ethan was already turning towards Forsyth, who was limping towards the gate.

Ethan roared again and ran towards him, but he was too late.

First, Forsyth disappeared through the gate.

Ethan didn't slow his pace. He just kept running.

It took a few seconds for Uma to realise what had happened.

Ethan had blinked out of existence.

Riyadh, Saudi Arabia

28th April 2010, 15:25 hours AST

E than stumbled as he entered a room he didn't recognise. There were no windows or furniture, just breeze block walls and a low ceiling peppered with bright fluorescents behind fake metal grills. It was more like a wide corridor, long and narrow, and cool, in stark contrast to the oppressively hot studio he had just departed. At the far end, Forsyth was standing by an open door, a triumphant grin on his handsome features. As he steadied himself, Ethan zeroed in on Forsyth's eyes, anger coursing through his veins like liquid oxygen as he thought of Uma lying helplessly, whilst this ... this monster assaulted her. Forsyth's words turbo-charged the anger. Suddenly, everything slowed down as Ethan assessed his options. There must have been twenty men in the room, standing between him and Forsyth, the majority in a uniform he didn't recognise, heavily patterned with a sandy camouflage. Some were holding wooden batons, others were empty-handed. There was no sign of other weapons. They looked Arabic, their faces gleaming with confidence. Ethan smiled at their first mistake: close-quarter fighting required specific skills. He doubted many had fought like this.

'I want him alive,' Forsyth shouted from the doorway.

The second mistake echoed around the room. Ethan backed towards the gate as two of the soldiers approached him, each one holding a short baton. Ethan stared at the three-foot wooden truncheons. They looked solid. He could do a lot of damage with one of those, but it would require a sacrifice. The soldiers moved wide, but before either could make their move, Ethan attacked the one to his right. The soldier reacted too late, swinging the truncheon over his head, but Ethan had closed the gap too quickly and the blow was weak. Ethan ducked, driving his right palm into the man's jaw, whilst at the same time parrying the blow with his left shoulder, then trapping the baton under his armpit before driving his knee deep into the man's solar plexus. As he straightened, Ethan brought his right arm up, taking the baton that was now caught between his rib cage and left arm. Without pausing, he crunched it down hard onto the man's skull. As the man slumped to the ground, Ethan felt a blow to his left shoulder – the sacrifice – from the soldier to his left. Grunting with pain, he whipped round to successfully parry the second blow. As the soldier came in for his third, Ethan deflected it with his own baton, holding the heavy wood horizontally in both hands, causing the baton to slide harmlessly to his left. As the soldier lost his balance, Ethan brought his baton down hard on the man's neck. Keeping the wall to his left shoulder, Ethan launched himself down one side of the room towards Forsyth, where the soldiers were bunched too tightly. Ethan used it to his advantage. Within the blink of an eye, four more lay groaning on the concrete floor.

Six down.

Ethan glanced at Forsyth, doubt now clouding the man's features as he edged into the corridor. He roared and lashed at another soldier who had rushed in, arm swinging too high, leaving his trunk exposed. Ethan attacked both sides of his rib cage in a flurry of strikes before driving the butt of the baton into his mouth. The man screamed, collapsing to the ground, blood spurting from his torn lips.

Seven down.

The remaining soldiers exchanged glances, unsure what to do. Three tried to move past Ethan, to create an overload from behind, but he launched himself at them in a blur of wood and broken bones that took him to the far side of the room.

Ten down.

A young soldier tried to parry his blows with his own baton, only to suddenly find it in Ethan's left hand. He howled in pain as his baton crunched into his raised arm, before slumping to the ground as two more batons thwacked into his temples.

Eleven down.

Ethan slid along the wall, the survivors now staying out of range, their faces slick with fear. He was five feet from Forsyth, whose face crimsoned with rage and something else – uncertainty. It was all Ethan needed to see.

He roared like a man possessed, launching himself at the remaining eight men who parted like a curtain, leaving Ethan a clear path through to Forsyth, who stumbled backwards against the far wall of the corridor. Ethan raced forward, raising his baton for the killing blow. Suddenly, however, he screamed as his right arm was almost wrenched out of its socket. He felt himself being jerked back into the room as if he was on a rubber band, then swung in a wide arc, before crashing headfirst into the breeze block wall. He slumped to his knees, trying to draw breath. Powerful hands gripped his shoulders. Ethan felt himself being pulled backwards along the concrete floor, back towards the gate. Someone stepped over him. He rolled onto his side, before gingerly getting to his feet and facing the mystery threat.

The two bodyguards from the TV studio were standing there, both breathing heavily. Behind them, the remaining soldiers were gathered in a semicircle, looks of relief on their faces. Forsyth was nowhere to be seen. The bigger of the two men stepped forward and beckoned Ethan to do the same. He looked familiar, his square jaw set in a determined grimace. Ethan rotated his shoulders, wincing as pain speared down his arm. He eyed the two batons he had dropped, assessing the new threat. The man was tall, easily six two and heavy, maybe two hundred pounds, with a four-inch reach advantage. Ethan feinted left and then right, but the bigger man easily matched his movements, refusing to be drawn in. Again, Ethan tried to tempt him forward, feigning attacks, but the giant moved deftly, like a man half his size, and Ethan was slowly driven backwards into a corner of the room without landing a blow on the man. The soldiers now advanced, batons drawn, smiles creasing their faces.

Forsyth appeared through the crush of soldiers and his appearance was like a boost to Ethan, who made his move, arrowing a kick at the man's groin. The man snapped an arm down, parrying the blow. He took Ethan's outstretched leg in an iron grip and pulled him off balance, knocking him to the ground. In a flash, he was on top of Ethan, raining blows down on his head. Ethan tried to parry, but it was no use. A pile-driver thumped into his cheek, exploding a constellation of stars across his retinas. Another followed, this time into his eye, and Ethan felt something crack in his cheek. Through the ringing, a man was screaming, 'I want him alive,' but the giant ignored the cry, wrapping his huge hands around Ethan's neck. Ethan looked up into the man's haunted face, and as he slipped into blissful darkness, he suddenly realised where he had seen him before – in the Camden townhouse. This was the man that had hurled him into the fire.

Oval Office, Washington DC

29th April 2010, 09:00 hours EDT

The Saucer Magnolia was in full bloom, its pink and purple goblet-shaped blossoms celebrating the morning sunlight that streamed in through the windows, bathing Uma in a warm glow. It was hard to believe that barely one month ago, she had been standing in the rose garden with Ethan, celebrating the launch of LEAP out to the world. How much had changed since then: 2,723 servicemen and women killed by a mysterious virus in Afghanistan; the Eyjafjallajökull Ice Cap exploding; Ethan nearly killed at their London HQ, itself destroyed; an oil platform burning out of control in the Gulf of Mexico; over four thousand people flayed alive by LEAP; Forsyth back in her life; and now Ethan had disappeared, presumably kidnapped. She stared hard at Ingram opposite, remembering his request that she relent on the law against copying. Back then, she had thought he might have been involved in the fire as a way of bringing her to the table when she feared Ethan might be dead. Now she was certain – he must have helped Forsyth introduce the virus. How else could it have happened? The LEAP system was the most secure system in the world. Besides which, who else could have told Forsyth of her decision to reinstate Ethan? It had to be Ingram. No one else knew. The problem was, she couldn't prove it. Ingram looked up, nodding at her, his face revealing nothing as usual. She resisted the urge to cross the lush carpet and rake her nails down his face, just like she had done with Forsyth. That had felt good, especially the headbutt. Seeing his stupid, handsome nose explode. She had no doubt it would soon be repaired, but it was going to hurt like hell until it was. What didn't feel so good was Ethan's reaction. That was her fault. She had released Anderson in the dressing room, knowing full well what would happen. The strange thing was, she didn't regret it. Forsyth had raped her. She had vowed not to tell anyone, but seeing him appear in the TV studio had unleashed a tsunami of carefully buried memories, that in turn had sparked a howling rage, which she had been powerless to control. And now Ethan was gone.

Uma sensed movement to her right as President Jamal Williams returned the phone to its receiver on the Resolute Desk. He nodded at each one of them gravely, before taking his seat next to Uma.

'So, where are we with LEAP, Edward?'

Edward Johnson, the US Attorney General cleared his throat.

'A class-action lawsuit has just been launched by four thousand or so families who lost a loved one in the LEAP massacre, but we're expecting this to be withdrawn as the victims are reinstated by Forsyth. However, I still think we are exposed for emotional trauma caused by the original accident.'

'And Forsyth? Do we know where he went?'

'He's back in Riyadh,' Ingram said. 'We've put out an arrest warrant for his detention, along with Crouch, whom we assume is with him, but the Saudis aren't cooperating. As you know, we don't have an extradition treaty with them, so we're stuck at the moment.'

'And the LEAP virus?' the President said.

Shane Williams, Chief Technical Officer of Green Ray, shifted uncomfortably in his seat. He'd never been in the Oval Office, and Uma could tell he was overawed.

'I've … we've … my team has finally located the virus. Without getting too technical—'

'And do you know how it was introduced?' Ingram cut across him.

'Not yet, but we're working on it.'

'So, we're pretty sure it was Forsyth?' the President said.

'Er, no, sir,' Shane said. 'At the moment, we can't trace the virus back to him, but it would take someone with a detailed working knowledge of the LEAP system to do what they did, and all fingers point at Crouch. As you know, he worked in the CBL Division.'

The President frowned.

'Carbon Based LEAPs, sir,' Ingram said. 'You, me, humans. He ran the initial programme after the White House bombings last year, which allowed you to LEAP everywhere with your security team.'

Shane nodded in agreement. 'Precisely, sir. He developed the framework for the current system before he disappeared. The man's a genius.'

He's a hopeless drunk, Uma thought. With a vendetta against her. She clearly remembered his large bulbous head slumped on the desk in the CBL centre, pasty face ravaged by alcohol. He'd engineered a terrorist attack on the President, making it appear that Uma was responsible. She also remembered that evening for a different reason. Ethan and she had blindly jumped together through the LEAP gate into the White House, knowing only that they could be killed. Probably not restored, but it hadn't mattered. They were together. Unlike yesterday, when Ethan had made the LEAP alone, to avenge her rape. She had sent him. Now he was gone. The realisation swarmed over her like ravenous locusts, and she suppressed the urge to cry out.

Dear God, what had she done?

From faraway she heard a familiar voice. It sounded kind, and she focused on its soft timbre. Gradually, the voice took shape and suddenly she was back on the sofa. The President was talking.

'The obvious play is to reinstate the people who lost their lives earlier this week. It would mollify the families and nullify Forsyth's threat, at least for the time being. It would also restore confidence in LEAP, which is much needed, particularly if we can show it was a virus.'

'Agreed sir. If we don't, we're in danger of completely derailing the programme. No one will ever use LEAP again, especially after that car crash of an interview yesterday.'

Uma glared at Ingram, but deep down she knew he was right. Her credibility was shot with the public after Forsyth's revelation about her restoring Ethan.

'If we decide to stick to our principals and comply with the LEAP Laws,' the President continued, 'what happens? Our goal of reversing global warming is dead. People simply won't use the system, especially once the volcano settles down and they cap the platform in the Gulf.'

'Restore those people and all that goes away,' Ingram said. 'It's the right move.'

'And then what?' Uma finally said something, but the three words sounded hopelessly inadequate.

The Attorney General leaned forward.

'Maybe we can do both, sir.'

'Go on, Andrew.'

'Well, we need to get ahead of this. Forsyth isn't going away anytime soon. Even assuming we can rebuild trust in the LEAP system, the public will never again trust the LEAP Laws, not after yesterday. However, there is a way around that. We could appoint an oversight board to enforce them.'

Uma made to speak.

'Hear me out. Not to reverse them, but to restore their credibility and provide exceptions, just like any business would in response to events. This is effectively an industrial accident. We're at fault. There's no getting around it. Make that the first variation – if people die in the LEAP system because of a system malfunction, then they get restored.'

The President had been observing Uma.

'I understand your concerns,' he said, placing a hand gently on her wrist. Uma pulled away, but immediately felt like a petulant child. 'I agree with the Laws,' the President continued. 'That's why I paused the restoration programme after the Afghanistan disaster. We're not rolling them back, but we have to respond to this.'

'And where does it —' Uma started to say.

'Why did you restore Ethan?' the President cut across her.

The question caught Uma off guard.

'What do you mean?

'Exactly that. Why did you bring Ethan out of his coma?'

Uma flushed again, this time at the memory of standing there in the hospital, feeling her resolve to shelve the LEAP programme crumble as she looked down at Ethan: tubes sticking out of him, his skin a deathly pallor, face bruised and cut from his brutal fight in the Homeland security cell at the hands of Grond.

'I couldn't stand the thought of losing him.'

'Isn't that the point? Not even you are immune, despite being a highly educated and rational scientist who created the laws because you recognised the danger of LEAP. But when it came down to it, you're only human. You couldn't resist its lure. To restore a loved one. To bring him back to life. I'm not sure I wouldn't make the same decision if Malena or the kids were in a coma.'

'What are you suggesting?' Uma said, knowing full well what he was suggesting. All she could think about was Ethan, trapped somewhere with that monster. Or worse still.

'It's too much for one person. It needs to be controlled by an independent body, as Andrew suggested. To remove the temptation.'

There was silence in the room, as he paused, sensing a big moment. A history defining moment that would alter the course of civilisation.

Uma kept her eyes down, refusing to look at Ingram or the Attorney General. She already knew Shane's answer. He had never agreed with the decision to delete the Anderson-infested Ethan. She clearly remembered the argument in New York all those years. What had he said? "Who made you judge, jury, and executioner?" And he had been right. She was all three, and look where it had got her.

'Agreed,' said the Attorney General. 'If we decide to travel down that route, I think we need to be proactive. There are many instances where it would be correct to revive someone.'

Uma stared at him blankly. She could think of one: what if someone disappeared thorough a LEAP gate, never to be seen again?

'For instance,' the Attorney General continued, 'anyone who has been murdered.'

'Anyone dying in the line of duty,' Ingram added.

Everyone looked towards Uma, who shrugged helplessly.

'Good, that's decided,' the President exclaimed. 'Andrew, start drawing up some ideas about how this can be structured. Uma,' the President turned to her, 'can you lead the restoration of those killed in the recent accident?'

She nodded.

'Anything else?'

The Attorney General raised his hand.

'We could offer a universal health programme. It'll avoid a million claims for clemency if someone dies through natural causes. Plus, it'll nullify a third of Forsyth's own offering. Put him on the back foot.'

'Won't that take time to set up?' Shane said. 'We'd have to train tens of thousands of technicians to offer that level of service.'

'True, but the optics will look great,' the Attorney General countered. 'That's all that matters at the moment, particularly with the midterms next year. It will begin to rebut the argument that LEAP is stealing jobs.'

The President smiled. Uma could tell he liked the suggestion.

'Great, let's do it. Anything else.'

'What about Ethan?' Uma's voice sounded small in the domed room. 'How do we get him back?'

The President turned to Ingram.

'We don't even know where he is,' Ingram said. 'Presumably somewhere in Saudi, with Forsyth. If he is, recovering him could be quite difficult. We don't exactly have good relations with the Saudis at the moment.'

'There must be something we can do?' Uma sounded desperate. Her tone drew a wry smile from Ingram.

'Well, conducting an illegal operation on foreign soil to recover a UK citizen from another jurisdiction hardly takes precedent. I suggest we take that up with our English counterparts at MI6.'

'Joseph's right, Uma. We can't just march into Riyadh and recover Ethan. It's not as if he was kidnapped. He was pursuing Forsyth when he disappeared. He went voluntarily.'

'It was a trap, designed to capture him. He was tricked.'

'What caused him to do that?' the President said. 'Forsyth clearly said something to him on the stand.'

Uma dropped her gaze. This was straying into dangerous territory.

'Shouldn't we be looking to neutralise Forsyth at the very least?' she countered. 'The copy feature of Forsyth's business is a problem. It contravenes the LEAP Laws, and will pull people into his business model. Not to mention, opening the door for copying on an industrial scale. Besides, if he's prepared to offer that, what else could he bring out next? Eternal life? It's a threat not only to LEAP, but everything we're working towards building.'

The President glanced at Ingram.

'Ideas, Samuel.'

'Well, I'm not sure what the doctor is suggesting. Assassinating an American citizen in another jurisdiction is not entirely, shall we say, legal.'

Uma wondered how many times Ingram had authorised exactly that.

'I'm not saying we kill him,' Uma said, thinking the exact opposite. 'We need to destroy his technology, not him. Get him back to the States, where he can stand trial. Along with Crouch. Without the tech and Crouch, the Saudis don't have an offering.'

'Let me take that up with the doctor offline, sir.'

'Good. Thank you, Samuel. In the meantime, let me summarise what we've agreed. We will restore the victims of the LEAP massacre. It will be the first exception to the LEAP Laws. Uma, can you work with Andrew on our first amendment, something that'll allow us to get ahead of the game with regards to resuscitating people? Andrew,' he nodded at the Attorney General, 'start developing a framework for an oversight body comprising officials from each nation using LEAP. Samuel, I need a plan of how you intend to repatriate Forsyth and

Crouch to stand trial. Work with Uma and your British counterparts to examine how we can get Ethan home safely.'

The President stood, a smile on his face, a sign of a job well done. The room relaxed until the next crisis.

The Acorn, Riyadh, Saudi Arabia

3rd May 2010, 12:36 hours AST

'Who's next?'

Mohammed stared down at his screen.

'The President of Belarus. He wants the full Health and BackUp services for his family.'

'How many are we talking about?'

There was silence as Mohammed checked his spreadsheet.

'Fifty-two people.'

Forsyth frowned.

'What service do they want again?'

'I said, Health and BackUp.'

'What, for all of them?'

'So they say.'

Forsyth did some quick mental maths. That was $156 million alone for the health monitoring. And the BackUp service ... No, that couldn't be right. He tapped away on a calculator to make sure his maths was correct.

Forsyth let out a gurgled laugh.

That was $2.6 billion annually. From just one family.

It was better than he had dared dream and getting better by the day, thanks to the Rae broadcast which had gone viral, playing 24/7 on news feeds around the world. All showing him being attacked by that woman. He winced as he felt his nose gingerly. It hurt like hell, but looked damn good. It was still broken, but the pain was bearable, especially after Crouch had removed most of the swelling and toned down the bruising by eighty percent. It gave his face a rakish look. Better still, it was a constant reminder to everyone that he was the victim here. He'd drawn the line at leaving the scratches, though. It made him look like a wife beater. Not a great look. So those had gone, but the broken nose remained.

'What are we up to?'

'To date, we've processed 110 orders. For a total of 1,234 people, including the Belarusians. That puts our booked revenues at $3.7 billion for Health and $43 billion for BackUp. In addition, Looks has pulled in just shy of $5 billion.'

Forsyth stood there, savouring the number. Already thirty billion over budget. In just five days. There was a lot more wealth in the world than the experts had projected. It wasn't just despots and gangsters requesting their services. The Armed Forces of multiple nations wanted BackUp; so did their governments for senior politicians. Celebrities wanted Looks and Health, as did sports stars all over the globe. The list went on. It hadn't even mattered that Green Ray had belatedly responded to the LEAP massacre with an offer to restore everyone – the damage had been done. Let them worry about the masses with their universal health care. It would take years to roll-out, and, in the meantime, Eternity would forge ahead, using the technology to achieve things Green Ray couldn't, because of the new oversight body they had just announced. It would tie them up in knots for decades.

'Does the Crown Prince know?'

Mohammed nodded.

'He checks the numbers hourly. This will strengthen his position with the factions. He's all but unassailable. Thanks to you.'

'Thanks to me,' Forsyth whispered to himself. It felt good. And long overdue.

There was a knock. An assistant entered, glancing at Mohammed, who nodded.

'Sir, we have been approached by the Daily Event. They want to run a one-hour interview with Mr Forsyth. Katrina Hoskins will be the host. What's more, she's happy to come here. They're suggesting a deep dive into your life, from an early age to now. How you came to run the world's fastest growing company.'

Forsyth smiled. He had had his eye on her for some time. She was beautiful. Intelligent. Feisty. Everything he liked in a woman. The chase would be interesting.

'I think that's a great idea. Set it up.'

The assistant disappeared.

'Do you think that's sensible?' Mohammed said.

'Why not? It's great for my profile. Did you not see how much coverage we got from last week?'

'That's precisely my point. It's too high profile. Your new partner prefers a much lower one.'

'Nonsense. You can never have enough coverage. Now, remind me, who are we seeing next?'

Forsyth made his way over to the double doors that lead into a full-size conference room which seated up to thirty people. His very own conference room, along with everything else that The Acorn provided. He had initially been reluctant to move his operations into the Crown Prince's private kingdom, but after the TV interview, he had finally relented. He'd been persuaded by the offer of one hundred hand-picked men that would form his personal security force, all under the command of Fox. All housed on the floor beneath his penthouse. One of just three, befitting Forsyth's new-found status. Fifteen thousand square feet of the most luxurious real estate in the world, providing everything that Forsyth could need: gymnasium, basketball court, three Michelin-trained chefs, cinema, IT suite for Crouch, swimming pool, spa, meeting rooms, private quarters. The list was endless. Forsyth failed to suppress a smile, studying himself in the mirrored door. He looked good. No, scratch that. He looked great. As befitted the most powerful man in the world.

Before Mohammed could answer, there was another knock at the door. Through the mirror, Forsyth saw Fox enter. The sight reminded him of the fight. Rae had fought like a man possessed, coming at Forsyth like an automaton. Had it not been for the American, Forsyth could have been badly hurt or worse. Not that there was any jeopardy in that. He could always restore himself, but pain reminded him of the weeks that he had endured after that woman had stripped him of his armour. That was far worse. Fox had prevented that from happening.

'What is it Fox?'

The tall man made his way across the lush carpet, stopping in front of Forsyth. He looked dangerous. Like Rae. Two men cut from the same cloth. Forsyth would be lying if he said he wasn't afraid of him. He was glad to have him on his side.

'It's been five days since New York. You promised me Rae.'

'And you shall get Rae,' Forsyth said, opening the door to the conference room. 'I've been clearing it with the Crown Prince. The day after tomorrow, you shall get your wish. Now, if you'll excuse me, I have an empire to build.'

Forsyth disappeared inside, leaving Ed standing there, staring at the mirrored door, his dead eyes dull in the reflected glass.

The Acorn, Riyadh, Saudi Arabia

4th May 2010, 20:25 hours AST

Katrina Hoskins stood, taking in the courtyard below. They were almost level with the tallest branches of the oak tree, and from her position, she could see a red squirrel scuttle along one of the uppermost fronds. It was swaying alarmingly, and, for a heart-stopping moment, she thought it was going to fall. But somehow it clung to the thin branch before stepping gracefully onto a stronger bough and disappearing into the foliage. She turned, watching her crew continue the setup. They had decided to conduct the interview at the far end of the room – correction, small hall – with its thirty-five-foot high ceilings framed by an unbroken pane of glass that curved a full 100 feet in either direction. She had no idea how they had managed it, but the effect was mesmerising. Across the entire expanse, the oak tree's huge limbs extended out towards the periphery of the frame. The team had set up two couches in the centre of the backdrop, meeting at a V. She would sit in one, her guest in the other. When the call had come through, she had been beyond excited. Her segment with Uma and Ethan attacking Forsyth had pulled in the highest viewing figures in the network's history. Now, both Forsyth and the Crown Prince had agreed to her idea for an exclusive interview in the nerve centre of their operations, The Acorn. The network had made the unprecedented decision to move the time of the interview to its prime-time evening slot. A guaranteed audience of ten million. At this rate, she would be holding her first Emmy by the end of the year.

Two enormous doors at the far end of the room suddenly swung open. Seconds later, a retinue of people entered, led by the unmistakable figure of Forsyth. He looked resplendent in a black cashmere sweater that accentuated his tight physique, with black chinos and biker boots completing his look. It shouldn't have worked – the man was over seventy – but somehow it did. His long hair looked perfect. His bright smile, just right. He caught sight of Katrina and beamed, making a beeline for her, arms outstretched in greeting.

'I trust that you and your team are settled in?' Forsyth said, ignoring Katrina's offered hand, and instead embracing her in a full hug that Katrina quickly pulled away from.

'They're perfect, thanks. In fact, everything is,' she replied, nodding towards the courtyard.

'Good, shall we get started?'

Katrina glanced past Forsyth at Nick, her producer, who nodded with a thumbs up.

'We're ready now, if you are.'

Katrina sat down, adjusting her mic. Forsyth did the same, all the time smiling at her. Christ, the man was hitting on her again. He was old enough to be her father. She was normally repelling men half his age, slimy TV types with fast tongues and fragile egos. It was yet another bone of contention with Brett, who still hadn't forgiven her for the Hawaii stunt, and now this. She was missing his mum's 85th today and was toying with the idea of surprising them all if the interview finished early. It would be close, but possible, if she managed to edit the material quickly. But first, she had an interview to record.

'Remember, this is going out tonight on our six o'clock special, so we've got limited recording time. Nick and I will then edit it this afternoon, giving you a final cut as agreed.'

'That's fine. There should be no problems, so long as you stick to our agreement. Nothing is off limits, except the Green Ray woman.' Forsyth's eyes glittered dangerously. 'Please don't mention her.'

Katrina nodded.

'I won't,' she said, but that was exactly where she would drive the interview. What was with him and Uma? He couldn't even refer to her by name. To Katrina's right, Nick counted down with a raised hand, raising his fingers theatrically before, finally, all five were showing. Face time, she intoned silently, turning to the camera and projecting her famous California smile at Forsyth.

'Welcome everyone. Katrina Hoskins reporting from Riyadh, where I'm delighted to bring you another worldwide exclusive. For the next hour, only on the Daily Event, I will be interviewing the current head of Eternity, the one and only John Forsyth.'

Forsyth saw the light on his video camera go red, stood up from his seat, clasping both hands Namaste style and mouthed, 'Thank you for having me,' before sitting down.

'So, Mr Forsyth—' Katrina began.

'Please, call me John.'

'OK, John, it's been a whirlwind week since you last appeared on our show in New York. Can you tell us exactly what happened with Ethan Rae when you both disappeared?'

'I would, Katrina, but I can't.' Forsyth flashed a thousand-megawatt smile at the camera, before continuing. 'Saudi Law prohibits me, but there will be an announcement in a few days that will reveal everything your viewers want to know about the criminal Ethan Rae, who is currently being held by Saudi authorities.'

'Criminal is a strong word, John. Would you care to expand?'

'As I said, I would love to, but can't. I'm sure you have much more interesting questions that your viewers need answers to, such as how a septuagenarian manages to look this great and run the fastest growing company in the world.'

'OK,' Katrina said, raising her eyebrows. This man was a piece of work. 'Let's start with that, shall we? It's not so much your age I'm interested in. After all, it's merely a number. No one is suggesting that any man or woman should be excluded from the workplace simply because of their birth date. What I would like to explore is that you look forty. I assume that's the result of your technology. That the real John Forsyth, in fact, looks a lot like the rest of us.'

A flash of fury rippled across Forsyth's handsome features as he realised the trap she had set him.

'I've always had an interest in health, right from when I set up my first self-improvement clinic back in the early seventies. Looking after your body was quite a novel idea back then: everyone smoked, drank too much and took drugs. I realised that if I was to achieve success, I needed to watch all three. I was trying to tap into the work of Napoleon Hill, who was the founding father of personal success. He wrote, *Think and Grow Rich*. It had quite an impact on me.'

Gotcha, Katrina thought. She'd seen Forsyth reference the book in any number of interviews, and had researched Napoleon Hill extensively. As far as she could tell, the man's only skill seemed to be an ability to reinvent himself. That, and committing fraud, which included embezzling money from his own charity. But she'd let it slide for now. Understanding Forsyth's obsession with Uma had become her focus.

'How so?'

'Well, it was published in '37, just as America was emerging from ten years of economic despair that affected millions of people, including my parents. His book was transformative for me as a child of The Great Depression. It laid out thirteen steps to get rich and became my bible. I followed all of them, and look at where it's got me.' Forsyth smiled, sweeping his arms round the vast atrium. 'Head of what will be soon the wealthiest company the world has ever seen.'

'You've talked a lot about that period of your life – born into abject poverty with your four siblings, all of whom died before your tenth birthday.'

Forsyth's eyes misted over, but Katrina had seen enough performances in her life to know that this looked off. Made up.

'Yes, that's right, Katrina. My father was a farmer in the Midwest. Lost everything because of the Wall Street Crash of '29: his cattle, his land, his home, and eventually, his sanity. It broke him, really. We had no home for seven years. We lived like vagrants in municipal shelters, travelling constantly from city to city. As you said, my two sisters and older brother all died. From measles. My dad became an alcoholic.'

'I don't think we can comprehend how difficult that period of history was. Not just for you, John, but for millions of Americans. How did you cope?'

'Simple, it's all about the survival of the fittest. Not just your body,' Forsyth patted his stomach, 'that's a given, it's about what's up here as well.' He tapped his forehead. 'Mastering this little fella is key too. Thoughts are things,' he said, dropping his tone conspiratorially, turning to face Katrina. 'You can become whatever you set your mind to.'

Katrina suppressed the urge to laugh out loud.

He's nothing more than a snake oil salesman, she thought.

'Well, you've done more than just survive,' Katrina said, looking around the room.

Forsyth waved his hand dismissively.

'These are mere baubles. What really drives me these days, Katrina, is enabling ordinary people to achieve whatever they want in this world, through sheer hard work and effort, just like I was able to.'

'How does that relate to Eternal? That's just for the richest people in the world to manage their health and looks, and safeguard their bodies with BackUp. How does that benefit the ordinary man?'

'We've just launched a charitable foundation called Eternity For All, to provide free healthcare for the poorest people in the Middle East. As I've said, without good health, you can't achieve anything. That's the starting point. We'll roll it out to Africa and India at the beginning of next year. It'll provide jobs and opportunities for everyone. They're the people that need it.'

Katrina looked at her notes. This was going nowhere. She needed to steer him back to Uma and Ethan.

'There's been a lot of reports in the press about how you acquired LEAP. That the Saudis stole the code. What do you have to say about that?'

'What I've said consistently. Why would they invest that much money in a fund dedicated to dismantling the industry that they rely most on for their current revenues? It makes no sense. The investment was to acquire the source code for LEAP.'

'And what do you say to Uma Jakobsdóttir's claim that unfettered copying of people or resuscitating the dead is an accident waiting to happen? That, if we're allowed to, it will lead to an uncontrolled population explosion which will be disastrous for the planet.'

Forsyth's facade seemed to crack at the mention of Uma's name. He stared at Katrina, eyes narrowing, and for a moment she thought he was going to stop the interview. Had she pushed too hard?

'That's she's a hypocrite,' Forsyth eventually said, his face breaking out into a wide smile. 'Remember, she's used LEAP twice herself. Once to revive her boyfriend back in '03 and there are reports that he did the same for her last year after the earthquake that destroyed his California residence. Besides, her argument is reductive. It's like saying we should do away with modern medicine. It saves and extends lives. One hundred years ago, there were loads of untreatable diseases. Take measles. It killed millions before a vaccine was developed in the fifties. Nature's way of controlling the population by culling the weak. It took my brothers and sisters. Now there's a cure. Are you suggesting that we should do away with that? And all cancer drugs, because allowing those people to live puts a strain on the world's resources. It's our God-given right to use new technology as we see fit. It's the story of mankind. It's our birthright.'

'What about the atom bomb,' Katrina countered. 'That was new tech, back in the forties. Taking your line of thought to its logical conclusion has resulted in 18,000 nuclear warheads that can destroy the world a hundred times over.'

'Different issue,' Forsyth shot back, sitting forward in his seat. He seemed to be enjoying the sparring with Katrina. 'Yes, it was new tech, but the atom bomb saved lives. First and foremost, we beat Hitler to it. Can you imagine if he had developed it first?' Forsyth shuddered theatrically. 'Remember, it shortened the war in the Pacific by three years, saving hundreds of thousands of American lives.'

Touché, Katrina thought, but Forsyth hadn't finished pressing home his advantage.

'Look, technology is neither good nor bad. There are unintended consequences of any new technology, but that's not a reason to limit its use.'

'Except that it's not neutral,' Katrina countered. 'You're just over-simplifying the issue to defend the consequence of using technology in any way you want and ignoring the environmental, social, and human ramifications. Isn't that Uma's point when it comes to LEAP and her oft mocked intransigence on her Laws?'

Again Forsyth flinched at the mention of her name, but Katrina needed to move on. Disappearing down this rabbit hole was not good for ratings.

'Besides which, at the moment, your business model only benefits the few. What my viewers would like to know is when do they get access to Looks, Health and BackUp?'

'Like most innovation, Katrina, in the early days, it's only available to governments, usually the military and the very richest. However, as it becomes more ubiquitous, it trickles down to the rest of the population. Remember, I ran the CIA fund for nearly ten years and saw it happen repeatedly. Eternity is no different. In time, the costs of providing the service will fall. It will seep out into the general population.'

In her peripheral view, John mimed a cutting motion with his hand.

Katrina turned to the camera.

'I suspect this argument will run and run, ladies and gentlemen. Unfortunately, we need to go to a commercial break. When we return, I will be interviewing the Crown Prince himself, who will give us some background on this amazing building and what else he has planned for the country as it prepares itself for an oil-free future.'

Katrina removed the mic from her blouse. As she did, Forsyth leaned in, placing a hand on her wrist.

'I told you not to mention the woman by name,' he hissed. 'I explicitly requested it. Remember, I can ruin you as quickly as I've made you. Just one word and you're history.'

His bright eyes flashed with anger as his grip increased on her arm.

'Ow! You're hurting me,' Katrina cried out, standing up, so that Forsyth was forced to release her. Katrina turned on him.

'Don't you ever touch me again,' she blazed back, jabbing a finger repeatedly at him. Forsyth stood up, drawing close to Katrina, who stood her ground. 'And before you follow through with whatever you're thinking, might I remind you that the cameras are still rolling. I'm sure that our viewers would be most interested in meeting the real John Forsyth.'

'You wouldn't dare,' he snarled.

'Everything OK here?' Nick said, approaching the couch.

Just as quickly, Forsyth suddenly smiled, a radiant blast of pure happiness, but laced with something else. Hunger, or was it desire? Katrina couldn't be sure, but it made the hairs on her arms prickle, fog-horning danger.

'No, everything's A OK,' Forsyth said. 'Just a difference of opinion, that's all. I look forward to reviewing the finished cut. Remember, I have the last say, so if you want to broadcast tonight, please delete all references to that woman, otherwise your bosses will have nothing to show your record audience back home.'

'We all have bosses, John,' Katrina shot back. 'The agreement says, sign off by the Eternity organisation, not you personally. The final cut will be delivered to the Crown Prince as requested by his office this morning. I would imagine he doesn't give a flying fuck about your spat with Uma. Now, if you'll excuse me, I have to interview the richest man in the world.'

Katrina turned away from Forsyth and started walking towards the entrance just as the Crown Prince entered the room. He waved a pudgy arm at her as Forsyth looked on, a mask of pure longing playing across his handsome features.

Al-Ha'ir Prison, 25 South of Riyadh

3rd May 2010, 22:47 hours AST

The heat crushed down on him, enveloping him in its grasp like a deep ocean from which there was no escape. He tried to raise his head off the thin mattress, but it felt granite heavy, so he just lay there, trying to regulate his breathing. Every breath hurt, as if hell-heated air was being pumped deep into his chest, regardless of how carefully he sipped at it. Ethan heard a scratching sound above and cracked an eyelid, wincing as it scoured the dry cornea like sandpaper. A rat appeared, inching across the ceiling like a furry arachnid, nose aquiver as it searched out danger. Satisfied, it scuttled down the wall, disappearing out of Ethan's peripheral vision, although he could still hear it scratching around the filthy cell for food. It would find none here. In fact, no sustenance of any description. Ethan tried to ignore the gnawing pain in his gut, uncertain if was just hunger or a more dangerous foe. He could feel the past shifting, waiting for the tectonic plates he had carefully constructed to crack open, so it could crawl up from the depths of his belly like an invading force of night terrors, slobbering and shuffling into the daylight with gleeful abandon. A past that promised unimaginable pain: the crack of a bullwhip, the flick of metal ripping into soft flesh, blood running freely down his back, and then the aftermath – lying face down on another dirty mattress in a similar cell, a lifetime of hurt compressed into each breath as he prayed for the sweet solace of death. Ethan suppressed a sob.

A rattling of keys made him sit up and he groaned as broken ribs competed with his fractured wrist from the beating he had suffered. Two guards appeared. They looked nervous, moving cautiously into the cell, keeping their backs to the wall, anxious to keep the man that fought like a demon in full sight. One threw some clothes onto the bed, nodding at Ethan, who stared at them. He'd worn these once before, knew what they meant. Ethan thought about refusing, but the beatings would follow and the pants would always go on. He rolled off the bed and stripped naked. As he bent to recover the thin material, they both gasped at his back – a riot of angry scars, the hard flesh rising and falling like a polluted sea. The other guard threw a pair of manacles onto the floor. Ethan stepped into those as well, clicking them shut. Emboldened, the man stepped forward, inserting Ethan's wrists into a matching pair of cuffs that were connected to their cousins by a thick iron chain.

Ethan stood there waiting, his stomach a tangle of emotions, as he prepared to be led out of the cell for his sentencing, and the inevitable punishment. His back flared with referred pain, an explosion of agony that knew no depths, just a headlong plunge into a bottomless abyss of hurt. The memory nearly collapsed him to the cell floor, but he fought the panic, holding tall.

He'd be damned if he'd let these brutes see his fear.

A sound made all three turn towards the door.

Forsyth was standing there, clapping slowly, a delighted smirk written across his handsome face. Behind him was the brute that had knocked Ethan unconscious.

'The great Ethan Rae. How the mighty fall,' Forsyth sneered, stepping into the cell. He stared at Ethan, his face a mixture of triumph and disdain. 'I've been hearing about your history.'

Ethan didn't respond, just focused on maintaining eye contact, pleased at the fear he could detect beneath Forsyth's thin veneer of bravado.

'I never took for you for a killer,' he said, moving closer and the two men either side of Ethan tensed the chains.

Ethan's face remained impassive.

'How does it feel to have been responsible for the death of your parents? I saw my mum killed by my dad. Strangled the life out of her with his own hands, he did, but to be their executioner ... Their own son.' He whistled theatrically. 'That's a whole different level.'

Ethan lunged forward, but the two guards were ready, taking the strain of the chains. Forsyth jumped back with a surprised shriek, but then grinned as he realised Ethan was trapped. Just how he liked them.

He stepped forward, more confident.

'I'm not entirely certain about the Saudi sentencing laws, but I doubt they'll be lenient, given this is your second offence. The world's going to change a lot whilst you're rotting in here for the next ten years.'

Ethan didn't respond, just kept his eyes focused on Forsyth's preternatural blue gaze, waiting for an opportunity. He just needed one chance.

Forsyth stepped forward more confidently, a lecherous smile playing across his face.

'Who will keep your girlfriend's bed warm whilst you're away? I've a good mind to revisit that. I have to say, she was a minx in the bedroom department. A real goer.'

Forsyth licked his lips.

'You leave her alone,' Ethan growled, pulling against the chains, but the men were ready for him.

'Ah, I see we've hit a nerve again.' Forsyth couldn't help himself, putting his face right up against Ethan's.

'Oh yes, I remember Uma well. I enjoyed fucking her. Nice and slow. And she loved it, so much so, that she got herself pregnant.' Forsyth laughed at the look of surprise on Ethan's face, the words hanging in the air between them like mustard gas. 'Didn't you know? Maybe that's because it was probably mine. But don't worry, she aborted it in January, so we'll never know whose it was.'

'You bastard,' Ethan whispered. 'You'll pay for that.'

Forsyth laughed, a fully belly laugh, and Ethan made his move.

He suddenly pulled back on the chains, wrong-footing both guards who stumbled as they struggled to adjust to the new tension. Without pausing, Ethan yanked the right-hand chain down hard and released it. The guard fell backwards. Ethan turned towards his partner, who was forced to step forward as he tried to maintain the tension. Ethan head-butted him before launching himself at Forsyth, who was hurriedly stepping back – but not fast enough. With two feet of slack in the chain, Ethan struck like a viper, driving his head into Forsyth's stomach and then whipping his neck up. He caught Forsyth's jaw a crunching blow and followed through, biting down hard onto Forsyth's nose as additional guards entered the cell. They began pounding Ethan with their truncheons.

As the blows rained down, Ethan managed to look up and, without taking his eyes off Forsyth, spat bloody gristle onto the cell floor.

'Get me Crouch,' Forsyth howled. Two guards broke away and tried to help him up, but he brushed them away and tottered into the corridor, watching the beating as the hole in his face poured blood.

'You'll pay for this,' Forsyth screamed as the cell door clanged shut.

The Acorn, Riyadh, Saudi Arabia

4th May 2010, 00:47 hours AST

Katrina stood, face pressed against the cool glass, staring down into the courtyard. Arab men talked in small groups, whilst vendors wandered amongst them, offering a selection of ice creams and alcohol, and scantily clad women gyrated on a rotating platform. Katrina smiled. It was definitely a different set of rules playing out in the Crown Prince's private kingdom. But why was she even surprised? It was no different from everywhere else. Now that would be a good story, except she would never get it past her producers – they wanted puff pieces, like the one she had just filmed. At least the Crown Prince's office had approved the unedited interview. She didn't imagine that Forsyth would take too kindly to the dodge, but frankly, she didn't care. Katrina had come across a hundred Forsyths in her life and had quickly learned how to play that game.

Nick cleared his throat, and Katrina turned. The team were all standing by the couch, equipment packed onto two trolleys.

'Boss, we've finished here. Are you going to LEAP now or stay the night and head back tomorrow?'

Katrina glanced at her watch, wondering for the hundredth time if she could make it to Greenwich. It was still early evening on the East Coast. Maybe if she left now? But there was no point. By the time she got there, the party would be over, Brett in bed, asleep. He wouldn't take kindly to being woken up.

'I'll probably stay here the night. Get some rest and experience more of this luxury before I get back to real life.'

Nick laughed.

'Us too. Do you still want to debrief?'

Katrina nodded. Over the years, they had developed a post-inter-view routine, whereby they would spend a couple of hours autopsying the approach and discussing what they could have done differently. She already had an inkling of what would be raised.

'Great idea. Where will you be?'

He nodded down into the courtyard below.

Katrina laughed.

'I'm not sure I'd be welcome down there. Why don't you come to my room? Give me thirty minutes to freshen up.'

Her suite was on the floor above and, like everything in this oth-erworldly edifice, was huge, five times the size of her apartment in Manhattan. She made her way into the bedroom, wondering whether to have a shower. The interview with Forsyth had left her feeling dirty. Another man trying to hit on her, which was old news, but his directness had been eye raising, even by Katrina's standards. She pulled a photo of Brett from her purse. It was a recent one, taken last autumn when they had somehow managed to spend an uninterrupted week at Martha's Vineyard, enjoying long walks on windswept beaches and evenings cuddled up in front of the fire, listening to Vivaldi's Four Seasons. It's how they had met. At Carnegie Hall, the year before. A charity concert given by the New York Philharmonic. He was different to every man she had ever dated. He wasn't much to look at, and quiet, but he was also attentive, treating her as an equal. She felt she could be herself instead of constantly wearing the mask she wore for the Daily Event. It was only recently that things had soured. He had asked her to marry him. She'd said yes, but he'd pushed for a date and now seemed to think he owned her. He kept pressing her to be home more often in the evenings, weekends as well, like a good wife, instead of focusing on her career. But she'd spent the last fifteen years carving out her career and now she was within reach of the ultimate prize – a prime time Emmy. And hopefully her own show where she got to call the shots and pick her own team.

The bell to her suite chimed, and she hurried to the door, wondering why Nick was so early.

Forsyth was standing there, holding a bottle of champagne, his perfect body now swaddled in a cashmere hoodie and joggers. Katrina's heart sank. She didn't have the energy to deal with him.

'Hi, John. What can I do for you?'

'I've come to apologise.'

'For what?'

'For earlier. My behaviour towards the end of the interview was unforgivable. I've come with a peace offering.' He flashed his best smile, holding up the bottle. 'It's Louis Roederer Cristal Brut. 1990. A great year, I'm told.'

Did the man ever stop, she thought?

'Apology accepted, but I'm going to have to pass on the drink. I've got a debrief with the team in five minutes. After that I'm returning to the US.'

Maybe the drive to Connecticut was worth it if she could avoid this randy old man who dressed like a teenager in heat.

She tried to close the door, but Forsyth caught the handle with his free hand.

'There's something else.'

Katrina took a deep breath, trying to control her rising anger. She really wasn't in the mood for this.

'What now? I've got to go.'

'I would like to offer you a world exclusive.'

That got her attention, and Forsyth knew it.

'Go on.'

'As you know, the Saudi's detained Ethan Rae after he followed me back through the gate.'

'And?' Katrina said, her eyes telegraphing that Forsyth would have to do much better than that.

'Well, Mr Rae broke multiple laws and will be sentenced tomorrow. There are suggestions he will get as much as ten years.'

Now, that sounded interesting, she thought.

'OK, what time's the sentencing?'

'First thing tomorrow, but there's more.'

'Go on.'

'I have it on good authority that they're going to punish him as well. As a warning to others thinking of LEAPing into Saudi, unannounced, without going through the proper protocols.'

'What do you mean?'

'They're going to give him fifty lashes.'

Katrina stared at Forsyth, both appalled and excited.

This was huge.

'That sounds barbaric. Can they do that?'

'They can and they will. And then the great Ethan Rae will disappear for the next decade.'

He could hardly control his excitement.

'The best bit is that I'm prepared to offer you exclusive access to both the sentencing and the flogging. As a peace token. I've already cleared it with the Crown Prince.'

Katrina stood there, head whirling. Viewing figures would go through the roof. Another daytime Emmy. She wasn't even sure that the regulators would allow a public flogging to be shown on prime-time TV, but that wasn't her concern. Her job was to bring great stories to the network, perform any interviews, voice-overs and, of course, ensure it got filmed. The rest was up to them.

She stood aside. Forsyth swaggered into her room, a hungry smile on his face.

'I thought that would get your attention,' he said, putting the heavy magnum of Champagne down on the counter.

'And what's in it for you?'

'A global broadcast of the great Ethan Rae finally getting his wings clipped.'

'You really have a problem with them, don't you?'

'It's just business. Green Ray is my biggest competitor. Removing the founder so publicly is in my best interests. Remember, the survival—'

'—of the fittest.' Katrina finished the sentence.

'Do I take it we have a deal?'

'Sure, in principle. I'll have to run it by my boss in New York. And my team, of course, but I can't see them objecting.'

'Great.' Forsyth reached for the magnum. 'Before you do, would you care to share a glass with me?'

Katrina looked doubtful, her mind already busy thinking about the calls she would have to make.

'One flute, I promise,' Forsyth winked at her. 'Both as an apology and a celebration of your scoop.'

Katrina shrugged her shoulders in resignation.

One drink with this old man wouldn't matter before she met the guys.

Katrina's Quarters, The Acorn

4th May 2010, 08:34 hours AST

The pounding continued, softly, imperceptibly, like a faraway jack hammer. It was on the periphery of her hearing, but was loud enough to be annoying. Katrina shifted her head, trying to shut out the noise, then realised with a sinking heart that the sound was inside her head. She sat up in the preposterous bed and rubbed her temples. Nope, it wasn't going away. She glugged deeply from a bottle of water, shards of recollection from the previous night beginning to pierce the jackhammers: returning to the room; Forsyth standing by the door; the scoop of the century following a half-baked apology; drinking the Champagne. But then, things got hazy. Nothing specific, but whatever it was made her skin crawl, guilt clawing at her insides like a caged rat. Had she slept with Forsyth? The pounding suddenly exploded like an IUD as the realisation drew her first tears. She had never been unfaithful to Brett. Had never felt the urge to. They had a strong relationship, built from the ruins of three failed marriages between them. She stumbled into the bathroom, suddenly aware that she was naked, an ugly bruise nuzzling her right breast. Where were her clothes, she thought? A bonfire of snatched memories ignited: of Forsyth nuzzling her neck, unbuttoning her blouse and bra, easing her slacks and panties down, leading her naked into the dining room, spreadeagling her on the huge table, stroking her long hair as she sucked his— Katrina vomited grey bile into the sink, retching long after her stomach was empty. The memories were coming hard and brutal now, and there was no escape from them. She stumbled into the shower, but even the scalding water couldn't wash away the shame that coursed through her veins. It was now a part of her. The realisation found voice in a howl of helpless rage as she wept hot tears that continued long after she had crawled back under the covers, eventually sinking into a troubled sleep of lost relationships and hollow awards.

A familiar voice awoke her, and she froze, heart beating so loudly that she feared he must have heard it from the living room.

'Hello, Katrina, are you there?'

She lay there under the covers, not daring to breathe as he entered the bedroom.

'Katrina,' he called again.

Suddenly the duvet was pulled back, and she shrank into the mattresses, both glad of the towel wrapped tightly around her and petrified that it offered scant protection. Forsyth stood there, a mocking smile sparkling his handsome face.

'There you are,' he said. 'Come on, you need to get up. It's your big day today.'

Katrina stared back up at him, limbs paralysed, mind numb, unable to process his normalcy after the horror of last night. Had she imagined it?

He placed a hand on her shoulder, and the touch transmuted her fear into fury.

'Don't you dare,' Katrina screamed, pulling away.

'Come now,' he tried again.

'What did you do?'

'I might ask you the same question.' His smile morphed into a lecherous sneer. 'You made quite a mess of my back with those long nails of yours.'

'Did you drug me?'

'Of course not,' he said. 'Why would I need to do that?' He glanced into the mirror behind the bed and adjusted his hair.

'I would never sleep with you,' she gasped.

'Well, last night would suggest otherwise,' he replied cheerfully, leaning in to kiss her.

She pulled back, striking out with her fist, which caught Forsyth a glancing blow on the forehead. He sat down on the edge of the bed.

'You do like to play dirty.' He smiled again, but this time it was a hungry glare, like a wolf hunting its prey. 'I like that.'

'You're going to burn in hell for this.'

'And how do you think that's going to play out? We're in a jurisdiction where women don't have any rights. A man can divorce his wife here, just by saying the words. Do you think anyone will believe you?'

'I'll destroy you,' she spat at him. 'Wait till I get back to the States.'

'Come now. Stop this nonsense,' Forsyth said, standing up, suddenly all business, 'You've got a trial to film. That's why I came to get you. Rae is being sentenced this morning and I'm as good as my word. Which is why you slept with me, I presume. To get the scoop of the century. You really are the dirty whore everyone knows you to be.'

'Fuck you,' she screamed at him. 'I will not film your mock trial.'

'Oh yes, you are,' he said smiling again, 'Because if you don't, everyone will get to see this instead.'

He picked up a remote control and pointed it towards the foot of the bed where a large screen silently descended from the ceiling. It was dark for a second, then suddenly flickered into life, showing the dining area from an acute angle, as if shot from a ladder. Forsyth and Katrina were talking animatedly. Katrina laughed gaily. And then Forsyth kissed her. She saw herself putting the glass down and wrapping her arms around his shoulders, kissing him passionately.

'Now, the sentencing starts in twenty minutes,' Forsyth continued matter-of-factly, 'so you don't have long to put your put face on, gather the troops and get your arse down to the courtyard. If you do, this little video will never see the light of day. Capeesh?'

Forsyth didn't wait for a response. He checked himself in the mirror, gently feeling the bridge of his nose and caressing his right eyebrow. Satisfied, he turned and left the room. Katrina didn't move, her eyes transfixed on the screen, as her now kneeling, hi-def naked version slowly unzipped Forsyth's trousers.

Washington DC

4th May 2010, 07:10 hours EDT

The man stepped through the doorway onto the rocky slope. He looked familiar, but she couldn't place him. Behind the figure, towering clouds framed Eyjafjallajökull, still belching ash into the atmosphere. The man was smiling, a broadcast of merriment and light. She felt herself respond just as the cloud lifted, momentarily igniting his long wavy hair in a blaze of gold, so bright that she had to shield her eyes. When she looked back, there were ten more men. They all looked identical. It made no sense. They were all walking towards her, faces glittering in the morning sunlight, eyes blazing with excitement. And then she realised what was happening. The doorway was spitting them out, one after another, like a freak-show production line. Another stepped through. Same clothes, same stubble, same sweep of hair, same preternaturally bright blue eyes. Ten became twenty, became forty, then eighty. The slope was becoming crowded, the men funnelling down, shepherded by its topography. To one side was a steep precipice; the other offered a river of molten lava that hissed and sputtered. They tumbled into existence with no pause, pouring towards her like human magma, cruel intent written large across hollowed-out faces. She felt herself edging backwards, but her escape was blocked by chunks of granite that towered three hundred feet above. But she needn't have worried. The men ignored her, arguing amongst themselves, until the first man seemed to notice her for the first time, staring at her nakedness with lustful abandon. She tried to cover herself, but fifty thousand eyeballs stripped her arms away. The first man pointed, and the others repeated the gesture. Suddenly, he was running towards her, bounding down the steep slope with ease, the mob matching his stride as one. They weren't angry anymore. They were laughing. A booming howl that swept over her like a sonic boom. With a sickening feeling, she suddenly realised who it was.

Uma screamed herself awake, heart beating so heavily she thought it would burst. She stumbled out of bed into the bathroom, splashing her face with cold water, but it was no good. Try as she might, the image of Forsyth haunted her like a cheap tattoo, his cruel laughter pinging around her head like a possessed pinball. Her first thought was to ring Ethan, but realised with a sinking feeling that he was gone. She stumbled back into the bedroom, but sleep was impossible as a billion Forsyths kept appearing, all jostling to see her naked. All laughing with that booming laugh that took her right back to San Francisco.

She struggled into discarded clothes, making her way into the office, but work was impossible. All she could think of was Ethan, alone in Riyadh, sitting in a cell. Worse still, dead. She felt her heart tear, stifling a sob, but her tears were all used up from last night. Damn the oversight board. She would restore him anyway if they refused, but deep down, she knew it wouldn't happen. It was the only way to prove to everyone that no person was above the LEAP Laws, not even her. The President was right; no one could resist the lure of cheating death. She had tried and failed. Twice: first with her father and then Ethan. And he had succumbed too. Maybe Forsyth was right to release it. He was only playing to people's hopes and fears. In fact, the ultimate fear, but if that was the case, her dream of reversing global warming was dead too. What was the point if no one ever died, or worse still, duplicated themselves? There was no point if there were more and more people pouring onto the planet. Her other dream reared its ugly head again, and she recoiled at Forsyth's handsome features.

The sight of him paralysed her, but it also unlocked a more recent memory – of him sitting in a TV studio. He was talking at her, a sunbeamer of a smile burning holes across her face. What was it he had said? Something about her double standards. She felt a flicker of anger. It felt good. She felt herself launch at his face, nails raking his perfect skin. That felt better. Her head smashed into his nose, soft cartilage collapsing underneath the blow. The taste of his blood on her lips. He was only human, after all. She could fight back; better still, hurt him. All she needed was the opportunity.

Uma stood up feeling refreshed, suddenly hungry. She made her way into the kitchen, thinking of her next move. A muted television on the counter top was broadcasting images of a blackened seascape in the Gulf of Mexico. The sight gave her fresh energy. The sooner they rolled out LEAP, the sooner they would strangle off the demand for oil. Shortly, no one would have to suffer the sight again. She opened the fridge and grabbed two eggs, a jug of milk, and some cheese. As she turned back towards the counter, her eyes strayed to the screen and Uma froze. Katrina Hoskins was standing in a large atrium, hair covered, holding a microphone. Beneath her, the caption read, "LIVE in Riyadh: Ethan Rae's sentencing."

The Acorn, Riyadh, Saudi Arabia

4th May 2010, 14:12 hours AST

Ethan hobbled through the cell door, the guards following at a respectful distance. In the corridor, two more men waited, both holding snubnosed submachine guns. They walked in front of Ethan who slowly shuffled along, shoulders bowed with the weight of chains that restricted his stride to just six inches. By the time he reached the elevator, Ethan was sweating freely, the heat crushing down on him as heavily as the metal restraints that bound his wrists and ankles. All five men crammed into the tight compartment, waiting, as the temperature seemed to tick even higher. As the lift lurched upwards, cool air poured down from the ceiling. It felt like heaven after the scorching humidity of the cell, and, for the first time in days, Ethan felt like he could breathe. He lifted his head as the lift doors opened into a plush atrium, where four members of the Royal Guard Regiment waited. They were bedecked in ceremonial uniform: a pristine white head-dress and thaub with crossed bandoliers. Across their waists, a gold belt sported an ornate gold-plated dagger to complement the golden scabbard in their right hands and from which protruded a slender grip wrapped in fine gold winding. The first group disappeared back down into the bowels of the earth as the smartly dressed soldiers stationed themselves in a square around Ethan, before marching forward slowly in lockstep, carolling him across the cavernous hall, their steel-tipped boots echoing loudly on the shiny marble.

As they approached two enormous glass doors leading out into a central plaza, a TV crew appeared, making a beeline for Ethan and his captors. There were three of them: a cameraman and a boom operator, both facing a woman with long blond hair that reached almost to her waist. She looked familiar, but had her back to Ethan as she talked into the camera. It wasn't until they neared that he realised who it was: Katrina Hoskins. She looked exhausted, dark shadows ringing red eyes that framed a tired face, thick with makeup. As they exchanged glances, Katrina stopped talking, and, for a second, Ethan thought she was going to burst into tears.

'I didn't—' The wooden scabbard caught Ethan in the stomach, doubling him over in pain as he gasped for air.

'No talking,' one of the soldiers grunted.

Ethan eventually straightened, allowing the group to resume its funeral pace. The TV crew followed at a respectful distance, but close enough so that Ethan could hear every word Katrina was saying.

'We have joined Ethan Rae in the Crown Prince's Riyadh-based palace, as he is being led out for his sentencing and punishment. According to the Saudis, he was arrested six days ago after he followed John Forsyth back to The Acorn and allegedly attacked him, hospitalising over ten of the Royal Guard Regiment. The Regiment is an elite squad of soldiers who are tasked with protecting the lives of the Royal Family, including their guests. Mr Rae has been charged under Sharia Law with over seven offences, including entering Saudi Arabia without the correct paperwork, trespassing on Palace grounds, attacking a guest of the Royal Family – which we presume is John Forsyth – inflicting bodily harm on members of the Royal Guard Regiment and endangering the life of the Crown Prince himself, who was in residence at The Acorn at the time of the attack. It is the last three that are the most serious. They fall under the Hudud category of the Saudi criminal code, which mandates severe physical punishments and, in some instances, can carry a sentence punishable by ...' Katrina paused and stared at Ethan who realised with a sinking feeling that she was also here against her will. Her eyes were filled with a sadness that knew no depth. What had Forsyth got on her to co-opt the US's hottest investigative journalist into this kangaroo court? '... death,' she finished with a finality that sent a chill through Ethan.

He hadn't expected that, but it made sense. The death of Rae would signal the end of Green Ray. It was brilliant and would be broadcast across the Western world with a clear message that Eternity had won. That LEAP had lost. What was worse, Uma had committed to observing the LEAP Laws moving forward and, after Forsyth's revelations on national TV, there was no chance Ethan would be reinstated. He was going to die today. The thought had never scared Ethan. In fact, until recently, he would have welcomed it. It would have been a sweet relief from the gnawing guilt that he had killed his parents, but now he had something to live for. Someone to protect. The thought that he might never see Uma again almost collapsed him onto the cold hard marble, a sobbing wretch in chains, wearing soiled prison clothes and nursing a hundred cuts and bruises. What kept him upright was the thought that she might be watching this. He didn't want her to remember him that way, so he summoned every ounce of strength, forcing each heavy foot forward into the courtyard, trying not to think about what Forsyth had said to him in the cell. Had Uma been pregnant? If Forsyth was telling the truth, which was a big assumption, it didn't make sense that Uma would have kept it from him. But equally so, why wouldn't she? They had barely begun to date. It was her body. She could do with it what she wanted, but a tiny part of him mourned the dead baby. If he died today, then his bloodline would end also, a realisation that shocked and saddened him in equal measure. Forsyth must be playing mind games, he reminded himself angrily. Trying to get inside Ethan's head to make him suffer even more. He tried to distract himself by focusing on what Katrina was saying.

'The death penalty can be imposed for a wide range of offences, including murder, rape, armed robbery, repeated drug use, apostasy, adultery, witchcraft and sorcery. Yes, folks, you heard it here, sorcery, and it can be carried out by beheading with a sword, stoning or a firing squad, followed by crucifixion. However, of the 345 reported executions in Saudi in the last five years, all have been carried out by public beheading, right here in Riyadh at Deera Square, which is known locally as Chop-Chop Square.'

The procession shuffled forward towards a colossal tree. Around it were gathered fifty or so people seated on soft sofas and deep divans. Everyone turned, staring at the strange procession. Ethan spotted Forsyth sitting next to a short, pudgy man, reclining in the biggest chair. Forsyth said something to the man and he laughed, his enormous belly wobbling with the effort. Ethan was led into the centre of the small gathering. Behind him, Katrina was still talking to her audience back home in hushed tones. It lent the whole proceedings a surreal feeling as he listened to a highlights reel of his own sentencing, punishment and perhaps death. Ethan glanced up at the tree, which must have been over one hundred feet tall. How had they got it here? It reminded him of the giant sequoias from the Reynolds estate. What the oak lacked in height, it more than made up for in spread, its gnarled limbs fanning out above the small gathering like an ancient umbrella. The guards stomped to a halt in front of a man who looked as old as the tree. His stooped shoulders were cloaked in a black Bisht with gold trim, his heavily wrinkled face was partly obscured by a red chequered Ghutra and his long white beard reached almost to his waist. As Ethan waited, the elderly judge slowly studied the small gathering before fixing his gaze on Ethan, with his lizard eyes that had delivered a lifetime of religious justice. An aide appeared with a lectern, on top of which lay the Koran. He placed the wooden stand in front of the elderly man who took the holy text in his right hand before speaking in a soft, gravelly voice. Behind Ethan, one of the guards translated, whispering into Ethan's ear. It took less than thirty seconds, but all he heard was, "26,000 lashes" and "ten years". Ethan sank to his knees, trying to process the number. How was that possible? He would never live through that. He had barely survived fifty. He was going to die today.

'Do you have anything to say for yourself?' The old man flicked his reptilian eyes towards Ethan.

There was nothing to say and, after a brief wait, the judge moved away from the lectern as the two guards yanked Ethan to his feet, leading him over to the tree trunk. One of his captors unlocked the chains, removing the heavy restraints. Ethan rubbed his sore wrists. For a crazy moment, he thought about running, but where would he go? Guards with guns were positioned at every exit. Besides which, how would it look on TV if the great Ethan Rae was filmed being dragged back to receive his punishment, crying like a baby? How would Uma feel? No, he would stay and die, with as much dignity as he could muster. Except that his back had other ideas. It was already rippling with tiny pinpricks of pain at what was to come. Ethan's resolve crumbled like a sandcastle washed away by the incoming tide. As the guards removed his shirt, Ethan heard Katrina gasp with surprise at what she saw. She then hurriedly explained to her breakfast viewers that the scar tissues were the result of a punishment that Ethan Rae had received several decades before – when he was a teenager – for killing his parents. He wanted to turn and scream at her. It made him sound like he had murdered them in cold blood. That's exactly what he had done, he thought grimly.

In his peripheral vision, he saw a man enter the courtyard. A great hulk of a man, cloaked all in black, his head covered by a black hood. In his hand was a heavy whip, a whip that Ethan remembered well. As he made his way towards Ethan, Forsyth stood. He was grinning, his face a triumphant mask, eyes glittering with joyous expectation of what was to come.

A guard pushed Ethan against the tree, whilst another pulled his arms apart, forcing his hands into metal shackles set into the trunk. Another did the same with his legs, so that he was spreadeagled, face pressed against the silvery grey bark. The rugged platelets felt cool against his limbs, calming almost, and Ethan felt his heart rate steady, his breathing evening out as he waited for the first crack.

When it came, he wasn't ready. The air compressed with the crack of a gunshot, the sound hanging for what seemed like an eternity. In the space, Ethan's life passed by him: Mark Brown, his parents, prison and pain, Uma, Anderson, Reynolds, the child he would never know.

The metal tip bit deep into his back.

Ethan screamed.

CIA HQ

4th May 2010, 16:28 hours EDT

The second hand inched across the clock face, but each halting advance felt like an hour, forcing Uma to relive the morning in excruciating detail. She shifted in her seat, wondering why she was even here. Whatever was agreed, it would be too late, at least for Ethan, but she had nowhere to go. Certainly not back to her apartment, where reminders of him lay everywhere: his rolled-up mattress in the corner of her bedroom where she would always find him in the morning, curled up, regardless of what time they got to bed. His fighting staff was by the front door, straight and true, waiting patiently for its owner. He practised every day in a space by the high-ceilinged windows, servant and master lost in a blur of wood and muscle as they set about dismantling the padded dummy. In the spare room, he had set up a small desk with three screens spread in a semicircle around two photos: one of Uma, the other of his parents. The parents he claimed to have killed years earlier, an act that had led to his previous internment. And just yesterday, history had repeated itself. She sighed heavily, willing the clock hands to speed up, but time would not be hurried. The images continued to tick through her mind: his bloodied torso, every sinew taut with pain; soiled trousers crimson black from the punishment. Eventually she had stopped watching, burying her head in a pillow, finally crying herself to sleep. No one called. No one came. And when she woke, her brain dumbly recalled the meeting with Ingram, her body responding on auto pilot, muscle memorying its way to this very seat, where she was now sitting, waiting for an audience with a man she despised.

As the clock dragged the minute hand to register half past the hour, a phone rang at the far end of the room. Uma stood as the middle-aged woman quickly answered it, speaking inaudibly into the receiver before replacing it in its cradle. She smiled at Uma.

'Director Ingram will see you now,' she said, showing Uma into a large room dominated by a huge desk. Ingram was nowhere to be seen. The woman seated Uma on a low settee which stretched the entire length of one wall, smiled at her again, and left. Not more games, she thought. Uma wasn't sure if she could stand another thirty minutes of this. However, almost immediately, a door opened to her right and the familiar frame of Ingram slouched into the room. He nodded at Uma and finished drying his hands on some paper towelling before returning to his desk. It must have been twenty feet away, which, combined with its low level, put Uma at a distinct disadvantage. Games within games, she thought.

'Good afternoon, Doctor. It would appear events have overtaken us.'

'There must be something we can do?'

'What do you propose? The British won't touch this. There's too much attention on your boyfriend. He is the News, and it's not going away anytime soon.'

Uma nodded, preparing herself for what was to come.

'That's not why I'm here.' She stood up and walked over to his desk. Even standing, she still only came up to his eyeline, but no longer felt at such a disadvantage.

'Enlighten me,' Ingram said, folding his arms and leaning back in his chair.

Uma swallowed hard. This was going to be harder than she had thought.

'Really? Are you going to make me say it?'

Ingram deadpanned Uma, forcing her to continue.

'I need your help,' she began. 'To get Ethan out of Saudi.'

Ingram didn't reply straight away. He just stared at Uma, his face impassive, grey eyes revealing nothing, but Uma could tell he was enjoying this moment. Something about his demeanour broadcast victory.

'And why would I want to do that?' he said after what seemed like an age, no hint of irony in his voice.

Uma remembered their last confrontation when Ingram had called her following the house fire. Then, she had refused to sanction the reinstatement of Operation Twin that would have saved his precious agents' lives. So much had changed so quickly and Ingram knew it.

'Because without Ethan, the LEAP programme will slow down.'

'No one's indispensable. Not even the great Ethan Rae. I can think of a hundred talented individuals who could take over the programme today and drive it forward just as quickly.'

'Because he's my boyfriend and I need him back,' she screamed silently at Ingram. 'Because I can't do this myself; I can't do it without him,' she soundlessly yelled at the tall man in front of her, but she would never let Ingram know that. Never allow him that satisfaction.

'No one has the talent of Ethan. Besides, he's the symbolic head of the programme. Do you know how that looks to the outside world? To see the head of LEAP whipped like a dog. Locked up like a common criminal.'

'What do you want me to do?'

'Go and get him.'

'We've been through this with the President. We're not guns for hire, Doctor. We can't just waltz into another jurisdiction and extract people at will.'

Uma doubted very much if that was true, but she knew Ingram would revel in that argument. It was one she could never win.

Uma swallowed hard, hating herself for what she was about to say.

'I can smooth the way for your copying programme.'

'Here you go again, Doctor,' his face was grim again, 'bending your ethics for your own purposes. Besides which, that bird has already flown the coop. Were you not listening to the President? There's an oversight board coming.'

'That could take months. I could talk to the President. Convince him to allow military exemption until the board is set up.'

'That won't be necessary.'

'Oh, and why's that?'

'We already have an exemption. It's called Eternity.'

Uma stared at Ingram, her gaze telescoping onto his huge forehead as she tried to absorb what he had just said.

'What do you mean?' she stammered.

'We've contracted them to perform that service. Everything we need, starting with the Intelligence services and, in time, everyone with a front-line role. It's Plan B in case this oversight board is not set up in time and doesn't approve my request that any member of the Armed Service be automatically enrolled in a backup. From today, over a million men and woman will shortly be protected. American families will never again have to face the trauma of seeing their loved ones come home in body bags or maimed for life or have PTSD.'

Time seemed to slow again, and Uma felt herself beginning to fall. She grabbed the edge of the desk.

'You can't do that.'

'That seems to be your stock answer to everything, Doctor,' Ingram continued drily. 'Of course we can. We live in a global economy. LEAP is moving too slowly, and after that little stunt you pulled in front of the President back in March, you left me with no choice.'

'The President won't allow it.'

'He has no choice, either. I'm protecting him from his own conscience. The midterms are approaching, and like all politicians, he's a slave to public opinion. Once they kick off, I'll tell him. It's a great story. No more American heroes returning home in body bags or with missing limbs. The optics are good for him, and, as you know, they're great for me. My job is to protect the country, including all of its servicemen. It always has been. Every day that we're in no-man's land, caught between a moratorium on restoration and the creation of a global oversight board, American heroes are dying out there. I won't accept that. Nor should you.'

Ingram dropped his head and started to read a document on his desk, leaving Uma standing there, unable to speak, a blizzard of thoughts turmoiling through her head: Ethan's bloodied back, her dream about Forsyth, his sneering laugh. Now this. There was no respite.

A full minute passed.

Eventually Ingram looked up. He seemed surprised to see Uma still standing there.

'Doctor, I need the room. I have work to do.'

Video Suite, The Daily Event Studios, Manhattan

4th May 2010, 17:12 hours EDT

The first lash cracked like a gunshot, ripping into Ethan's exposed flesh. His shoulder exploded in a puff of pink as the whip head bit deep. The whip master steadied himself, adjusting the ornate handle in his grip, before lashing the fifteen-foot thong back across his right shoulder and then flicking it forward. This time, Ethan's other shoulder puffed red. Next, the lower back. Again and again it struck like a black mamba, exploding into the skin, until Ethan's back was a river of blood, but there was no respite as the popper now lacerated Ethan's muscles, slicing into the deltoids and trapezius along his upper shoulders before ripping through his teres muscles and latissimus dorsi. Like a modern-day snake god, the popper bit deeper and deeper, now cutting into the rhomboids and splenius muscles, but still there was no end. Crack and cut went the bullwhip. Crack and cut. Ethan's screams were long since silenced by the onslaught, his arms now rigid as he hung from the iron manacles like a joint of meat. On and on it went, the whip master pounding the whip like a metronome, lash after lash, strike after strike, until Katrina lost count. Tears sprang unbidden as she forced herself to watch over what she had witnessed in person less than ten hours ago.

'Stop it, please stop it,' she cried, turning away from the screen. The video editor paused the frame mid lash, the bloodied popper flicked back towards the camera like the tongue of a snake, Ethan's ruined back river-red in the foreground. She sobbed silently for several minutes, head bowed in hands, her senses overwhelmed by the bloodletting she had witnessed. No, it was worse than that. What had she done? Reporting on this barbaric act, facilitating that monster's private vendetta against LEAP.

A knock at the door pulled her back into the room. She raised her head as Scott Parker, head of the news division, entered. His smile froze as Katrina turned.

'Now's not a good time, Scott,' she sniffed, wiping tears from her face. They tasted metallic, the iron-like fragrance infusing the editing suite like a bad smell.

'Now's a great time. I just wanted to tell you that this recording has broken all viewing records, not just for the Daily Event but nationwide, for any factual programme. Ever. It's Emmy time, baby, Emmy time.' He whooped with excitement, moving to high five Katrina, who just stared at his raised hand with horror.

'Fuck off, Scott,' she snarled, knocking his arm away. 'How can you celebrate this barbarity?'

Scott lowered his hand, a puzzled frown on his perma-tanned face.

'Not computing, Katrina. You filmed this ... this shit show. We're all watching it because you presented it. It's a bit late to grow a conscience, don't you think?'

Katrina lowered her head, a fresh set of tears welling up, her face reddening at his truth. He was right. She had enabled this. She should have refused to film the segment, but even as the thought sprang up, another crowded it out – of her, kneeling in the lounge, her fingers on his zipper and ...

She had no choice. Her career, her engagement to Brett – everything obliterated in a moment. Everything she had spent her career working towards. All the hustling. Accommodating arseholes like Scott. Fighting off all the other slimy producers with their wandering hands and dumb sexist jokes. Being portrayed as a blond bimbo with no brains. She'd had no choice, but that was her cross to bear now, silently. In the meantime, she somehow had to work, reporting the news as she had done for the last fifteen years. All the while, images of Ethan's back kept exploding across her mind like a deranged IUD. She'd be damned if this would derail her. She needed to fight back and she had the perfect way to do it.

She sat up a little straighter, wiping away coppery scented tears.

'You're right, Scott. We should be celebrating.'

'That's more like it,' he grinned, relieved his hot anchor had stopped blubbing like a cry-baby.

'In the meantime,' she said, 'I'd like to do some follow-up pieces: maybe we can get Forsyth back in to discuss the fallout from yesterday's ...' Her eyes flicked to the screen. She still couldn't bring herself to say it, despite her new resolve. All she could do was nod at the frozen image.

'There you go,' Scott said. 'Anything you want – it's yours. I'll get Todd and Mandy on it right away. In the meantime, gather the troops. I've booked Masa Masa for this Friday. We are going to have a party to end all parties.'

He turned and left the room, leaving Katrina staring in horror at the screen as fresh tears began to leak through her fragile facade.

Saudi Prison Hospital

5th May 2010, 03:32 hours AST

W arm air rushed over the car like a windy river, buffeting his face even though they were only going forty. It felt good. The road ahead was clear, the night sky peppered with stars, and the desert spread out before them like a sandy sea. He remembered his first driving lesson just ten weeks earlier. Nobody cared. He'd seen young boys, barely able to peer over the steering wheel, roaring around in battered BMWs and souped-up Mercs. He'd done it, too, driving to school every day, and home again in the afternoon. It gave him an incredible sense of freedom. Therefore, when, towards the end of the meal, his father had tossed the keys over, he'd caught them with a smile. The perfect end to a perfect evening. The food had been good – steaming hot Kabsa rice dishes topped with roast chicken and lamb, infused with cloves, cardamon, cumin, and saffron. They'd sung Happy Birthday, the other diners smiling at the happy family. One of his father's colleagues had recommended the restaurant, but it was a forty-five-minute drive back into Riyadh, most of it along Highway 65, which at this time of night was deserted. Even then he had driven carefully, staying within the speed limit, checking his mirror, smiling as he caught sight of his mum laughing at something his dad had said. They looked happy.

'Did you hear that?' she said, winking at him.

'What?' he shouted above the roar of the road. 'I can't hear you.'

'Your dad's joke.'

'One sec,' he shouted, feathering the brakes as they approached a junction, before glancing into the back seat.

'It's a terrible joke,' she said.

'You found it funny,' his father said, making a face at his wife. 'Let Mark decide.'

'I've just been on a once-in-a-lifetime holiday,' his father said. 'I tell you what, never again!'

His mother laughed again. So did Mark.

'Oh, that's terrible,' Mark said, glancing both ways. He gunned the motor, pulling into the road.

An explosion of pain blossomed across his retinas like an atomic flash,

Someone screaming: animalistic, inhuman.

The whip head biting deep, his skin popping open like a burst balloon.

Blond hair, once so vibrant, now bloodied and limp.

Another flesh-cutter slicing through his skin like butter.

Teeth clenched so tightly, they must surely shatter.

His father on the tarmac, neck cocked sideways like a broken action man.

White bone protruding from his thigh.

Smooth skin, alabaster white, eyes glazed over, their light snuffed out.

Ethan opened his eyes and groaned. He was lying face down, his head buried in a pillow. It smelled sickly sweet. Of death and a lifetime of pain. For a moment, he thought he was going to be sick. He tried to move, but a million nerve endings broadcast their opposition, the pain radiating out across his back like bloody ripples in a pool. He lay there for several minutes, absorbing the hurt. Then he tried again, screaming this time as he collapsed back into the pillow. But he persisted, remembering the first time. Or was this the first time? His young body ravaged by fever. If he could do it then, he could do it now, but the weight on his back was immense, holding down on him like a hydraulic press inlaid with hot coals. He whimpered, biting down on the soiled pillow until he thought he would choke, but gradually the pain faded into the merely intolerable. Again, he moved, this time shifting his arms. Again, he collapsed. Lying there, he tried to gather his energy. The attempts blurred into each other, every failure a small success, inching him higher. Each time, he drew strength from his sixteen-year-old self. He felt young wounds tear open, hot blood seeping over dried blood, fresh pricks of pain layered on top of decades of hurt. He ignored them with a practised determination. With a final shriek, he forced his wrecked body into a sitting position.

Ethan sat there for a long time, eyes closed, recovering his strength. The room looked identical to the one he had lain in for six weeks after the first time: a single bulb hanging forlornly above his head; the only furniture, his rusty bed, the enamel long since faded; bare mattress soiled with blood and worse. He touched a toe to the rough gravel and left an imprint in the sand. In the corner, a camera flashed its angry red eye at him. To his right was a dirty window. Through the cracked glass he could hear sounds of the prison he would now call his home for the next ten years. Five hundred and twenty weeks. Nearly 190,000 days. The maths was as fresh in his head now as before. He would not see Uma for over four million hours. The thought made him weep. It was unbearable, a pain which cut deeper than anything his back could muster. He collapsed back onto the filthy sheets with a gut-wrenching sob that matched the sound of his heart tearing in two.

Green Ray Offices, Manhattan

6th May 2010, 12:32 hours EDT

The table stretched away into the distance, a smooth plane of wood that seemed to carry on forever. Uma wondered how long the tree had stood, and what it had witnessed before being chopped down to serve as an inanimate object for supporting papers, coffee cups, and sweaty elbows. The walnut was cracked in places, but the craftsman had burnished the wood to a high sheen. Polish on a dead body. It felt barbaric, this once proud tree cut down in its prime, then carved up, body parts now on display for everyone to see. She touched the wood. It felt cool. Uma resisted the urge to crawl under its dark legs and curl up in a tight ball. Hidden away from Ingram, from Forsyth and, of course, from LEAP. Her thoughts turned to Ethan, as they had done every minute of every hour for the last two days. Of him lying in a cell in some dusty prison, wounds festering. He had never spoken about his time in jail, and Uma had never pressed him. She didn't need to, his scar tissue was proof enough of the horrors visited on him as a sixteen-year-old boy, still mourning his parents. Deaths that he blamed himself for. He would be revisiting all of that, and it was her fault.

Shane still hadn't worked out how they had obtained Ethan's atomic code and stolen him back to Saudi. It was ingenious really. It had finally made her accept that LEAP had long since ceased to be under her control. She'd known for months, since last March, when Ingram had handed her the letter she'd written to Reynolds all those years ago. She just hadn't been willing to accept it, until last Wednesday in the TV Studios of the Daily Event, when she had intentionally weaponised Ethan, unleashing him on Forsyth. It was hard enough to plug the leaks caused by LEAP. Impossible when she was also causing the crack, through which an entire dam of problems was now pouring.

'Doctor, what do you think?'

Uma dragged her eyes away from the wood, glancing across at Maisie Collins.

'Sorry, I was miles away.'

'The presentation. What do you think?'

Uma pulled herself back into the room, studying the sea of expectant faces gathered round the huge table. They were the cream of her Green Ray team, handpicked to kick-start an initiative she had been thinking about since the Climate Change Conference in Copenhagen the previous December. It had occurred to her, as she stood on the dais with the President announcing that LEAP would be free to every nation on the planet, that it would not be enough to reverse all CO_2 emissions. She'd realised that other initiatives would be needed to run alongside the system in addition to what she had started with the Green Ray fund. Today was the day, of all days, when members of her team had presented their recommendations to her.

'I like them. I think we should go with each one.'

'Are you suggesting we split the budget three ways?' Maisie said, a look of disappointment on her face as several members of the team also exchanged worried glances.

'No, quite the opposite. Give five billion to each programme,' Uma said. She'd already decided prior to the meeting that each initiative needed equal focus and, therefore, equal capital if they were going to make an impact.

'I beg your pardon,' Maisie said, struggling to keep the excitement out of her voice. 'Did you just say five billion each?'

'I did,' Uma said, smiling for the first time in what seemed like ages. It felt good. Finally, something she could control. That would have a direct impact on the planet, with no nasty side effects. It reminded her of the work she had been doing before the US government hijacked her life less than twelve months ago, particularly the SMART meters and the wind farms. Both were working well. They had shelved the Electro. Who needed a car, even if it was electric, when LEAP was in town? They'd budgeted over ten billion to develop and subsidise the Electro. Well, that money could go towards these three projects. Huge projects. To begin with, Trillions, a reforestation programme, aimed to plant four trillion trees, which in time would absorb twenty-five trillion pounds of CO_2 from the atmosphere. Then Oceanic would clear the world's oceans of over two hundred billion tons of plastic. Finally, Elemental would recycle the base elements from every municipal garbage dump in the world. All in five years. 'We can't afford to wait on any of this. In time, LEAP will recycle everything so we won't need to chop down trees or manufacture more plastic or extract any element from the ground. However, whilst that scales, all three are needed. We can't afford to wait. And if more money is needed, we'll provide it.'

There was silence in the boardroom, but not for long. Suddenly, everyone was standing and clapping, whooping with excitement. Maisie gave Uma a big hug, tears streaming down her face. Uma joined in, crying silently into the younger woman's shoulder. Others approached, hugging her, mistaking her tears for tears of happiness, though she was actually being crushed by the sadness that weighed upon her.

Someone cracked open a magnum of champagne. The pop startled Uma back to reality: Forsyth and that night in the Pyramid. Her nightmare had started with a bottle just like that. She pulled away from the huddle, quietly exiting the room into the reception area. At the far end, a TV screen covered one wall. Emblazoned across it was the handsome, perma-tanned face of John Forsyth.

Uma stumbled back onto the sofa, transfixed as the giant face laughed at something offscreen. As the camera panned back, Katrina suddenly appeared. The woman who had narrated Ethan's barbaric punishment as if she was voicing a cooking show.

'Turn it up,' Uma screamed at the receptionist, who fumbled for the controls. 'Turn it up!' she shouted again. She wanted to run and hide, but couldn't move, her limbs frozen, black spots pinging across her vision.

'... that has nothing to do with me,' John Forsyth's husky voice boomed across the reception at Uma. 'Remember, Rae attacked me. I'm not the aggressor here. I tried to escape. He followed me.' He rubbed his nose self-consciously and continued. 'Followed me through the gate and into my apartment back in Saudi.'

'How did he do that?' Uma heard Katrina ask through a long tunnel, as if she was three hundred miles away, not thirty feet.

'No idea. I would imagine that Rae breached our gate security and followed me through to do ... to do, I don't know what,' Forsyth said with a shudder. Again, he touched his nose, wincing with pain.

'Do you think the punishment meted out to him was warranted? Ten years and 26,000 lashes seem extortionate for what he did.'

'When he got to the other side, he continued his attack. I think he was trying to kill me. He was completely deranged. Like a madman, really. He hospitalised twelve of my men. He just kept coming, like ...' Forsyth sounded genuinely scared. 'If it hadn't been for my security detail ...' he nodded at a man offscreen and the camera panned to an unsmiling Ed Fox, '... I'd hate to think about what might have happened. Do you think that's disproportionate?'

John Forsyth looked into the camera, his brilliant blue eyes searching out Uma's, boring a hole into them. She could picture Ethan attacking Forsyth. She had seen him do the same thing on countless occasions. The thought brought a half smile to her lips, but it was cold comfort. Ethan wasn't coming home anytime soon, thanks to Forsyth's carefully laid trap.

'Besides which, it's a good job he followed me through.'

'How so?' Katrina said, frowning.

'Well, here in New York, attempted murder is a Class B violent felony. If convicted, Rae could have been sentenced to twenty-five years to life in prison. Compared to that, he's got off lightly.'

'But the whipping seems barbaric: fifty lashes every week for the next decade.'

'Many would say America's record of capital punishment is just as barbaric. I'm not saying Saudi's is any better, but my point is that we must respect the laws of other countries. And in this case, the laws of Saudi permit the courts to combine physical punishment with the sentence. It's a system that has existed for hundreds of years.'

'It still sounds barbaric to most of our viewers and, quite frankly, having watched the flogging, I would have to agree,' Katrina said with a shudder.

Uma cried out in anger. The scream returned motion to her jellied limbs. Suddenly she was standing, raging at the outsized image of Katrina Hoskins, sitting there, all prim and proper, faking her way through yet another interview, whilst Ethan rotted in a Saudi cell.

'Jane, have my car meet me at the front,' Uma shouted at the startled receptionist.

'Yes, ma'am. Where are you going?'

'The Daily Event.'

Daily Event Studios, Manhattan

6th May 2010, 13:23 hours EDT

The room was cool after the heat of the studio. Katrina felt half human again as she wiped away the thick makeup from her face. Blotchy skin appeared as the mask disappeared, to reveal black circles that ringed swollen eyes, red from too much crying. She sighed heavily, staring at her reflection in the mirror, wondering what to do. Forsyth had triumphed again, manipulating the interview to present himself as a victim. For the thousandth time that week, Katrina questioned if she could have done anything differently. But each time, the same cul-de-sac appeared, of her kneeling in front of John Forsyth like a Times Square hooker. The thought made her feel defeated and humiliated in equal measure. She wished the ground would open up and swallow her down into its depths, never to see the light of day again. She wasn't sure how much more she could handle. She was trapped in a vicious circle, at the beck and call of Forsyth every time he wanted to broadcast his message to the world. Worse still, she felt responsible: she had filmed Ethan Rae's sentencing, then his flogging, and continued to allow this ... this monster, to control the narrative.

A commotion outside her dressing room door dragged her eyes away from the mirror. Two people were arguing. One of them sounded very familiar, her angry voice clearly audible through the door. Katrina's heart sank as the door slammed open. Uma appeared, followed by a red-faced assistant.

'I'm so sorry, Katrina. She just barged in.'

'Call security, Sarah,' Katrina said, throwing the dirty cotton pads onto the desk.

'Why are you allowing this man to broadcast his poison on your show?' Uma yelled at Katrina.

'Please leave my dressing room,' Katrina said, turning to face Uma. The woman was enraged, her cheeks flushed, her eyes also red with crying. It felt familiar.

'Why did you film that filth in Saudi?' Uma shouted at her, brushing away Sarah's vain attempts to restrain her. 'If you touch me again, I'll break your arm,' she snarled at the young assistant, who, after glancing at Katrina, retreated to the doorway, where other members of the production team had gathered.

'It's none of your business,' Katrina retorted.

Two security guards appeared and approached Uma. One placed a hand on her shoulder.

'Please, miss, you need to leave,' he said.

Uma reacted as if she had been scalded, heeling him in the shin. He yelped with surprise.

'How dare you touch me! Do it again, and I swear to God you'll never work again.'

The guard glanced towards Katrina for some guidance.

'You need to leave,' Katrina said again. 'Please,' she added more softly, with pleading eyes.

'Not until you've answered my questions,' Uma screamed back. 'Why are you allowing him to do this? What has he got on you?'

A look passed between the two women – not even a fraction of a glance, but Katrina may as well have laid bare her soul. In that instant, Uma knew.

'He's got to you, hasn't he?' she said softly, her shoulders slumping, rage dissipating like a deflated balloon.

Katrina blushed scarlet.

'It's OK, Joe. I've got this.' Katrina stood up.

The two guards didn't move, unsure of what to do as all the anger drained out of the room.

'You can go,' Katrina said again, nodding at Sarah. 'Please don't disturb us.'

The men retreated to the door, one of them rubbing his shin. As Sarah closed the door, she glanced back.

The two women were standing there, silently, staring at each other, tears rolling down their faces.

Daily Event Studios, Manhattan

6th May 2010, 15:46 hours EDT

'What do we do now?' Katrina said. She was slumped in her chair, Uma opposite, perched on a low couch that ran along the back of the changing room. They had been talking for over two hours. Uma was exhausted, but also exhilarated, as if a huge weight had been lifted from her shoulders. She could tell Katrina felt the same way. Her eyes had recovered their intensity. She had even managed a smile as the poison leached from her body, washed away by all the tears and the unburdening of her dirty secret. Uma had started first, unprompted, haltingly, as if the words were stuck inside of her, ashamed to reveal themselves to the outside world. A trickle became a torrent until they poured out like hot bile until every drop of shame had been expunged from her body. Until the silent ache that had possessed her for all those months faded away like an exorcised demon. Katrina had spoken in a low monotone whisper, clearly terrified, the memories still raw, right up to when she had found herself kneeling in front of Forsyth. She couldn't bring herself to continue, and Uma didn't push. They had simply sat in silence, united by their shared trauma until now.

'We fight back,' Uma said.

'How? He has our recordings. My career would be over,' Katrina said, her eyes misting over, the fear in her voice palpable.

'We need to rescue Ethan first. Right that wrong.' Uma glanced at Katrina, who nodded. 'Then we can get Forsyth.'

'How? Ethan's in a heavily guarded jail. Forsyth's got 24/7 protection, organised by a man called Fox. I think he's ex-military. Follows him everywhere. Besides, how do we even get to them? They're in Saudi; we're stuck here.'

Before Uma could answer, there was another knock at the door. Katrina's assistant appeared, an apologetic look on her face.

'I'm so sorry,' she said, taking in the two women. She glanced at Uma, who smiled back, silently apologising for her earlier behaviour. The woman nodded, turning to Katrina.

'There's a production meeting at half past. To discuss tomorrow's show.'

Katrina glanced at her watch.

'I forgot,' she said, groaning. 'Give me ten minutes.'

Sarah nodded, before retreating from the room, shutting the door as she left.

'I'm so sorry, business calls. Maybe we can continue this conversation later. After my meeting. You're welcome to stay here.'

Uma shrugged.

'I need to get back to the office as well. You're welcome to come over this evening.'

Katrina started repairing her makeup, gathering her thick blond hair into a bun and savagely tying it back. Within seconds, the inscrutable anchor that Uma had detested since her first meeting was back.

'Sounds good.'

They both exited the office, making their way down the corridor towards the production room. To get to it, they had to pass through the studio. It looked so different to Uma's previous experiences, the cameras now silent, hot lights dark, the deserted stage, like an abandoned living room. As they made their way across the set, Uma passed the gate through which Ethan had disappeared. The memory made her heart ache. She stopped, thinking of the last time she had seen him. The memory was quickly replaced by an image of him hanging from the manacles, spreadeagled, his back a mess of torn flesh. She stumbled, reaching out to steady herself against the gate. The metal felt cool. What had Shane said? Someone, probably Crouch, must have hacked their system to obtain Ethan's atomic code. They would have then uploaded it, allowing Forsyth to execute his trap. Shane was still desperately trying to locate the leak. This gate was useless. Simply a receiving station, a two-way tunnel, that allowed anyone with the prerequisite clearance to jump between the TV studio and, presumably, somewhere in Riyadh. To be of any use to them, it had to be a sending gate attached to a monitor, so they could access both the jump coordinates and security.

The realisation hit her like a thunderbolt. She turned towards Katrina, her mind whirling with possibility.

Of course. Why hadn't she thought about it before?

'I know how we can get to Forsyth,' she said, her face flushed with excitement.

Transamerica Pyramid, San Francisco

8th May 2010, 10:06 hours PDT

Uma paused at the threshold of the conference room before entering. Katrina stayed in the corridor giving her time, recognising what Uma was about to face, but Uma couldn't move. It was as if some invisible barrier was holding her back. She felt powerless to push through it, despite her earlier confession. It was one thing to talk about her rape, but quite another to revisit the scene of the crime. She took her time, not fighting it, just standing, staring straight ahead, trying to control her breathing, which was coming in short ragged bursts. It made her feel lightheaded. She leaned against the doorjamb for support. Feeling something on her cheek, she realised with some surprise that she was crying. Hot, silent tears had appeared unbidden. Random senses surfaced like flotsam from a lost wreck: a forked flash of brilliance, the heavy rumble of thunder, her aching shoulder. But mainly, it was the laughter. A hard booming laugh, right from the belly of the beast. A sneering laugh, mocking her stupidity. Uma felt herself flush red as shame flooded her veins like caustic soda, dissolving her new-found dignity. She stood there, transfixed by the cruel sneer. An image of a hollow skull exploded across her retinas, its eyes flaming cobalt. It looked so real, her mind infusing it with a solidity it didn't deserve. As she sank to her knees, the Pacific sky parted for a second and bright light flooded the conference room, bathing Uma in warm sunshine. In that moment, the spell broke and Uma struggled to her feet, making a beeline for the wall-to-ceiling windows.

San Francisco bay glistened beneath her, its famous bridge arrowing across the Golden Gate straight into Marin County and beyond. The last time she had seen that view was the first time she'd slept with Forsyth. The memory threatened to topple her brittle resolve. She inhaled sharply, shifting her gaze into the bay, pausing at the rocky smudge of Alcatraz Penitentiary. She was too far away to see the prison buildings, but the sight transported her mind's eye to another fortress, this one in a sea of sand, its hot dusty buildings baking in one-hundred-degree heat. A room appeared, its walls climbing high to a domed roof through which the prison guards could taunt the prisoner below. He was strung up by his arms, face concealed beneath a black hood, but Uma knew who it was. As she reached down to him, the whole cell rushed upwards, and she found herself inches from his bloodied back, the torn flesh clearly visible. This time, she didn't collapse. This is why she was here. To save Ethan. Now she had the means to do it. Without a further glance, she strode purposely across the carpet, where she had laid less than four months earlier, and into the video conferencing suite.

Her feet crunched on broken glass as her eyes swept over the destruction they had wrought in their brief fight. Nothing had changed, but everything had changed: the collapsed bookshelf, hardbacks littering the floor, the smashed laptop. Behind it, the empty magnum, still embedded in the video screen like a macabre art installation. She could still picture Forsyth's bald pate raked by her nails, his temple dripping blood, his formerly preternatural eyes, now a dull blue. She followed the flat tune of his whistle into another room, staring at the

Eternity terminal, untouched since her revenge. Now all she saw was an old man, walking with a frame, his once handsome face ravaged by the loss of his silicone implants and Botox. Where his nose should have sat, a ragged hole bubbled bloody mucus. His lips hung like dry leather across toothless gums so that the lower half of his face carried the pinched look of a village elder, except around his cheeks and forehead. Here, the skin seemed too big for his skull, giving the impression that his entire visage had slipped two or three inches below where it should have been.

Katrina entered the room, her eyes meeting Uma's, whose smile widened further.

'This is how we fight Forsyth,' Uma said. 'This station should at least get us to Riyadh. If we're lucky, into the palace where Forsyth is holed up.'

She tapped the space bar, and the screen lit up.

'It looks like someone has been here recently.'

'What do you mean?' Uma dragged her eyes away from the screen and followed Katrina into another room – Forsyth's LEAP room – which looked almost identical to the one they had just left. Except on the desk there was evidence of a half-eaten meal.

'This is how they did it,' Uma said, her voice pinched high with excitement. 'This is how they broke into the system, introduced the virus and stole Ethan's code.'

'Why didn't you think of it earlier?'

'I couldn't,' Uma said, 'and no one else knew. I didn't tell anyone after Forsyth disappeared. No one has prosecuted him. Ingram won't touch him.'

She stared at the bottle of neat whiskey next to the plate.

Suddenly she was in a different room, staring at another balding head, but this one was bulbous, deep under eyes shadowing Professor Crouch's face like dark clouds which were framed by beetroot cheeks that had consumed way too much alcohol.

Uma picked up the bottle.

'And I know exactly who did it,' she said. 'Come on, we have a lot of work to do.'

Route 509, South of Riyadh

13th July 2010, 11:36 hours AST

The Range Rover was travelling along the dusty road at speed, a plume of dust billowing out from behind as its back tyres caught pockets of sand that had crept onto the empty four-lane highway leading out of Riyadh. The two men sitting up front were silent. Ed took a long swig from the litre bottle of water sitting in the middle compartment between him and the driver. Even with the air-con set to max, it felt humid in the cabin. He could already feel the cauldron of heat into which he would soon step. A cauldron in which he would get to exact his punishment for an hour. An hour that would whip by in a blur of blood and screams, leaving him anxious for the next week to pass. Ed traced the crosshatched leather of the bull whip handle in his lap before gripping it tightly. It felt solid, part of him. A second skin that delivered his judgement like an avenging serpent, keeping him satiated until the next opportunity. He glanced back into the passenger seat where his prisoner glared back at him. That's about all he could do as his arms were trussed tightly together by plastic ties which were secured to a metal chain around his waist. That itself was connected to a pair of metal shackles restraining his thighs and ankles. His face was partially obscured by a leather helmet they had fashioned to prevent the man from biting or headbutting them. In fact, as they had discovered, Ethan Rae had an endless supply of attacks he could deliver with his body at any moment. Over the past ten weeks, he had hospitalised four of the prison guards, which had now led them to this point.

Ed Fox settled back into the cushioned seat, staring out of the window. Sand disappeared away into the distance on either side of the Range Rover. He hated the place, but he hated Ethan Rae more. It was a fair trade. He spent his days organising Forsyth's security, waiting for his moment, and every seven days he would make the thirty-minute drive from Riyadh out to Al-Ha'ir Prison, where they picked up Ethan Rae and transported him back to The Acorn to restore his body from the previous week's whipping. Without it, he would die. Hell, he was half dead anyway when they collected him from the prison hospital. His wounds, left untreated, would quickly fester in the heat of the tiny room, and on more than one occasion, they had nearly lost him, but that was the point. Forsyth wanted Rae to suffer, and hell, he was succeeding in his wish. Crouch would restore the half-dead man, complete with full memories right up to the last second they put him through the chamber. In that way, Rae would never forget his pain. Piled up, week on week. Month on month. And eventually, year on year, as he received his punishment. That was fine by Ed. At least Rae got to come back every seven days, fully restored, like new. Unlike Jo and Angel. They were never coming back. They had, in fact, died, suffering excruciating pain as the car burned around them. It was only fitting that Rae got to experience his own pain and Ed was more than happy to deliver each flick of it for the next ten years.

The SUV slowed as it approached the main gates of the prison. Set on a sprawling complex off Route 509, twenty-five miles south of Riyadh, it may as well have been a thousand. No one could escape, but if they did, they wouldn't last a day in the surrounding desert. If the facilities didn't kill them first. Prisoners were piled in, five to a cell built for two. In fact, that was Ed's pervading memory of the place: sweat, shit and piss. An ugly odour overhanging the crumbling buildings, one that was complemented by rotting flesh when they collected Rae from his hospital bed.

The vehicle pulled up outside the punishment centre and Ed got out. The heat hit him like an angry fist. He quickly joined the four waiting guards under a plastic gazebo, which offered them scant protection from the midmorning sun. They were jumpy. With good reason. News had spread about the crazy-mad Englishman who fashioned deadly weapons out of body parts. They eyed the Range Rover warily as Ed's driver opened the passenger door and unclipped Rae, before yanking him out of the back seat onto the dusty road. He landed with a whoosh of winded breath as the guards abandoned the shade and systematically started lashing out with their short sticks. They had all decided weeks ago that a predictive strike was better than a beating. Remind the prisoner who was boss. Ed wasn't sure it worked, but it made the guards happier.

Two of the guards grabbed Rae's shoulders, dragging him towards the main doors where four others were waiting. Ed accompanied them to the central atrium, where he removed a small cine camera from his pocket. Forsyth insisted on it. He wanted proof that the beating had been delivered. Insisted on watching it, in fact, before a copy was sent to Rae's girlfriend. Every week. As a reminder of the living hell, her boyfriend now inhabited. At first Ed had worried about the Jakobsdóttir woman, worried that he wasn't carrying through on his promise to Jo and Angel, but this was better. She got to suffer, just like he was suffering. It was worse than death; a fitting punishment for her.

The four guards manhandled Rae towards two posts driven deep into the centre of the square. Resembling a miniature amphitheatre, it was ankle deep in sand soaked black by Rae's blood which was surrounded by covered seats, all of which were empty. Whilst two of the men held their prisoner securely by his shoulders, the others unlocked his arms from the waist chain and cut the wrist ties, before manhandling him between the posts where they forced his forearms into the manacles then snapped them shut. Everyone seemed to relax.

One of the guards removed Rae's hood, then the ankle shackles, before ripping his shirt away to reveal the smooth white flesh of his back.

Ed adjusted the focus and pressed the Rec button before handing the camera to a guard. Satisfied it was recording, Ed stepped into frame, talking quietly at the flashing red light.

'Week ten. We're 500 lashes in.'

Ed unfurled the bullwhip, making a beeline for his prisoner, the fifteen feet of leather trailing behind him like a sleeping snake. He took Rae's hair in his fist, pulling Ethan's head towards him.

'How does it feel?' he growled. 'You're one percent into your punishment. Just 25,500 lashes to go.'

Al-Ha'ir Prison, Saudi Arabia

13th July 2010, 11:55 hours AST

Ethan hung there, trying to locate the voice. Was it in his head? He'd done the maths a thousand times over. Knew the toll: fifty every week for the next 520 weeks. It was simple. He was good at maths. His teacher had told him so. What was his name? Mr McKenna. His bushy moustache always twitched with suppressed merriment when one of his classmates got a question right, but Mark was his favourite: mental maths, their friend. It promised certainty when life offered none and he recited the computation under his breath:

'520 weeks; 189,803 days, including the leap years,' he muttered. '4,555,272 hours, 273,316,32—'

The blow caught him on the ribs. An explosion of pain blossomed up his right side, burning everything in its path, including the voice. All he could hear now was someone screaming, a high-pitched wail that made his throat hoarse.

The voice returned.

'What the fuck are you talking about?' it said, as a pair of giant desert combat boots suddenly filled his vision. Ethan lifted his head, following the khaki trousers up to a camel-brown T-shirt. Broad chest, thick forearms, both tattooed. One said, 'JO' nestled inside a heart, the other, 'ANGEL' similarly framed. He couldn't crane his neck further, but the trousers suddenly bent at the knees and a face appeared. It looked familiar.

'You're not Mr McKenna,' Ethan said. 'Where is he? Are you the relief teacher?'

The thickset face frowned. It was handsome in a crumpled sort of way, framed by a black buzzcut that matched a four-day-old stubble. The man's skin was infected by a pasty white complexion, out of which dead eyes stared back at Ethan with a boiling rage.

'What have I done to you?' Ethan said, or had he thought that?

Either way, the face smiled, but it was humourless.

Ethan suddenly remembered where he'd seen him. Inside a burning building, smoke everywhere, those same dead eyes emerging from through the flames. He'd felt himself being lifted and then nothing.

'You tried to kill me,' Ethan acknowledged, wondering why he wasn't dead. Maybe he was. His wrists hurt. That was strange. Why didn't his back burn, or his leg ache, or his forearm? In fact, come to think of it, all the wrong things hurt: his chest was on fire, cheek bone similarly blazing, shoulder burning whilst his head just smouldered. He tipped his neck back, scrunching his eyes shut. That made no sense. Glasgow, at this time of year, was cold, the afternoons thick with heavy clouds, the arctic wind whistling in off the Clyde.

'Welcome to hell, Rae. You're never leaving this place.'

'My name's Mark. Mark Brown,' Ethan said, fully taking in his surroundings for the first time. The soldiers were standing in a small semicircle around the khaki giant, their dark faces flushed with spite; the hot sand beneath his feet was spattered with black mud; the empty seats were shaded beneath a ramshackle roof that gave way to a bottomless blue sky beneath a broiling sun.

'I want to go home.' His lower lip started to quiver. Ethan clenched his teeth together, trying to swallow the ache, but it was too late. A sniffle escaped as unwanted tears leaked down his cheeks which felt hot with embarrassment. A guard guffawed and pointed at Ethan, whose resistance evaporated. He wept, long baleful cries that echoed round the small enclosure, growing in size as rivulets of tears streaked his face.

'You do, do you?' the man said, his tone grim, eyes grimmer. 'Jo and Angel were on their way home when they were—' The words choked on his own cry, a roar of rage that momentarily paused Ethan's pitiful crying. '—burned alive,' he gasped, unfurling the whip. A gunshot cracked above Ethan who shrunk back into the restraints, his wail morphing into a scream. A soldier appeared, holding a small video camera that he brought up close to Ethan's face.

'Smile for the camera,' Khaki boots growled, cracking the bull-hide leather. 'It's for your girlfriend.'

Through his tears, a distant memory tugged at Ethan. He didn't have a girlfriend. Wait a second, he thought. He remembered being in a pool with a woman. A real stunner. Way out of his league. Thick black hair. Petite. She was nuzzled close to him, her face inches from his. God, she was beautiful, he thought. The kiss felt so natural, their lips melting together. What was her name?

'Uma,' he mouthed. 'Uma,' he said louder, a surge of longing overwhelming his senses. 'Can I see her?' he asked hopefully.

The giant bent down, bringing his face close to Ethan's, hands grasping his cheeks.

'You'll never see her again.'

'Who's Jo?' Ethan said, staring at the black ink on the man's forearm.

The giant paused, confusion crowding his eyes.

'What did you say?' he whispered, bringing his lips close to Ethan's ear. 'Never say her name again.'

That's where he had seen him, Ethan thought. In a room, soldiers everywhere, a handsome man in the corner, grinning like a maniac. Batons were flying, crumpling into someone's face, screams of pain. Suddenly, the giant was in front of him. It was Forsyth he was protecting. He was in a TV Studio, Uma beside him, the next second crumpling forward, something protruding from the back of her neck. Poor, beautiful Uma, lying dead in his arms. He started sobbing again, but through his tears, he knew the man was talking to him.

'—gets a weekly tape to remind her who's in charge.'

Was he talking about Uma? She was alive. His heart lifted. She was alive. The whip cracked like an electric cable. Ethan shrank back, his back blossoming in a bouquet of referred pain.

'In fact, I might take it to her this time. Make sure she watches it. Or maybe I'll just kill her.'

'You're a dead man,' Ethan roared, straining against the chains, but the man just laughed at him, aiming a kick at Ethan's midriff, catching him just below his rib cage. Ethan felt the air suck out of his lungs. He collapsed back, the chains taking his full weight. For a moment he could only hang there, struggling to breathe, black specks pinging across his vision. Gradually the pain cleared. It was as if a cloud had lifted. His recent memory was restored: his tormentor was no longer a stranger, Uma was alive but in pain, Forsyth's taunt was ringing in his ears.

He had to get out of here and he knew when he could escape – the moment Crouch put him through the transporter. When he stepped out, he was whole, fully recovered, his body strong, mind clear, but every time he stepped out, there were ten guards plus the Khaki giant they called Fox, waiting for him. They gave him no chance, trussing him up like a turkey for Christmas, but there had to be a way. It was his only hope. Otherwise ... He blinked in the heat. How could he survive the next ten years of this? He would go mad. Caught in an endless cycle of pain and suffering with an hour's respite each week when they restored his mutilated body.

A movement in front of Ethan drew his focus back to the amphitheatre. Fox had rewound the whip. It was now curled in his right hand. Ethan tensed his body as Fox disappeared out of sight behind him.

Suddenly, the first crack of fifty shattered the afternoon sky.

Route 509, Riyadh, Saudi Arabia

13th July 2010, 13:08 hours AST

E d slumped in his seat, half dozing, as the Range Rover roared north along Route 509 into the outskirts of the city. Outside, single-storey low rises sat forlornly in neat rows, as if crushed into the hot earth by the relentless sun burning overhead, their brick burned to the same colour as the desert. Despite the air con, every pore in his body oozed heat and dust, just like everything in this godforsaken country. He hated it all, but so long as Rae was here, he would stay. It was a small price to pay for the revenge he got to exact each week, but once it was over, the next seven days stretched out in front of him like the Najd plateau surrounding Riyadh. His only companion – nightmare inducing memories of his dead wife and daughter. He sighed heavily, studying the camera in his blood-spattered hands, wondering how Rae's girlfriend would react. Worse still, wondering whether she would even watch it. He wouldn't, if it was his wife. Scratch that, he had no choice. His dreams were infected with ferocious petrol fires and screams, but if the Jakobsdóttir woman didn't watch, what was the point of sending it? Maybe he needed to accompany the camera each week, just to make sure. He would take it up with Forsyth when he got back to The Acorn, but first, he had to deal with the TV crew from the States. As head of Forsyth's security, he had very little to do, but one of the few jobs was to vet anyone who came into contact with the great man. Nothing and no one came onto Forsyth's floor without Ed's say so. Today, it was that reporter from the Daily Event, back for more interviews. He was amazed that she had even turned up. He'd heard the rumours about what Forsyth had done to her, and cringed. Women were meant to be respected, better still, honoured, just like he had with Jo during the fifteen happiest years of his life. And more latterly with Angel. He'd wanted to be a role model to her across everything: life, love and loss. The realisation that he would never see her enjoy a first date or go to college crushed the blood from his heart, hardening it even further. Forsyth could do what he wanted to his women, so long as he let Ed avenge his own.

The American producer and his convoy of trucks were already waiting as they pulled up outside the enormous gates ringing The Acorn. As Ed got out, two members of the Royal Guard Regiment emerged from the gate house in full battle dress, hidden black shaded sunglasses, their snubnosed Heckler & Koch HK33s lending them a menacing look. But Ed knew differently. Just like the Afghans, it was all show. Drop them in a fight and they folded, just like Forsyth had discovered with Rae. He nodded at the three men.

'What is it this time?'

'Another documentary,' Nick Lovell said, eyeing first the guards and then Ed's blood-spattered tunic warily. 'We're here for ten days, hence all the kit.' His eyes flicked over the three trucks.

'Why didn't you teleport them?' Ed said. 'It would have saved a lot of time.'

'American companies can only use LEAP, which is banned here, so we had to do it the old-fashioned way. By plane into King Khalid.'

'Where are you setting up?'

'Same place as last time, except we've brought a video-editing suite. The plan is to shoot the footage in the morning, then edit it here, before sending the finished reel back to the States in time for the morning show. We'll set that up in Ms Hoskins' quarters, if that's OK?'

Ed shrugged. He didn't care where they set up.

'Fine. Let's do it. Show me what you've got.'

Ten more soldiers appeared with an assortment of scanners. They disappeared into the trucks with some of Nick's team, whilst he waited in the guardhouse with Ed, who didn't engage with him. Ed couldn't get Uma out of his head: that she was avoiding the pain of seeing her boyfriend flogged half to death. Why hadn't he thought of it earlier? This place had dulled his brain. One of the Guard Regiment entered with a query about the last truck, which contained equipment that had not been on the previous manifest. He insisted Ed inspect the equipment, despite Nick's protestations.

'What did you say it was?' Ed asked, lifting one of the panels in the rear of the containers.

'I've already told you,' Nick replied. He was sweating heavily in the afternoon heat and his cotton suit was soaked through. 'It's a mobile post-production suite to edit footage from the multiple sites we'll be shooting across. We assemble those panels into a small room, complete with all the equipment, so we can work on the footage, visual effects, soundtrack, audio, everything. Do you need to see it?'

'Nah, that's fine.' Ed was already wondering if he could catch Forsyth before he disappeared for the evening. 'But we need to do the security checks on your team.'

'Again!' Nick exclaimed. 'It's the same personnel as last time. And we were vetted at the airport for over an hour.'

'Hey, not my rules,' Ed said. Actually, they were his rules, but Lovell didn't need to know. 'Once we've finished, take the trucks through to the service elevators. These two will show you.' He nodded at the soldiers, who stared back impassively. 'The maintenance crews will take the equipment up to the Oak Suite. We can inspect everything there.'

'We need two of my men to accompany them. Last time they broke a camera lens. Cost, twelve thousand dollars.'

'No one's allowed back there. Visitors can only access designated areas,' Ed said. Another of his rules. He didn't want unauthorised personnel wandering around the Palace.

Nick folded his arms.

'Sorry, I have strict instructions not to let the Saudis unpack our equipment again, unless you want to pay for any breakages.'

Ed shrugged. He was now desperate to catch Forsyth. The thought that she wasn't watching the videos bored into his head like a wood beetle.

'Fine, let's do the clearance now. I'll escort them upstairs with the equipment.'

Ed returned to the Range Rover and pulled the team manifest. There were six names on it. He returned to Lovell, who had been joined by his team. Each man handed their passport to him. He did a quick check. Everything looked in order.

'Where's Ms Hoskins?'

'Forsyth took her straight up to her room.'

I bet he did, thought Ed, but didn't press the issue. At least he knew where Forsyth was.

'Our men will drive the trucks. Your team can cram into the Range Rover unless you want to walk with these two.' He nodded at the soldiers. All six Americans bee-lined for the SUV and the gates cracked open, allowing the convoy to pull forward. It was like stepping through a portal into another world: lush green lawns stretched away on either side of a four-lane drive, along which were planted hundreds of Phoenix palm trees, their scaly trunks loping fifty feet up into the humid afternoon. As they crested the brow of a low hill, the Crown's Prince's kingdom within a kingdom appeared, shimmering like a desert mirage in the valley below. The Acorn shone in the centre. Steep steps climbed up to its capule, planted like an inverted cup inside a polygonal redoubt and covered with rough wooden scutes that supported the shiny glass pericarp. It rose, oval-like, six hundred feet above the complex, before tapering off into a gleaming observation deck.

The four vehicles wound down into the natural hollow, following a main avenue that was bridged by pairs of inverted scimitars. They towered over the vehicles, their blades crossing overhead, before splaying outwards on either side of the broad road. The convoy swung around the base of the Acorn, disappearing down a service tunnel cut into the redoubt, eventually drawing to a halt in a subterranean garage beside a huge elevator. Workers appeared from nowhere, unhitching each container, before swarming inside and emptying the equipment into the elevator. Everyone crowded inside. The lifts lurched upwards at a snail's pace, the bulk of the equipment being emptied on the second level, before they continued upwards to Forsyth's floor.

The procession wound its way silently to Katrina's quarters, and Ed rang the bell. Within seconds the door was opened by Katrina Hoskins. She looked hot beneath the pale brown hijab covering her head. Ed could have sworn she'd been crying. Nick stepped forward into the apartment, followed by the equipment.

'Where do you want this setting up?' he said.

'Through there, please,' Katrina said, pointing towards a large conference room, before turning towards Ed.

'What can I do for you, Mr Fox?'

'I understand Mr Forsyth is here. I need to give him something,' he said, fingering the camera.

She glanced down at his bloody hands and stiffened.

'He's just stepped away.'

'OK. Do you know where he's gone?'

'No, but he said he'll be back in the next fifteen minutes. We need to finish planning the next week.'

I bet you do, Ed thought, noticing the red mark on her wrist. Katrina caught his gaze and hurriedly pulled her sleeve down.

'You're welcome to wait. I'm just in here, preparing some lunch.'

He followed her through into the ridiculously large kitchen which would have served a small restaurant. There were signs of a recent scuffle – broken glass was scattered across the tiles along with fruit from the bowl. An upturned vase lay on the island unit, long blooms lying forlornly in the spilt water.

She started to gather up the stems.

'Here, let me help you with that,' he said, placing the camera on the central counter before crouching down and picking up the fruit.

'That's OK,' she said, but Ed ignored her, sweeping both fruit and glass up before crashing everything into a bin.

An uneasy silence settled in the kitchen as Katrina finished collecting the stems before wiping the counter down. Finally, they both stood on opposite sides of the island unit, arms folded, staring at the camera.

'Do you miss your family?' Katrina suddenly said. 'I miss my boyfriend on these trips. Terribly.' She subconsciously rubbed her forearm, her eyes misting over.

Ed just stood there, unable to answer, paralysed by the mention of his wife and daughter.

Katrina nodded at his forearms, mistaking his silence for annoyance at her directness.

'Sorry, I didn't mean to pry. It's the reporter in me.'

Ed looked down at the blood-spattered tattoos. He walked to the sink and ran the hot water tap over them. The woman unsettled him, so much so, that he debated whether to leave and speak to Forsyth later.

'When did you say Mr Forsyth would be here?' he said, turning to face Katrina as he dried his hands.

Before Katrina could answer, Nick entered the kitchen.

'All done,' he said. 'I'm going to unpack and maybe we can meet in ...' he glanced at his watch, '... an hour to discuss the schedule over the next ten days.'

Katrina nodded. Suddenly she was alone again with Ed, a heavy silence filling the vacuum left by Nick's conversation.

'What's on the camera?' she tried again.

Ed stared at her.

'You really don't want to know.'

'Try me,' she said, her tone spiky with indignation. 'It's literally my job.'

Ed grabbed the camera, turning to leave, but Katrina sprang forward, her tone slightly hysterical.

'Why do you work for Forsyth?'

Ed stopped and turned.

'You're working for him.'

'No, I'm not. I work for the Daily Event.'

'Are you sure about that?' Ed said, glaring at the lilies on the countertop. Katrina flushed red before shooting back.

'Is it something to do with Jo and Angel?'

The words exploded in Ed's head like detonating mines.

'You know nothing about me,' he bellowed, launching himself across the island unit, but she was too quick, sprinting out of the kitchen and down the hall into the conference room. Ed followed, propelled by a primeval urge that he only ever felt on the battlefield. His eyes were drawn to a silvery capsule that had been erected in the corner of the room. It must have been twenty feet in length and was accessed at one end by three steps leading up to a doorway in which Katrina suddenly appeared.

'Did Forsyth fuck them as well? Is that why you're here? Torturing that poor man?' she taunted him, before disappearing into the editing suite.

Ed roared and sprinted across the conference room, taking the steps in one leap. He could see her sat at the desk, grinning. He lunged through the doorway, but as he did so, he disappeared.

Transamerica Pyramid, San Francisco

13th July 2010, 03:53 hours PDT

When Ed came to, he was in darkness, his whole body aching. He sat there for several seconds, trying to clear his head. Gradually, flashes of memory sparked across his synapses: that blond bitch taunting him about Jo and Angel; a surging anger; chasing her into the conference room; leaping up the steps; suddenly finding himself in another room; moving so fast he lost his footing, crashing into ... Everything went hazy again, the gloom enveloping him. He tried to stand, but could barely move. There were bindings on his feet, his wrists secured with plastic, and his chest and thighs restrained by something – rope, maybe. It came to him in a flash: the room was tiny. No window. A computer screen against one wall. A metal table right in front of him. That's what he'd smashed into. Movement to his right. Black hair. Long and curly. A searing pain across his right arm, blossoming out, like all the best pain, across his chest and back. He knew that pain. Had trained for it. He'd been tasered. Not once, but twice. No wonder he ached. Inky blackness faded as his eyes registered a thin strip of light in front of him, low down. Another light, this one blinking red above his head. A dull green glow to his right, enough to make out dark shapes. He was still in the same room. Why would that reporter want to kidnap him? For what Forsyth had done to her? Why not take Forsyth? What use was he? Ed heard voices, a key turning in a lock, a blaze of light searing his vision, whispered conversation, both female. He opened his eyes.

The Jakobsdóttir woman and Katrina Hoskins were sitting across from him, separated by the metal table he must have crashed into. Both looked tired, especially Rae's girlfriend, her face pale, dark shadows ringing swollen eyes, which kept flickering to the camera sitting between them like an alien artefact. A smile flickered across his lips: she had watched it. But the small victory felt hollow, despite the knowledge that it had achieved his purpose, and he realised it was no longer enough. It felt strange to be so close to the other person responsible for Jo and Angel's absence. She was smaller than he remembered. Ed felt the familiar surge of rage that had driven him to this point. He glanced down, testing the restraints. Plastic. Their second mistake. The first was the tabletop concealing his wrists. Ed flexed his arms, feeling them give slightly. He could stretch, weaken the ties. Two minutes max. For now, he needed to buy time.

'What am I doing here?' he asked, looking back and forth at the two women, but neither could hold his gaze, their eyes fixed on the camera in front of them. Eventually, Uma spoke.

'I ... I ...' she tried haltingly, but whatever she wanted to say couldn't be said. Katrina shifted uneasily in her seat and Uma tried again, this time in a rush of words, barely a whisper.

'I want to apologise for the pain I've caused you.'

It sounded hollow to Ed. Worse still, insincere.

How did they know, he thought? He'd told no one. Forsyth had guessed, but that was after a conversation with Ed. He glanced at Katrina, remembering what she'd said in the kitchen. Had his secret spilled out during one of her moments with Forsyth?

'It's a bit late for that,' he spat back, working the ties, repeatedly clasping his hands together, then pulling his palms apart, before collapsing them. Generating heat. It would soften the plastic.

'I never intended for it to happen. I created the LEAP Laws for a different reaso—'

'You're a goddamn hypocrite,' he cut in. 'One rule for you and your boyfriend, whilst the rest of us had no choice. No say in who got to live or die.'

'You were in the carbon programme?' she said, without waiting for his answer. 'That wasn't my idea, you know. To restore all those soldiers.'

'So, you would rather have us die as well, whilst you got to restore each other?'

'No, that's not what I meant,' Uma said. She looked close to tears, Ed noted with some satisfaction. He could feel the plastic heating up. Wouldn't be long now.

'What she means ... meant to say is,' Katrina continued, 'that had the army not interfered in your life with its restoration programme, you wouldn't have been around when Jo and Angel died. Wouldn't have had to suffer through their deaths.'

Ed stared at her incredulously.

'Please don't say their names,' he whispered, his voice dropping so low, they both had to lean forward. 'There's nothing you can do to bring them back, but I will make you pay for my pain.'

The Jakobsdóttir woman glanced at the bloodstained camera between them.

'Hard, isn't it? To see your loved one suffer, unable to do a goddamn thing about it.' He choked on the final few words, his anger rising. It gave him strength and he could feel the ties stretch.

'Please stop,' Uma said, tears spilling down her face. 'I am truly sorry for what you've gone through. I would do anything to make it right.'

'Would you?' he screamed at her, leaning forward and flexing his shoulders. 'Just like you did with the victims of the LEAP virus?'

Uma started to sob.

'Thought not,' he said.

An uneasy silence descended on the room. Uma and Katrina continuing to stare at the camera. Ed summoned every ounce of strength to break the restraints.

'Why am I really here? You didn't go to all this trouble to make an apology.'

'You're right, we didn't,' Katrina said. 'We want to rescue Ethan from the hell he's in.'

'Rae is never leaving that place,' Ed snarled. With a roar, he pulled his hands apart and the ties snapped. He stood up with such force that the chair spindles along the back snapped in two. In a flash, he grabbed the table with both hands, lifting it high above his head. Katrina screamed, falling backwards and scrabbling away, but Uma seemed to freeze, looking up at the heavily muscled man, waiting for the table to fall.

Suddenly, the door to the small office was flung open and a man entered. In one stride, he was standing protectively behind Uma.

Ed paused, staring at him in confusion, and at the gun pointing at his chest.

That wasn't possible, he thought.

'Put the table down, Ed,' a voice thundered, his ears confirming what his eyes refused to accept. Without hesitation, he brought the table down hard towards Uma's head.

An explosion rocked the room. Ed's head whip-lashed back. His legs buckled, and he crashed to the floor. Uma scrabbled forward, but she already knew he was dead.

'What have you done?' she screamed, looking back at the man, who straightened and shrugged. But all Uma could see were two words engraved in black ink on his forearms.

"Jo" and "Angel".

Transamerica Pyramid, San Francisco

13th July 2010, 04:02 hours PDT

Eddies of smoke hung like early morning mist over Fox, who hadn't moved, a helmet of blood broadcasting that he never would. Katrina was slumped in the corner of the room, face in hands, weeping softly. Behind her, a large figure was leaning against the door frame, also unmoving, but head intact. Uma looked down at Ed Fox, his face frozen in a slap of shock. The bullet had bulls-eyed his forehead, killing him instantly. Now her carefully laid plans – ten long weeks in the making – were also lying motionless on the floor of the office. It wasn't meant to happen like this.

'Why did you kill him?' she said, already knowing the answer.

The figure by the door shrugged.

'He was going to kill you. What choice did I have?'

'You could have just wounded him.'

'My – his – training just kicked in. It was a split-second decision when I entered the office. He was standing over you with the table. There was no time to think. It was simply self-preservation. Him or you.'

Uma nodded. That was precisely why they'd chosen this man. He was an expert in everything they needed to rescue Ethan. She felt surprisingly calm and clear-headed, as if the last seven years had prepared her for this moment. For all the ugliness and the deaths that had followed her decision to release LEAP into the world. For all the fights and the pressure that she had withstood to keep the LEAP Laws intact, but which had been slowly, inexorably taken from her, along with Ethan. So that now, in this moment, after deciding to breach the Laws herself, she was prepared for the consequences of that decision. It had come sooner than she expected, but nevertheless, she felt prepared.

'We've murdered someone,' Katrina said suddenly, her voice slightly hysterical. She stood up and started pacing. 'What have we done?' She turned on Uma. 'Why did I let you talk me into this? We're finished before we've started.'

'He deserved to die,' the man said. 'Did you see what he did to Ethan?'

'Of course I did,' Katrina snarled, turning on him. 'I was there, remember, commentating on it.'

'Well, I did it,' he replied, advancing across the room and towering over her. 'I've whipped him five hundred times. I remember everything.' He sank to his knees and started to cry, arms wrapped around his chest, rocking backwards and forward, his whole body shaking uncontrollably. 'What have I done?' he wept.

Open-mouthed, the two women watched the giant cry. Eventually, Uma placed a hand on his shoulder.

'We talked about this, remember?' she said, taking the man's face in her hands, lifting it towards her own. The eyes of a killer stared back at her. The man who had whipped Ethan to within an inch of his life. She didn't know whether to strangle him or hug him.

'I know,' the man sniffled. 'I didn't expect this ... this pain. I can remember every single stroke. As if I'd done it.'

Uma hugged him tightly.

'We can always reverse this, you know,' she said, releasing him. 'Restore Fox from his last LEAP when we brought him over. Send him back to Saudi. He won't remember any of this. Neither will you. We could stop it now.'

'No,' the man said suddenly, standing up and wiping his tears away. 'If we don't do it now, we'll never rescue Ethan.'

'Don't we need to report this to the police?' Katrina said dumbly, nodding at the dead body.

'We can't,' the man said, shaking his head.

'But we've killed someone.'

'It was self-defence,' he said.

'And how do you explain ... you?' Katrina said, nodding at him.

'We don't,' Uma said.

'Don't what?' Katrina said.

'Do either,' Uma said. 'Tell the police or explain Ed.'

'But we can't undo this.'

'Of course we can,' Uma and the man said in unison. Uma couldn't help but smile. They'd done it repeatedly. They'd restored their father. They'd restored Ethan after the coma.

'No, I mean, I can't unsee this.' Katrina nodded at the body on the floor of the office. 'I won't forget it.'

'We can wipe your memories if that would help,' the man said. 'From your last LEAP. You'll be none the wiser.'

Katrina stared at him.

'You can do that?'

He nodded, a half smile on his face.

'Why do you think we fought so hard to keep the LEAP Laws for so long? This is going to get fucked up pretty quickly once those restraints are removed.'

'I'm not sure I want that,' Katrina said, before adding, 'but maybe it would be good. I've just witnessed a murder. I'll have to live with that, knowing I was party to it.'

'It was self-defence,' Ed repeated, his tone hardening. 'He was just about to kill me ... you.' He nodded at Uma.

'Either way, it's messed up.' Katrina started to cry again.

Uma squeezed Katrina's shoulder. This was tough for her. Uma had been dealing with LEAP for decades; Katrina less than an hour. She had already experienced a lifetime of unintended consequences. She remembered when Ethan had been entangled with Anderson. Later, she had reinstated him after he had been strangled by Grond. Poor dear Ethan, now languishing in a Saudi jail somewhere, on a seven-day carousel of punishment that would eventually drive him insane.

'Remember why we're doing this. It's to save Ethan.'

'I know,' Katrina sniffled. 'I just never expected this to happen.'

Uma nodded. She had, but just not so soon.

'Guys, this is all well and good, but I need to go.' Ed stepped forward, recovering the camera from the floor of the office. 'I've already been gone nearly an hour. If I don't get back soon, all of this will have been for nothing.'

He's ... I'm right, Uma thought. They needed to hurry if they wanted to make this work. If Katrina continued down this line of thinking, well ... She shut the thought down quickly, as the abyss of what she'd started opened up in front of her.

'How do we get rid of the body?' Katrina said, wiping her eyes.

Uma exchanged glances with Ed. They'd done this before. She remembered the fight as if it had just happened, the outcome the same. Except, on that occasion, it had been her sister lying there in a pool of blood, half her neck blown away. Reynolds had sat there, feigning care, eventually posing the same questions Katrina had just asked.

'We can put him back through the scanner,' Ed said.

'You can do that?' Katrina said.

'Yes, we've done it before. A long time ago.'

He turned to Katrina, taking her hands gently in his.

'Once this is over, as we agreed, we'll restore Ed Fox, wipe his memories back to the LEAP he made following you. He'll be alive and none the wiser. Ethan will be safe.'

Katrina nodded, processing the information.

'It'll be as if none of this had ever happened,' she said, looking more reassured. A tight smile formed on her mascara-smeared face. Uma didn't have the heart to tell Katrina that the memories never went, that she still carried the scars of Fredrik's death, Eva's death, the four thousand that had been flayed alive. Ed Fox's family. All of them. As if she had lined everyone up and pulled the trigger herself. This was all happening because of LEAP, but it was too late now. She had crossed the Rubicon. This time, there was no going back.

The Acorn, Riyadh, Saudi Arabia

14th July 2010, 06:30 hours AST

Uma wrenched herself up, arms flailing, heart pounding, trying to locate the incessant beeping that had torn her from an uneasy sleep and now bored into her skull like a possessed drill. A ghoulish glow to her right broadcast 6:30 and she smashed a fist down on the clock. The noise stopped abruptly. Uma collapsed into the pillows, lying there, staring into the blackness, an overwhelming sadness crushing down on her. She suppressed a sob, as a memory she had no memory of surfaced through the cloying darkness: a woman, sitting on a sofa surrounded by cushions, holding a fistful of cards, laughing, her eyes sparkling with life. Next to her, a young girl, maybe ten with long blond hair matching her mum's, was giggling and wagging a finger at … him – Ed, her father. Uma gasped: Jo and Angel. She missed them so much. It was a crushing sense of finality to match the day when she had visited Ethan in the hospital, lying there, sprouting tubes from his throat and mouth. Except it was worse, far worse. She had brought Ethan back; Jo and Angel were never coming back. The finality of their deaths stretched out before her into old age and beyond. She had killed them, or as good as. Self-loathing joined the desolation of his loss. She lay there trying to process what she had done. Another memory: Angel was running towards him, hair streaming in the afternoon sunlight, a paper fluttering in one hand. Uma felt Angel's arms around her neck, soft hair tickling her cheek as Angel excitedly pulled away, showing Uma the picture ... of him, Jo and Angel at the beach. Uma felt herself smile at the memory, a soft glow, warming her insides like hot chocolate on a cold winter's afternoon. She groaned, the realisation smashing into her like a breaking wave: her baby. What had she done? Uma curled up into a tight ball, cradling her belly, and cried. For Jo. For Angel. For her dead child.

When she awoke, Uma lay there for several minutes, gathering her strength to push through the blackness that had resettled over her like an old friend. She knew what was happening, but it was hard to fight the suffocation of Ed Fox's desolation. It infused every pore of his body. For the hundredth time since she had run the programme that fused her brain into his head, she questioned the decision. So far, nothing had gone right, from the moment she had been forced to kill Ed to save herself, and now this. She hadn't expected it to work seamlessly. Separating out his brain functions that she needed from those that weren't necessary had been fiendishly difficult, despite her experience of repairing her father's resetting memory. She'd left brain-stem function alone. That controlled his sense of balance, reflexes, breathing, digestion. The same with his parietal lobe function, including senses, spatial and visual perception, reading and writing ability. Again, it all was necessary for her plan to work. It was the frontal and temporal lobe workings that had proved trickier. She'd pretty much kept her frontal lobe intact, including problem solving abilities, personality, her emotional traits and judgement. The temporal lobe had proved more difficult, particularly his memories. She needed access to his longer-term memory to ensure she knew everything about The Acorn, his schedule, who he knew and, of course, where Ethan was being held. It was all contained in his hippocampus, located in the temporal lobe and fairly easy to isolate using the quantum computing power of LEAP, but – and it was a colossal but – she didn't have a clue about Ed Fox's individual memories. That would have taken too long, way longer than the ten-week deadline she had given herself, during which Ethan had suffered 500 more lashes. She couldn't delay any longer. So, everything had come across, hence, what she was experiencing. God knows what it was doing to his mind. It was both foolhardy and dangerous, but what choice did she have? Every avenue had been blocked off. She needed to rescue Ethan.

The thought propelled her out of bed. She stood, swaying dangerously, wondering where to go. The answer arrived a millisecond later. It was a weird sensation, as if her brain was on a slight delay as it searched out a new set of instructions. She flipped a light switch and the room came to life in a soft glow of yellows and oranges. It both looked familiar and new, like déjà vu. It was like she had been here before yet had never pulled back the luxurious red curtains or trod the carpet or entered a mirrored bathroom with a shower the size of her entire bathroom in DC. She stood there staring at her reflection, momentarily too shocked to move.

Ed Fox stared back, his eyes framed with dark circles. She rubbed her chin self-consciously, recoiling slightly at the sandpapery roughness before tracing the outline of his hard chest muscle, and marvelling at the size of his biceps. She held up his hand, turning it slowly. It felt detached from her body, as if she was wearing 3D glasses and inspecting a giant avatar's hand. It was big, like a slab of concrete, nails bitten to the cuticle, hairy fingers, and a scar on his right palm that ran to his wrist, where "Angel" lurked like a dark spirit, fuelling the emptiness in his heart. She flexed her biceps again. She'd never been this strong. It felt good to have such physical strength. Her eyes wandered down his chest, past his ripped abs to his manhood, proudly erect in the soft glow of the bathroom. He – she – was massive. She stroked it and felt her buttocks tense as tendrils of pleasure feathered up her glutes and lower back. A groan escaped his lips. She grasped it more tightly, rubbing her hand faster and faster, up and down his penis, until, with a grunt of pleasure, she ejaculated into the basin. Uma gasped with surprise, as black dots pinged across her vision. She sat down heavily on the toilet, completely misjudging the distance. Fox was six two; she was five two. Those twelve inches were playing havoc with her distance perception. Her brain simply couldn't handle the change. It thought it was in a tiny petite body weighing in at barely fifty kilos, not in some hulking body builder.

Her vision cleared. She stood up, noisily urinating into the basin, marvelling at the tidiness of it all. Just a quick shake and she was good to go. She switched on the shower and stepped in, the hot jets washing away the indecision she had felt earlier, along with some of the blackness. She could control that, she realised. After towelling down, she wandered back into the bedroom, opening the drawer containing his gym kit. Her brain was already speeding up, as if assimilating the additional memory into her own. She finished dressing. Next stop: the kitchen. It was the same layout as Katrina's. She realised with a wry smile that it was exclusively Fox's memory that she was unconsciously accessing. Boy, Katrina had laid her trap well, taunting him with her reporter's precision. Uma found herself bristling at the intrusion of her questions about Jo and Angel. Worse than that, she was beginning to boil with anger and suddenly found herself raging against the reporter as she remembered chasing Katrina into the conference room. She was acutely aware that if Fox had got hold of her, Katrina would have died, just as she would have done when he stood over her – Uma – with the table. That anger coursed through her veins like liquid hate. Uma gasped at the sudden realisation that Fox hated Uma – both of them: the other Uma in San Francisco and herself – in equal measure, for what she – they – had done to Angel and Jo.

Uma opened the fridge, selecting a Tupperware marked "Monday 14.7 breakfast". She didn't remember making it. Presumably one of the chefs must have prepared it earlier. She grabbed a spoon and wandered into the living room, sitting down at the large dining table. It could have seated twenty people. Again, that wave of emptiness gnawed at her insides like a rabid dog, consuming any vestige of contentment that she had generated in the bathroom. Uma spooned at the cold meal, feeling both nauseous and hungry, before trying some. It was cold porridge, topped with blueberries, raspberries and crushed nuts, which presumably Fox's body craved, because she wolfed it down. As she returned to the kitchen for more, a loud buzzing diverted her stride towards the front door. She glanced at his watch. 'Damn,' she muttered. Fox was due to meet some members of the security team at nine for a sparring session in the gym. He – she – was late. It must be them. As Uma approached the door to his apartment, she stopped dead, unable to continue, her eyes fixated on a familiar object resting on a low table. She must have stood there a full thirty seconds before grasping the thick leather handle. It felt solid and reassuring, but conflicting sensations exploded across her limbs: Ed's joy as the whip head bit deep, lancing the boil that contained the poison of his hatred for Ethan and herself for taking Jo and Angel from him. With revulsion, she realised she was now both the architect of Ethan's predicament and the deliverer of his punishment, each strike of the bullwhip, a fitting damnation for her selfishness in weaponising Ethan to get back at Forsyth.

The doorbell rang again, followed closely by loud knocks. Uma dropped the whip as if it was a hot coal. She immediately felt better, as if the absence of touch somehow muted the memory, removing its power. The pause allowed her to think more clearly. This was why she was here – to put a stop to this. She had to stay focused. If she didn't, Ed Fox would not make it through the week and all this would have been for nothing. Ethan would remain stuck here, experiencing that pain every seven days. Feeling more centred, Uma took a deep breath and opened the door to Ed Fox's apartment.

Three men were standing there. She recognised them immediately: Silva, Harris and Petty, all mercenaries that were here when Fox had arrived at The Acorn. Two smiled in welcome, but the third, Petty, scowled at Uma. A flash of memories, feelings and encounters scudded through her mind: Petty had wanted Fox's job as head of security. He disliked all Americans. No, it was worse. He hated Americans. Silva had told him the story after a training session: Petty's unit had been hit by friendly fire in Helmand Province. A US Air Force F-15 Eagle had mistakenly struck their position during a firefight with Taliban fighters. Three of his buddies had died instantly, and Petty was given a medical discharge for PTSD, ending up in Saudi selling his services to

Forsyth. Uma scowled back, suppressing an overwhelming urge to hit him.

'Ready, boss?' Silva said.

'After you guys,' Uma said, momentarily stunned by her deep gravelly bass, ripped hoarse by Fox's cigarettes, but no one gave her a second glance. They travelled in silence to the floor beneath where the wellness centre was located. Katrina had described The Acorn in detail, plus Uma had Fox's memories to draw on, but seeing it in person was a whole different experience. The deserted gym was no different. Aside from the gleaming arrays of space-age equipment which looked like instruments of torture, there was a boxing square, grappling cage, fifty-metre pool, hot and cold plunge baths, spas and saunas galore. They made their way over to some shiny bikes with arm handles that moved in tandem with the pedals. The three men adjusted their seats before hopping on, and Uma followed suit. For the next twenty minutes, she peddled as fast as she had at any moment in her life, but was pleasantly surprised at how effortless it felt. Despite his smoking, Fox was clearly a fit man. Eventually, Petty alighted, making his way over to one of the weight machines, where he adjusted a pin in the stack of metal, before lying horizontally on a backrest. Above him were two hand grips attached to two bars protruding out of the main column. He adjusted himself and grabbed the handles before pushing the bar upwards, not once, but five times in quick succession, grunting with the effort. Uma, who had never been in a gym in her life, looked on with interest.

Petty finished his set, nodding at Uma.

'Beat that,' he grunted.

'Is that all you've got?' she said, before even realising it. Without thinking, Uma removed the pin, reinserting it across the weight marked 200 kilos. She looked over at Petty and winked, smiling when he responded with a scowl.

How was she expected to lift that? Uma thought. It was fifty percent over her own body weight, but Fox seemed to know what he was doing. It felt like an out-of-body experience as she felt him lie down, pulling his shoulder blades together and arching his back. He gripped the bar slightly wider than his shoulder width and inhaled before pushing the bar up to his full arm extension, exhaling at the same time. He held it for a moment, then lowered it back down towards his chest, before repeating the movement. Five times in total. Uma sat up, glancing at Petty, who dropped his eyes. Fox was a beast. She couldn't help smiling at the power in her limbs. It felt good. People would think twice before pushing her around again.

As the quartet completed their routines, they moved through more machines which seemed to exercise specific muscle groups. Each time, Fox knew exactly what to do. Each time he bettered Petty, who seemed to get more and more wound up, but could do nothing about it. As they finally completed their sets, Petty addressed Uma for the first time.

'I saw you with that American reporter yesterday. Trying to muscle in on Forsyth's action, are you?'

The other two smirked at each other.

Uma answered before she could stop herself.

'Forsyth's a pig. Any man that has to drug his women is no man in my book. He's a lowlife, a rapist, plain and simple.'

'Look at you,' Petty replied in a mocking tone. 'Judge and jury now, as well as punisher.'

Uma couldn't stop herself.

'Do you have a problem with that, Petty?'

'I do. You turn up here, ten weeks ago, all high and mighty as Forsyth's right-hand man.' Petty pushed a finger into Uma's chest. 'Next thing we know, you're whipping Rae to avenge your little bitches.'

Uma could feel the anger pulsing through Fox's veins, but wasn't sure if that was also hers. However, she sensed the other two didn't seem surprised by Petty's outburst. What's more, they expected Fox to respond. That was fine by her.

She grabbed his finger, jerking it down savagely, before wrenching it sideways, applying just enough pressure on the proximal interphalangeal joint. Petty screamed and backed away, holding his hand.

'You bastard,' he screamed at Uma. 'You've broken my finger.'

'Actually, it's a dislocation of the middle joint of your index finger. I've torn your ligaments, that's all. It should pop back into place.'

Petty launched himself at Uma, but Silva stepped between them.

'Whoa, slow down there, buddy. You know the rules.' Silva nodded towards the boxing ring. 'Sort it out in there.'

'With pleasure,' Petty said, ducking under the lowest rope before rolling onto the canvas. He beckoned for Uma to follow. She stood there, uncertain what to do, but eventually took her cue from the others and joined him in the ring.

'What's it to be?' she said to Petty, lightly dancing around the shorter man. Uma couldn't help but smile. Fox was clearly a fighter.

Petty moved fast. One second he was backing off, the next, spinning in a wide circle, right leg perpendicular to his body. Uma instinctively pivoted her chest backwards so that Petty's heel passed harmlessly in front of her chin. She straightened. How had she done that? There was no time to consider it, as Petty launched a flurry of punches at her face. She parried them effortlessly, before unleashing a pile driver at the smaller man's head that he did well to avoid, then she followed through with a vicious kick of her own. She barely had time to admire how high she had managed to get her thigh before she repeated the attack, again spinning high in the air, and this time she felt her heel connect.

Petty collapsed to the canvas where he lay, momentarily stunned, before sitting up. He seemed to notice his distended finger for the first time and grabbed it in the other hand, before wrenching it hard right, all the while staring at Uma. She heard the click. Suddenly he rolled away, pulling his knees up behind him, inverting his arms, both palms flat to the canvas next to his ears. He kicked his legs upwards and, as his body flicked up, he snapped them down hard so that he landed on his feet. Petty turned to Harris, who handed him a short staff. It reminded Uma of the one Ethan had used whilst laying waste to Ingram's men in the Carbon-Based LEAP centre in Washington. How was Fox with weapons? Even as the question formed, she mouthed "Bōjutsu" and knew the stick was a bo. It relaxed her immediately. She circled Petty as he moved back into the centre of the ring, twirling the short staff in his hand. Without warning, he lunged forward, slamming the wooden pole overhead, bringing it down towards Uma's head in one fluid movement. She flung herself to one side, but Petty stabbed the staff forward, catching Uma square in the stomach. She felt the oxygen suck out of her lungs, collapsing backwards onto the canvas. Petty pressed home his advantage, leaping on top of Uma and pinning her arms down with his knees, as he rained blows down on her unprotected face. Again, instinct kicked in. She felt her whole body jackknife upwards. Petty was thrown sideways, allowing Uma to free one arm. She put it to good use, repeatedly punching her opponent in the ribs. Petty cried out, and Uma freed her other arm. She formed a double fist, crashing it into Petty's unprotected right side. Everyone heard the ribs crack. He rolled off Uma, groaning.

Uma got to her feet and went over to Petty, who was still sitting on the canvas, clutching his chest. He scowled up at her.

'You need to move faster if you want to dole out the insults,' Uma said, reaching down to help him up.

The next second, she was sailing through the air, landing with a thud on her back. Petty arrived a second later, his elbow arrowing into her unprotected ribs. She felt a crack, grunting with the pain.

'That's for the ribs and finger,' Petty grimaced, as he exited the ring.

Uma slowly got to her feet, feeling her rib gingerly, before ducking under the ropes. She followed the others into the changing rooms where she quickly showered and got dressed. As she returned to the gym, a suited man entered the centre and approached her. Uma recognised him, without even realising it: Mohammed, Forsyth's assistant.

'Mr Fox, it's time,' he said. 'We need to go.'

Without thinking, Uma answered, 'Where?'

Mohammed frowned at her.

'Mr Forsyth wants to see you.'

The Acorn, Riyadh, Saudi Arabia

14th July 2010, 08:47 hours AST

U ma froze on the threshold of the apartment that the small Arab was inviting her into, an unmistakable sound assaulting her eardrums. It punched deep into her brainstem like a recoiling how-itzer. She clenched both fists, trying to slow her heart rate, resisting the urge to curl up into a ball, but it was no good. The laughter had triggered a slew of images, smells and feelings that she was helpless to control, so she simply stood there, gripping the doorframe, waiting for them to play out.

'Commander Fox,' Mohammed said. 'Are you OK?'

Uma stared at him, momentarily confused.

Who was he talking to?

And then she remembered.

'Yes, thank you. I think I broke some ribs in my sparring session with Petty.'

'You should get those seen to.'

Uma nodded, feeling better as her reaction faded, to be replaced by the familiar rage, tinged with shame. The feeling energised her. She had nothing to be ashamed about.

Mohammed turned and continued down the corridor, stopping as it doglegged right, beckoning for Uma to follow. She caught him up, and they entered together. Even by The Acorn's standards, it was impressive, but also soulless in equal measure, all hard marble, faded light and dark colours. A fitting abode for Forsyth. One to match the blackness of his heart, Uma thought, as she followed Mohammed down a wide staircase that must have been fifty-feet high. It framed the entire main living area below, which seemed to be divided into different living spaces. They skirted a tinkling fountain set in black granite, then continued past an informal dining square ringed by huge cushions which surrounded a giant circular brass table, standing six inches off the floor and inlaid with black onyx. Up ahead, Uma spotted the familiar figure of Forsyth, his long hair tied back, giving him the look of a faded rock star. He was sitting next to Katrina on a low couch, his arm draped over her shoulder. Uma's heart dropped. She had forgotten about the news anchor, and that she was facing her own personal nightmare with Forsyth. Katrina's eyes flicked across Uma's, a mixture of relief and revulsion at the sight of Ethan's punisher. As they approached the seating area, Katrina retreated to the far side of a low table. Forsyth frowned, which morphed into a wide smile as he caught sight of Uma and Mohammed.

'Commander Fox, why so glum? It's a beautiful morning.'

Uma attempted a smile and nodded at Forsyth.

'My ribs,' was all she could think to say. 'I was just telling Mohammed, I hurt them sparring this morning. In the gym.'

'You soldier boys, always fighting.' Forsyth stood, moving towards Uma, who thought for a second that he was going to hug her like he had done in the TV studio. She instinctively felt her whole body stiffen, but he instead walked over to where Katrina was standing. She edged round the table towards Uma and Mohammed, forcing Forsyth to follow her, until they were all standing in a tight circle. Uma's fist clenched as she stared at Forsyth, remembering the last time she had seen him in Manhattan. It felt like yesterday. She could feel her nails raking down his face, her head crunching into his nose. With a surge of excitement, she realised she could end him here, right now. Fox's huge hands would snap his neck like a twig. It was intoxicating, the knowledge that she could end this monster's life in a second, but that wasn't the plan. She was here to rescue Ethan. Forsyth could wait till later.

'I have a job for you,' Forsyth said, nodding at Katrina, who scowled back at him.

Uma looked over at Katrina, who stared blankly at her, eyes devoid of recognition. Of course, Uma had forgotten: Katrina didn't know about Fox. She had opted to have her memories wiped by five hours to forget Fox's murder. Uma couldn't blame her. Living with all this suffering was hard work.

'I need you to take Miss Hoskins to Professor Crouch. She's going to film a restoration.'

Uma stared blankly at him, causing Forsyth to frown with annoyance.

'Keep up, Commander. The Hungarian PM dropped dead yesterday, on the floor of the Upper Chamber in Budapest. He had a massive stroke that Health didn't pick up. Fortunately, he bought BackUp and his wife has come to collect him. She's waiting in the other room. I want you to escort everyone to Professor Crouch's office, where Miss Hoskins will film the reunion – Prime Minister Kovac's wife has agreed – and it'll be broadcast across the Americas, Europe and Asia. Great publicity and should generate lots of business.'

Uma stood there, dumbfounded. She had no idea the programme had advanced so quickly.

'Step to it, Commander,' Forsyth said, clapping his hands vigorously. 'Time is money.'

The woman dabbed at her heavy eyelids with a small hanky grasped in her pudgy hand. Uma was surprised she could even lift it to her face, given the number of heavy gold rings that drenched her fingers. She was muttering something in a language Uma was not familiar with, presumably Hungarian. Katrina stepped away in frustration.

'Cut,' she said, glaring at her producer Nick, who stepped forward, smiling. He glanced at the translator, who followed him over to the heavyset woman.

'Mrs Kovac, I know it's difficult, but could you stop whispering? It's ruining the audio.'

The translator spoke quickly in Hungarian, the woman nodding enthusiastically as she had done on the previous six occasions.

'Nick,' Katrina said, 'it doesn't matter. We can pull this out in post-production. It's not ideal, but we'll be here all day at this rate.'

Nick turned back to the elderly woman who had started to cry again, each intake of breath building towards what they all now knew would be a ten-minute explosion of wailing.

'OK, Mrs Kovac. It doesn't matter, you're doing so well. Your husband is ready now. You will see him in two minutes.'

As the translator delivered the message, the old lady gasped and burst into tears, grasping Nick to her ample bosom.

Uma watched them, her mind a whirl of conflicting emotions. On one hand, Fox's rage threatened to break out into violence as images of Jo and Angel rippled to the surface, each one a reminder that this could have – should have – been them. That he should have been standing here, meeting his wife and daughter. The ache was unbearable, but on the other hand, equal feelings of horror stormed over her like acid rain, burning away Fox's longing, as she thought of the billions of life extensions that Eternity could offer. Uma swallowed. She wasn't sure how much more of this she could stand. As she watched, Nick counted Katrina in again. They restarted the interview, this time ignoring the woman's mutterings. The camera focused on the gate. To one side, the bulbous silhouette of Crouch's bald head filled a screen. He had insisted that he be in shot, his simpering request delivered with a blast of neat alcohol that made Uma gag.

Suddenly, an older man stepped through the gate. Two orderlies caught him as he stumbled forward and, after steadying his legs, slowly guided him over to the woman who had fallen silent, mute with shock at the sight of her recently dead husband. Then, with a shriek, she waddled forward, embracing him in a cacophony of wails and screams of happiness.

Uma looked on, still fighting Fox's rage, thinking of when she had resurrected Ethan. That indescribable feeling – part happiness, part relief tinged with anger and longing – as he had walked through the gate fully recovered after lying unconscious in a hospital bed for so many months. As the man cupped his wife's face in his hands and kissed her gently on the lips, she felt herself tear up at the memory. Who was she to deny these people their loved ones? she thought. Was she doing the right thing with the Laws? She was no longer sure. The only thing that she was sure of was that she needed to get Ethan out of here before living inside Fox drove her mad.

Al-Ha'ir Prison, Riyadh

20th July 2010, 09:36 hours AST

The clicking of boots on the concrete was deafening in the narrow corridor. She wanted to claw at her ears to deaden the sound, but if anything it seemed to magnify, until, as they reached the door, each step felt like a gunshot, exploding hollow-point bullets deep inside her skull. It had started the moment they had left the outskirts of Riyadh in the Range Rover. An ambulance had appeared behind them, its lights flashing, siren wailing and the noise live-streamed danger, sending her imagination into overdrive as to how she would find Ethan. Not that she needed any prompting. Fox's memories had already done the damage: ten weeks; ten collections. She knew what she would find, the memories conveniently replaying over and over in her mind's eye across the previous week as it snail paced to this moment. Every second, both sleeping and waking, was filled with one stinking mess of a memory. And that wasn't even the worst of it. What Uma hadn't been prepared for was the conflicting emotion of Fox's reaction: grim satisfaction at finding Rae like that, along with a morbid excitement that he would get to inflict it all again. It infected every pore of his hulking frame, tearing at her own revulsion, leaving her exhausted each morning, traumatised by the evening, dreading the nighttime of terror that lay inside her own head. The man didn't seem to sleep. As the morning of Ethan's eleventh punishment arrived, Uma had robotically gone through her routine, equally revolted at the tingle of excitement Fox felt at getting to punish Ethan all over again, along with a creeping dread that she would have to witness Ethan's pain first hand. She had considered returning to America. The LEAP gate was only one floor away, promising sweet oblivion from this nightmare, but it wasn't really an option. She hadn't survived a week inside this monster's head to give it all up now. Shortly, she would return Ethan to America. In the meantime, she had to contain her emotions and continue to act like Fox, otherwise she would never liberate Ethan or herself from this living hell. One, she kept reminding herself, she was responsible for delivering him into. As they had pulled through the prison gates, her resolve had nearly cracked, the last seven days suddenly magnified into this moment as each of her senses catapulted into overdrive: a droplet of sweat on a guard's cheek, the crosshatching leather on the handle of the bullwhip, the overpowering smell of antiseptic burning her nostrils, the explosion inside her ear drums.

The four soldiers in front of her suddenly stopped, causing Uma to nearly walk into the back of them, all too aware that this was the moment. There were two prison guards outside the room, both with sidearms. One of Uma's companions leaned the stretcher he had been carrying against the wall before handing one of them a single sheet of paper. The man studied the document for what seemed like hours. Then he studied the five men carefully. Uma felt herself nodding down at him, realising that she could have crushed his skull with one blow of Fox's fist. In fact, she could kill all of them in this moment, but now wasn't the time. It calmed her nerves slightly. She enjoyed being strong. The guard nodded back at her and produced a key, which he placed in the lock, twisting twice. The door swung open like a coffin lid. It took her a few seconds to realise he was expecting her to enter first.

Uma forced a size ten into the cell before stopping, unable to move as the smell of sweat, vomit, urine and excrement enveloped her like a cloud of mustard gas. And something else: death. She gagged, covering her mouth and nose, but it was no good. She felt herself retch, hunching her shoulders, trying to disguise it as a cough. Behind her, the men shifted. She heard one of them speak questioningly and forced herself to continue, one leaden step at a time. As her eyes adjusted to the gloom, she could make out a cast-iron bed at the far end of a narrow room, windows along one wall, blackened with blinds that did nothing to keep the midday sun at bay. She belatedly registered the heat. It must have been over one hundred degrees in the cell. Sweat sprang freely across her entire body, stinging her eyes with salt. She blinked, finally staring at the bed, but it was empty. What she had assumed was Ethan was, in fact, two dirty pillows streaked with sweat and blood.

Her heart sank. Had they already taken him? Was this a trick, because they had found out Fox was in fact Uma and this was now her cell. She half expected the clang of metal behind her, but as she turned back towards the door, one of the guards just shrugged. nodding past the bed.

'Floor,' he said.

Uma tortoised further into the room until the edge of a dirty mattress appeared. Her heart leapt, then sank, but she forced herself forward, eventually rounding the rusted bed-frame. A naked figure was lying there, curled up into a foetal position, its back a sea of oozing pus that was speckled with black. As she collapsed to her knees, a cloud of flies suddenly lifted from the ruin, buzzing angrily around her head.

'Oh God,' she heard herself whisper. 'Oh God.'

The body moved slightly, as if responding to her words. As she watched, its head turned.

All of a sudden, she was staring into Ethan's eyes.

Uma fainted.

The Acorn, Riyadh, Saudi Arabia

20th July 2010, 10:36 hours AST

Uma kept her eyes straight ahead, not daring to look down at the trolley clunking along the corridor in front of her. Four members of the Royal Guard Regiment were stationed around it: one pushing, two ahead, another with a restraining hand on Ethan's, thankfully, covered body. Uma wished she could forget everything from the last hour. She swallowed hard, almost retching as the taste of Ethan's cell caught in her throat. It was everywhere: on her clothes, in her hair and crawling across her skin like a malevolent swarm of scarabs. When she had come to, a guard had been bent over her, waving smelling salts in her face, his colleagues tittering like small children by the cell door. As Uma had got unsteadily to her feet, they'd entered with the stretcher before unceremoniously dumping Ethan's half-dead body onto the soiled canvas and carrying it out to the ambulance. Apparently, Fox liked to travel with Rae, but she had declined, much to everyone's hilarity. She had followed in the Range Rover, trying not to think of Ethan up ahead. Forsyth would pay for this.

The lead guard stopped outside a room. He stood aside, beckoning Uma, who stared dumbly at him, wondering what he wanted. Fox came to the rescue, and she hurriedly stepped forward, stooping her head to a scanner that confirmed it was his eyes. She repeated the exercise, placing a huge hand, palm down, on a square of glass beside the doorframe. A lock clicked and the guard entered, followed by the creaking trolley. Bringing up the rear was a reluctant Uma. They processioned across a low-lit foyer around which glass-sided rooms were gathered like empty fish tanks. At the far side, it opened out into a larger office that was dominated by a floor-to-ceiling continuous curve of glass, in front of which the unmistakable figure of Crouch stood, looking out onto the dusty skyline of central Riyadh. As they approached, he turned to meet them.

'How is our patient?' he said, lifting the corner of the sheet that covered the gurney. Uma felt herself gagging again as Ethan's eyes flickered open, his head turning towards Crouch, lips moving.

'What's that?' Crouch said, leaning in.

Ethan mumbled again, barely a croak, and the professor crouched lower, his temple nearly touching Ethan's mouth, which suddenly opened and clamped onto Crouch's cheek. He howled, pulling away, a pudgy hand clasped to the side of his head, blood leaking down his neck. Uma could have sworn she saw the tiniest of smiles flicker across Ethan's red lips. As she watched, he spat something in Crouch's direction, who removed his hand to pick it up. Half his lobe was missing. Uma couldn't help herself and smiled. Despite his pain, Ethan was still fighting. Poor, brilliant, pig-headed Ethan.

'What's so funny?' Crouch squealed, dabbing his ear with a tissue.

'You were warned,' Uma said, looking down at the small man whose face was now puce with rage, blood soaking into the off-white collar of his lab coat. 'This man is dangerous. You shouldn't have got so close to him.'

Crouch made to strike Ethan, but as his fist came down, Uma stepped forward, blocking his arm. Crouch cried out in surprise.

'How dare you touch me,' he screamed, turning on Uma, who drew herself up to Fox's full height. She stared down at the tiny man, realising she could knock him over with one blow. Better still, she could probably end his life. Her arm itched at the thought. It would be so easy. Just one strike, but then what? Uma glanced at the four soldiers, who looked on in shock at the standoff between the two men. It calmed Uma down. What she was doing was out of character for Fox. She needed to be careful. This wasn't the plan. She was here to free Ethan, not satiate her desire for revenge over some petty squabble. Fox's muscles relaxed.

'I thought you wanted him conscious. Knocking him out won't help anyone.'

'Fox's right, you know.'

Even before Uma whirled round, she already knew who it was.

Forsyth was standing by the open door to the office, smiling his one-hundred-watt smile into the room. He sauntered over to them, staring down at Ethan like someone would inspect a crushed insect on the heel of their shoe. He grabbed a handful of Ethan's hair. Uma felt Fox's body tense. It was involuntary, as if she had no control over this hunk of muscle she was visiting temporarily. She clenched a fist, listening intently to Forsyth's exchange.

'How does it feel?' he said to Ethan, 'to suffer like this. Just like I did after your whore ruined me.'

Suddenly, Uma realised how effective her revenge on Forsyth had been. Removing his looks had truly been a devastation for him, but, she conceded, it had also sown the seeds of this current nightmare. She had inadvertently fed his desire for revenge in much the same way as Forsyth's actions with Eternity were now feeding hers. The circularity of it was not lost on Uma, but as she stood there staring down at Forsyth, she realised that only one of them could live. Once again, the thought both terrified and excited her in her equal measure. She couldn't believe that she was plotting to kill someone, but being in this body empowered her in ways she had never imagined. It was as if Fox's physical strength and size were adding heft to her thinking. Or was Fox's own desire for revenge spreading like poison, corrupting her soul? It made her think of Ethan and Anderson. The entanglement had poisoned Ethan's mind, almost destroying him. It had taken Uma's own death to give him what? The strength to control Anderson's worst excesses. To reassert his own personality and belief system. Was the same happening to her? Was Fox controlling her now? The scary bit was that, whilst Uma detested the possibility of that happening, she also found herself attracted to the power she felt. Not just his physicality, but his certainty of purpose. None of the second guessing that seemed to cripple her every move. For the first time since entering Fox, she considered whether she should stay. Finally finish Forsyth off. She stared hard at the man who had driven her to breach her own Laws. He was talking to Crouch.

'Rae needs to remember everything up to this moment.'

'Don't worry, he'll keep his memories, all five hundred and fifty of them.' Crouch grunted in pain, his hand still clasped to his ear.

'Good,' Forsyth said, glancing at Uma.

'Got the camera?'

Uma held it up. Fox wouldn't let her forget that.

Forsyth grunted with satisfaction, releasing Ethan's hair. His head flopped back onto the trolley.

'OK, let's do it.' Forsyth clapped his hands. 'I've got to get back to the shoot. We resume at two.'

Of course, Uma had forgotten that Katrina was shooting all of this week. She silently prayed that Forsyth had behaved himself.

Crouch made his way over to some screens and nodded at the four guards who seemed to know what to do. They removed the blanket covering Ethan, and lifted him from the trolley. Uma turned away as they carried him over to a doorframe and, with no hesitation, threw him through it. Ethan disappeared. Forsyth wandered over to where Crouch was busy on his screen. Uma followed, stopping at a respectful distance as Forsyth glared at her, but she was now in earshot.

'How are you progressing?' he said to the professor.

'Nearly there.'

'You've been saying that for weeks,' Forsyth said, his voice thick with impatience.

'It's not easy. What do you want me to do?'

'It was your idea,' Forsyth said. 'It's your greatest creation, you said.'

'I know it is, but for it to work, I need to infect the entire system. Every gate, every person. It has to be a catastrophic failure. From which there will be no coming back.'

'I know. That's why I love the idea,' Forsyth said. 'My question remains the same: when?'

Crouch stopped typing and looked up.

'You'll have it in five days. By the end of the week – LEAP, Jakobsdóttir, Rae. All of them will be a footnote in history and we will be the only viable teleportation system on Earth.'

As Uma absorbed the news, Ethan stepped back through the doorway into the room.

The Acorn, Riyadh, Saudi Arabia

20th July 2010, 11:01 hours AST

Ethan was standing there, naked from the waist up, his wrists encased in metal manacles that matched those round his ankles. He blinked once, as if not sure where he was. A wave of pain seemed to sweep his body, recognition registering across his face as he took in Fox, Forsyth, Crouch and the waiting soldiers. His shoulders sagged slightly, head sinking to his chest as if defeated.

'What are you waiting for?' Forsyth turned on Uma who had remained stock still, paralysed by what she was seeing. She could have reached out and caressed his face. It was completely unmarked: no grime, no sweat, no blood. Just beautiful, perfect Ethan, standing there in the middle of the office. As if he had just stepped into the room, the nightmare he was currently caught in, a distant memory. All Uma wanted to do was gather him in her arms and hold him tightly, but that was impossible.

Forsyth's admonishment forced movement into her reluctant limbs. She stepped forward, guiding Ethan towards the entrance. It was only then that she realised his back was completely clear of scars, as was the wrist that he had damaged when Reynolds' castle collapsed; Crouch had removed all visible signs of his suffering. As their eyes met, she nearly collapsed to the floor. It was like staring into the heart of a supernova, all hot rage and boiling violence, and something else: a seething hostility that tore at her heart with its hatred. She felt Fox reciprocate and tensed, but was a fraction too late. Without warning, Ethan suddenly knelt. As she instinctively bent towards him, he drove upwards, head first, towards her chin. Fox's training kicked in and he easily parried the blow, knocking Ethan to one side with his forearm. Before Uma could react, he clasped both hands together and clubbed down on Ethan's neck. Ethan collapsed to the floor as the four guards stepped forward, raining more blows down on his head and shoulders.

'Hold him, goddamn it,' Forsyth was shouting at her. 'Hold him. No more accidents today. Get his hood on.'

The guards hauled Ethan to his feet and, as Uma applied a choke-hold, one of them approached with the leather hood. Ethan began to struggle.

'Hold still,' she said, applying more pressure to his neck. 'It'll be worse otherwise.' Ethan's back was now pressed into Fox's chest and groin, Fox's left arm wrapped around Ethan's neck, hand locked into his right bicep. Uma could smell Ethan's hair. The sensation made her want to kiss his neck. At the same time, she couldn't shake that look he had given her. She knew it was directed at Fox, but there was no consolation in the knowledge. She could feel Fox applying pressure and it made her want to weep, but it did the trick. Gradually, Ethan stopped wriggling long enough for the guard to pull the black leather contraption over his head.

'Get him out of here,' Forsyth barked. 'Fox, bring the tape directly to my quarters. I shall enjoy watching it today.'

He returned to where Crouch was working as the four soldiers guided Ethan back through the empty foyer, towards the elevator. Uma followed at a safe distance, fingering the small object in her pocket. She didn't really need it, but there was no point in taking any chances. This was where she had decided to spring her attack. It was an enclosed space, giving her twenty seconds alone with the soldiers, more than enough time to disable them without fear of anyone interrupting her.

As the doors slid open, Uma stepped in first, ensuring she would be behind the soldiers as the elevator descended. This was the moment. A guard punched the button to their floor and the door slid shut. Her time had started. She withdrew the two tasers, one from each pocket, and pressed the small units into the necks of the two guards directly in front of her. There was a crackle. Both men collapsed forward into their companions. The front two turned, but Uma already had the tasers against their necks, delivering a ten-second burst to each of them. One of the soldiers went down, but the other turned towards her, still standing, a puzzled frown on his face. Uma pressed the taser again. Nothing. He said something in Arabic, but she didn't wait, bringing her forehead down onto his nose with all her might. There was a sickening crunch, and he fell to the floor, unconscious.

Uma stopped the elevator, pressing the button for Katrina's floor. As the elevator lurched upwards, Uma turned towards Ethan.

'We'll have you out of—'

Ethan's knee crunched into her groin and Uma sank to her knees, an explosion detonating inside her right testicle. She tried to stand, but the ache intensified, enveloping her stomach, then chest in a bloom of pain that she thought would never end. Ethan's knee now drove into her face and she felt the cartilage in her nose crumple. Stars pinged across her vision as she tried to parry his double-fisted blows that rained down on her head and shoulders. Uma roared and launched Fox's body at Ethan, driving him across the elevator and into the opposite wall. She felt the compartment shake as he slid to the floor, momentarily winded. Uma hobbled to the panel, hitting the stop button as Ethan struggled to his feet. They turned to face each other, circling warily, stepping over the unconscious guards.

'Ethan, I'm here to get you out.'

His eyes flamed at her through the slits in the black hood. He rushed her, but this time she was ready. As he ploughed into her waist, she double fisted her hands, crunching them down onto his back. He collapsed onto one of the guards, and Uma turned him over.

'Ethan, it's me. Uma. Please, I'm here to help.' Uma realised how stupid it must sound. Even sane, it would have taken some absorbing, but Ethan had endured ten weeks of torture at the hand of Fox and his eyes said as much. She avoided them, trying to convince herself that he understood. That at some level, she had conveyed what was happening.

'I'm going to unlock your manacles now. We're going back to the US. There is a gate to take you home. Do you understand?'

He nodded.

Uma's heart lifted, elated that she had reached him, pushing the signs aside that said otherwise. She heard Fox's voice in her head, "The eyes, watch the eyes."

'Good, I'm unlocking your manacles and removing this horrendous mask.'

She unbuckled the straps and pulled the leather from his head, before unclipping a set of keys from the belt of one of the guards. The ankle bracelets first. Then the wrists.

"The eyes," a voice screamed inside her head, but Uma blocked it out. She knew what she was doing.

As Uma stood, Ethan struck.

A blur of metal, the manacles whipping across her face. Stunned, she slid to the floor. In a flash, Ethan was straddling her, hands pressed around her neck, thighs holding down her arms. He was surprisingly strong.

She finally looked into his eyes.

No recognition. No humanity.

'I'm going to kill you,' he snarled.

The pressure built, black spots snow-storming her vision as she stared up at Ethan, his face a mask of rage, eye slits lasering hate.

'Ethan, it's me,' she tried to say, but no words formed, just a strangled gargle as Ethan kept the pressure up, his eyes locked on Uma's.

Fox's body instinctively jackknifed wildly, trying to dislodge Ethan.

Not like this, she thought, not at the hands of her lover, but Ethan's hold was tenacious. He wasn't going to be denied again.

Her vision spotted over and she weakly tried to hook a leg over his neck, but it was way too late. She could barely lift her foot off the ground.

As her eyes finally closed, all she could see was Ethan's face staring down at her. The face of a madman.

The Acorn, Riyadh, Saudi Arabia

20th July 2010, 11:23 hours AST

Uma's eyes flickered open, remembering the fight. Remembering his raging eyes and hate-fuelled hands slowly throttling her life-force away. She shifted position, suddenly aware of Ethan's dead weight above, his face inches from hers, back to normal, as if he was asleep, the slightest grin playing across his lips. Uma groaned. Everything ached, her throat sandpaper sore as desert-dry lungs cautiously sipped the air. Everything foghorned danger. Time was running out, but all she could do was lie there, trying to process what had just happened. However many times she reminded herself that Ethan thought she was Fox, Uma couldn't shake that feeling of pure terror. That her boyfriend had tried to kill her.

So why was she still alive? The question galvanised her jellied limbs, and she heaved Ethan aside, sitting up. Three of the tasered guards lay unmoving. The fourth, the one she had headbutted, was crouching, truncheon in hand, staring at her, his eyes wide with confusion and fear. He must have come to, seen Ethan throttling her and hit him. It occurred to her that this one knew what had happened – he'd seen

Fox turn rogue. The realisation demanded action, but all Uma could do was rationalise that it didn't matter. She would be long gone by the time he told Forsyth his story. Back in San Francisco with Ethan. She remembered her arrangement with Uma. The deal had been that she would be swallowed back into the system, Fox reinstated and then released. It felt strange to be presented with her own death, not once, but twice in two minutes. First Ethan, and now this. Were these her final few moments alive? She liked this body. Liked that feeling of power when she defeated Petty in the ring. Realising that she could have killed Crouch with a single blow, and do the same to Forsyth. And then there was the conversation she had overheard. That required further investigation, but if she were to stay ... Uma glanced at the guard, baulking at what she would have to do. Killing Fox had been in self-defence, the same with Eva, but this would be ...

She shut the thought down and struggled over to the guard, who feebly tried to block the blow as Uma drove her fist into his chin. Satisfied he was unconscious, she turned towards the control panel of the elevator and pressed Katrina's level. It lurched back into motion. The movement seemed to jolt her head back into the moment. All of this could wait. For now, she had to complete her mission, which was to return Ethan to Uma. Then they could regroup and work out what to do next. She rolled him over, then cupped her hands under his armpits, pulling him upright into a standing position. She stooped slightly, letting him fall against her shoulder. He collapsed onto it. Uma straightened, marvelling at how light he felt.

Once outside the lift, she strode down the corridor towards Katrina's apartment – towards her escape gate. Inside the conference room, she stood on the top step of the editing suite, staring at the door, circling around the decision that she wanted to make, but couldn't. Forsyth and Crouch's conversation bothered her. If they were planning something, she owed it to Uma and Ethan to discover what it was, otherwise all of this would be for nothing. If she left now, her cover would be blown. There would be no coming back as Fox. They would have to find another way, which might take months. Or never. Staying was the correct decision, but a new thought suddenly took hold: Kill

Ethan. Fox's desire for revenge suddenly surfaced, colliding head on with her new plan.

Uma could feel Ethan's neck in her hands, and imagined a vicious wrench to the left, his vertebrae snapping.

She suppressed a sob.

Fox's rage and hate were running riot, infecting her decisions and guiding her actions. Again, the feeling was overwhelming, drawing her, like the scent of blood draws a wolf. Her finger was on the trigger, the slightest pressure dispensing death.

'Shut up,' she growled. 'I'm in charge.'

Scared of what might happen if she delayed, Uma quickly opened the door, hunching Ethan off her shoulder and letting him fall backwards.

He disappeared.

Without a backward glance, Uma made her way out of the conference room, back towards the elevator.

Manhattan –TV Studio

21st July 2010, 07:55 hours EDT

E than sat perfectly still with his eyes closed, trying to imagine what had happened, but it was no good: nothing. All he could remember was having breakfast with Uma in her DC apartment, discussing their approach to the interview, and then she had stepped through the gate, Ethan following close behind. Their destination – these studios, where he was currently sitting. Instead, he had emerged in Uma's apartment in DC, the same place he had just left, but now it was twelve weeks later. It was very disconcerting. To have lost three months of your life only to discover that the world had kept on turning. That it was, in fact, a completely different place to the one he had departed: that the 4,240 victims of the LEAP virus that he was meant to be discussing with Katrina had in fact been reinstated by Green Ray no less; that all lawsuits from the victims' families had been dropped; that, in his absence, an oversight board had been proposed and was currently taking shape, led by Ingram and comprised of every nation that had accepted the LEAP technology; that Green Ray no longer enforced the LEAP Laws; that, in fact, they were undergoing a revolution with fifteen draft amendments already suggested, including the full reinstatement of all murder and road traffic accident victims; that a universal health care system to rival Eternity's was in the works; and that the volcano had settled down with no noticeable activity since 6th June. Not that it mattered. Following the reinstatement of the LEAP massacre victims, identification of the virus and announcement of the universal health care, usage had slowly tripped up. Yesterday, there had been eighty-two million LEAPs across a twenty-four-hour period.

Ethan should have felt elated, but he felt flat. Worse still, he felt deeply uneasy, particularly after his late-night debrief with Uma, who had explained his true whereabouts during all this time. He shifted in his seat as a wave of hot licks inflamed his back at the thought. It was bad enough to experience that nightmare once, but to have it repeated, and on a weekly basis ... Ethan shuddered. No wonder the version that had stepped through the gate yesterday had been a gibbering wreck; a homicidal maniac that didn't know where or who he was. But he had no recollection of that, either, thanks to Uma. She had decided to put that version back into the LEAP system and restore him – to the Ethan that he had been twelve weeks ago. Her logic was brutally sound: Saudi Ethan was a broken man. She had bitter experience of losing Ethan for nearly five years as he festered in a mausoleum north of San Francisco. He admired her honesty, understood it even, but as the long night gave way to dawn, Ethan had begun to experience the familiar flutter of resentment that had plagued his years after being brought out of the coma: What right did Uma have to do what she had just done? Had Uma just murdered him? The Ethan, that is, who had arrived from Riyadh. He had been a person: flesh and blood, just like him, with thoughts and feelings. Didn't that Ethan have rights, however damaged he might be? And if so, what did that make him? An interloper? An aberration, recalled at the whim of his girlfriend because she couldn't face dealing with a deranged Ethan.

He opened his eyes, suddenly panicking at the image of a roaring fireplace in a deserted fortress, miles from anywhere. He could feel the heat on his skin, mimicking the growing inferno inside of him, raging at Uma's constant manipulations: taking his blood when she had first introduced him to LEAP; failing to tell him that Shane had entangled him with a killer called Anderson; excluding him from the LEAP rollout programme. Hell, she'd done this before, restoring him to an earlier version of himself in an effort to purge Anderson from his system and, in the process, wiping months of memory. Why was he even surprised at her actions now? This was who Uma was. What she did. Manipulating the rules to fit her goals. The problem was that Ethan didn't seem to know what they were anymore, and she didn't seem open to sharing them with him.

A noise by the door pulled him back into the room. Uma was standing there with Katrina. They were talking animatedly, but he was too far away to hear what they were saying. Uma caught sight of him and her face lit up with happiness. He half returned the smile, standing as she approached. She gave him a warm hug, ruffling his hair.

'I'm never letting you out of my sight again,' she said. 'Are you ready to do this?'

Ethan nodded, but he didn't feel ready. He felt rushed. Worse still, unsure, but Uma had been insistent. They had to get ahead of Forsyth, unlike last time. So, once again, he had reluctantly agreed, despite the obvious fact that he was missing weeks of context and was totally reliant on Uma for his information – the Uma who had a long history of misleading him when it suited her purposes.

'Are you sure?' she said, sensing his reluctance.

'Sure,' he replied. 'Just tired. It's a lot to take in.'

Katrina joined them, smiling at Ethan.

'I have to say, I'm pleased to see you're in one piece after what you've been through.'

Ethan studied the news anchor. He was aware of her role in his rescue, or at least the bits Uma had wanted him to know. The story didn't fully add up, though. There was something else, which he couldn't quite work out, but neither woman wanted to get into it. Once again, he had a feeling that Uma was holding something back.

'If you're ready, Ethan?' she continued. 'We're on in one minute.'

Ethan nodded and followed them onto the set of the Daily Event, where more makeup artists quickly applied the finishing touches to his face and neck. How many times had they sat here? It felt like a confessional, but it was the best way to reach the widest possible audience. Ethan could see the producer count Katrina in, and suddenly they were live.

'I'm delighted to announce that I am joined this morning by Uma Jakobsdóttir and Ethan Rae, the joint heads of Green Ray. Yes, you heard me correctly. Ethan Rae is here in the studio after his daring rescue from Saudi Arabia in the early hours of this morning.'

Ethan felt the camera on his face. He tried to smile, but it came out as a tired grimace.

'Uma, would you like to explain how you did it?'

'Yes, thank you, Katrina.' Uma clasped Ethan's hand in her own and squeezed hard. 'We've been working on getting Ethan out of Saudi for quite some weeks now. I would like to add that this was not a government-sanctioned rescue, but one we organised privately.'

'Yes, I wanted to ask you about that. Just to get that right, you want to go on record that this was a privately financed prison break in a foreign jurisdiction. It sounds illegal to me. How does that sit with your partners?'

Wow, Ethan thought. Katrina really wasn't holding back, but as they had discussed in the prep session, all the elephants in the room had to be confronted head on, otherwise they would be torn to pieces by the press. It suddenly occurred to him that that was going to happen, anyway.

'Yes, of course,' Uma replied evenly. 'As I've always maintained, Ethan was imprisoned on some trumped-up charges after being kidnapped from American soil. And as you've seen on TV, and witnessed firsthand by yourself, subjected to the most horrendous torture on a weekly basis.' Christ, Ethan thought, there were videos of his whipping? He hadn't even considered that and felt a surge of pain across his back, as his hands involuntarily clenched into claws, crushing Uma's. She flinched, glancing sideways, but continued, 'There was no way we could just sit back and allow that to happen. We had to get him out of Saudi. The Americans, as you've rightly said, did not want to be involved in this mission. I'm here to say, on record, that they played no part in the rescue.'

'So, tell me, how did you do it?'

'With inside help, fortunately. From individuals that work for Forsyth, but realise how rotten his regime is. That's all I can say, I'm afraid. Any further detail might reveal their identities.'

Another part of the story that didn't add up, Ethan thought. How had a lowly Saudi guard managed to spring him out of a high security jail, then spirit him back to America?

'Quite. I understand your reluctance.' Katrina turned to Ethan. 'Tell me, Ethan, can you remember any of your time in Saudi? It must have been traumatic.'

No, not really, was what he wanted to say, because he hadn't been there, but Uma had been insistent. They couldn't reveal that to the public, and there it was, he realised. Yet more deceit from her, and he was now a party to it.

'Yes, I remember every second,' he lied, drawing on long-buried memories that he never thought he would have to voluntarily dredge up. 'The punishment was organised so that I forgot nothing.' He fell silent, feeling the flicks of pain cut into his back, and this time, his clenched fists were real. 'More pain than any man can bear. And then in the days afterwards, they didn't treat me. I was coming in and out of consciousness as the wounds from the flogging festered. Eventually they went ...

He fell silent, tears forming as he remembered the days in the hospital bed stretching into weeks, then months. The heat, the dust, the smell of death, the stink of rotting flesh. That sense of abandonment. He had never felt so lonely in his life. Not far off how he was feeling now. He turned to Uma.

'... but, thanks to this lady at my side, I'm back. Ready to continue my work to roll LEAP out. Put a stop to Eternity. It's diabolical what they did to me: the flogging, reinstating me, retaining my memories. Forsyth and Crouch are monsters, and we need to put a stop to what they are doing. That is what I am going to dedicate my time towards.'

But all he could think about was that Uma was just as bad, and he, too, by extension. They were copying people – him – and using the technology to suit their own purposes.

Katrina smiled, and Uma squeezed his hand.

'It sounds horrendous, Ethan. How do you survive that level of stress and torture?'

Ethan paused for a second. Now there was a good question.

'I'm strong. Remember, I had ten years' practice when I was sixteen. Back then, it felt much worse. I had just lost my parents and been sentenced to ten years. I didn't understand a word of what was happening. I was all alone. Had no one to help me. At least this time I have Uma. Without her help, I would still be there.'

Katrina nodded and then smiled, the interview at an end.

'Thank you, Ethan. For coming in today at such short notice and sharing your experience with us.' She smiled into the camera. 'Don't go away, folks. After the break, we will be speaking to Ben Jones, our Louisiana anchor who is reporting live from Baton Rouge. It's eight days since BP installed a containment cap on the ruptured wellhead, but fears have been raised that it might not hold after engineers detected seepage, heralding a possible methane gas leak on the seabed.'

As they wrapped up after the segment, Ethan and Uma retreated to Katrina's makeup room. Ethan felt tired, unsure of what to do next. The more he thought about it, the more he regretted filming the segment, but it was too late. He was now on record. Whatever Uma had planned and wasn't telling him, he was now part of. As they gathered their belongings, there was an anxious knock on the door. Katrina's assistant entered without waiting for a reply. Ethan knew instantly that something was amiss.

'You need to turn the TV on. Forsyth's holding a press conference in Riyadh.'

Oval Office, Washington DC

21st July 2010, 16:37 hours EDT

U ma instinctively clenched her hands, balling them into tight fists as Ingram entered the room, the President close behind him. They both sat down opposite her. Nobody spoke for a moment. In the silence, Uma could feel the room's enormous power, crushing down on her shoulders like an oxen's yoke. She swallowed hard, wishing Ethan was here, but the President had specifically requested that he not attend. Truth be told, Uma was relieved, since she had some inkling of what was going to be discussed, but Ethan had not reacted well, accusing her of withholding information, of cutting him out of the loop. How could she tell him she had inhabited Fox? That she had killed Fox. As Fox. He wasn't ready for that level of detail, and the fewer people who knew about it, the better. Besides which, a tiny part of her had wanted to see how he would react to losing three months of his life. The lost years in Reynolds' castle were still a painful memory for her and had been precipitated by a similar episode as she tried, then failed, to disentangle him from Anderson.

The President smiled at Uma. He looked tired and Uma realised she wasn't the only one with problems. He had the midterms coming up in November, and it already looked like he was going to get a drubbing.

'What on earth is going on, Uma?' he started.

She glanced at Ingram, who stared straight ahead, his face like stone, but she could have sworn a glimmer of satisfaction shimmered across its rocky face.

'I rescued Ethan,' she said.

'In direct contravention of Director Ingram's order not to.'

'That's not strictly true, sir. The director refused to help me.'

'Yes, because it would have represented a very public act of aggression in another jurisdiction,' Ingram countered.

'With respect, sir, I think if Director Ingram wished to rescue Ethan, he would have been sitting here weeks ago. Besides, I took these actions as a private citizen. They might have been illegal, but so was his original kidnapping.'

'I understand that, but we just happen to be your partner in LEAP. We are guilty by association. Besides which, after what happened in Saudi this morning,' the President said with a wave of his hand, 'that is the least of our worries.'

Uma couldn't disagree there. After Katrina's assistant had turned on the television, they had been presented with a smiling Forsyth being interviewed. Beside him sat a manacled Ethan. It had been so simple, really. Once again, Uma had been blinded by her tunnel vision, this time to rescue Ethan from the hell she had delivered him into, never for one moment thinking the obvious – that Forsyth would just regenerate Ethan. Why wouldn't he? It was part of his business model, yet she had missed it. So had Katrina. Worse still, Ed Fox was sitting in the frame as well. He – or more accurately – she should have returned with Ethan, but hadn't. Instead, a confused Saudi guard had appeared with a broken nose and a broadside of Arabic, along with a scribbled note from Fox, explaining that he couldn't return whilst Forsyth remained free. He said that Uma could lay the blame for Ethan's escape on the guard he had sent through, and that she would know what to do with him. She'd had no choice but to store him in the LEAP system and

ponder how her plan had unfolded so catastrophically quickly. Forsyth
had joyfully announced that Uma was lying. That Rae had never left
Saudi. That he would, in fact, serve out the rest of his sentence. That
the person who had appeared at Uma's side on US national prime time
TV was, in fact, a copy, not the original. It was further evidence of
there being one rule for Uma Jakobsdóttir and one rule for everyone
else. Not only had she reinstated her loved ones in contravention of
the LEAP Laws, but she also copied them when it suited her.

'Who exactly is the original Ethan?' the President asked.

Uma had rehearsed her answer to the question, even though it
wasn't true.

'Our Ethan is. If you follow the timeline from when he followed
Forsyth through the gate back to Saudi, we rescued that version and
brought him back here.' Except that wasn't even true. The Ethan they
had brought back was a mumbling psychopath, his brain destroyed by
the trauma of receiving fifty lashes weekly. She had restored the original
Ethan from before the original LEAP out to Saudi. God, it was a mess.

'That's your interpretation,' the President said. 'Forsyth's is equally
viable. They have an exact copy of the man that followed him through.'
He sighed heavily. 'We have two Ethan Rae's and no one knows who
is the original one.'

'They both are.' Ingram spoke for the first time. 'That's the problem
with the technology. LEAP is redefining what it means to be human.
We need to get a handle on that. Quickly.'

Uma stared at him in shock. This was what she had been saying for
years. What angle was he pursuing now?

'Regardless of what is happening with Rae, Forsyth's making a
mockery of us. He's destroying people's trust in LEAP. First, it's
your—' he narrowed his eyes at Uma '—and by association, our refusal
to reinstate people killed in the LEAP massacre. Then they discovered
that the woman in charge has been merrily ignoring her own Laws and
arbitrarily restoring Rae in a botched rescue attempt on foreign soil.'

'It wasn't botched, sir,' Uma said. 'We rescued Ethan.'

'It really doesn't matter what you think. It looks that way to the
public, and in this game of politics, perception is everything. Forsyth is

right. It appears that there is one rule for you, whilst everyone else gets to live by your Laws. It looks arbitrary; worse still, elitist. Not exactly the ticket we ran on.'

'If I may, Mr President,' Ingram said, smiling at Uma.

'Of course, Joseph. Go on.'

Uma held her breath. Here it comes, she thought.

'The new LEAP Oversight Board meets tomorrow for the first time in New York, at the United Nations HQ. We now have a representative from each nation that has signed up for the LEAP technology. This could be our, shall we say, first order of business to decide what to do.'

'What's that supposed to mean?' Uma shot at him.

'Well, we need to decide some guidelines on future copying. Give the public some clarity on what is allowed with LEAP, otherwise there might be a clamour for other copying to take place.' Uma relaxed. For one awful moment, she thought he was going to suggest that they discuss what to do with Ethan. Even Ingram wasn't that cold-hearted. 'Who wouldn't want to?' he continued. 'If we're not careful, it'll be chaos. A business could simply duplicate its best people instead of hiring new ones. Worse still, firing all the others. Sports franchises could copy their best players. Can you imagine if Oklahoma had nine Kevin Durant's on their first team? I think we need to announce this soon. It will give us the run on Forsyth and recover some of the damage that has occurred with this latest incident.' He glanced at Uma, who felt herself flush with a mixture of helpless rage and embarrassment.

'I think that's a good start, Joseph.'

'What about Forsyth and Eternity?' she said. 'They will continue with their business model. What's stopping him from approaching every business, every sports franchise with the same offer Director Ingram just outlined?'

'What are you suggesting, Doctor? That we invade Saudi? Take him out?'

Uma shrugged.

'Given what's at stake, yes, we should consider that.'

The President stared at Uma. He looked so disappointed in her, as a father might a daughter.

'I thought you were different, Uma. Invading countries like a spoilt child because you're not getting your way. We've already got one ruinous war in the Middle East. I will not commit more troops to invade a country, which until last year was our closest ally in the Gulf. That is simply not going to happen. If Forsyth goes down that route, we'll deal with it through the courts. There's a multitude of ways to stop him: prohibiting dupes in the workplace would be a good start.'

Uma stared at him. He didn't have a clue what LEAP was capable of. None of them did. They could have a million dupes of one person inside one million different people. Just like she had done with Fox.

The President gathered up his papers.

'There is one more thing, sir.'

'Yes, Joseph.'

'What do we do with Rae?'

Uma froze. She should have known he wouldn't let it pass.

'What do you mean?' the President said.

'Well, he is currently the first copy in human history. That throws up all sorts of ethical and legal issues. Clearly, it's in breach of the LEAP Laws, which we all agreed would now be managed by the Oversight Board. If we want to appear to be standing firm, shouldn't we do something about it?'

'What are you suggesting?'

'Do what the doctor has done on multiple occasions – return him to the LEAP machine. Put him back where he came from if the Saudis insist on keeping their version of Rae. It's a good time to draw a line in the sand. Show people what the natural order of things will be in this new world.'

'You don't get to decide that,' Uma shouted at him.

'Neither did you, Doctor, but it never stopped you,' Ingram shot back.

'OK, folks. Calm yourselves,' the President said. 'Joseph is right, Uma. It's not for you, or me, or Joseph to decide, but we need to decide. Maybe it should be the first order of discussion when you convene this new board. Let them debate it and vote on the outcome. In the meantime, put Rae under house arrest.'

'But he's the original,' Uma heard herself saying. 'The one in Saudi is the copy.'

'Let's not go down that rabbit hole again. Joseph, start the process.' The President rose, turning to leave.

'Uma, I'm sorry it's come to this, but I'm sure you'll agree it's for the best if we want to get control of the public's perception that LEAP is being run for their benefit, not yours.'

Then he was gone, closely followed by Ingram, who didn't even look in her direction, leaving Uma sitting there, alone, as the weight of the room crushed the air from her lungs.

United Nations, Manhattan

22nd July 2010, 09:57 hours EDT

The East River glimmered in the early morning sun, already high in the sky, forcing Uma to shade her eyes from the glare. It was going to be a hot day, in the high nineties. The familiar red livery of a large Circle Line cruiser was visible on the water, its decks full of tourists as it cut a furrow towards her, emerging from underneath the famous cantilevers of the Queensboro Bridge, then onwards towards the southern tip of Manhattan and the Statue of Liberty. Directly opposite, Belmont Island was a tiny sliver in the water, its fifty-seven-foot beacon a warning to all river traffic. Uma's gaze wandered a few inches north to Roosevelt Island, the southern tip a mess of diggers and concrete as the Franklin D. Roosevelt Four Freedoms State Park took shape. At least, that was what Katrina had told her. She had run a feature on the UN the previous year, explaining that the tip of the island would feature a bust of the famous president along with the Room, an open-air space that was meant to articulate the four freedoms of Roosevelt's legacy to America – freedom of speech, freedom of worship, freedom from want, and freedom from fear. Uma didn't feel free. Far from it. She felt trapped by what was about to happen next, hemmed in by the familiar machinations of Ingram, as he effortlessly manoeuvred her into agreeing to this kangaroo court. She realised ruefully that he had started months ago. From the moment that American soldiers had been infected in Afghanistan, there had been a constant worrying pressure to set up the Oversight Board. And here they were, facing a tribunal to decide Ethan's fate, and she felt far from confident: Ethan was not the original, but in fact, the copy. Two people knew: herself and him, Katrina now safe in her ignorance. But it wouldn't take much digging to reveal what she had done.

A polite cough behind Uma caused her to turn. Katrina Hoskins was standing there.

'Are you ready?' she said, stepping forward and taking Uma's arm in hers.

'As ready as I'll ever be,' Uma replied. They made their way to the elevators that would take them down to the ground floor of the UN Headquarters. From there, they entered the wide reception area with its 100-foot-high glass curtain frontage, set within a metal grid that climbed far above their heads. Around them, delegates from over 180 countries filled the vast space, waiting to enter the main meeting room. Uma and Katrina were forced to wait as the mass of people slowly shuffled forward. Against the far wall, a mural stretched fifty feet above them, depicting women and children praying, wrung hands held to the heavens, sobbing heads bowed to the ground. In the bottom right, three wild cats, jaws bared in a silent roar, seemed to be leaping out of the picture, whilst above them, a knight in shining armour galloped towards a group of women on a black charger. The painting felt familiar, and Uma suddenly realised it reminded her of the huge tapestries hanging in the Reynolds' Great Hall where Ethan had been holed up. She wondered how he was doing. Hopefully better than when she had seen him last night. Ingram had been good to his word. Ethan was stuck in her apartment in DC, four agents outside the door. As he had grimly reminded her, the room was nicer, but it was still a prison. Uma prayed it was temporary, but feared that it might not be.

'It's called "War and Peace" by Brazilian artist Candido Portinari,' Katrina said, nodding at the tapestry. 'That one's called War and behind us is Peace,' she continued. 'You have to pass this one as you enter the General Assembly Room, and Peace as you leave. It's designed to remind everyone what they're fighting for when in session. The paintings will be moved at the end of the month. Sent back to Brazil to be restored.'

Uma nodded, only half listening, willing the crowd forward so she could get this finished, but progress was glacial as they slowly filed past a series of exhibits to remind delegates of the horrors of war: an arms expenditure clock calculating the daily worldwide spending on weapons next to a resource comparison diagram showing the allocation of military spending compared to humanitarian causes – currently $1,747 billion to $32 billion – and finally, just before they entered the room, a huge black-and-white photo, depicting the familiar mushroom cloud. It reminded Uma of her father. He had been involved in the Manhattan Project towards the tail end of the Second World War. It had turned him into a fervent anti-nuclear campaigner. As they passed the statue of Saint Agnes, discovered in the ruins of a Roman Catholic Cathedral in Nagasaki after Little Boy had flattened the city, Uma shuddered. Her father had often spoken about the US's two strikes on Japan. He had seen it as a betrayal. The bomb had been sold as a deterrent to the scientific community, yet politicians had made it into a weapon of mass destruction. The parallel with LEAP was not lost on Uma. Was her father's oft-repeated warning about to come true again, that mankind simply wasn't ready for this type of technology? Had LEAP already become the world's latest weapon of mass destruction, she wondered, thinking of the soldiers killed in Afghanistan and more recently, the thousands who had died a painful death, the skin stripped from their bodies?

Finally, they entered the chamber, a four-storey theatre, with concave walls to the west and east, centring in on a stage that was raised up on a green carpet dais, which hosted a green marble desk, normally reserved for the President of the General Assembly and the Secretary-General of the United Nations.

'My seat is this way,' Katrina said, giving Uma a long hug. As she moved away, Uma suddenly felt as alone as she'd felt in a long time, despite the hundreds of people about her, more so even than when Ethan had been in a coma or subsequently interred in Reynolds' castle. Back then, as now, she had a focus, which had carried her through some very dark days, but back then, Ethan had only been her business partner. Now he was so much more. She feared she was about to lose him for good, and it was all her fault. Uma shuffled down an aisle, past seated delegates, until she was shown to her own seat, right in front of the stage. A front-row seat to witness her own humiliation. Uma sat down, craning her neck, looking up at the UN emblem embossed on a gold background which rose behind the rostrum. Suddenly, the hall fell silent as a familiar figure made his way onto the rostrum and sat down: Edward Johnson, the US Attorney General, who was the interim President of the LEAP Oversight Board, pending the appointment of a permanent one.

Uma took a deep breath.

Here we go, she thought.

Uma's Apartment, DC

22nd July 2010, 12:32 hours EDT

'Welcome to the opening session of the new LEAP Oversight Board. We are gathered here today as a new community, charged with managing a new technology that was gifted to the world on 18th December 2009 in Copenhagen by Uma Jakobsdóttir and our very own President Jamal Williams. A new technology which promises to deliver so much to the world. Not least, a chance to reverse global warming, perhaps the single biggest threat to our planet since a meteor exploded over Chicxulub in Mexico sixty-five million years ago. But it also promises so much more than that: improved health care, more efficient use of our precious resources and the chance to solve global hunger. However, as with all new technology, LEAP is a double-edged sword, also representing a significant threat to humankind; a threat, that if we don't actively manage, will speed up the depletion of our planet's precious resources, especially if we allow untrammelled copying and the resurrection of our loved ones. Each one of you here today has been chosen as a custodian of your country's commitment to ensuring that doesn't happen, principally through the four founding Leap Laws. Four laws that each of our nations has committed to enshrining into local law by the end of the year. Four simple LAWS: no copying, no resurrection of the dead, no merging of minds or species.

Simple, but also deceptively complex, throwing up a tsunami of ethical and moral conundrums that we have never dealt with before, but need to address.

'That is why we exist – to chart a course through the minefield that is LEAP. It has already thrown up our very first challenge: what to do with the world's first LEAP copy, Ethan Rae? He is an exact duplication of himself, each version of him a human being, inheriting all the rights of Ethan Rae, which is obviously not possible under our legal systems. One current version lives in DC, here in America, the other is serving a ten-year prison sentence in Saudi Arabia. Unfortunately, the complexity of our job here today is further complicated because Saudi Arabia is not currently part of the LEAP Oversight Board. But that complication should not deter us from sending out a clear message to everyone that uses the LEAP system, that they cannot copy themselves, and our job here today is to decide one thing, and one thing only: which of the two Ethan Rae's is the copy and which is the original. Once we have established that fact, the copy will be returned to the system and reduced to its base elemental atoms, with all associated files of that copy being permanently deleted from the system.' There was a low murmur in the hall. The AG let it die out, before continuing.

'Now, I know that sounds barbaric, but the alternative is more horrifying. If we allow untrammelled copying of individuals through the system, we risk a population explosion of such a magnitude that it will accelerate the stripping of natural resources from this planet of ours. To show what I mean, please consider the following. If every person of every nation present here today, excluding the nine states that comprise the Eternity axis, created just one copy of themselves, our population would increase overnight from 6.8 billion to 13.75 billion. If they made two copies, it would go to 20.6 billion. It would be as if a swarm of locusts had descended on our planet. The human race would become unsustainable. We would, in essence, cease to exist as a species. That is the magnitude of the decision we are making today.'

Ethan muted the TV as Uma sat there, staring at the screen. She had already heard it once, and it got no easier to absorb on a second telling.

This was her fear. This was why she had introduced the LEAP Laws. She should be ecstatic that they were being formalised in such a public setting, providing the guidance that she had longed for. Except that it was no longer so straightforward, as the man she loved stood to lose his life once they worked out what she had done.

'What are you not telling me?' Ethan suddenly said, turning towards to her.

'What do you mean?' she countered, folding her arms defensively.

'Please, don't bullshit me,' he continued, pacing in front of her. 'Something is off here and I need to understand what it is, so I can help you get out of this mess.'

Uma felt herself reddening. There was no way Ethan was ever finding out what she had done with Fox. He simply wouldn't understand.

'You know everything,' she said. 'I would keep nothing from you.'

'That's not true, is it?' he said. 'I can think of two off the bat: my entanglement and what Forsyth did to you.'

'I couldn't tell you those things,' she stammered, her face reddening even more. 'I explained why.'

'Stop,' he screamed, throwing the remote against the wall where it shattered. Uma recoiled as if he had slapped her, suddenly in another time, another life, another place: Ethan had destroyed a phone in the top room of her parents' house in Reykjavík the night she had discovered he was still entangled with Anderson. It had heralded the beginning of a nightmare that had taken over seven years to subside.

'That's what you do. You hold things back from me. It's like a poison, eating away at my sanity.' His voice was soft, pleading. 'Please don't do this again. I don't think I – we –can survive that.' Ethan turned away, wiping his eyes.

Uma stared at him, aghast, a wave of guilt sweeping over her like an electric current. He was right. She compartmentalised information. The latest, her dead baby. She was doing it again. It was likely to result in Ethan being snuffed out like a candle. The one man who had stood by her, who loved her unconditionally, and she was driving him away with her lies and deceit.

It stopped today.

Uma stood up, feeling lighter than she had felt in weeks. 'I'll tell you everything, but not here.' She looked around the room, remembering how Ingram had seemed to know her every move. He was probably listening to them right now. What she was about to tell Ethan would hasten his permanent deletion if he found out. Taking his hand, she led him to the bathroom, flicking the light switch on. The fan droned into life, and Uma opened both taps in the sink and bath before spinning the control on her power shower to max.

Uma turned to Ethan, drawing him close. She spoke, slowly at first, but soon the words were tumbling out as she unburdened herself: what had happened to Katrina; their plan to kidnap Ed Fox, Forsyth's head of security, and her mind merge with him; his subsequent shooting; that she had wiped Katrina's memories; how the dupe of Fox, the one containing her mind, had refused to come back after rescuing Ethan, instead sending the hapless soldier. After she had finished, she stepped back from Ethan, feeling lighter than she had in years, staring at him through the cloud of steam that now swirled around them. It reminded Uma of another moment, when she had shared her first kiss with him in another steamy encounter in a different country, his soft lips on hers. The moment she had first fallen for him.

He stared back at her for what seemed like an eternity. Then he leaned forward, hugging her.

'Thank you,' he whispered.

'There's something else,' she continued. 'I was pregnant.'

He pulled away again, his eyes questioning.

'You know I won't have children,' she said simply, hugging him tightly. 'I lost a part of you that day, but I don't want to lose you as well.'

'I don't care about the baby,' he whispered back. 'All I want is your honesty.'

'What do we do now?'

Ethan shrugged.

'I don't know. Once they find out I'm the copy, they'll return me to the system. Your reputation will be destroyed forever. I'm not sure there is anything we can do, other than pray that your dupe gets me out of Saudi,' he said.

Uma sat down on the side of the bath as his words slowly sank in. Then she began to sob. Deep, mournful lungfuls of regret that leached out of her, as his dispassionate analysis confirmed what she had long feared.

The Acorn, Riyadh, Saudi Arabia

22nd July 2010, 01:23 hours AST

The woman burst through the door and stood there, swaying as her eyes adjusted to the dim light. A movement to her left drew a giggle. She sashayed towards the bar, shaking a finger at the man standing there, trying to prise the cork off a magnum of champagne. The pop caused Uma to jump, even though she was expecting it. Champagne exploded out over Forsyth and his companion. They both laughed as Forsyth upturned the bottle over the woman's head. She squealed in mock surprise as the freezing liquid engulfed her in a bubbly shower that made the silk dress cling to her body like Saran wrap. He tossed the bottle aside, kissing her deeply before licking the frothing liquid from her face and neck. For a horrific moment, Uma thought they were going to take it further, but the woman eventually pushed him away.

'I'm going to change into something more drier,' she slurred, tottering away on six-inch heels. Forsyth collapsed on the couch beside Uma.

'Hey, Fox. Why so jumpy?' He looked over at Uma, his eyes glistening despite the gloom.

The man missed nothing. What could Uma say?

That the sound of an exploding cork reminded her of when he had raped her last October.

That her boyfriend had tried to strangle her two days ago.

That Ethan was currently being tried in Manhattan to decide who was the copy. Uma couldn't escape it; no one could. Deep down, she knew where that was heading. Only one Ethan could live.

That the sight of Ethan being ejected from the LEAP gate earlier today had crushed her spirit.

That being forced to watch Ethan being flogged had drained what energy she had left, leaving her barely able to stand.

They had travelled up to the prison in Range Rovers that afternoon, foreboding clouds of sand towering over them like a biblical punishment sent by God as a sandstorm blew in over the vast Al-Nafud desert. Ethan was sitting next to her, trussed up like a Christmas turkey, Forsyth up front, his mood now jubilant after his rage of seeing Uma parade Ethan on early morning TV. It had been Crouch's idea to spit Ethan back out. It was so simple, really. Too simple. Uma should have thought of it, but she had been focused on all the wrong things: on getting used to Fox's body, but mainly on rescuing Ethan, to assuage her guilt for weaponising him at the TV studio. That's all that had mattered to her. Now she'd made things worse. Here, and in America. She couldn't imagine the chaos in DC after Forsyth's hastily convened press conference. Ingram would be having a field day. For the hundredth time, she wondered how Uma was coping. As badly as she was, no doubt, trying to work out how their plan had failed so spectacularly. The only saving grace was seeing Ethan, sitting in the studio, looking healthy and relaxed. Uma had realised immediately what had happened. She would have done the same, swapping the raging monster she had saved in Saudi for an earlier version of Ethan, probably from the last LEAP he took. It was not lost on her that they had turned full circle, spending three months working on a rescue that had created the one thing they had sought to avoid – duplicates of Ethan, one stuck in prison, the other missing three months of memories. They were no further forward. They had, in fact, taken ten steps back.

'Tired, I guess,' Uma said. 'It's been a long day.'

'It sure has,' Forsyth said, 'but now we get to celebrate, right? Your fuck up has actually worked out well for us. I really couldn't have planned it any better. Imagine the shit-show back in DC with a duplicate Ethan running around. Those lily-livered Democrats will be a having a collective thrombosis over the ethics of that one.' He laughed drunkenly. 'Not only that, you've discredited that woman even more. I really couldn't have done it any better if I'd tried.'

He put an arm around Uma's shoulder, who recoiled at the unwanted contact. Just one twist, she thought, imagining his neck in Fox's hands. Forsyth would be dead, but she would not make that dumb mistake again. He'd have a hundred copies of himself in Back-Up. She needed to bide her time, discover what he had planned before making her move. If she got that far. Her hastily conceived cover-up was paper thin. Forsyth was suspicious, that much was clear. He had grilled her for close to an hour about how Ethan had escaped. Uma had stuck doggedly to her story: that it had been one of the prison guards who had tasered the others and had tried to strangle Fox, before escaping with Ethan. It barely felt credible, but Uma had the battle scars to prove it, which had been her excuse for not being the one to whip Ethan. At least she hadn't had to deal with that nightmare. The broadcast from America had halted the interrogation before Crouch had suggested the workaround and the whole ugly roadshow had moved onto punishing Ethan. Uma knew this wasn't the end. She knew that Forsyth would revisit her story later and eventually put two and two together. Her time was limited, but she was at a complete loss about what to do.

'Come, I've got a surprise for you,' Forsyth said, standing up, his eyes glittering dangerously. He hauled Uma off the couch as a woman entered the room. She stood, head bowed, arms crossed, her hands hidden beneath the sleeves of a long chiffon abaya, loosely held with a plaited rope belt. Beneath it, she was clearly naked.

'Ta-dah!' Forsyth announced theatrically.

Uma stared blankly at the woman.

'My gift to you. For an unexpected job, well done.'

He beckoned the woman over and she flung her arms around Uma, who stood there, unsure what to do, except hug her back.

'Oh, come now, I thought you would be a little more grateful.'

Uma stared down at the woman who was barely five two, her face partially covered by long flowing locks of red hair. She glanced up at Uma and smiled, her ruby-red lips parting suggestively, and Uma's heart dropped at what Forsyth had just presented to her. Worse still, what he expected her to do.

'I am,' Uma replied, 'but like I said, it's been a long day.'

The woman squeezed Uma's hips, then reached a hand up to the nape of Fox's neck, gently drawing Uma's face down towards her own. She kissed Uma, whose first reaction was to pull away, but she was aware of Forsyth's eyes on her. Uma reluctantly placed her hands on the woman's buttocks, hoisting her up, so her face was level with Uma's. The woman smiled at Uma, but her eyes were expressionless.

How many men had she done this with? Uma thought.

She felt Forsyth's gaze pull away as the other woman returned from the bathroom, now dressed in a sheer negligee. Forsyth whistled and stumbled over, swinging the woman round in a circle, before kissing her eyes, face, then neck, then working down to her breasts which he nibbled through the translucent material. Uma put the woman down, but she seemed to infer that more was needed and, taking Uma's hand, she led her into another room, dominated by a long table. Cameras glinted in every corner. Uma realised where she was. Had Forsyth raped Katrina here, and was she now expected to sleep with a prostitute, whilst being videoed for Forsyth's later pleasure? There was no end to the man's depravity.

The woman closed the door before trying to unbutton Uma's trousers. Uma backed away.

The woman looked up.

'You no like,' she said, glancing back at the door, her face slick with fear. The woman slipped out of the robe, and stood there naked, her arms drawing self-consciously over her breasts. The woman was clearly terrified of Forsyth. With good reason. If she didn't give his head of security a good time, what could she expect? A beating. Or worse.

'Yes, I like,' Uma responded lamely, repeating what she had said to Forsyth, 'but it's been a long day.'

'I help,' the woman said. 'I massage.'

She removed Uma's shirt, then her pants, before gently guiding Uma over to the table, making her perch on the edge. Uma reluctantly complied, trying not to panic. Was this some cruel joke of Forsyth's? Did he know? Uma was too tired to make any sense of it. The woman climbed onto the table and started to massage Uma's shoulders, sliding her hands down her spine, feathering the skin with her long nails. She drew her hands round to Uma's chest, crushing her breasts into Uma's back. Uma felt tiny tendrils of pleasure butterfly out across her upper torso. She groaned, glancing down at her waist.

Fox was almost fully erect.

That explains so much, she thought, pulling away from the woman and recovering her pants and shirts.

'I'm sorry, I can't do this,' she mumbled, quickly donning her clothes. 'We sit, yes?'

The woman looked up at Uma, then glanced towards the door.

What was going on? Could she be that afraid of Forsyth, or was there something else at play?

Uma put a finger to her lips, motioning for the woman to stay put before turning to examine the room. There was one only way in and out. If something was going down, they were effectively trapped, which left Uma with no choice.

She crept over to the door, grasping the handle, but as she did, the door burst inwards, knocking her to the carpet.

Uma sprang to her feet as Fox's training kicked in, but it was no good.

Within seconds, the room was filled with soldiers from the Saudi Royal Guard Regiment. There must have been at least twenty, including Petty, who was leering triumphantly at Uma. He jabbed the butt of his rifle towards her stomach. She easily parried the blow, but others stepped forward, pounding their gun stocks into her chest and back. Uma collapsed to her knees, groaning. Petty took aim, this time whipping the barrel across Uma's face. She felt a searing pain in her cheek and fell forward, mouth leaking blood, vision birthing stars. She had a loose sense of arms roughly pulling her into a sitting position. Suddenly she was on her feet, swaying, gathering her senses, assessing her chances, even as the circle of testosterone and gun oil closed around her.

A familiar voice cut through the fog.

'You didn't really think you would get away with it, did you?'

Uma focused on the figure in front of her. Forsyth was standing there, a glass of champagne in one hand.

'How much did they pay you?' he asked.

'When did you find out?' Uma spat back.

'Rae's escape was just too easy. There's no way you would have allowed that to happen unless you had been compromised. And your behaviour since then has, to say the least, been strange.' Forsyth glanced at the prostitute on the table. Uma followed his gaze. She looked terrified.

'Anyway, it doesn't matter. You can still be of service to me one last time.' Forsyth glanced at Petty. 'You're in charge for the time being. Bring him and the girl to Crouch's office.'

The Acorn, Riyadh, Saudi Arabia

22nd July, 2010, 02:08 hours AST

The pupil's centre was black, set inside a shifting orange sphere flecked with yellows and reds before fading into a cyan iris, which Uma realised was a kaleidoscope of blues and greens, itself orbited by repeating pairs of alternating rings: the inner, royal blue; the outer, a lighter turquoise. She recognised it immediately: a hydrogen atom. As she watched, the eye seemed to blink at her, then started to fade. Within seconds, the screen was black. Uma frowned, shifting her position, trying to energise her hands, but it was no good. They remained stubbornly numb, thanks to the thick twine that bound her wrists. She looked over at Salma. That was her name. She'd heard some guards use it. Her head was bowed, eyes shut, hands similarly tied, heavy breasts clearly visible through the open abaya she had grabbed from the floor as they were both led away from Forsyth's quarters. Behind her, by the doors to the laboratory, stood members of the Saudi Royal Guard, including Petty, who flashed a triumphant smile in her direction. She ignored him, focusing instead on what Crouch was doing as he busily tapped away on his keyboard. As the atom faded on his screen, another took its place. An oxygen atom which suffered a similar fate to the hydrogen eye. Others followed in quick succession: carbon, nitrogen, calcium, phosphorus atoms appeared, each one disappearing from the screen. Behind Crouch, Forsyth watched the professor, his back to Uma. There wasn't any effort to conceal what was going on, but then, why should they? For all they knew, Fox was a simple soldier, not a quantum physicist who recognised the constituent elements of every human being on the planet, but had no idea what it meant.

Crouch tapped the keyboard with a satisfied flourish, before leaning back in his seat and stretching his pudgy arms above his head.

'Is it ready?' Forsyth asked, the excitement in his voice palpable.

'We're ready,' Crouch said. 'We just need to infect Fox and deliver him back to the US. They'll never know what hit them. When they do, it'll be too late.'

'Very poetic,' Forsyth said. 'Their Trojan Horse is now ours.' He turned to look down at Uma, his million-watt smile causing her to glower back, as she realised he was referring to the fake editing suite they had used to liberate Ethan back to the States.

'Scowl all you want,' Forsyth sneered at her, 'it will not help. In approximately two hours, LEAP will cease to exist, leaving Eternity as the only viable provider of teleportation services on the planet.'

Uma stared at Forsyth, aghast. What did he mean? Cease to exist. How was that even possible? She eyed the guards loitering by the entrance to the laboratory with renewed urgency. She had to escape, but how? There were seven soldiers, plus the three mercenaries. There was no way she could overpower all of them.

'What are we going to do with her?' Crouch nodded at the woman beside Uma.

'I don't know,' Forsyth said absentmindedly. 'Give her to the team for a job well done.'

'You'll pay for that,' Uma muttered.

'And what are you going to do?' Forsyth laughed, 'Rescue her like a knight in shining armour? She's a fucking prostitute, for God's sake.' Forsyth was suddenly all business. 'Let's get this show on the road.'

He clicked his fingers. Petty stepped forward, motioning for two of the guards to follow him.

Uma scanned them as they approached, looking for weapons. The guards each had a G36, the assault rifle grasped diagonally across their chests. It would be unwieldy close up, but carried a thirty-round detachable box magazine, which might be useful for later. A Glock hung from Petty's waist, the holster open for a swifter release. That was more like it: seventeen rounds in the magazine, plus one in the chamber. Perfect for close quarters. One second. That was all the time Uma would need to remove it from Petty's holster and fire. Another five to empty the magazine. The realisation both horrified and excited her in equal measure. That Fox could do that so quickly; that she knew just what to do.

'Finally, got your promotion,' Uma snarled at Petty as he approached.

Petty smiled victoriously down at her, as the two guards shouldered their rifles before hoisting Uma to her feet.

'I always knew something was off about you,' he replied. 'You're nothing but a dirty Yank, fighting for the other side, just like all the rest.'

'You're not leadership material, Petty,' Uma chided. 'I heard you couldn't even cope with some friendly fire. Cracked up, caved in. Blubbed like the big baby I know you are.'

Petty roared with anger. He threw himself at Uma, shaping up to deliver a haymaker onto Uma's unprotected head. As his front foot came forward, Uma tore her left shoulder out of the guard's grasp, raising her bound hands to parry the blow and, at the same time, throwing her right knee hard into Petty's unprotected rib cage. He screamed in pain as her knee cap crushed his already cracked ribs. As he doubled over, she wrenched the Glock from its holster, then fired up into Petty's head before turning on the two guards who were still struggling to un-shoulder their rifles.

Two more shots boomed.

Uma swivelled towards the doors.

Fifteen bullets left, seven targets.

First, Silva, hand reaching for his Glock.

Uma felt a searing pain in her leg, but kept firing.

Harris' head snapped back.

The remaining soldiers were bunched tightly. She emptied the magazine into them, her finger pressed to the trigger long after the gun fell silent.

Six seconds, ten dead or dying.

Uma blanked her rising horror and limped over to Forsyth and Crouch cowering by the screens. They both looked terrified and without pausing, she clubbed Forsyth on the back of the head with the butt of the Glock. His skull crunched satisfyingly, and he slumped to the floor.

Uma glanced at Crouch who sat there, transfixed by the gun, but Uma ignored him, instead hobbling over to the injured men, but it was too late: Silva and Harris were dead, as were three of the soldiers. The other two were fading fast. One had taken a bullet in his throat, from which bloody air bubbles sputtered weakly as his life ebbed away. The other was holding his midriff, black blood oozing between his fingers.

Uma suppressed a sob. What had she done?

A sound by the screens dragged her attention back into the room. Crouch was laughing.

'You'll never get away with this,' he chortled, tears streaming down his face.

Uma stared at the dishevelled professor, the manic cackle slowing her tears. He was right, the gunfire must have alerted someone. Although, she thought, it was nearly three in the morning and this side of the facility was deserted. Partly, Forsyth's instructions – no one got in without his prior authorisation – but also the sandstorm had shut everything down. She glanced over at the floor-to-ceiling windows. Normally, at night, the view of downtown Riyadh was breathtaking, the glowing U of the Kingdom Center towering above the brightly lit spire of Al Faisaliah Tower and the skeleton of the half-completed Makkah Clock Royal Tower, but tonight it was a wall of blackness as the mile-high storm rolled over the city. There would normally be guards at the elevators, but these had been disabled by the fine sand that had wormed its way into every exposed nook of the Acorn, setting off fire alarms and smoke detectors. They'd been shut down after five that afternoon and would be disabled for at least twenty-four hours as the mega storm, currently fifty miles wide, inched its way over Riyadh's five million residents who were now cowering in their houses. It gave her more time to turn this around, but how? She stood up, wincing, and looked down. Blood leaked out of her torn trousers. Harris? He must have got his shot off. She knelt again to recover a knife from one of the dead guards before shuffling back to Salma.

Slowly, the woman raised her head.

Uma baulked. In the harsh light of the office, she looked even younger, barely in her twenties.

'Please, no die,' she said, her eyes bleeding fear.

'I'm not going to kill you,' Uma said, stooping to cut the rope that bound Salma's hands, before handing the knife over.

'Cut,' Uma said holding out her bound wrists. The woman complied, slicing through the rope. Uma took the knife from her and knelt again. Taking a handful of the abaya in one hand and, using the sharp blade, she cut through the material. Satisfied she had enough, Uma bound it tightly around her thigh, but the blood still oozed. She needed a windlass to ratchet the tourniquet. Without thinking, she grabbed one of the Heckler & Koch rifles, knocking out the pin that held the hand guard in place, before twisting it off the gun to reveal the piston assembly. She forced the spring-loaded rod back inside the assembly until it popped out. Uma sat down, thigh flat to the floor, placed the metal rod over the knot and tied another half knot around it. She twisted the tourniquet a few times, stifling a cry as shooting pains lanced up her leg into her groin. Satisfied, she tied off the ends of the abaya. Her leg throbbed like hell, but at least the bleeding had stopped. She hobbled back over to the screens, pulling up a chair beside Crouch. He glared at her through rheumy eyes, cloudy with drink, as she grabbed his keyboard and mouse.

'Don't touch that,' he squealed.

One of Fox's heavy fists shot out sideways, catching Crouch square on the jaw. He slumped forward in his chair without a sound.

God, that felt good.

'Now, let's find out what you've been getting up to.'

The Acorn, Riyadh, Saudi Arabia

22nd July 2010, 03:09 hours AST

Forsyth's eyes snapped open, then focused in on the bodies laid out neatly in front of him. For a moment, he just sat there, struggling to process the three men. Then he remembered: Fox. He had moved fast, blisteringly fast, disabling, disarming and removing the top of Petty's head in the same movement, before turning the gun on his two guards. They both looked peaceful, as if asleep, their bloodstained khaki shirts the only clue that they would never wake up. Forsyth's whole face throbbed rhythmically, metallic breath ragging through his nose, lips bulbous, vision snowballing a blizzard that matched the pea-souper clogging up his brain. He felt different. His hands were tied; his feet were bound. He looked over towards the door where seven more bodies were laid out in a long row like some sort of offering – or warning, perhaps – that said, "Don't fuck with me." Crouch was slumped at his desk, a body beside him. It looked familiar, but Forsyth's eyes were drawn back to the dead men at his feet. The top of Petty's skull was missing. He suppressed the urge to vomit. He had never seen a dead person before, except Al Rahman, but he was not like this. Forsyth's area was intel, helping people live their best lives, living longer, looking better, not this. It was barbaric. Fox was a monster. He swallowed hard, gasping as the pain in his mouth overwhelmed his senses. It felt like a cheese wire was slicing up through his gums into his nasal cavity and beyond. Tears leaked down his cheeks and he screwed his eyes shut. He sat there, waiting for the ache to subside, not daring to explore what was causing such torment, fearful of what it must have done to his looks.

A groan from the bank of monitors drew him back into the room. His eyes flickered open, searching for where the sound of life had come from. They widened in confusion, then horror.

Forsyth instinctively looked down and screamed at what he saw.

A blood-soaked abaya barely covered his heaving breasts.

The Acorn, Riyadh, Saudi Arabia

22nd July 2010, 03:12 hours AST

Forsyth came to again suddenly, his eyes trying to open, but just one obeying. His head throbbed and so did his mouth which was leaking blood. He licked the place where his front teeth should have been. Pain chiselled up into the roof of his mouth. He groaned and sat up, surveying the devastation with his good eye. Dead bodies were everywhere; Fox nowhere to be seen. But he had left his whore. She was sitting on a chair, staring at him, her eyes bulging with fear, wrists and ankles bound, her face swollen and bloody. He struggled to his feet, grimacing as he stood. The right side of his cheek felt distended, and the nerve endings in his gums continued to siren that something was very wrong. He stopped in front of a blank screen, jutting his front teeth forward over his lower ones. He gasped out loud. All four of his front incisors were missing. Forsyth screamed, this time with anger. Fox must have knocked them out, but why? He knew Forsyth could restore them. Next to him, Crouch groaned. Forsyth shook him by the shoulders. He needed him conscious to sort his face out. There was no way he could be seen like this, but like a bad car crash, Forsyth's gaze was drawn irresistibly back to his mouth. Fox had made a real mess. To what end, he thought again? And where had Fox gone? He wouldn't get far. Unless he had another gate somewhere. A LEAP version that he could use to escape back to America. As realisation dawned, Forsyth punched the screen in frustration before picking up a keyboard and smashing it down repeatedly, until it was a shattered pile of black plastic.

Crouch groaned again, opening his eyes.

Forsyth pulled him into a sitting position.

'You need to help me.'

'What happened?' he mumbled.

'Fox happened.'

Crouch looked at Forsyth, frowning.

'Your mouth?'

Forsyth turned on Crouch, holding a hand to his lips.

'Fox kicked me. I need you to thort it.'

Behind him, the woman was babbling incoherently, but Forsyth ignored her.

'Crouch, can we deliver the viruth today, thill?'

Forsyth had organised rolling interviews throughout the afternoon in preparation for Green Ray's demise. He could taste victory, but had to sort out his face first. The thought made his heart beat wildly as an image of an old man with weeping sores appeared in his mind's eye. He wasn't going back there. Never. And the woman responsible would pay dearly for her actions. This afternoon, if he had anything to do with it.

The whore was rocking back and forth in her chair, moaning.

Forsyth turned to study her. She was staring straight at him, face contorted with panic, but his eyes were drawn to her mouth. Fox was a monster. Her front teeth were also missing, her nose punched sideways. He'd ruined her looks as well.

Forsyth turned back to Crouch, who was now tapping away on his keyboard.

'Can you fith me? Now.' It hurt to speak, each movement of his lips agitating the bloody gap where his beautiful teeth had been.

'OK, give me a moment,' Crouch mumbled. 'Shouldn't we raise the—'

'No,' Forsyth cut him off. No one could see him like this. He needed to think, but couldn't. The woman was screaming now, a high-pitched wail that vibrated his brain cells, like nails ripping across a blackboard. He turned on her. She was frantic, straining against the rope, staring at Forsyth as if he was a ghoul from the depths of hell.

'Thut up,' he roared, but it was no good. She continued to scream. He marched over and punched her hard in the cheek. The silence was instant, but it didn't relieve his headache. If anything, his mouth hurt even more. He made to speak but caught himself. The lisp. Fox had ruined his voice. He sounded like a moron.

'Crouch,' he shouted. 'Repair me. Now.'

The Acorn, Riyadh, Saudi Arabia

22nd July 2010, 03:24 hours AST

Crouch watched as Forsyth emerged from the doorway, a broad smile on his handsome face. He immediately sought out a screen to inspect his repaired teeth, laughing with delight at his restored face and turning sideways to inspect his cheek.

What an idiot, Crouch thought. So preoccupied with his looks and presenting the perfect image of himself. Such a waste of energy.

Forsyth picked up a telephone, quickly punching in some numbers.

As he waited for it to be answered, he flashed one of his brilliant smiles at Crouch, who nodded back.

'We need to deliver that virus today,' Forsyth said. 'It would've been better with Fox, but we can return to the previous plan.'

'That's fine. I've multiple ways into their system.'

'What about her?'

Crouch looked over at the woman tied to the chair. She stared back at him, wild eyes bulging over the tape that Forsyth had stuck over her mouth. He'd had no choice. After coming to, she'd continued to scream as if the very gates of hell had opened up. Nothing either of them could do would quieten her cries. Again, Crouch had suggested that they call some guards, but Forsyth didn't want anyone to see him. It was comical, really. She was still trying to speak, but at least it wasn't an ear-splitting shriek. Crouch shrugged, unsure of what was being asked of him.

'Could she deliver the virus?'

'What will it add?' he said. 'I understood Fox. There was an element of poetic justice in him delivering the virus back through LEAP, but her?' Crouch shrugged again, wondering what Forsyth was after.

'It doesn't matter—' Forsyth began, but turned away as his call was answered. 'Please get someone up here right away. We've had some problems in the lab. And find Fox. When you do, bring him here.' He paused, listening. 'I know, I know, he won't get far in this storm.' Forsyth glanced towards the window. It was a mirror, blackened by the sandstorm hurricaning just two inches away.

As he ended the call, the woman started screeching loudly, her face red with the exertion of trying to make herself understood through the tape.

'For Christ's sake, shut up.' The back of Forsyth's hand caught her cheek so hard that her head snapped back, but it didn't stop her. As she recovered, the wailing started up again. Forsyth's fist landed hard on the other cheek. This time, she was still.

'Right, where were we?' he said to no one in particular. 'Let's get on with it then. I want it fully operational by the time we go live this afternoon.'

Crouch half nodded, distracted by a series of messages flashing on his screen. As he read them, a clammy shiver engulfed his body as if he had been submerged in a barrel of icy water.

'What's up? What's wrong?' he heard Forsyth's voice from faraway.

'Nothing,' Crouch muttered, dragging his gaze from the screen towards his erstwhile boss.

The Acorn, Riyadh, Saudi Arabia

22nd July 2010, 03:53 hours AST

The solution had been devastatingly simple, as all the best solutions are. It had just required Crouch to think about the body in more primitive terms, something his brain wasn't attuned to doing. Part of his difficulty had been Forsyth's insistence on something theatrical, like it had been when people were stripped of their skin. It was easy to do through the LEAP system, but the virus had shown its hand immediately, thus alerting Green Ray. This had allowed them to shut down the system as soon as the reports of what was happening trickled in. This time, he had built in a thirty-minute delay to infect as many LEAPers as possible. That had required something more subtle, but he had done it. All that remained was to devise a delivery mechanism and decide when to do it. For the former, they had wanted to use Fox, but now he was gone, so Crouch had intended to return to his original plan – inserting the virus into the system through a million access points. According to the usage stats, morning and evening were the prime times for travel as everyone teleported to work and back again. The system was now recording over one hundred million LEAPs at peak commute time across central Europe alone, which included parents dropping their kids off at school and continuing onto work. It was less in America, partly because of different time zones, but also because more Europeans had been affected by the volcano, so were further ahead with the rollout. So, that was the plan: a minimum of one hundred million people would be infected. It was irreversible this time, too. A double virus: one to kill as many people as possible; the other to infect the system itself, including everyone stored in it. There was no coming back from that reputational hit. It would obliterate Green Ray and that woman, leaving Eternity as the only viable teleporter in the world.

Crouch glanced at his watch. Just one more minute. Then it would all be over. Moments in his career flashed before his eyes, punctuated by unfamiliar feelings. He recalled his relief at getting the job from Reynolds, which had quickly turned to resentment as his young boss had ridiculed him weekly whilst visiting the Nevada facility. But that was nothing compared to the embarrassment he had suffered after his fall in San Francisco, the trip on the lip of the door coming to represent everything about the Reynolds' Airline collapse. He had gladly felt nothing during his descent into alcoholism, drifting from one high school job to another, until the US government had pulled him from obscurity with a chance to resurrect his career as head of their Carbon Based LEAPs unit. Crouch welled up as he remembered the moment the agents had offered him everything his heart could desire. It was so much more meaningful the second time, because he now appreciated what he had lost. Except the job turned out to be a poisoned chalice, plunging him into a nightmarish plot to assassinate the President of the United States, which he was too weak to turn down. Waves of guilt washed over him at the memory, but Forsyth had saved him with an offer to head his fledgling operation in Saudi. The promise this time was not money, but the restoration of his reputation by heading the pre-eminent teleportation service in the world. Gratitude warmed his heart as he remembered accepting the position. However, that familiar sinking feeling returned when he realised he had replaced a man child with a megalomaniacal septuagenarian for a boss. He remembered his sense of betrayal after the CIA had tricked him into enabling an attack on US bases in Afghanistan. It didn't matter that everyone was restored. He had facilitated the massacre just like the attack on POTUS. That was when he realised his Ground Zero was that woman. Her actions, to divert Reynolds on 17th December 2003 at 10:45, were the first beat of the butterfly's wings. His life had unravelled from that moment onwards. Anger coursed through his veins. He would have done – *had* done – anything to avenge that moment. To make her pay for that act. Crouch had gladly supported Forsyth's own vendetta. Initially, with the virus that stripped the skin from all those people, he felt nothing, the alcohol once again protecting him from any sense of guilt. Which brought him to his final act. He was waiting for it to end. The familiar feeling washed over him: relief.

Relief that it was over.

Relief that he would neither have to hide anymore, nor take orders from puerile infants and old-age pensioners.

Relief that he was now released from his living hell.

H_2O comprised sixty percent of all humans. That was the key. A simple inorganic compound, each molecule comprising just three atoms: two hydrogen, one oxygen. All he had to do was separate them into their constituent parts. Better still, have them teleport in situ, from the target's body. Instantaneously. He had tested it on mice, but never humans. Until now.

'What's wrong with you?' Forsyth asked, coming over.

'Nothing,' Crouch mumbled, staring at the clock counting out on his screen. As he did so, there was a commotion by the door as members of the Saudi Royal Regiment entered the room. They were panting heavily after climbing the stairs and stood, chattering in Arabic, surveying the surrounding devastation. Forsyth turned to meet them.

As he passed the woman, his pace suddenly slowed. One moment, he was striding purposefully. The next, he seemed to pause in mid-air, his body visibly shrinking into his clothes. Three of the soldiers screamed, but Crouch couldn't see what was happening as Forsyth was facing away from him. Then slowly, his body toppled over onto the woman, his head striking her thighs. There was a great tearing sound, and the trunk sheared off at the neck, falling to the floor. The woman stared down at the skull nestling in her lap. She started to scream, great howls of pain and rage. Crouch rushed over to see what was left of Forsyth.

His face had slipped sideways, lightly tanned skin now a dark brown, leathery in texture and melted to his bones like cured meat. His once beautiful nose was now a sludge of adipose tissue. It was unmistakably Forsyth. His recently restored, perfectly white teeth were frozen in a Munchian scream, his black hair still luxurious, spilling down his shrivelled cheeks and over his shrunken skull. Where his brilliant blue eyes had once glittered, hollowed-out sockets bored into Crouch. Two of the soldiers joined him. One started talking gibberish, whilst the other lifted Forsyth's body from the floor, as if it was a blow-up doll, and laid it beside the three corpses in front of them.

More guards arrived. One gently removed the skull and laid it on the floor at the head of his body. The rest just stood there, staring at the woman's nakedness, as only men can do. One laughed, and another made an obscene gesture as he cut her ropes, pulling her up roughly into a standing position. The woman screamed, swinging an arm at the guard, who easily evaded it. He grabbed her dress, pulling it open further. Her breasts spilled out, and he cupped one of them in his hand, making a sucking sound with his lips. Everyone howled with laughter. Crouch turned away in disgust. As he did, he could have sworn the woman screamed his name, but couldn't be sure. He exited the facility, not stopping until he was safely locked inside his suite.

He pulled a bottle of Rittenhouse from the credenza, weighing it in his hands, feeling its coolness against his palms. Finally, he broke the seal, pouring himself a shot. As the cool liquid sliced down his throat, Crouch smiled for what felt like the first time in months.

Home at last.

Al-Ha'ir Prison, 25 miles South of Riyadh

22nd July 2010, 03:59 hours AST

Uma hunched forward, peering out over the steering column at the dust storm swirling outside the Range Rover. She beamed the headlamps for a second, but had to look away as the dizzying kaleidoscope of sand threatened to overwhelm her visual cortex. As the lights faded, she stared back into the impenetrable wall. It had battered the SUV all the way out of Riyadh, driven by a shamal that at times threatened to suck the vehicle up into the mile-high vortex of desert sand accompanying the gale force winds. Uma glanced over at Salma, who smiled back sweetly. The woman brushed a stray hair from her face, struggling to find her hand in the oversized sweatshirt that Uma had pulled from the back of the Range Rover, along with sweat pants and trainers that were also way too big for her. The woman hadn't spoken since her duplicate had stepped out of the gate in the lab. Instead, she had sat there, staring at her twin, an uncomprehending look on her face. Except it wasn't an exact copy. Uma had put Forsyth's mind inside the woman's, much like she had teleported hers into Ed Fox. After infecting the real Forsyth with the virus, the idea had come to her as she stared at his handsome face. It was too easy for him to simply die once the virus destroyed his perfect body. She wanted him to suffer, like he had made her suffer. Like he had made Ethan suffer. Like he had made all the women suffer, with his sickening fetishes and vain glorious preying. Except this time there was no way back for him. No one would believe the rantings of a common prostitute. She had particularly enjoyed putting Fox's boot through Forsyth's cruel mouth. It would be bad enough for Forsyth to live out his life stuck inside the very sex that he clearly despised, but to lose his looks as well … That was the sweetest of revenges.

After leaving the lab, they had made their way to Forsyth's quarters. She knew exactly where the recordings were – or at least Fox's memories did. In his bedroom, in a drawer, over 200 discs were neatly laid out, their holders labelled in much the same as the computer folders on his laptop in San Francisco. After hurriedly throwing them into two pillowcases, they had continued down the deserted stairwell into the bowels of the Acorn where Uma had recovered her Range Rover. She had intended to head east towards Doha Port where she would blag a berth on a container ship heading back to the Caribbean. Fox, it seemed, had contacts in every harbour that he had been stationed at. She had explained to Salma that she could go anywhere. Uma would pay. She could access money. However, within minutes of exiting the complex, Uma realised she still had unfinished business.

Taking the goggles from her lap, she pulled them over her eyes. Once she was certain they fitted snugly, she rolled up the balaclava around her neck, covering her mouth and nose, and finally looped it over head.

'Close your eyes,' she muffled at Salma. 'And count to thirty before breathing.'

Salma nodded, pulling the hoodie low over her face before adopting the brace position, head burrowing into her thighs. Satisfied, Uma cracked the door open, but she was no match for the howling gale which ripped the handle from her grasp. Instantly, a fist of sand punched into the cabin. Uma stumbled out, struggling to maintain her balance as she wrestled with the storm to gain control of the door, before slamming it shut. She knocked on the glass twice as agreed with Salma, before standing and trying to gain her bearings. Everywhere she turned, a roaring torrent of sand blasted into her, tearing at her goggles and face mask. She coughed as the tiny particles quickly permeated the thick cotton mask, choking her nostrils with dry dust. Beginning to panic, she reached out a hand, searching for the outline of the Range Rover which was pointed towards the prison. She worked her way down the wing, then onto the bumper. Satisfied she was facing the right way, Uma stepped forward, half running, half stumbling blindly along the forecourt, arms outstretched, until she felt the reassuring so-lidity of the Al-Ha'ir Prison wall and eventually, as she tracked left, the intercom. She pressed the button and waited, but nothing happened. She pressed the button again, holding it down. This time the port-hole unlatched. She pushed her ID through the small opening, which snapped shut, leaving Uma standing there, waiting, wondering if this was the moment her luck ran out. Suddenly, the door cracked open. Uma bundled inside, turning to help a guard she didn't recognise force it shut against the weight of the storm. Uma pulled off the googles to let the man know who it was, but he still eyed her suspiciously, hand on his holster as he retreated towards his desk.

'Where is everyone?' Uma said, looking around the empty room, normally bustling with ten or more guards.

'Who are you?' the guard said.

'You know who I am,' she said, nodding at the card in his hand.

'Yes, but why now? It's late.'

'I need to speak to Rae. On behalf of Mr Forsyth.'

'It's very early for a visit, Mr Fox.' The guard handed Uma her ID, who shrugged as nonchalantly as she could. 'Besides, it hasn't been authorised.'

'You know how Forsyth is. Always changing his mind about things.' Uma kept her voice calm, but her heart was racing.

'I'm afraid we shall have to get clearance.'

'From who exactly?' Uma deadpanned. 'Mr Forsyth?'

'I suppose,' he said.

'Well, he's currently asleep. Do you want to be the one that wakes him at four in the morning? Be my guest. Here is his personal cell.'

Uma handed the guard her mobile.

'The network is down.'

'Call him on the landline,' Uma countered, nodding at the phone on the desk. 'I've got his room number in The Acorn.'

Uma stared hard at the man, who eventually shrugged. John Forsyth's rages were legendary. He needed this job. Besides which, what could one man do in this storm?

'OK, you can go, but be quick.'

Uma nodded and followed him down the corridor.

'Where is everyone?' she asked again.

'The storm,' the man grunted by way of explanation.

Uma relaxed. This was going to be easier than she could have imagined.

As the guard opened the door, the same smell of sweat, blood and death assaulted her nostrils, but she was ready this time. He remained by the entrance as Uma entered the cell. She could feel his eyes on her back and halfway across the room, she stopped and turned.

'I need privacy if you don't mind. Lock the door, wait outside. I'll knock when I've finished.'

He stood there for several seconds, clearly deliberating what to do, before slamming the door shut with a hollow clank. Uma heard the key turn. This had better work, she thought.

Behind her, Ethan groaned. She walked over to his mattress and knelt by his side. Even though she had prepared herself, she still burst into tears at the sight of his back, oozing red puss from the beating he had suffered that morning. It was inhumane. That was why she was here. Now Eternity was incapacitated, no one would survive being transported through one of their gates, which meant Ethan was stuck here. Like this. She couldn't take him with her. He would never survive being carried to the SUV in this storm, let alone a ten-hour drive to Qatar. Besides which, there was no point. She had been following the kangaroo court in New York: only one Ethan could live.

Realising that if she delayed any longer, she would be unable to go through with it, she took the pillow from his bed and gently lifted Ethan's head, passing the thin cushioning underneath. Without pausing, she pushed his face down into it.

'Goodbye, Ethan,' she whispered, increasing the pressure on the back of his head.

United Nations, Manhattan

22nd July 2010, 21:58 hours EDT

Uma stared at the table in front of her, wondering what to do. Each desk was fitted with earphones, allowing delegates to listen, either to any speakers on the rostrum or to interpreters translating in one of the many booths that ringed the hall. In addition, there was a fixed receiver, a microphone control, and buttons for electronic voting, which Uma was excluded from doing. That was reserved for the 182 delegates who were shortly to decide Ethan's fate. Once again, Uma felt powerless, like she had done on so many occasions over the past months, except this time, it felt different. For a start, Ethan, whilst grateful for her honesty, had added nothing beyond her own hope that somehow she, as Fox in Saudi Arabia, could rescue Ethan again. To face what? Unless he could destroy Eternity, they would be plunged back into the same nightmare: Ethan in New York facing annihilation, and another restored Ethan in Saudi, facing ten years in a hellhole. The one she rescued hadn't even lasted three months, before his mind had splintered. Plus, she faced humiliation, the likelihood being expulsion from any future involving LEAP. Just at the moment it was beginning to do some real good.

As the clock ticked towards 10 p.m., the lights suddenly dimmed in the hall, which fell silent as Ingram and the Attorney General appeared on the rostrum before taking their seats. What was he doing here? Uma thought.

Edward Johnson tapped the microphone.

'Welcome back, ladies and gentlemen. We shall shortly start the vote on our first resolution, regarding the matter of Ethan Rae. Before we do, there has been some new evidence which has only come into our possession in the last few hours.' There was a low murmur in the auditorium as Uma saw the familiar figure of Shane Williams, CTO of Green Ray, step up onto the low dais right in front of her, a file of papers in his hand. He stood there, waiting, oblivious to her presence as Uma felt the air suck from her lungs. As she stared at him in horror, he glanced over, their eyes meeting for a millisecond, and in that moment, she knew he was going to give evidence against her. She felt a surge of emotions, part anger, part sadness at his betrayal, but a part of her also understood. He had been one of the first people to trample over the LEAP Laws, three of them in one go, when he had copied Ethan, resurrected a dead assassin and merged his atomic code with Ethan's brain. It was a trifecta of breaches. Shane had always regretted his decision, but interestingly, hadn't wanted to delete the merged man. That had been left to Uma, who had deleted Shane's creation, wiped his programme and restored Ethan. The opposite of what was just about to happen. All she could think of were Shane's words. 'You can't control this, you know,' he had shouted at her. 'The genie's out of the bottle now. It will not be easy to put back.' Oh, how right he was, she thought, except here he now stood, trying to do exactly that. But the genie had long since bolted.

On the dais, Ingram and Johnson appeared to be deep in conversation, before the Attorney General glanced down at Shane and motioned with the palm of his hand to wait, before turning and addressing the hall.

'I've just been informed by Director Ingram that his office has received fresh evidence different to that which I was intending to share with you. He has convinced me it will be far more persuasive in clarifying exactly who is the copy.'

As he turned, looking up towards the UN emblem, an enormous screen slowly lowered down from the ceiling. At first it was blank, but then a fuzzy red rectangle materialised, which slowly solidified into a deep wine-coloured carpet. As the image tracked back, a settee appeared. An icy trickle of fear slid down Uma's spine as Ethan appeared in the frame, sitting on the sofa in her apartment in DC.

'Are we live?' Uma heard him say from a thousand miles away.

'Yes,' a voice answered.

'Good afternoon, everyone. I have some information that I would like to share with you. Information that will help clarify who is the copy.' He paused for a moment, staring into the camera, but it felt like it was directed to Uma. It was like he was staring into her very soul. His kind eyes looked both sad and determined, comfortable at knowing that what he was going to say would put things right. 'There's no easy way to say this, so I'll come straight out with it. I'm the copy.' There was a roar behind Uma. She avoided Shane's accusatory glare, her limbs turning to jelly and galaxies of light clouding her vision. 'After being rescued by Uma, an act of kindness that I will forever be grateful for, I realised quickly that I couldn't live with the memories of what happened in Saudi.' He closed his eyes, clearly collecting himself, before opening them and continuing haltingly.

'As many of you know, I was imprisoned many years ago when I was a teenager. On that occasion I received fifty lashes. It took nearly six months to recover from that, but the mind takes longer.' Tears brightened his eyes which glistened like dying suns on the huge screen. 'Even now, there's not a day that goes by when I don't relive some of those memories.' He shuddered, the words slowing to a crawl. 'However, what I recently experienced was a whole other level of pain. Fifty lashes a week. That was what I was receiving.' Ethan's tears fell freely now, his voice almost a whisper. Uma sobbed, the ramifications of what he had done now clear.

'I couldn't sleep that first night back, wracked with terrible dreams. The next day, I could barely function. No man should have to go through that. LEAP offered me an escape, so I took it. A six-week escape, rolling back my programme to the morning I was kidnapped after following Forsyth through the Eternity gate. It worked,' he said, his voice stronger. 'It wiped my memories, allowed me to live, free from my nightmare in Saudi. And more importantly, to continue my contribution to the rollout of LEAP. But that doesn't matter. I realise that now. I broke the prime Leap Law. I copied myself to save myself. I am guilty as charged. I should have sought help through the proper channels, but we were under enormous pressure to counter what Eternity was doing, so I made that decision myself. One, I now realise, I had no right to. No one with that amount of power should. No one is above the Laws. Which is why your role moving forward is so critical. I am so grateful that the future management of LEAP is now in the right hands.' Ethan's voice had steadied, his tone growing stronger as he continued. 'I have therefore decided to voluntarily put myself back into the system, after which all my files will be deleted. In fact, I have already signed the paperwork to that effect. Tomorrow morning, I will be returned to the system. I am of sound mind. No one has pressured or coerced me to do this. My actions have been entirely my own. I conferred with no one, sought no one's help, and ran the copying programme myself. That's all I have to say. Thankyou.'

As Ethan stared into the camera, the screen went blank.

Uma's Apartment, DC

23rd July 2010, 10:28 hours EDT

U ma shifted her position, returning blood to legs long since numbed by the position she had been sitting in for the last hour. Beside Ethan. It felt so innocuous, a scene they had shared on countless occasions in the short time they had been together, but of course, this was different. This was the end as she knew it. Uma was at a loss as to what to do, numbed by the rapidity with which events had progressed after Ethan had dropped his bombshell in the General Assembly Hall of the United Nations. It reminded her of the night she had spent with her father when she had restored him following his failure to return home after a routine afternoon hike up into the Þingvellir National Park. The search parties sent out to look for him had found nothing, except her father's backpack in a deep fissure, lying amongst the sharp rocks that littered the crevices. He was almost certainly dead. Uma had immediately restored him from the last LEAP backup, embracing him tightly as he had emerged from the chamber. Of course, when she told him what she had done, he had been furious.

'You can't do this!' he had scolded her. 'It will upset the natural order of things.'

'But you might be dead,' she had wept, all too aware of what he was suggesting. She was also confused. Only the week before, they had made a monumental breakthrough with the LEAP system, one that effectively cleared the way for her to launch LEAP out to the market. She couldn't understand why he would want to miss that.

'But what if I'm not? You can't have two of me running around!'

He had ordered her to transfer him back into the system and then delete his program. She had refused. What daughter wouldn't? This had made him even madder.

'The line "With great power comes great responsibility" exists for a reason,' he lectured her.

And here she was again, sitting with the only other man she had ever loved, but it was different this time. Back then, with her father, they had talked for hours after his decision. Tonight, she had barely said a word to Ethan, trying to work out a way round the problem until her brain cells were a tangle of Gordian knots that made her head ache and heart want to burst.

As she shifted her weight, Ethan looked down, smiling sadly. Uma thought her heart was going to fracture in two. After two hours, all she had were five words.

'Why did you do it?'

He took her hand, pulling her round to face him before kissing her gently on the lips.

'Ever since my parents died, I've lived with the guilt of causing their deaths that night, of not being able to protect them. It's defined my life, driven my success, fed my loneliness, which no amount of charitable donations could fill. Until I met you. You gave me a reason to live and I vowed to protect you with my dying breath. To ensure that you could achieve everything you were put on this earth to achieve. You're doing something important here, Uma. Work that will save the world. I can't allow that to be ended by some trumped-up charges when your actions were driven by a simple goal to save me. You can't be caught up in another copying scandal. It will end your career, which would be disastrous for Green Ray. You're the figurehead of the movement. You need to continue the work. That's why I did it, and would do it again tomorrow. And the day after and for all eternity.'

'I thought we were going to grow old together,' she cried, burying her head in his chest.

He hugged her tightly, and Uma responded, gripping onto him as if her life depended on it.

After what seemed hours, there was a knock at the door. It was a CIA agent. He was young, barely out of college.

'Excuse me, Mr Rae,' he said, his youthful face filled with admiration as he shook Ethan's hand. 'It's time.'

Ethan stood and looked down at Uma. She avoided his gaze. All she could think of was her own culpability. She wouldn't have needed to save him if she hadn't intentionally summoned Anderson and pointed him at Forsyth that day.

Ethan gave her one last kiss, his soft lips melting into hers. She lingered, feeling the softness of their touch. At some point, they pulled apart.

Uma felt herself sob, her eyes blinded by more tears. By the time she wiped them away, Ethan was standing by the gate in her apartment.

He smiled sadly at her, turned towards the gate and, as she watched, he blinked out of existence.

Washington DC

'Hi, Uma. It's me.'

The raspy voice, ripped dry by a thousand cigarettes, was unmistakable. Uma sat up in bed, heart beating wildly. Her mouth tasted like old cigars.

'Where are you?' she said, flicking the light on by her bedside table. She had been lying wide awake, fully clothed, in the darkness of her bedroom, churning through the events of yesterday.

'On the Saudi/Qatari border.' His voice sounded strained, as if he was trying to hold it steady.

Uma glanced at her watch. It must be past midday in Saudi. If indeed he was still there.

'I've been trying to get hold of you,' Uma said, trying to remain calm. That was an understatement. She'd called Fox's number every fifteen minutes throughout the long night. It was the only thing she could think to do after Ethan's death. She kept seeing him, standing there sadly, before turning and ... The memory triggered another wave of tears as she reminded herself for the hundredth time that she was responsible for this mess. But there was a way out. Fox's refusal to come back with Ethan after rescuing him was now the only way to save to Ethan. She had to get him to rescue Ethan all over again.

'I saw,' Fox said in a monotone. 'There's been a storm. It knocked out all mobile networks. We've just emerged from it.'

There was silence on the phone. Uma had so many questions, she didn't know where to start.

'Are you OK?' she tried.

'I've been better.' Fox suppressed a laugh, which choked out into a sob.

'What's going on?' Uma said, the first inkling of alarm leaching up her spine. 'Why didn't you come back? With Ethan, the first time. As agreed.'

More silence.

'I thought I could be more useful here,' he said.

'That's why I wanted to speak to you. Something—'

'I haven't got long,' Fox cut in. 'I'm sending you a file. It contains evidence of Crouch's involvement in the troop and LEAP massacres. We've got him, Uma. We've finally got the bastard.' He was speaking quickly, as though afraid Uma would interrupt him. As she listened, he filled her in about the virus Crouch had made, and how Fox had applied it to Eternity using Forsyth as the delivery agent. How it had destroyed the system, along with Forsyth.

'You mean he's dead?' she said, her tone suspicious, not daring to believe Forsyth was no longer around.

There was a brief pause.

'He's dead.' There was a hint of relief in Fox's voice, but once again it sounded fraught, as if he was struggling to contain his emotions.

'And there's no way back for him?'

'Like I said, this virus is irreversible. I've seen nothing like it before. Every H2O atom in the body is infected. Each one contains a countdown clock which teleports it back to the main system, thirty minutes after transmission. It's embedded in the system's code, so if someone uses Eternity, they will suffer the same fate. The entire system is useless. It's finally over.' Fox sobbed again, as Uma felt herself breathe for the first time in days. It was over. She could barely believe it, except it wasn't over. Far from it: her Ethan was dead. Fox was her last hope. He was talking again.

'There's something else.'

The line crackled and hissed. For a second, Uma thought she had lost him.

'Ethan ...'

'What did you say?' Uma's heart skipped a beat.

'Ethan is dead.'

'I know. That's why I've been trying to call you.'

'No, I ... here.'

A cold cloud enveloped Uma's body as she tried to untangle what Fox was saying.

Suddenly, the static disappeared. In the silence that followed, Fox spoke, his rough voice choked with emotion.

'I killed him so you could free Ethan in New York.'

Black dots misted across Uma's vision.

'Ethan's dead,' she said.

More silence, stretching into eternity.

'Can't you restore him?' Fox said eventually, his voice barely audible.

'They scrubbed the backups. Every one of them.'

Time seemed to stand still as they both absorbed what the other had said.

'Come home, Uma,' Uma eventually managed.

'I can't,' the gruff voice sobbed.

'Why not? What will you do?'

'You'll know.'

Before Uma could say anything, the line suddenly went dead.

'Please, don't go,' she whimpered, but the only sound she could hear was cold static hissing in her ear.

Nine Months Later

Virginia

2nd May 2011, 06:23 hours EDT

The lawns fell steeply away from the house, rolling down to the slow-moving river which steamed lazily in the early morning heat where the water wasn't shaded by the towering oaks lining the far bank. Underneath their cool canopy, swarms of mayflies were already gathering, their delicate triangular wings buzzing noisily in the humid air. Opposite, where the grass had faded to mud, three whitetail deer stood in the shallows, the two fawns sipping cautiously as their mother stood guard. A noise from further up the bank drew her furtive glance back towards the large mansion, but after scanning the white lime-stone structure for signs of life, she eventually risked a quick drink. One hundred feet above her, Ingram stood on the balcony outside his bedroom, staring at the family, a glass of iced tea in his hand. He loved this time of day. No one around, just the sounds of the river below, the unbroken forest spread out before him, the sun just beginning to crest the treetops, its fiery fingertips warming his face. He yawned, looking at the pile of paperwork on the table beside him, a brief speech he had prepared for the press conference on top. Normally he would review them on the way into work, but LEAP had put paid to that. The President had mandated that all federal staff should use the system as a way of forcing take-up. He hated it, but the inconvenience of losing his morning commute to teleportation was more than compensated for by the benefits that it had already brought, particularly after what they had achieved yesterday.

He toasted the river and collected the paperwork, before carefully opening the sliding doors back into his bedroom. His wife of forty years murmured in her sleep as he tiptoed into their en-suite bathroom, where he showered and dressed. It was a quick turnaround this morning. They had worked late into the night, tying up loose ends from yesterday's momentous operation. Six months ago, he would have probably stayed at the apartment in DC, but LEAP had rendered that obsolete. He had spent every night of the last ninety at Oaklands. His wife had never been happier. He had grown to love the place even more, savouring his early morning sojourns on the balcony in every weather, contemplating how he could better serve his country. Ingram crept back into the bedroom and kissed his wife on the forehead before making his way downstairs. Polly, their four-year-old golden retriever, ran up to greet him. After a quick cup of coffee, he entered his office where he had positioned the LEAP gate. Operating it was already easier, the list of allowable destinations now displayed on the new iPad, only released last year. Today, as with most days, he clicked on the one labelled, "White House", but unlike most days that he travelled there, this was a good day. A day for celebration. A day he was going to enjoy, basking in the brief public glory of a job well done for his country.

Without a backward glance, Ingram stepped through the gate and disappeared.

Unknown Location

2nd May 2011, 11:57 hours EDT

The tall man stumbled slightly as he entered the room, not because he had lost his footing, but because he wasn't where he was supposed to be. He did a double take, inspecting the small room, a mystified frown wrinkling his long face which grew even more creased as the door opened and Uma entered. She closed it, facing Ingram across the table, the door behind her.

'Doctor, I wasn't expecting you,' Ingram said, his eyes narrowing slightly. 'Where are we exactly?'

'Somewhere that's safe,' Uma said, her hand gripping the door handle tightly. She was surprised at how nervous she felt, but Ingram had always affected her that way. He seemed as cool as ever, casually walking over to one of the chairs before sitting down.

'I hope you've got a good reason for kidnapping me. I assume this is what you've done,' Ingram said, gesturing around the room.

'You're a hard man to get hold of.' That was an understatement. Ingram had ignored all her requests for a meeting following Ethan's death, not that it made any difference once she had decided on her course of action. They would have still ended up in this room, having this conversation. The thought emboldened her. She had been waiting for this moment for months. The realisation steadied her nerves. She was in charge here, not him.

Ingram looked at his watch, unaware of the missing hours.

'I've got a meeting with the President in two minutes. You may have read about what happened last night.'

'I know, that's why I brought you here.' Uma had timed his entry into the room carefully, leaving everything the same to mimic the LEAP he had been expecting. She savoured the moment that would shortly arrive, then withdrew a remote from her pocket and pointed it at a large screen on the wall. The television sprang into life. She quickly changed channels, bringing up the White House Press Briefing room. The shot, taken from the back of the small theatre, showed every seat occupied, each reporter facing the familiar lectern, embossed with the President's seal and flanked by two US flags.

Uma studied Ingram carefully. He still hadn't noticed the time difference. She suppressed a smile as the on-screen digital clock flicked to midday. The camera zoomed in on the famous lectern as Jon Court-ney, White House Press Secretary, appeared stage left, before taking his place in front of the wooden stand. He waited for the room to fall silent, before addressing the assembled journalists.

'Good afternoon, ladies and gentlemen. After the momentous an-nouncement by President Jamal Williams last night, I would like to welcome Director Ingram on stage with some important and ground-breaking news.'

The room fell silent. Uma looked over at Ingram, who didn't seem to react until, as they both watched, Director Ingram limped onto the stage. He looked old and he stumbled, just as Ingram had.

'I've underestimated you, Doctor,' he said, his face impassive.

Uma realised that was as much admiration as she was ever going to receive.

'Where do you think this little show is going to get you? If that's a copy—' He nodded at the screen. '—what do you expect him to say that can possibly harm me?'

'Watch,' is all Uma said.

The man on stage began haltingly, stooping slightly as he leaned into the double mics. 'Ladies and gentlemen, as has been widely trailed on all the networks, I'm pleased to confirm that, shortly after 3:39 a.m. yesterday morning in Pakistan, American Navy Seals successfully shot and killed Osama Bin Laden, the leader of al-Qaeda, in his compound in the Pakistani city of Abbottabad.'

Ingram tried to continue, but was drowned out as every man and woman stood and applauded. Slowly the room quietened down and Ingram resumed.

'I have to say this achievement is the crowning glory of all my years in the Intelligence service, driven by my desire to avenge the attacks on the Twin Towers in New York City, the Pentagon and the downing of Flight 93 in Shanksville, Pennsylvania. Nearly three thousand Americans died on 11th September 2001. I made a vow that day, to myself and the American people, that I would dedicate my remaining career to bringing the vicious murderers behind those cowardly attacks to justice. Nearly a decade on, we've finally succeeded—' There were whoops in the audience. Ingram raised a thin arm to acknowledge them. '—after years of painstaking intelligence work, involving millions of agent hours to locate the mastermind behind the 9/11 attacks. As the President confirmed in his address last night, our forces were able to bring all that effort to fruition in an operation code-named Neptune Spear, when two stealth versions of our Black Hawk helicopters landed inside Bin Laden's compound, located and executed him. The entire operation took just thirty-eight minutes. No Americans were killed. In addition, we were able to recover a treasure trove of information about al-Qaeda, contained in ten hard drives, dozens of mobile phones, almost a hundred thumb drives, and thousands of documents. This will hopefully lead to the further weakening of the al-Qaeda infrastructure, and eventually wipe their threat from the face of the earth.' Everyone clapped again. Ingram waited for the applause to subside, before continuing. 'I have one further announcement I'd like to make.'

Uma held her breath.

This was the moment.

The moment she had spent months planning for. Months of slowly siphoning off Ingram's memories from the system, learning his routines, and sometimes, briefly inhabiting the lanky body late at night, practising his speech and familiarising herself with his mind, when the real Ingram was asleep, tucked up in bed with his wife.

Ingram was sitting stock still, his back arched upright, hands resting on the table, exuding calmness. It was as though he was watching daytime television.

She turned back to the screen, wondering how he would feel in thirty seconds.

'I am honoured to have played my small part in the extermination of Bin Laden and, having restored the pride to our wonderful security services, I feel it is time to hand the baton over to a younger person. Immediately after this announcement, I will have a meeting with the President to tender my resignation as Director of the National Intelligence.'

That got Ingram's attention. The blood drained from his face as he stared up at the television, his shoulders slumping, long limbs sagging into the chair. In an instant, Uma saw him age ten years.

That was more like it.

'I'll reverse that decision as soon as I return,' he said, a slight tremor in his voice. 'You'll be prosecuted under the new LEAP Act for the unlawful hijacking and impersonation of another human being.'

'Whoever said you're going back, Director. Oh, I beg your pardon, Mr Ingram.'

Before he could respond, Uma was standing in the corridor. 'There are only two ways out of this room,' she continued, nodding at the LEAP gate and the door handle. 'Both will put you back into the LEAP system. Enjoy your retirement.'

The door slammed shut.

Oval Office, Washington DC

2nd May 2011, 12:30 hours EDT

U ma stood facing the Resolution Desk, her back almost touching the white marble fireplace over which an imposing portrait of George Washington hung. To her left, a bronze bust of Abraham Lincoln stared impassively into the room, book-ended by a cast of Martin Luther King, Jr. to her right, and, above which, Norman Rockwell's "Working on the Statue of Liberty", depicted workers hanging precariously from the welcoming torch as they cleaned it against a brilliant blue Manhattan sky. So much history, she thought, but it no longer phased her, being at the centre of all this power. Not like before. Back then, she was barely surviving, wracked by nightmares, uncertain of her future, mourning her past. Back then, she had been railroaded into releasing LEAP, against her better judgement, attacked at every turn by a power-hungry CIA Director, and pursued by a perverted Septuagenarian. Back then, she had been forced to reinstate troops against her wishes, along with the victims of the so-called LEAP massacre. Back then, she had finally lost control of LEAP, as it was handed over to an oversight board comprising delegates from all active nations using the new technology. That was all in the past. Now she was in charge.

The room felt like home.

The curved door to her left suddenly opened and President Jamal Williams entered. He looked tired, with good reason. Neptune Spear had kept everyone up late into the night, and the day had been filled with debriefings on the Libyan and Syrian civil wars, along with on-going protests across the Gulf. Uma stepped forward, smiling warmly. The President responded, shaking her hand in his famous double grasp. He motioned for her to sit. She complied, wincing slightly as the arthritis in her knees objected. She would have to fix that later.

'Joseph, why didn't you come to me first?' the younger man asked, but before Uma could reply, he continued, 'I'll get straight to the point. I would like you to reconsider your decision to stand down. At least until the end of my term.'

Uma stared at the President for a good thirty seconds before reply-ing. Not because she didn't know what to do or had any doubt about what she was going to say. It was the obvious play, one she had expected the President to make. In fact, she was counting on it. The only reason Uma had proffered her resignation in the first place was to see the look on Ingram's face. It was a fitting revenge – to remove the one thing he wanted most in the world. It had been worth the risk. She needed Ingram in the role. It was the only way she could make sense of Ethan's death. The mere memory of his name triggered a crushing longing that permanently lurked in the recesses of her soul like a black hole. It slowed time to a standstill: each second a day; each breath, a lifetime; each beat of her dead heart, an eternity. It swallowed up any glimmer of hope for the future. It leadened her limbs with guilt. She had triggered the events that resulted in Ethan's death. She was responsible for his absence, and would have to live with that knowledge. Somehow right that wrong by any means necessary, including this. Uma breathed deeply, drawing strength from her nascent resolve.

'That's very kind, Mr President,' she said. 'However, it just feels like the right moment to step back, to allow younger blood into the role, particularly as we move into this new era. You don't want a dinosaur like me holding back progress.'

'That's precisely why I want you to stay. LEAP has heralded in a new age for humanity, one infused with great hope, but also great risk as we begin to examine what possibilities this new technology offers, particularly when it comes to national security. We need old hands to guide the tiller. Hands that have experienced life, as we say, and have the interests of this great nation at the centre of their moral compass.'

Uma relaxed back onto the couch, enjoying the moment. She really couldn't imagine this going any better. He was desperate for Ingram to stay on. She would be lying if there wasn't a small part of her that had enjoyed the last six months, despite the crushing loneliness that she had to live with. It had allowed her to piece together the remaining pieces of the jigsaw around Ingram's involvement: he was behind the attacks on the US troops, knowing that the massacre would force Uma to restore them and pave the way for an independent body to oversee LEAP. Uma had to give it to him – everything he did was for the good of the country, but there was also an undercurrent of personal hubris running through his decisions. One came with the other. She would be careful not to let the same thing happen to her. All this power was intoxicating.

'I think for that to happen, I will need involvement in the Oversight Board, especially as they begin to roll-out the new LEAP Laws that each signatory country has enacted in their local jurisdictions.'

'What do you have in mind, Joseph?'

'The new presidency of the LEAP Oversight Board will shortly be filled. If I stay on, I would like to put my name forward. It would allow me to keep my finger on the pulse of international reaction to the LEAP Laws. To understand how committed each country is to the new rule book, particularly when it comes to national security.'

The President smiled. 'Always one step ahead, Joseph. I should have seen this one coming.'

Uma smiled back.

'Not at all, Mr President. I fully intended to resign this morning, but if you feel our great nation would benefit from two more years of my oversight, I would be happy to continue as Director of the NSI.'

'Good, that's settled then.' The President stood up, shaking Uma's hand. She also stood, assuming the meeting was at an end. 'One more thing, before you go. I don't suppose the good doctor will be happy with this announcement. Whilst it's no reason not to go ahead with your suggestion, I would like to keep her on board as much as we can. She has had a hard time of it lately. I think there is so much more for her to offer, particularly when it comes to the environment.'

'Don't you worry about Uma,' Uma said. 'We've been getting on so much better since Ethan Rae's death.'

Epilogue

FDR Drive, Manhattan

21st September 2011, 13:34 hours EDT

Katrina Hoskins swore softly, regretting for the umpteenth time her decision not to LEAP directly from her apartment to the venue, but she'd needed to go into the office to collect her interview notes and was now running late. There was only one gate serving the entire network's staff. The line of people queuing to make trips had run to over one hundred. It was quite incredible how quickly the technology had been adopted and was, now, well, like any other form of transport – great, until it didn't work as intended. So, she was now being belatedly driven, and was sitting twiddling her thumbs beneath the rusted ironwork of the Queensboro Bridge, debating whether to walk, but it was at least two miles. A quick call to Nick, her producer, confirmed her worst fears: the room was set up, her guests waiting. Important guests, perhaps the most important she had ever interviewed given the events of the last six months. At least it wasn't going out live, she reassured herself. On the Daily Show, the LIVE element had been everything, but now she had her own show, Big News, thankfully pre-recorded, broadcasting four times weekly across the prime-time slot at 7:30 p.m. Eastern time. That's what three Emmys got you. There was a tap on the tinted glass of the Escalade, and two women climbed in, both sweating profusely. As Katrina scooted into the middle seat, she praised her decision not to walk. Eventually, the traffic began to move as Abi and Mary applied the finishing touches to her hair and makeup. Shortly, the majestic sweep of flags along United Nations Plaza came into view. Katrina stared up at the 195 fluttering pennants. Each one signified a country that now had a double role: both as a member of the UN, but also a founding member of the LEAP Oversight Board. She quickly scribbled a note under additional questions: "Why share the UN building?"

Nick was in the reception area to meet her and they were both escorted through the marble hall before being whisked up to the 38th floor, the executive suite of the Secretary General of the UN. It was a maze of offices and meeting rooms, but finally Katrina stopped outside a set of double doors. She took a deep breath, counted to five, and entered the room. To her left, the Big News film crew were gathered around a plethora of cameras, lights and mics that faced an L-shaped black leather couch on which two familiar figures were sitting.

'Director Ingram,' Katrina said, shaking the hand of the tall man who had stood up to meet her. 'How are you?'

His face broke out into a warm smile.

'All the better for seeing you,' he said, standing aside as Katrina crouched down beside the woman on the couch. They hugged each other like long lost friends.

'Uma, I've missed you,' Katrina whispered in her ear.

'Me too,' Uma said. 'It's been a while.'

'I was thinking that on the way over,' Katrina said. 'The last time I saw you was in the General Assembly Room, before ...' Her voice trailed off, unsure what to say, even though she had practised it a hundred times that morning.

'It's OK,' Uma said, sighing heavily, her eyes watering. There was an awkward pause before Uma smiled at her brightly with a determined smile. 'I hear you finally got married,' she continued, studying the large ring on Katrina's finger. 'Wow, that is a whopper. I'm so happy for you.'

Katrina blushed. 'Yes, finally. We tied the knot after the awards ceremony last September.' She fell silent, realising her Emmys were borne from suffering that had directly affected this woman. 'I'm so sorry,' she eventually said. 'That was insensitive of me.'

'Please, don't apologise. As I've come to realise, Ethan is everywhere. I don't want to dishonour his memory by not talking about him.' She smiled again, but it faded quickly. An awkward silence descended on the room before Nick stepped forward.

'I'm really sorry, folks, but we need to run the interview. We're already ten minutes late.'

'Of course,' Uma said, recovering her smile. 'We have so much to talk about. Please,' she motioned for Katrina to her take her seat opposite them as Director Ingram sat down beside Uma.

Katrina quickly studied her notes as Abi applied more makeup and one of the crew mic'd her up. Suddenly, John was counting her in. Seconds later, she began.

'Good evening, ladies and gentlemen. I am joined here today by the recently elected President and Vice President of the LEAP Oversight Board, Director Joseph Ingram and Doctor Uma Jakobsdóttir.'

She turned towards her guests.

'My first question is for Director Ingram. Firstly, many congratulations on your new appointment, but please, can you explain to our viewers how you will balance this role with the already considerable demands of your current role as Director of the NSI?'

'Thank you, Katrina,' Ingram smiled at her, a warm embrace that Katrina felt herself responding to. 'You have to remember that my role here is more decorative than anything. I will open each of our biannual sessions and attend major functions, but the real work will be carried out by Doctor Jakobsdóttir here as Vice President. She has a wealth of experience, as the, shall we say, mother of LEAP: she devised the initial LEAP Laws before sensibly handing over their management to the LEAP Oversight Board.'

Katrina turned to Uma.

'I might ask the same question of you, Uma. Firstly, congratulations. Thank you for giving the Big News your first interview since the events of last year, but again, how on earth can you balance running Green Ray with this new role?'

'Good question,' Uma smiled. 'I'd be lying if I said it was going to be easy, but I'm used to it. Remember, I ran Green Ray single-handedly for nearly seven years. More recently, I balanced it with the role of US Energy Secretary. But I don't mind the work, it's important. As Director Ingram said, I am ideally placed to straddle the two roles. On one side, Green Ray runs the LEAP system and pursues other environmental programmes. I'm ably assisted by our new CEO, Grant James, who takes a lot of the day-to-day decisions. On the other side, the LEAP Oversight Board is an independent body comprising the 195 nations that have signed up to use LEAP. It is tasked with ensuring that the LEAP Laws are adhered to. As you know, I developed the Laws and feel passionately about them, as discussed frequently with yourself on previous shows. However, I now also accept that they are too big for one person to control. I am simply a mouthpiece for the nations that use the system. Each country has now enshrined the Laws into local law. Our job is to administer the multitude of requests that filter through daily requesting exceptions to the Laws, which are, in turn, debated. If agreed, they are enshrined into the local laws as addendum to the LEAP Laws. It's an excellent system and allows us to be fair.'

'There is a lot to unpick there, Uma. Could I start with the latest members of the Board? You have recently admitted Saudi Arabia. Was that a wise move after their behaviour with Eternity?'

'Of course. As Director Ingram will explain, we now understand the events of last year, but to specifically answer your question, we want to be an inclusive organisation. After the collapse of Eternity, we were, of course, delighted to invite them into the fold.'

'Yes, about Eternity. Do you know what happened there?'

'That's a question for the Director of the NSI,' Uma said, nodding towards Ingram.

'Thank you, Uma. Yes, we have uncovered a great deal about what happened last July in Saudi Arabia, thanks to people whom we can't name for security reasons. It would seem that Eternity was infected with a catastrophic virus that was meant for the LEAP system but ended up frying their own system and rendering it completely inoperable. Unfortunately, John Forsyth was killed in the outbreak.' Katrina suppressed a smile. There was nothing unfortunate about the death of the Forsyth. He had raped her, co-opted her into filming Ethan Rae's punishment and running interviews which were effectively adverts for his business. She was not at all sorry, especially after receiving a package in the mail, two weeks ago, containing what appeared to be the master disc of her and Forsyth. There was no note. Katrina had shredded the disc that morning. 'Professor Charles Crouch also died, from alcohol poisoning. We have subsequently discovered that he was behind the attacks on American personnel in February, which, had it not been for the quick action of Uma and Green Ray, would have resulted in the deaths of over three thousand soldiers. Not only that, but we also have evidence to prove that he was behind the code that killed so many people in the so-called LEAP massacre. It was a heinous move by John Forsyth to shut Green Ray down. It should have been called the Crouch massacres. Again, had Uma and Green Ray not acted so swiftly, thousands of families would have lost loved ones that day. And finally, we have evidence to show that Forsyth planned to use his Doomsday virus to kill over one hundred million innocent people, again, to discredit Uma and Green Ray. It was all designed to remove them as viable competitors so Eternity could monopolise teleportation. Now, I appreciate that is a lot of information to process, so I will hold a series of detailed briefings at CIA HQ in Langley so journalists can see for themselves what that monster Forsyth had planned, along with his sidekick Crouch, who is being likened to Josef Mengele, the infamous doctor of Auschwitz, for his complete disregard for human life.'

'Director, that is quite an incredible story. Can you share with us the brave men and women who helped you uncover this information?'

'It was just one person,' Ingram said. 'That's all I'm prepared to say to safeguard his—' he smiled mischievously, '—or maybe, it's her identity.'

'Understood, Director. I can't wait to understand the detail behind your assertions. So, forgive me for my next question,' Katrina shifted uneasily on her seat, 'but I feel obliged to ask it, so our viewers have full closure on this matter. It concerns Ethan Rae.' Katrina paused, staring at Uma. 'I feel conflicted, because I know Ethan was also your partner, but do you know what happened to him in Saudi?'

Uma's eyes misted over. Her lower lip quivered as she considered the question.

'As I said before the camera rolled, memories of Ethan Rae are everywhere for me. I am at peace with what happened to him here in New York. He made the ultimate sacrifice to uphold the LEAP Laws, laws that we ourselves had broken, which proved that no one person could run them, and which Ethan was fully committed to preserving the integrity of. We knew the risks of handing control over to the Oversight Board. We discussed it at great length in making our decision. It could have been either of us that died, but the Laws are the Laws. No one, absolutely no one, is above the Laws.'

She looked over at Ingram, who nodded sagely, before continuing. 'To answer your question, we only know what Director Ingram's agent told us. That assumes Ethan died because of his injuries sustained from repeated whippings as he served out his punishment in Saudi Arabia. As I've come to learn, you have to respect the laws of individual nations. How can I expect otherwise if I'm asking LEAP nations to respect the LEAP Laws? I can't have my cake and eat it too.'

'Well, it must be hard for you to lose both your business partner and lover. On behalf of my viewers, I would like to extend our condolences to you.'

Uma nodded, her eyes misting over.

'Thank you, Katrina. That means a lot to me, but I would rather discuss what we have got planned, both with Green Ray and also the Oversight Board.'

'Yes, of course. Shall we start with Green Ray?'

'Yes, let's start there. Firstly, I would like to celebrate a small mile-stone we achieved yesterday. Mark it in your diaries. It was a historical moment in the history of the human race: yesterday was the first time that the combined LEAPs across the system exceeded five billion.'

'Can you explain to our viewers what that means exactly?'

'Yes. So, measured over a twenty-four-hour period, there were over five billion journeys conducted using the LEAP system, ranging from lengthy trips, including London to Sydney, right down to one-mile jumps from home to school. But the real history making is that in less than one year we have removed twenty-five percent of global emissions. Emissions, that this time last year would have been spewed into the atmosphere. So far this year we have eliminated four giga tonnes of CO_2 from the atmosphere. That's four billion tonnes and roughly equal to eight times the mass of all humans on the planet. It's a fantastical amount and something I am so proud of. As would Ethan be.' Uma's eyes misted over again. Katrina could have sworn that Director Ingram's did too.

'Uma, that is an incredible achievement. You should be proud of yourself.'

'Katrina, it's only the beginning. As you know, we are pressing ahead with our Trillions, Oceanic, Elemental, and global healthcare programmes.'

'Again, please explain what that means for our viewers.'

'With Trillions, we've already planted one hundred million trees and, through Elemental, recycled over fifty million tonnes of waste which is now serving as base material for the LEAP gates, meaning that manufacturers now have access to raw materials without having to mine them. We have recently made it a condition of gaining access to our healthcare service that each member country has to commit to the Trillions and Elemental programme. In return, every citizen will receive a base coverage of health. We are gradually moving towards a circular economy whereby nothing is wasted: all food and other trash is now put into the LEAP system at source, before being sold to manufacturers who can make whatever products they need. In time, these initiatives will make huge inroads into both industrial and agricultural emissions, which together comprise nearly one third of annual CO_2 output globally.'

'Incredible. What would you say to your critics that LEAP has created mass unemployment across industries which overnight have seen
their demand disappear? I'm talking principally about transportation,
but it's also beginning to apply to both mining and farming as more
food is, as you say, recycled through the system.'

'We're creating alternative jobs quickly – over fourteen million since
last year alone – through our four programmes, but also in the LEAP
gate installation and maintenance.'

'I understand that, but these are high-end jobs. Some of the job
losses are spread across lower-skilled industries, like baggage handlers,
dockers, rubbish collectors. These people can't just swap to another
high-knowledge job. The transport industry alone worldwide has lost
millions of jobs, far in excess of the ones you have created. That lag will
take years to bridge, and, in fact may never be narrowed.'

Uma paused before answering.

'There's no simple answer here. LEAP was always going to cause
disruption as the economy corrected, but what I would say is that
we've worked really closely with every government to ensure the pain
is minimised. So, for instance, in Sweden and Norway, they are now
charging a flat monthly service fee for a gate, plus a one-off charge for
making a LEAP based on distance and usage. That money is then used
to make interim reparations to any worker affected by the transition.
It's a monthly payment, more like a universal salary, which will be
paid until that individual finds a job in the new economy. In China,
the government has been far more cautious, restricting the rollout of
LEAP internally, both as a means of transportation and Elemental.
We're working closely with them to at least guard against the worst
swings in the economy, but I'd be lying if it hasn't caused problems. In
Switzerland, they're trialling a layaway service whereby citizens who
have been affected by the move to LEAP can choose to be archived in
the system for up to ten years free of charge, whilst the economy picks
up.'

Katrina stopped Uma with her hand.

'Just a minute. Are you telling me they're effectively archiving
themselves in some weird form of suspended animation?'

'Well, when you put it like that, it does sound strange, but Switzerland is a progressive society. They already allow assisted suicide. Have done since 1941, in fact. This is no different, so long as the motives are not selfish. I might add that it is carefully monitored. The person wishing to, as you say, be archived must initiate the routine, be active in setting the time they wish to remain in storage for, and must also step through the gate themselves.'

'It sounds barbaric,' Katrina said, turning her nose up. This wasn't quite where she had wanted to take the interview. It was macabre, and she wanted to move on, but Uma hadn't finished.

'My point is that we're in a new world with new rules and new possibilities. This is one of them, and people are exercising their right to store themselves. I might add that over 10,000 of their citizens have taken up the offer, and they have received over 250,000 applications from other countries of citizens wishing to do the same.'

'OK, one area that I wanted to address is how are you going to enforce the LEAP Laws moving forward? You yourself have fallen foul of them in the past. How do you police them?'

'I'm glad you've asked that, Katrina. As I've explained in the past, the body is changing constantly. Well, we can monitor that for any irregularities in the atomic structure between LEAPs. If something has changed, then it will be picked it up almost immediately. The same with resuscitation. I'm pleased to say we've already agreed forty-three instances where a person can resuscitate a loved one, including a victim of murder and victims of road traffic accidents. Industrial accidents are also covered and any law enforcement personnel losing their life in the line of duty. Once agreed here by the Board, these exceptions are then enshrined into local law in each country. They have twelve months from the vote to do so or they risk having their LEAP operating licence withdrawn.'

Katrina looked up. Nick was motioning for a commercial break. They had already overrun.

'Fascinating, Uma, really fascinating. I could talk all evening about this, but I'm afraid we have to go to break. When we return, we will talk more about some of these exceptions.'

The camera lights dimmed. Katrina stood before turning to address Ingram and Uma.

'I thought that went well. Thank you so much.' She looked at her watch. 'We have fifteen minutes before the next segment. If you'll excuse me, I need a restroom break.'

When she returned, the TV crew and Ingram were nowhere to be seen. Uma was standing by the windows, looking down into the East River. Katrina joined her, admiring the panoramic view through the floor-to-ceiling glass frontage. Directly in front of her, the thin green sliver of Gantry Plaza State Park skirted the far shore before fading into the urban sprawl of Long Island City, Sunnyside Garden, Elmhurst and beyond towards Queens, a recently shuttered JFK Airport and Long Island.

'I've been meaning to talk to you for months,' she said, 'in private, but couldn't because of what you've been through. I wanted to know if you'd received a package recently. In the mail, containing, you know ...'

Uma looked over and smiled.

'I did – the master disc.'

'Do you know who sent it?'

'A friend, I think,' Uma said.

'Well, if you do speak to them, please pass on my thanks.'

'I will,' Uma said softly. 'Are we ready to continue? I have a lot to do.'

'Yes, of course. Please come and sit. We'll be finished in twenty minutes.'

As Uma turned, Katrina stared at her in surprise.

'I never knew,' she said.

'About what?' Uma asked, her eyes following Katrina's down to her waist.

'Oh, that,' Uma smiled. 'Yes, I'm three months,' she said, patting her belly.

Book 4 in The Race is On series will return in October 2024.

Ed Fox will return in a spin-off series in February 2025.

What Next!

Did you enjoy ATOM INC? You can be the difference.

As an Indie Author, reviews are **THE** most powerful tools in my quiver when it comes to getting attention for my books. It's the only way I can compete against the financial might of the big publishers who can command unlimited budgets for advertising and an army of marketeers to promote their writers.

However.

I have my own army.

An army that the big boys would love to get their hands on.

My faithful readers.

An honest review of my book is worth a thousand ads. And ten thousand marketeers! It provides social proof of my writing to other readers and more often than not, persuades them to hit the BUY button.

So, if you enjoyed this story, I would be eternally grateful if you tell others what you thought about ATOM INC on the book's Amazon page—it can be as short as you like.

Thank you so much.

Fancy some exclusive swag?

Building a relationship with my readers is the very best thing about writing—I'm blessed to call many my friends and a few even help me with my writing; spotting typos, correcting research errors, suggesting plot improvements or simply agreeing to join my infamous ARC teams!

I email a newsletter every three weeks with details of new releases, special offers and signed giveaways. Oh, and the odd snippet about my life in Leeds and that of my writing buddy Max—an aged, often bad tempered, but very lovable brown Labrador.

In return, you'll receive the following gifts, which are all exclusive to my club and can't be obtained anywhere else:

1. A free prequel novella called MAD, introducing The Race is On series—amongst other things, it explains why Uma's father created LEAP and how Uma became a copy of her sister. It's a doozy and one of my favourite stories, although the plot nearly cleaved my mind in two! If you've downloaded this previously but still want the dossier and ss below, just sign up and collect the dossier and ss.

2. A short dossier that answers some of the questions that you might have as a reader about ATOM INC, including what is made up and what is actually fact. And how I merged the two.

3. My date and time ss which I created to track the timelines in ATOM INC—sounds small, but endless hours were poured into this baby and I want you to see the blood, the sweat and the tears in those cells as I worked to create a sense of urgency across Reykjavík, London, Riyadh, Afghanistan, LA, Virginia, Washington DC, New York City and San Francisco.

If you want to unsubscribe at any time, it's simple to do and I promise never to share your details with anyone. To join the club and receive the novella, dossier and ss, just scan the QR code below, or type

the following link into your browser: https://ocheaton.com/atomin
c-mad-offer/

I've dreamt of becoming a writer for years and, like many, believed
there was at least one book in me. Having passed that hurdle, I've
discovered there're loads and look forward to sharing future stories
with you as I create them.

OC

Leeds, England

About OC Heaton

I write what I love to read—big issue tech-nothrillers, with a side of sci-fi, that are super well researched inside a complex plot full of twists and turns.

When I sit down to write a book, I have three non-negotiables:

1. It needs to concern a current or recent real world issue that I can deeply research (I love research!) and weave my fictional story into. Hopefully, so tightly that you struggle to spot where one stops and the other starts.

2. It has to have a complex plot full of twists and turns that'll leave you guessing right until the end.

3. It must contain grey characters, even the good guys. This makes sense to me. First, as a reader I hate stereotypical/one-dimensional characters and second, grey is real life,

right?

When I'm not writing I relax in my hometown of Leeds in the UK with the love of my life and our two daughters.

 And Max—my aged, often bad tempered, but lovable Labrador—who features a lot in my newsletters. It rains a lot in Leeds but that works out well for me—loads of time for research and, of course, writing!

Here are some ways that you can talk to me:

Email: oc@ocheaton.com

Web: www.ocheaton.com

Facebook: https://www.facebook.com/ocheatonauthor

Instagram: https://www.instagram.com/ocheaton

The Race is On Series Listing

MAD—Prequel novella to The Race is One Series

1986. Reykjavik, Iceland.

Brilliant quantum scientist Jakob Arnasson is on the brink of immortality. After years of fervent anti-nuclear activism, he has finally brokered a nuclear disarmament summit between two of the world's greatest powers: the USA and the USSR.

But on the eve of the talks, Jakob is forced to use his LEAP teleportation device to save his own life — an action that has far-reaching consequences. It resets his memory to the day of his first "leap", in 1954.

Thrust into a future-altering weekend without any recollection of why he should be there, Jakob's responsibilities suddenly multiply when the CIA recruit him for a dangerous covert operation to save the talks.

And just as he looks set to lose everything, a much greater threat appears on the horizon...

FREE to download when you join my Readers Club. Just scan the QR code below, or type the following link into your browser: https://ocheaton.com/atominc-mad-offer/

LEAP—Book 1 of The Race is On series

One small step could ruin mankind's greatest leap...

Ethan Rae is known for his billions, but his latest business venture is about to really put him on the map: a quantum teleportation system that would solve global warming for good. Known as LEAP, the system is capable of providing Earth's ultimate second chance...until it falls into the wrong hands.

When playboy CEO Samuel Reynolds III snatches LEAP out from under Ethan's nose, he adds insult to injury by attempting to destroy

Ethan's business partner, Uma Jakobsdóttir. But this is no malicious whim. As the daughter of its creator, Uma enforces the LEAP Laws.

Because of its potentially devastating capabilities, LEAP users must not clone people, revive the dead, or merge minds and species. But in the race to recover their precious piece of tech, Ethan and Uma are faced with sacrifices that push their resolve to breaking point.

From the frozen wastelands of Iceland, to the leafy suburbs of London and the mean streets of New York City, LEAP is a technothriller that will keep you questioning what it means to be human.

LEAP is **free for Kindle Unlimited Readers!!** Or BUY IT at your local Amazon store. Either way, just scan the QR code below or type the following link into your browser: https://geni.us/WOFbk9

Green Ray—Book 2 of The Race is On series

No good deed goes unpunished...

Six years after the near-catastrophic hijacking of LEAP, Uma Jakobsdóttir is determined to find a safer path to environmental salvation. So, with her father's invention back under wraps, Uma turns her attention to the $85 billion-dollar Green Ray fund with the intention of renewing the planet—minus any teleportation.

But when the capabilities of LEAP are discovered by the U.S. government, it sets its sights on using the device to protect the country against economic collapse. When the White House proposes a new set of rules for LEAP—ones which would only allow the teleportation of goods, not people—Uma's objections are steamrolled by powerful forces.

Then the President's life is endangered, and the rules of the game suddenly shift again—leaving Uma in ethical turmoil as she races to stop the full power of LEAP from being unleashed on an unsuspecting world...

Green Ray is **free for Kindle Unlimited Readers!!** Or BUY IT at your local Amazon store. Either way, just scan the QR code below or type the following link into your browser: https://geni.us/K8SbJA

ATOM INC—Book 3 of The Race Is On series

You've just read this!

Dedication

To the one and only love of my life, Lillian. And, of course, our girls.

Acknowledgements

My thanks go to my partner, best friend, adviser and sounding board in this latest adventure, Lillian Ayala. Your love, enthusiasm, patience and wisdom know no bounds.

I am also extremely grateful for the assistance I received from the following individuals whose input helped me shape, write and eventually publish ATOM INC: my editor Julie Hoyle. My battle hardened team of BETA readers who very kindly gave up their time to read ATOM INC prior to publication: Anamaria, Dave Johnson, Chris Wood, Gordon Wood, Miriam Good and Fi Glover.

Copyright